"*Sand Daughter* is a fascinating snapshot [of] the world of the Crusades. Twelfth-century Arabia is beautifully re-created, but this is ultimately a story about people and not places. Thankfully, Sarah Bryant provides characters to care about aplenty. Not just a love story, a thriller, or a straight historical but rather an impressive blend of all three. The author's research is impeccable and applied with the lightest of touches. This is an epic filled with emotion and rich with atmosphere—as heady as the hashish smoke swirling around the desert tents."
                                                        —*Historical Novels Review*

PRAISE FOR

The Other Eden

"This riveting adventure proves irresistible from beginning to end."
                                                        —*Booktrust*

"Lush, sensual, musical, and dangerously seductive, *The Other Eden* is a rare vision of a corrupt, irresistible paradise. Enter this novel at your peril; leave it only with profound regret. *The Other Eden* will haunt you and your dreams."   —J. D. Landis, author of *Lying in Bed*

Sand DAUGHTER

Sarah Bryant

BERKLEY BOOKS, NEW YORK

THE BERKLEY PUBLISHING GROUP
Published by the Penguin Group
Penguin Group (USA) Inc.
375 Hudson Street, New York, New York 10014, USA
Penguin Group (Canada), 90 Eglinton Avenue East, Suite 700, Toronto, Ontario M4P 2Y3, Canada
(a division of Pearson Penguin Canada Inc.)
Penguin Books Ltd., 80 Strand, London WC2R 0RL, England
Penguin Group Ireland, 25 St. Stephen's Green, Dublin 2, Ireland (a division of Penguin Books Ltd.)
Penguin Group (Australia), 250 Camberwell Road, Camberwell, Victoria 3124, Australia
(a division of Pearson Australia Group Pty. Ltd.)
Penguin Books India Pvt. Ltd., 11 Community Centre, Panchsheel Park, New Delhi—110 017, India
Penguin Group (NZ), 67 Apollo Drive, Rosedale, North Shore 0632, New Zealand
(a division of Pearson New Zealand Ltd.)
Penguin Books (South Africa) (Pty.) Ltd., 24 Sturdee Avenue, Rosebank, Johannesburg 2196,
South Africa

Penguin Books Ltd., Registered Offices: 80 Strand, London WC2R 0RL, England

Published by arrangement with Snowbooks, Ltd.

This is a work of fiction. Names, characters, places, and incidents either are the product of the author's imagination or are used fictitiously, and any resemblance to actual persons, living or dead, business establishments, events, or locales is entirely coincidental. The publisher does not have any control over and does not assume responsibility for author or third-party websites or their content.

English translation of "The Crusades Through Arab Eyes" © 1984, 2004, from original edition by Amin Maalouf 1983, reprinted with permission from Saqi books. Michael Sells, Excerpts from *Desert Tracings* © 1989 by Michael Sells and reprinted by permission of Wesleyan University Press.

PRINTING HISTORY
Snowbooks edition / 2006
Berkley trade paperback edition / October 2009

Library of Congress Cataloging-in-Publication Data

Bryant, Sarah.
   Sand daughter / Sarah Bryant. —Berkley trade pbk. ed.
     p. cm.
ISBN 978-0-425-22980-4
1. Women, Bedouin—Fiction. 2. Crusades—Third, 1189–1192—Fiction. 3. Knights Templar (Masonic order) 4. Jinn—Fiction. I. Title.
   PR6102.R935S36 2009
   823'.92—dc22   2009019239

PRINTED IN THE UNITED STATES OF AMERICA

10   9   8   7   6   5   4   3   2   1

For an end to crusades

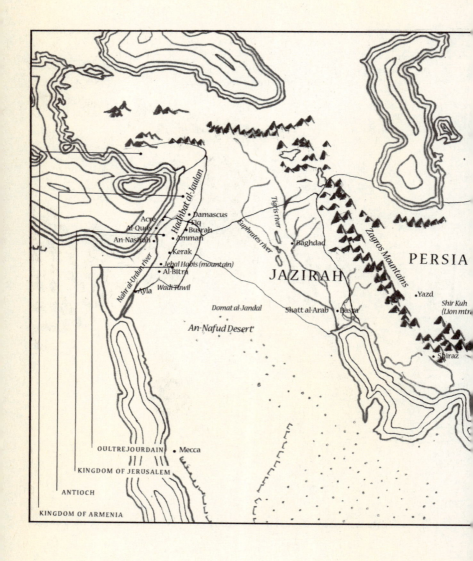

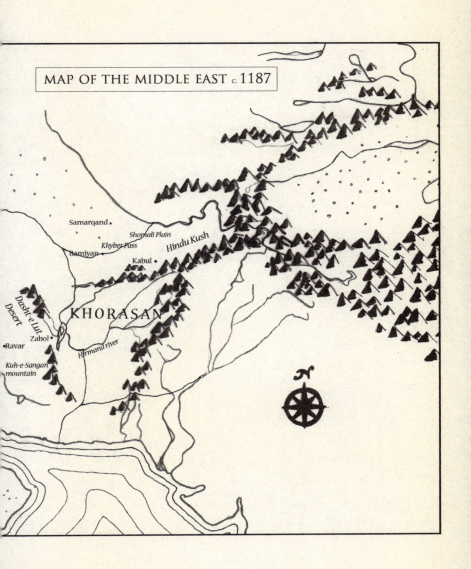

MAP OF THE MIDDLE EAST c.1187

Samarqand

Shomali Plain

Khyber Pass
Hindu Kush
Bamiyan

Kabul

KHORASAN

Dasht-e Lut
Desert

Zabol

Ravar

Hirmand river

Kuh-e-Sangan
mountain

N

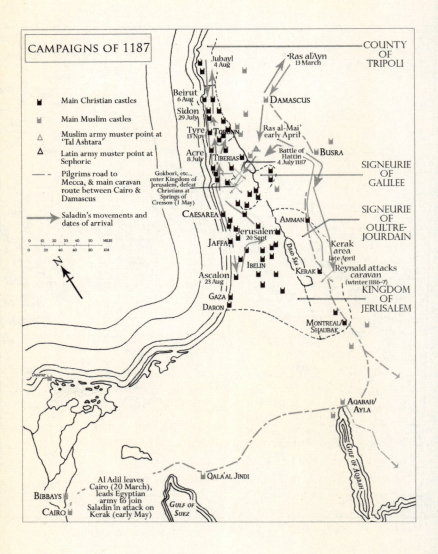

CAMPAIGNS OF 1187

■ Main Christian castles

▪ Main Muslim castles

△ Muslim army muster point at 'Tal Ashtara'

▲ Latin army muster point at Sephorie

- - - Pilgrims road to Mecca, & main caravan route between Cairo & Damascus

➤ Saladin's movements and dates of arrival

0 10 20 30 40 50 MILES
0 20   40   60   80 KM

N

COUNTY OF TRIPOLI

Jubayl 4 Aug

·Ras al'Ayn 13 March

Beirut 6 Aug

DAMASCUS

Sidon 29 July

Tyre 13 Nov

TORONN

Ras al-Mai' early April

Acre 8 July

TIBERIAS

Battle of Hattin 4 July 1187

BUSRA

SIGNEURIE OF GALILEE

Gokbori, etc., enter Kingdom of Jerusalem, defeat Christians at Springs of Cresson (1 May)

CAESAREA

AMMAN

SIGNEURIE OF OULTRE-JOURDAIN

Jerusalem 20 Sept

JAFFA

Kerak area late April

IBELIN

DEAD SEA

KERAK

Reynald attacks caravan (winter 1186-7)

Ascalon 23 Aug

KINGDOM OF JERUSALEM

GAZA

DARON

MONTREAL/ SHAUBAK

DUMYAT

AQABAH/ AYLA

GULF OF AQABAH

Al Adil leaves Cairo (20 March), leads Egyptian army to join Saladin in attack on Kerak (early May)

QALA'AL JINDI

BIBBAYS

CAIRO

GULF OF SUEZ

GLOSSARY

ARABIC WORDS

alif—the first letter of the Arabic alphabet

Ayyub—the name of the ruling dynasty to which Salah ad-Din belonged

ba'a—the second letter of the Arabic alphabet

banj—a medieval version of hashish

Bedu—Bedouin; an Arab nomad

caliph—the leader of an Islamic state, considered a direct successor of Muhammad

dervish—a Muslim ascetic/mystic

emir—any of several types of leader, including military commander and prince

farsakh—an ancient Arabic unit of distance, approximately six kilometers

Franj—literally, "Franks"; a medieval Arabic term for any Europeans in Palestine, regardless of their country of origin

hadith—traditional sayings attributed to Muhammad

hajj—a pilgrimage to Mecca

imam—a Muslim prayer leader, similar to a Christian minister

kufiyya—a man's headscarf

Ma'dan—marsh Arabs (from Jazirah/Iraq)

Mamluk—elite slave-recruited Muslim soldiers, later a ruling dynasty

Muharram—the first month of the Muslim year

mujahid (pl. *mujahiddin*)—a Muslim holy warrior
oud—a classical Arabic instrument, like a lute
qanun—a classical Arabic instrument, like a zither, played with
    metal plectra
quartan fever—malaria
Sayyid/Sayyida—Sir/Lady
Sidi—"my master," usually used by a servant
souk—the commercial quarter of an Arab city
sultan—a Muslim leader, directly beneath the caliph in hierarchy
wadi—a river bed or valley, generally dry

ARABIC PHRASES

alhamdulillah—praise be to Allah
Allahu akbar—God is the greatest
as-salaamu alaikum—peace be upon you (equivalent of "hello")
Inshallah—if God wills it
ma'as salaama—go with peace (equivalent of "good-bye")
Wa alaikum as-salaam—and upon you is the peace

PERSIAN/PASHTO WORDS

aghundem—to dress, to put on
betaan—a shaman; prophet
Bibi—a female title of respect; "lady"
harquus—facial tattoos
Hewad—homeland
husay—a falcon
kavir—a salt desert
Khan (fem. Khanum)—title for a leader
mateledal—to wait for
meerre—literally, "warrior"; colloquially, "husband"
Psarlay—spring
setar—a stringed instrument like a lute, but with a very long neck
tut—mulberry

OTHER

league—a medieval European unit of distance, approximately 2.2
    kilometers
Outremer—the catchall name for the Frankish territories in the
    Holy Land at the time of the Crusades
Saracens—a medieval European term for Arabs

Sand
DAUGHTER

Prologue

"THERE is Kerak Castle," said Yazid, pointing to a low mountain in the middle distance, topped by fortress walls. "That is the home of Brins Arnat."

Rahil clutched her grandfather's hand more tightly. Like all Muslim children in Oultrejourdain, she had been brought up on tales of the Franj prince's savagery, but she had more reason than most to dread this place. It had haunted her dreams for as long as she could remember, for it was Kerak who had killed her parents. They had been taken prisoner in one of Arnat's many raids as they made their own pilgrimage when she was two years old. And so, although Rahil had never laid eyes on the castle before, she nevertheless knew it by the intimacy of fear, just as she knew her parents' faces in her nightmares, though she had long forgotten them by day.

Now the only family left to Rahil was Yazid, and though she loved him devotedly, she would have given anything to have been left at home. She had even asked him if she could stay with a neighboring family; but in the end, her grandfather had felt that it was wrong to impose on others for so long. The trip to Mecca was long and unpredictable, and besides, he had said, it would be good for Rahil to make the hajj now, while she was young, instead of leaving it until the end of her life, as he had.

They drew closer to the hilltop fortress. Danger radiated from its walls like the miasmic shimmer of heat on a noontime desert. Rahil tried to convince herself that what she felt was merely fear, not foresight. She tried to concentrate on the caravan's size and the strength of its defenses. Surely, she thought, even Brins Arnat would think twice before attacking a group of such size and might. Surely he would be interested in the wealthy pilgrims, with their rich trappings and their high ransom potential. Surely he would not touch an old man and a ten-year-old child in nondescript clothing, carrying only enough money to pay their way at the caravanserais.

Yet as the castle loomed closer, Rahil found that she was sure of nothing but her own terror.

As Rahil looked up at the castle, Brins Arnat looked down at the caravan with a quickening of his pulse that was all too rare since his wife had begun locking her door at night and then, to spite him, those of the serving wenches. He did not, of course, think of himself as Brins Arnat, though he was pleased that in their club-tongued way, the Saracens had the sense to refer to him as "Prince," for he thought of himself as the Prince of Oultrejourdain. The other Frankish nobles called him simply Kerak, after his mighty southern fortress.

Now in his sixty-first year, he could hardly remember Europe. It was more a conscious act of forgetting than not. Kerak had been his father's second son, with no birthright but with an ambition that soared well beyond any reasonable expectations. As an adolescent he'd railed against his filial insignificance, finding his destiny at last in the Pope's call to avenge the fallen County of Edessa.

Kerak had all the prerequisites to rise to the top of the Holy Land's frontier society: flexible ethics, a way with a sword, a faculty for sycophancy, and a handsome face. Still, securing his place had not been simple. He'd married a wealthy widow, then promptly been captured and incarcerated in a Saracen prison for sixteen years, during which time she died, and he honed his hatred of all things Arabic. Upon his release Kerak married again, another, wealthier widow, who brought with her the title to a dusty piece of property at the extreme south of the Frankish kingdom, known as Oultrejourdain.

In Oultrejourdain the disinherited son at last found significance, and he used it to beat that wild territory into submission. But though his people called him "Prince," he was not quite satisfied, for there was one Saracen who still did not respect his will. The would-be prince was determined to break him, and there below his castle walls, practically within spitting distance, was his opportunity.

"You have a leery look in your eye, Messire," spoke a voice behind Kerak. "What is it you are thinking of?"

Kerak turned from the caravan to face Gerard de Ridefort. The Grand Master of the Knights Templar stood looking back at him calmly, his white tunic fluttering in the morning breeze. His face was properly obsequious, but there was a glimmer of derision in his blue eyes that sent a hot spike of anger rising in Kerak. Though allies by necessity, Kerak and de Ridefort bore little love for one another.

Perhaps they were too much alike. De Ridefort, too, had risen from humble beginnings, by virtue of similar qualities. But while Kerak had chosen the sword to hack out a name for himself, de Ridefort had slithered his way to the top by political maneuvering. Age and dissatisfaction had ground Kerak into a plump, redheaded devil with a ruddy drunkard's face marred by a dead, milky eye— the remnant of a run-in with a Saracen blade. De Ridefort, though just as atrophied within by his own brand of bitterness, had clung to his bland, blond looks and still presented a good approximation of most ladies' ideal knight. Kerak hated him for it.

"What do you want?" he snapped.

De Ridefort bowed slightly, the sun glinting on his gray-streaked golden hair. "You requested my presence."

Kerak was about to bluster when he recalled that this was true. He had called for de Ridefort as soon as he had spotted the caravan. "Yes . . ." he said, then, "yes," again, with more conviction. "You see the heathen caravan passing below? It is armed, and it should not be. Take the garrison and teach them a lesson."

De Ridefort looked at Kerak as he might a fractious child bent on some disastrous amusement. "Forgive me, Messire, but are you certain that this is wise? We are currently bound by a truce to the Sultan Salah ad-Din—"

"That truce was none of my making!" Kerak cried.

"But if you break it," de Ridefort answered carefully, "the war that follows will be."

"Yes . . . and the nobles will thank me for doing what the king is too spineless to do."

"Careful, Kerak," said the Master, with a twist of smirk in his voice, though his expression remained pious. "Remember who it is that keeps you."

Kerak eyed the caravan, framed now in sections between the crenellations of the battlement. A few more minutes and it would be too late; and so, although he longed to check de Ridefort for his arrogance, he kept his temper. "Kill the guard," he said coldly, "and put the pilgrims in the dungeon. If the women protest, rape them. If the men draw weapons, kill them."

De Ridefort's expressions were like fine watercolor drawings: never overt but always giving clear voice to his thoughts. Now he wore a look of refined disgust. Observing this, Kerak approached him with a tender smile until they were close enough to kiss, and for a moment the Templar Master wondered if Kerak was mad enough to do just that.

Instead, fixing his eyes on de Ridefort's, he said, "You are hesitating, Messire, which leads me to wonder whether there is something to the rumors that you have . . . how shall we put it . . . a particular 'friend' among the Saracen tribes?"

De Ridefort shut his eyes against the cruel glint in Kerak's, but he could not shut out the words, nor the rush of guilty hatred that ensued.

"The king may be an idiot, Messire," Kerak continued, "but he is still the king. A word from me and the whispers about you might become a good deal more."

"You think that he would take the word of a madman over that of the Master of the Temple?" de Ridefort snapped, his pastel composure finally succumbing to a bright flush of anger.

Kerak shrugged, looking once more at the caravan. "Madmen generally speak the truth, while politicians lie by profession."

De Ridefort looked at Kerak for a long time, wondering why, of all the nobles in Outremer, it had to be this one who formed the buttress of his plan. Still, as both of them knew, he had no choice but to obey him. So, with the slightest of bows he said, "Messire," and turned to rouse the garrison before he had to witness the satisfied smirk on Kerak's face.

Part One

One

Wadi Tawil, Near Ayla
Winter Grazing Lands of the Hassan Tribe
Late February, 1187 CE

"KHALIDAH!" Zaynab called for the third time. "When I find you, girl, I'll have your hide!" She looked around, one hand on her hip, the other shading her eyes from the late-morning glare. Then, muttering, she walked off toward the horses' grazing area.

From the sandstone cave high on the slope above the camp, Khalidah and Bilal watched her go. "I think I'd prefer a beating to what Numair and Abd al-Hadi are planning," Khalidah said.

"How do you know what they're planning?" Bilal asked, drawing circles in the dust with his finger.

"Don't pretend to be stupid, Bilal," she said, for he had watched with her that morning as her father's twin, with whom he had fought on and off for control of the tribe since their own father died, had arrived with a retinue of armed horsemen and a magnificent mare. The mare was, quite simply, the most perfect that Khalidah had ever seen: a flaxen chestnut, her wedge-shaped head high and proud, her tail flickering out behind her like a lightning strike. But though Khalidah loved horses beyond almost anything, the sight had filled her with the blackest despair. Among the tribes, where horses were family and a good war mare worth more than a man's life, a horse like that one was beyond value. She could not be sold or traded, only given as a gift of the highest honor: not unlike a sheikh's only daughter.

Bilal gave her a long, hard look. "Most girls would swoon at the prospect of marrying a man like Numair."

The words stung like a slap. "You think I should be happy to be traded for a warhorse?" Khalidah asked coldly.

"Your words, not mine."

"Speak plainly!"

"Fine," the boy said defiantly. "Don't marry your cousin; marry me."

It wasn't the first time he had said it, but it was the first time Khalidah thought he might mean it. She looked at him more carefully than she had looked in a long time. Like her, Bilal was just shy of sixteen. He was still more child than man, smooth-cheeked and scruffy in a worn-out robe that showed too much of his wrists and ankles. Still, he was well built, with a fine, open face, skin the color of parchment, and black-fringed eyes of a startling blue unseen among the tribes, which he hated for exactly that reason. He would be the kind of man most girls dreamed of. Yet even if the decision had been hers to make, Khalidah would not have considered his proposal seriously.

"I can't marry you, Bilal," she said, continuing the thought aloud. "You know that."

"Because I am the fatherless son of your own father's servant?"

"No! You know that my father loves you like a son."

"Very well, then. You are my best friend, Khalidah—"

"And you are mine," she interrupted, "and that is exactly the problem. We bicker like old women; we know each other too well. I think for a marriage to work, it is best not to know too much about one another." Bilal frowned, and Khalidah wondered whether she really believed this. "I mean, honestly," she continued more loudly, to cover her own doubts, "how could I act subservient to you when you're the little boy who used to pee the bed?"

"Khalidah!" he wailed.

"Besides, do you really think that you could beat me?"

"You want a husband who beats you?" he asked incredulously.

"Of course not!" Khalidah cried, wondering how the conversation had come to this. She thought for a moment and then, deciding it was better to change the subject, she said, "As for beatings, I suppose Zaynab really is too soft on me. She always threatens, but she never does it."

"I wish I could say the same."

Khalidah looked at Bilal with a mixture of pity and envy. "She's your mother, and my nurse. That is why she beats you and only threatens to beat me."

"Perhaps . . ."

Khalidah looked down at the assembly of black tents fluttering in the late-winter breeze. Beyond the tents, the horses and camels and goats grazed the scrub; beyond them, the desert seared white to the mountains on the horizon. At that moment, somewhere between the desert and the cave, the men of her family were constructing her fate, and Khalidah knew that she could not hide from it forever.

"Come on," she said, and started down the hill.

When they arrived at the camp, Bilal wandered off in search of something to eat while Khalidah made her way to her father's tent. The men's section was silent when she reached it, its flap rolled up to show the space bereft of all but empty coffee cups and a smoldering fire. Khalidah's heart sank further: they had already decided. She was about to walk on when a movement caught her eye. She peered into the tent's shadows and then leapt back again in alarm. Far back in one corner a man was sitting, beckoning to her. He was a young man, perhaps five years older than she was, with black, wide-spaced eyes over a straight nose and a mouth that looked ready to smile. His beard was trimmed close, his hair cut short under an embroidered skullcap, his clothing odd: a short robe over baggy trousers with an embroidered woolen waistcoat on top. Most intriguing of all, he held a *qanun* on his lap—the most difficult and beautiful of the traditional instruments.

Nevertheless he was a stranger, and no doubt one who belonged to Abd al-Hadi. Khalidah had no intention of entering the tent. Apparently surmising this, the man set the *qanun* aside and came toward her. Instinctively, Khalidah drew away, but he caught her arm. She was going to scream—she ought to have screamed—and yet something made her hold back. Even years later, she would come no closer to defining it than to say that it was a kind of recognition: that sudden, rare recognition one feels for a person who is about to alter the course of one's life irrevocably.

Into that pause, the man spoke: "There is no time to explain, Sayyida—they will be back in a moment—but I must implore you to say yes."

"What?" Khalidah demanded, recovering herself enough to snatch her arm away.

His sigh was full of the inevitable, his voice low and full of music. "Please, Sayyida. Promise me that you will say yes to whatever they ask of you."

"You are a madman!" she cried.

He smiled. There was sun in it, the kind that drives for a blinding moment through storm clouds. "I'm not, more's the pity. They are coming now. They must not see us speaking together. But please, Sayyida, say yes, and buy me time to explain . . ."

And then he was gone, settling back into the tent's shadows like a mouse into its hole. Khalidah blinked after him for a moment but then, hearing her father's voice and her uncle's ricocheting laugh, she turned and fled to the women's quarters.

She had been hoping for time to compose herself before she faced Zaynab, but her nurse was sitting at the front of the tent with the flap half-raised, a wedge of sunlight falling across a garment she was stitching. Looking at her in this domestic pose, Khalidah wondered why Zaynab had never remarried. Khalidah had been too old for a nursemaid for years now, Bilal was a man in the tribe's eyes, and a woman as attractive as Zaynab was, still young enough to bear children, must have had offers. Though Khalidah liked the romance of the possibility that Zaynab still loved Bilal's dead father, she doubted that this was the reason for her persistent widowhood. She retreated into stony silence whenever Khalidah asked about him, and Bilal said that she refused even to tell him his father's name.

"So kind of you to make an appearance," the nurse said dryly.

"Have you been looking for me?" Khalidah asked, trying to make her voice sound normal.

Zaynab looked up as she bit off a thread and gave her a wry smile. "As you and my no-good son must know very well." But she said it affectionately. "You have too little respect for your elders, Khalidah. Not everyone is as forgiving as I am."

Noticing the anxious furrow between her brows, Khalidah felt a pang of guilt. "I'm sorry to have worried you, Zaynab."

"Hmm." She raised one eyebrow, set to chastise further, but when she looked closely at Khalidah she changed her mind. "Are you all right? You look pale."

"I'm fine."

Zaynab did not seem convinced, but she only said, "Good, because the men have asked you to join them at the noonday meal. You must change your dress."

"Zaynab!"

"Yes, I know. You'd much prefer to wear rags and break your neck riding with Bilal. Inside, please. You look as though you've been rolling in a dung heap."

Grudgingly, Khalidah followed Zaynab into the tent. It was unusually spacious, even for a sheikh's tent; or, more to the point, unusually empty. The women's section of a Bedu tent was intended to house a harem of wives and their female children, but Abd al-Aziz's was occupied only by Khalidah and Zaynab. Though Khalidah knew that this was a mark of shame on her father, she could not wish it otherwise. The living quarters of other girls were hot and crowded with squabbling women and crying children, thick with the smells of cooking from the adjacent kitchen and the babies' dirty swaddling. She knew that they pitied her for her solitary existence, but Khalidah never woke without being thankful for the silence and ordered calm.

Zaynab let the flap fall. With an effort Khalidah pushed her strange conversation with the minstrel out of her mind and began to take off her dirty clothes. A moment later, a serving girl came in with a basin of hot water and a towel. The steam rising from the bowl was heavy with the smell of roses.

"Where did we get perfume?" Khalidah demanded.

"A gift from your uncle and cousin," Zaynab answered, without meeting her eyes.

"Since when do they bring us gifts?" she grumbled. "Usually it's misery." When Zaynab said nothing, Khalidah realized that she had been hoping her nurse would contradict her. A lump rose in her throat.

"Your father will handle them," Zaynab said at last, "but in the meantime, I won't have you dishonor him in front of his brother."

To avoid Zaynab's eyes, Khalidah began to wash, but she asked with careful nonchalance, "Who is the man they brought with them?"

"They brought a number of retainers with them, as always."

"I do not think that he is a retainer. He looks like a musician."

"Ah, yes," Zaynab answered. "He's Abd al-Hadi's new minstrel. They say the sheikh has taken a shine to him and brings him everywhere."

Khalidah nodded as though this information were of only perfunctory interest to her and continued her bath in silence. When she was finished, Zaynab approached her with the dress. It was the traditional double dress of the tribes, made of deep blue wool and heavy with Zaynab's own embroidery.

"It's so hot . . ." Khalidah began halfheartedly.

"It brings out the color of your eyes," Zaynab said in a tone that brooked no argument. This was her standard reply when Khalidah complained about clothing, but it made little sense to the girl. The color of her eyes—a deep, coppery gold—was not generally considered an asset. It reminded people of her mother, and most wanted to forget that Brekhna had ever existed.

Nevertheless, Khalidah stood obediently while Zaynab tied her sash, loaded her with jewelry, and pinned up her red silk headscarf. When Zaynab was finally satisfied, she led Khalidah outside and made her wait while she brought tea from the kitchen in an elaborate silver pot. She handed the pot to the girl and gave her a gentle push in the direction of the men's section. Then, as Khalidah had hoped, she retreated back inside.

Sheikh Abd al-Aziz's reputation for eccentricity was widespread. His daughter's unconventional education was generally agreed to be the primary example of this, along with the fact that he had married only once, despite that wife's having died early on and left him only a single, worthless daughter. A more acceptable madness was his passion for horses. Though many tribesmen shared it to the extent of bringing their best horses into their tents at night, none of the Hassan went as far as to give them a room of their own, decorated as richly as the sheik's, complete with woven tapestries and filigreed lamps.

This stable lay between the men's and the women's quarters. During the day it was empty, and long ago Khalidah had discovered its usefulness both as an escape route during tedious gatherings and for eavesdropping on the interesting ones to which she was not invited. Looking around to make certain that she was unwatched, Khalidah slipped inside the stable. She lifted her skirts out of habit, though the floor was pristine, having already been cleaned for the coming night. Setting the teapot down beside a copper watering pail, she put her ear to the cloth wall.

A man with an affable, expansive voice, like her father's but smoother, was saying: "I realize that this must seem abrupt to you, but the Franj have been testing the treaty of late, and I fear there may not be time for lengthy negotiations." This would be Abd al-Hadi.

"*One* Franji," her father answered, his own voice cool and meticulous. "Brins Arnat."

"Yes, and Arnat may well be more powerful than the rest of them put together, since their king appears to be his puppet and the Templars his lapdogs. Arnat flouted the truce when he attacked that caravan at midwinter, and as far as I have heard, none of his own people have done anything about it—least of all King Guy."

"Salah ad-Din is said to be negotiating the prisoners' release."

"Arnat does not negotiate," said Abd al-Hadi, his agitation more apparent against his brother's calm, "except with the point of his sword."

"Our swords, too, have points," Abd al-Aziz countered.

"I have no desire to fight the Franj," his brother said. "Don't look at me like that—as if I were a coward! It is not cowardice, but wisdom. If that hotheaded Sultan challenges Arnat, it will be all the excuse the Franj need to begin another war. And since it seems unlikely that Arnat will suddenly decide to listen to his king or appease the Sultan, I would prefer to be as far from both of them as possible, as soon as possible."

"Then why this proposition?" asked Abd al-Aziz, his own voice neutral. "What do you think an alliance with me will be worth to you when my grazing lands are covered by Franj fortresses?"

"More than it will be if I'm skewered on a Franj sword."

"More, then, than Allah's rewards to a fallen warrior of the Faith."

There was a taut, bitter silence. Then Abd al-Hadi said, "The Franj are rash and impatient. They will overreach themselves one day, and these lands will be ours again. When I have lived to see that day, I will meet Allah gladly." After another long silence he continued, "Either way, we have strayed from the purpose of our conversation."

"Indeed," Abd al-Aziz answered slowly, and Khalidah could almost see his face, narrow and intelligent with a wash of contempt, the black eyes bright with the thoughts he was not speaking. "I can see the wisdom in your suggestion, but Khalidah is not prepared for marriage."

And there it was: the word she had known she would hear. Presupposing it had made it no less bitter. She longed to think that her father was stalling out of love for her, that perhaps he would not really let this happen, but she could not quite deceive herself.

"She is nearly sixteen," countered Abd al-Hadi. "Most girls her age are married already."

"Khalidah is not like other girls. She is headstrong, unruly, and she has not had the benefit of a mother's guidance."

"Has her nurse not educated her?" her uncle demanded.

Abd al-Aziz sighed. "She has tried."

"And if she has failed, why then do you keep her?"

Abd al-Aziz said nothing.

"I surmise from your reticence that there have been other offers."

Still, Abd al-Aziz didn't answer.

"Blood is weightier than gold, Brother. You cannot tell me you would prefer Khalidah to marry outside the clan, especially when you have no heirs to carry on the bloodline . . ."

Khalidah turned away, disgusted. There had indeed been other offers of marriage. Not many, to be sure—she had her reputation for unruliness and her mother's mysterious ancestry to thank for that—but she was still a clan chief's daughter. She had listened to all of her suitors' petitions through this same woven wall, and, as always, the labyrinthine negotiations had reached their bottom line—the sum of her worth. But though Khalidah's father was wealthy, she liked to think that she would not have been easily bought even if he had not been.

Nevertheless, Abd al-Aziz was human, and therefore not without a secret longing. Whereas other men lusted for gold or status, he longed for unity. The only thing he regretted more than the loss of his wife was the division of the Hassan. As far back as Khalidah could remember, her father had been trying to find a way to reunite with his brother, but Abd al-Hadi had never been willing to settle for less than his brother's complete abdication.

Never until now. Khalidah thought of the golden mare—the color of hope and longing—and knew that Abd al-Hadi had finally found her father's price. She picked up her teapot, hoping that it wasn't too late.

Two

THE men's section was crowded with Abd al-Hadi's retainers. They were busy tearing at a roasted sheep on a massive platter of rice, which was laid out by the fire. Around the rugs were piles of cushions woven in brilliant patterns, and on the cushions the men reclined: Khalidah's father, thin and stern; Abd al-Hadi, with a similar face but the build of a well-fed king; her cousin Numair, who had been a petulant boy when she had seen him last and was now a tall, bearded man, handsome but just as sullen; and, finally, the minstrel, whose eyes bored into her from the shadows.

"It is not like you to await an invitation to sit," her father said dryly.

Realizing that she had been staring at the minstrel, Khalidah quickly inclined her head to her father and uncle and said her *salaam*s. Then she poured a little of the now-tepid tea into the sand in the obligatory sacrifice and set the pot down.

"I'm sorry to have kept you waiting, Father," she said.

Abd al-Aziz began to answer, but his brother interrupted, smiling, "Who would not wait a lifetime for such grace? Last time I saw you, you were a skinned-kneed child. Come, Sayyida, sit by me." Abd al-Hadi patted a cushion between himself and Numair. Reluctantly, Khalidah sat down, twitching her headscarf forward to hide her expression.

"No, put it back," Numair said, pinning her with snake's eyes. "Let me see your face."

Both the request and its manner put her back up. Khalidah glanced at her father, hoping that he would chastise her cousin, but he told her, "Do as he says," looking as though he would rather have said something quite different. Reluctantly, Khalidah pushed back her scarf, its decorative coins tinkling as they fell behind her shoulders. She could feel Numair's eyes burning into her right cheek and the minstrel's on her left, cool and appraising but no less intent. She sensed acutely the dark undercurrents battling beneath the placid scene.

"Try the mutton, Niece, it is superb," Abd al-Hadi said, reaching into the sheep's rib cage for a kidney.

Khalidah's stomach flopped over. A roasted carcass made her queasy at the best of times, and at the moment she was already feeling nauseous. "Thank you, Uncle, but I have eaten already." She poured herself a glass of cold tea and sipped to hide her discomfort.

Her father and uncle exchanged a look, and then Abd al-Aziz cleared his throat. "Daughter," he said, "you know that I have long wished to see the two branches of the Hassan united again, as they were under my father. Now my brother has come with a proposal that would achieve this, and end our constant warring." He paused, as if steeling himself. "He suggests that you and your cousin Numair marry."

Khalidah leveled her eyes at her father. "And how have you answered him, Father?"

"I haven't, yet."

"And why not?" she continued, not caring whether the men thought her too bold.

After a long pause, her father said, "When the Franj's late king died, he left their state in chaos and his sister Sibylla to claim the crown. Of course she declared her husband king, and so we are saddled with Guy, a weak, insipid man by all accounts, far too willing to listen to the loudest voice in a crowd and too stupid to remember anything but the last words it said."

Khalidah set her tea glass down but said nothing, for although none of this was news to her, her father seemed to want his guests to believe that it was.

"Unfortunately," he continued, frowning, "the loudest voice at present is that of Brins Arnat, and Arnat has no respect for Salah ad-Din's truce."

"What about Count Tripoli?" Khalidah asked, earning herself a raised eyebrow from the minstrel, an indulgent smile from Abd al-Hadi, and a look of cold suspicion from Numair. "He is respected by his people, and he in turn has always respected Salah ad-Din. Can he not intervene on the Sultan's behalf?"

Abd al-Aziz indicated to Khalidah to pour him a glass of tea. When he recorded its temperature he gave her a pointed look, but rather than comment he set it aside and said, "This is precisely the problem. Many Franj think the crown should have passed to Tripoli—Tripoli himself thinks so—and it's divided their kingdom. So Arnat sits in his fortress at Kerak pulling Guy's puppet strings and calling for Saracen blood, while Tripoli sulks in the north. The Templars are behind Kerak; the Hospitallers too, no doubt. It is only a matter of time before they goad King Guy to war, and Salah ad-Din will be all too ready to meet them when it happens."

Abd al-Aziz lapsed into silence, staring at the tapestry that separated the men's section from the stable. When Khalidah was certain that no one else was going to speak, she ventured:

"Forgive my ignorance, Father, but what does this have to do with my marriage?"

Again, an unfathomable look passed between the brothers. It was Abd al-Hadi who answered, "The Hassan are wealthy and powerful, but right now we are like a snake with two heads. Both my brother and I feel"—and Khalidah knew that she did not mistake the coldness in his tone—"that the time has come to stop spilling our own blood: to reunite our clan into a force that can withstand both the Franj and the Sultan."

Khalidah was well aware that there was more to this than either man was saying, more even than what she had overheard; yet what they *were* telling her was strange enough. That they would wish to unite against the Franj made sense, but she knew that her father supported Salah ad-Din, and the conversation she had overheard made it clear that he would willingly fight for him. Why then speak of withstanding him?

Finally, she said, "And when did you plan for us to marry?"

This time, when Abd al-Hadi looked toward his brother, Abd al-Aziz didn't look back. Attempting a smile, Abd al-Hadi said, "Given the situation, I would suggest we hold the henna ceremony tonight."

It was only through respect for her father that Khalidah didn't throw her tea in her uncle's face. The henna ceremony was the first in a series that would last a week, at the end of which she would be Numair's wife. It should have been preceded by a formal request for her hand and a negotiation of the marriage contract, conducted over the course of months. What Abd al-Hadi was proposing was a disgrace, an indemnification of her own honor and her father's, as the only time a girl was married so quickly was when her purity was in question or her father had some dire need of her bride-price.

Nobody moved. It was so quiet that the creaking of the wooden tent poles in the breeze seemed like a storm in a forest. The minstrel had stopped fiddling with his *qanun* and sat staring at her over his master's shoulder, with a desperate look in his eyes. And she wanted nothing more than to scream, *Why? Why should I trust you? Why should I do what any one of you asks of me?*

Yet she could not shake that earlier feeling of recognition, or her sense, however unfounded, that the minstrel's was the only request she had heard that day untainted by self-interest. So in a small, cold voice Khalidah said:

"Uncle, you do me too great an honor. But as you have asked, I most humbly accept my cousin's proposal and look forward to joining your family as a daughter." And then, without waiting for a reply and with nothing like humility, she stood and left.

KHALIDAH didn't go back to the women's quarters, but walked away from camp toward the scrubland where the horses were grazing. She did not want to think about what she had just done, nor why. Instead she watched the new mare. Among the horse-breeding tribes, the Hassani line was considered the finest, but the gift horse blazed out among them like Venus among lesser stars. *And yet*, Khalidah thought, *you too are only chattel*. She pictured the golden mare leading a whooping column into battle. No doubt she would throw herself among the spears and swords with a lion's courage, and Numair—for Khalidah had no doubt that Numair did not really intend to part with this horse—would only curse her when she fell. The mare danced, graceful despite her hobble, and Khalidah sighed.

"She is beautiful, isn't she," said a low, musical voice at her shoulder.

Khalidah whirled. Abd al-Hadi's minstrel stood behind her, looking, as she had looked, toward the new horse. "You!" she sputtered. "Why are you tormenting me?"

"This isn't the place to discuss it, Sayyida," he said softly.

"We shouldn't be discussing anything, anywhere," Khalidah said.

"No," he agreed. "I should be practicing dance tunes and you should be combing your hair or bathing in lime juice or whatever women do to prepare for a henna ceremony." He smiled in a way that told Khalidah she had not imagined the irony in his tone. "Instead, we both stand contemplating Zahirah. No doubt this means something; but I am a musician, not a philosopher."

"Zahirah?"

"The gift horse."

Khalidah glanced from the horse to the man. There was also something regal in his bearing and a pride in his keen black eyes that set him in relief against the desert. He looked like a man others would die for; even as she thought it, the idea appalled her.

"If you have something to say to me," she said shortly, "then say it—preferably in plain terms."

"I have a good deal to say to you, but we must find somewhere safer. I have enough troubles without being caught alone with a sheikh's daughter."

Khalidah stared at him in the way she knew unnerved most people, but he just looked calmly back at her. Finally, against all her better judgment, she said, "Do you see those rocks above the camp?" She pointed, and his eyes followed her finger to the sand-stone outcropping where she and Bilal had hidden from Zaynab that morning. He nodded.

"Pretend to be examining the horses. When you have walked once around the herd, go up there. On the eastern side, you'll find a small cave. I will be there." She turned to go, and then turned back. "Have you a name, minstrel?"

"Sulayman," he answered.

Khalidah nodded and hurried away. She rounded the camp and then made her way up the hill, keeping to the rocks when she could and hoping that no one was watching. She settled into the cave's shadow, her eyes on a hawk wheeling in the deep blue sky until Sulayman appeared, backlit by the afternoon sun, his face momentarily in shadow and his head surrounded by a bright nimbus. For a second Khalidah felt she was looking at something more than human, and that he in turn was looking into her. Then he knelt beside her and the illusion was broken.

"Thank you for trusting me, Sayyida," he said.

"I do not claim to trust you," Khalidah answered.

"Well, then, for listening." Khalidah conceded this with a nod, then waited for him to go on. At last he said, "There is no easy way to say this, so I will simply say it. You are in grave danger. I did not mean to unsettle you earlier, but it was imperative that you accepted Numair's proposal unconditionally."

"Why?"

"Because you wouldn't have survived the night if you had not. He intends to have your tribe's lands at any cost."

"And so he would murder me in my bed?"

"Precisely."

"And how exactly would he do that with only a handful of men to support him, and all my tribe around me?"

Sulayman sighed. "Things are not quite as they seem. Several miles to the west of here, there is another camp. A camp of your uncle's warriors, substantially fleshed out with Franj mercenaries."

"Franj mercenaries!" She paused, considering the possibilities, not least of which was that Sulayman was mad. "How do you know this?"

His head gave an equivocal tilt. "A rich man's minstrel hears things, many of which he'd rather not, most of which he shouldn't. I will not endanger you by identifying my sources. But rest assured, they are trustworthy."

Of course he was lying; he had to be lying. Bedu raids were first and foremost about honor. Surprise attacks were honorable. Hiring Franj to fight one's battles was not.

"It's senseless," she said, more to herself than to Sulayman. "Our lands are not worth his honor."

"Perhaps not now," Sulayman answered, "but they could be. If, for instance, your cousin controlled a port city adjacent to them."

"Well, he does not."

"Not yet. But I have heard he has wrangled a promise from someone in a position to make it, that he will be given lordship of Ayla, in exchange for certain services."

It was just strange enough to be true, and Khalidah could not come up with a compelling reason for Sulayman to be lying. "So what, then?" she asked at last. "I have no choice but to submit to Numair and become Lady of Ayla? To live in a palace like a canary in a cage, turning a blind eye while the Franj drown pilgrims and slaughter children? Or does my honorable cousin intend to throttle me on our wedding night?"

She had intended sarcasm, but as she spoke the words, she found she could easily imagine Numair doing just that, with the same calm, predatory stare he had cast on her earlier. "He'll cut my father's throat after the wedding, I suppose," she said, her tone suddenly defeated. "Perhaps his own father's, too. He'll take our wealth and our horses, and what's left of the tribe will wander the deserts like outcasts . . ." She shook her head. "There must be an alternative."

"Indeed . . . that is why I am here."

"You? Do you intend to fight off Numair's raiders yourself?"

"Hardly."

"Then I suppose you mean to run away and hide."

"Precisely," he answered. "And I intend to take you with me."

"Will I find then that you are a long-lost prince?" Khalidah laughed bitterly. "You must think I'm a fool! You could be working for anyone—for Numair himself."

He nodded, squinting into the afternoon glare. "I could be. But we have sat here alone for some while now. If I had intended to kill you, I'd have done it already."

Khalidah smiled to herself, but she said nothing. It was better to let him believe this for the time being. If she needed to disabuse him of the idea of her vulnerability, surprise would work in her favor.

"Even if I agree to go with you," she said at last, "I don't see how it's possible. They're bound to notice if I'm not at my own henna ceremony. Then my father will be after us, and he knows every sand grain of this desert . . . as do my uncle and cousin."

"You'll go to the ceremony and leave afterward. By the time your people are in a condition to follow, we'll be far enough away that it won't matter."

Khalidah wanted to take exception to the implicit command, but she couldn't. The fact was, despite what she had said—despite the pure, mad folly of it—she had known that she was going to go with Sulayman the moment he suggested it.

"What are you going to do to them?" she asked, still trying to sound equivocal.

"Don't worry about that. Just make sure you drink nothing but water tonight."

"Do you plan to poison the wine?"

He smiled. "Only to modify it."

Khalidah shook her head. "And so we ride away, and leave my father and Zaynab and Bilal and all the others to the mercy of Numair and his Franj."

"I don't know much, Sayyida, but I do know that your cousin is essentially lazy. There is always a risk in battle, and if he can claim your lands without one, that is the option he will prefer. I intend to make it clear that you are still alive; as long as Numair believes that, then your people should be safe."

"Should be?"

He sighed with an infuriating note of tolerance and said, "This is the best I can do, Sayyida. It is this, or certain death. But of course, the decision is yours."

"Who do you think you are?" Khalidah demanded.

To her surprise, Sulayman smiled, his eyes creasing to half-moons, teeth flashing white against his dark skin. Again, Khalidah had the bewildering sensation that she was in the presence of someone who deserved reverence. "I'm afraid that's a question without an answer," he said. "But what you really mean is, who am I to you? As to that, I'm little more than a messenger from someone who does not wish to see you harmed. I can lead you to a safe place, where there are people who can help you. But first you have to trust me."

"In fact, I do not," Khalidah answered. "I need only agree to ride with you."

Sulayman shrugged. "As you like."

Khalidah looked at him, her eyes brighter and more golden than her headscarf's coins. "Numair intends to keep Zahirah for himself, doesn't he?"

She thought she knew the answer, but Sulayman surprised her, saying, "No. She is a gift . . . or rather, a bribe."

"For a Franji?"

He nodded. Khalidah considered this, her eyes fixed on the grazing horses far below. Even at a distance, Zahirah's graceful form was unmistakable. "I'll go with you," she said. "But Zahirah is mine."

Three

WHEN Khalidah returned to the tent, Zaynab was waiting for her with another rose-scented basin of water. She had expected a scolding, but Zaynab didn't even ask her where she'd been; she simply helped her off with her dress and began to wash her hair. At last Khalidah couldn't stand it anymore.

"Say something, Zaynab," she implored.

Zaynab squeezed the water from Khalidah's hair and then sat down behind her to comb it out. "It's you, Khalidah, who are withholding words."

Cold water trickled down the inside of Khalidah's shift and she shivered, wondering how Zaynab could have found out so quickly. She was trying to decide how best to answer her when the woman continued bitterly, "It isn't like you to submit so silently to so great a dishonor. To think, they haven't even given you time to gather a trousseau!"

Giddy with relief, Khalidah's words tumbled out. "What use is a trousseau anyway? I would never wear all those dresses, jewelry makes it difficult to play the oud, and the lot of it weighs down the pack camels needlessly when it's time to move."

"And what does this cousin of yours bring with him to sweeten the bargain?" Zaynab continued, ignoring Khalidah's argument. "No gold, no camels or goats, just a horse!"

"She *is* a very fine horse . . ." Khalidah ventured.

Zaynab snorted. "I might have known you'd say that. But you can neither wear nor eat a horse—unless you are a Franji, filthy creatures—and anyone can see that she is not intended as a brood-mare. It is of little use to anyone else that your father will look fine riding her at the front of a caravan—or, as Allah wills it, to charge the Franj."

Little do you know, Khalidah thought sadly. "What would my mother have done?" she said aloud.

Zaynab frowned and came around to face Khalidah, holding a pot of kohl and a fine brush. "If Brekhna had been here," she answered as she began lining the girl's eyes, "it would never have come to this. Look down, don't squint!" she admonished; then she sighed. "Your mother was my friend, but there was a good deal about her that she kept close. She was unpredictable, some said fickle. But one thing I can tell you, she saw right through Abd al-Hadi's bluster to his weak-ness. She would never have married you to his son. But Brekhna is not here, and there's nothing I can do to stop this farce."

Khalidah heard the apology in the words, and she leaned for-ward to kiss Zaynab's cheek. "It is not your responsibility to stop it. If it buys peace for the tribe, then it is worthwhile, and in the end . . . well, I'd have been married one way or another. What dif-ference is there between husbands?"

Zaynab's look turned shrewd and slightly pitying. "I think you would find that there can be a very great difference; but that doesn't signify now. At any rate, I will be with you in your new home, which I hope will be a comfort to you."

"You intend to come with me?"

"Of course I do, if Numair will have me. What use will your father have for me once you are gone?"

"What about Bilal?"

Zaynab sighed. "Bilal is not a child any longer, and for all I love him, I cannot show him how to be a man. I leave that to your father, just as he has left it to me to show you how to be a woman. Besides, Bilal and I have never brought each other much joy. Per-haps we will love each other more for the separation." She paused, shook her head. "Anyhow, you will have children of your own soon, and then you will need my help as you never have."

Khalidah had a sudden image of a long line of little boys, all looking up at her with cold, reptilian eyes. To hide her horror, she turned toward the front of the tent. "Do you hear that?" she asked.

Someone had taken up a drum, playing a fast beat. A flute joined in with a reedy syncopation. The next moment, Khalidah's frayed attention was snared by a rippling, reverberant trill that grew in volume until it plunged like a cliff bird into skimming flight. She had heard a *qanun* played once or twice before, but never like this.

"You're still in your shift!" Zaynab called sharply.

With a start, Khalidah dropped the tent flap she had been about to lift. "I'm sorry. It's just that music . . ."

Zaynab gave her a keen, appraising look. "Indeed. Put on your dress, and then you can go see."

It was then Khalidah noticed the dress spread out on her bed: silk the color of heart's-blood, the yoke and hems covered with Zaynab's colorful embroidery, which always suggested birds and beasts without ever quite breaking the laws against idolatry. Zaynab must have been working on it for a long time; she had no doubt intended it for a happier occasion than this. Tears pricked Khalidah's eyes as she touched the soft fabric.

"At least you won't be married in rags," Zaynab said, pretending not to notice. "We can make others once you have gone to—"

She bit off the rest of the thought and busied herself with helping Khalidah dress. When she was finished, Khalidah and Zaynab stepped outside. In the space of a half hour, the camp had been transformed. The short desert twilight had deepened to night, and a full moon was cresting the sandstone hills. The camp itself was alight with fires and lanterns, and the stars had retreated from the competition. Despite the evening chill, the flap had been turned back from the front of the sheikh's section, and people were spilling out from the bright interior into the flickering shadows.

With Zaynab in her wake, Khalidah made her way through the crowd toward the fabulous music. They parted for her, wishing her good luck and happiness. She saw both men and women, which was strange. Normally the henna night was segregated, the women and men celebrating separately. But then, Khalidah reminded herself, nothing about this wedding was right, and by the next morning none of it would matter anyway.

In the men's section, a group of women sat in a tight circle by the stable wall. They were women she had known all her life, and yet when they looked at her now she saw wariness beneath their smiles, and she burned with shame for what they must be thinking. Sulayman glanced up from his *qanun* and for a moment their eyes met; then he looked back at his flashing plectra. Numair watched her with predator's eyes, while Bilal sat in his shadow with a brooding look. Her father and his brother were deep in conversation and did not notice her at all.

Looking from one to the next, Khalidah felt suddenly lightheaded. Well aware that fainting now would only add credence to everyone's suspicions, she greeted the men quickly and then went to sit among the women. She barely heard as they began to sing the traditional songs extolling her beauty and virtues. She held out her hands obediently for Zaynab and sat staring at them as her nurse began to draw intricate patterns with the tube of henna paste. Khalidah had of course attended many henna ceremonies before her own, and normally she fidgeted until the unfortunate artist sent her away, usually with her tattoos only half-finished and admonitions not to touch the paste until it had dried (which she invariably ignored). Now, Khalidah's stillness was such that Zaynab asked her repeatedly if she was well.

In fact, Khalidah was wondering the same thing herself. Dizziness had become dislocation. It was as if a scrim had come down between herself and the world, and nothing looked quite real. She watched as if dreaming while the men drank wine and passed the hookah, growing loud with false merriness, and the people outside the tents danced and the women painted their hands and sang hollow words.

Sulayman played a melody that seemed to grow ever more intricate, mirroring the latticed paintings on her skin. When she thought that Zaynab wasn't looking, Khalidah stole glances at him. The lamplight flickered golden against his cheek and his fingers moved like river reeds, the plectra's metal rings flashing. Then, as she watched, a figure emerged from the shifting light and shadow of the tent wall behind him, hovering against the corporeal scene like an image from a fever dream. She was a woman, her white robe richly embroidered at the collar, cuffs, and hem, as was her headscarf. She wore no veil, and her dark hair hung down her back in long plaits beneath the scarf, wound with beads and cowry shells. Her face was fair skinned, marked at the forehead and cheeks with some kind of patterns, and her features had a fierceness that reminded Khalidah of a hunting hawk. Her eyes were as golden as Khalidah's own.

Abruptly, the music stopped. The woman faded back into the white-and-gold tapestry behind Sulayman, and Khalidah realized that she was standing, her patterned hand reaching toward the place where the woman had been, where now Sulayman sat alone, his hand resting on the *qanun*'s strings as another man's might on the belly of his lover.

"Khalidah!" Zaynab hissed. "Say that you recognized the song . . . say something, or the minstrel is dead!"

Khalidah looked at her father, who looked back with cold eyes. She could think of nothing to say but the truth, and so, though she knew that it was nearly as bad as their suspicion, she said, "I am sorry, Father. The music the minstrel was playing . . . it seemed as if . . . that is to say, it put me in mind of my mother, and it seemed for a moment that she was here with us . . ."

Her father continued to look at her, though now his expression was inscrutable, and Khalidah's heart sank. All at once Abd al-Hadi roared with laughter. "Ah, the look on your face, girl!" he said. "Truly, you have seen little of the world if Sulayman's pandering can capture your imagination so. Now, if they're finished with you, how about a song?"

Khalidah looked around in confusion. She still wasn't entirely certain how she had come to be standing in her father's tent, with so many suspicious eyes on her and her heart scurrying like a hare in a hawk's shadow. She hated singing to an audience at the best of times; now, it was unthinkable. So she offered up her hands, covered with intricate pipings of sticky, green-brown henna paste.

"I cannot play my oud with these hands."

"From what I have heard, your voice needs no accompaniment," her uncle answered without missing a beat.

She took a deep breath, said, "As you wish, Uncle," and stepped toward the fire. She settled herself between her father and Abd al-Hadi, with her back firmly to Sulayman, and said, "What would you have me sing?"

Abd al-Hadi seemed already to be losing interest in his own idea. "Oh, anything," he said, pulling a piece of meat from the roasted goat at the center of the gathering and contemplating it. "Perhaps a love story. 'Layla and Majnun'?"

He rolled the meat with a bit of rice and tossed them into his mouth. Khalidah swallowed around the lump in her throat. Though it was indeed a love story, she could think of few less befitting a marriage celebration than that ballad of star-crossed lovers driven to madness and death. But, as with the rest, she had no choice but to obey her uncle's order.

A few lines into the ballad, a silence fell over the guests. Khalidah's voice was a spear that pierced and pinned them, made them listen; and, listening, they felt the faint stirrings of a profound remembrance, as if they had wept with Layla, or raved with Majnun among the wild beasts. At last it was over. Khalidah fell silent as the final notes were lost on the wind. For a moment no one moved, and no sound was heard but the half-remembered echo of Khalidah's song. More than a few people, not realizing it, were silently weeping. Then the murmuring began and time resumed. Khalidah tried not to notice the strange look some of the people gave her, a mixture of awe and fear.

"Wonderful!" roared Abd al-Hadi. "Your Khalidah is truly a jewel among women—eh, Numair?"

He nudged his son and Numair looked up, his eyes like caves in his sandstone face. "Indeed," he answered. "A voice so extraordinary almost makes one wonder if the stories about her mother are true." He looked at Khalidah for a moment with detached intensity before he smiled. Abd al-Hadi laughed again, too loudly, and Abd al-Aziz took a sip from his cup to hide an expression Khalidah could imagine only too well.

Khalidah herself was exhausted. If she had not known it to be impossible, she would have said that while she sang she had been with Layla, walking every step of her tragic road. If she closed her eyes she could even see her: slight, frail-skinned, unremarkable except for her eyes, wide and deep as the night sky above a half smile of recognition. She reeled, and the room darkened. She knew that she had to get out, away from this celebration of her purchase, from the duplicitous smiles and the lamplight's flickers of illusion. She was unaware of having reached out for support until Zaynab's arm came around her, wiry and warm. At that moment she could have wept, and Zaynab seemed to know it.

"You must excuse Khalidah now," she said to the men. "This has been a long and exciting day for her"—this she said with a distinct irony—"and she needs to rest."

She stood up, still firmly supporting Khalidah without appearing to, and when they had been dismissed, she led her toward their own quarters.

Four

ONCE Zaynab had pinned the flap into place, Khalidah sank grate-fully onto her bed, unpinned her headscarf and jewelry and laid it aside, then began unwinding her sash.

"Let me do it," Zaynab said.

Khalidah shook her head. "I'm not a child anymore."

It seemed to Khalidah that there were many things Zaynab wanted to say to that, but instead she watched silently, looking oddly helpless as Khalidah undressed and combed her hair and climbed under her quilt. It occurred to Khalidah then that she had no idea how she would know when it was time to meet Sulayman. From there worry widened into panic. After all, she had no reason to trust him, no reason anymore to trust anything . . . and yet she knew with mounting clarity that she could not possibly remain where she was.

Sighing, she turned over. The hanging lamp was trimmed low. Across the room in her own bed, Zaynab was a dark bulk with a faint glint of open eyes. "You are thinking of the man with the *qanun*," she said softly.

Again, Khalidah wondered if Zaynab could have found out about their plan; then she realized that the woman had drawn an entirely different conclusion. "Why would I think of him?" she answered.

"I saw how you looked at him, Khalidah."

"Well, it wasn't what you think. Zaynab . . ." Khalidah faltered among the first lies that came to hand, but in the end she discarded them all. "What I said to my father was the truth. When he began to play, I saw my mother. *Saw* her—not just a memory."

Zaynab said nothing. Khalidah listened to the guttural patter of the drums, the low warble of the reed flute that seemed to have replaced Sulayman and his *qanun*. The filigreed lid of the lantern threw golden constellations across the dark cloth of the roof. They wavered gently as the tent swayed in the breeze.

At last Zaynab said, "I never knew that you remembered her."

Khalidah sighed. "Neither did I. But the woman I saw . . . I'd have known her anywhere."

Zaynab was silent again for a time; then, slowly, she said, "I suppose it's little wonder that the boy's music brought her back to you. Your mother played the *qanun* too."

A flash of white cloth and golden eyes, a faint drift of music: a memory. Khalidah sat on a high dune looking out across a universe of sand. A woman in white sat beside her. Her headscarf had slipped back, revealing four plaits of dark hair with deep red lights, like fire beyond a nighttime horizon. She held a *qanun* on her lap, but she did not play it. The wind blew across the strings, pulling faint harmonics from them and whipping them away again.

"She used to take me out," Khalidah said tremulously, "away from camp, into the desert."

"That's right," Zaynab agreed, "though I'm surprised that you remember. You were barely walking then. Brekhna had a hunger for open spaces and solitude. She never liked life in the camp, though she bore it for your father's sake and for yours. What else do you remember?"

"Not much. A feeling . . . a look. The color of her hair. Inside it looked black, but in the sun it was like the coat of a dark bay horse. The way she smiled, as if it were meant to cover something that it couldn't, quite. And then . . . and then, she was gone. I cried for her, but she never came. And then you came into our tent, and after a while I stopped missing her so much. I forgot her face . . . I thought I did . . ."

"She was a caged bird," Zaynab said in an odd, dreamy tone.

"Your father is a good man and a good leader, but—Allah forgive me my boldness—your mother should not have married him. She could never belong to him, as a wife must belong to her husband. I saw it in her at once, as she must have seen—" She faltered, and Khalidah had just enough time to wonder what words Zaynab had suppressed before she was speaking again. "She couldn't forget the ways of her people," she said, her voice even softer, more laconic than before, "and though she never said it, I always thought that she had loved someone else, once." Zaynab sighed. "But we are women. Our feelings don't matter in the world of men. You and Brekhna and I, we're all alike, except that in the end she had the strength to look truth in the eye. That's why she left. Perhaps there was Jinn blood in her after all . . ."

Zaynab's words slurred into sleepy silence, but Khalidah was wide awake. "Left?" she whispered. "What do you mean, left?"

Zaynab said nothing.

"My mother died!"

Zaynab answered with a snore. All at once, Khalidah realized that the camp had fallen silent. It was far too soon: a henna night celebration often lasted until dawn, as hers had had every appearance of doing when she had left. Khalidah pulled on a simple woolen dress and wrapped a shawl around her head, then lifted the flap.

In the flickering light of the fires people lay sprawled and curled. She crept outside and nudged the first person she saw, a plump old gossip called Rusa. The woman mumbled something unintelligible and then settled back to sleep. There was a cup in her hand, with a little wine still left in it. Khalidah pried it from her grasp and tasted the dregs. The bittersweet tang of poppy was subtle but to her—thanks to a long bout with a wasting cough as a child—unmistakable.

She was looking down at Rusa, wondering where Sulayman could have acquired enough opium to drug an entire wedding party, when a hand closed over her shoulder and whipped her around. The man who held her was one of Numair's retainers, though she could not recall his name. He had thin features, and the light of the dying fires sharpened them and hollowed his eyes, which fixed on her with a greedy look not unlike his master's.

"Take your filthy hands off of me!" Khalidah hissed, struggling against him; but he had caught her off guard, and he was too big for her to throw him.

"Unlike these fools," he said, while she fought his hands like a netted butterfly, "I never touch wine. It's too easily adulterated . . . as you have proven."

"How dare you speak to me this way!" Khalidah said. She had chosen outrage, hoping to stifle her fear, but his words chilled her to the bone. The suggestion of complicity was bad enough, but what really worried her was the fact that he would challenge her at all. Whereas he ought to show deference to a better who could, at a word, have him executed, he displayed only contempt—as if, to him, she were already dead.

"Sayyida." He inclined his head ironically. "Your cousin would be very disappointed to find that you had a hand in this." He gestured to the sleeping guests. "But you must admit that it looks suspicious. After all, you're the only one still awake—"

"Other than you."

He regarded her with cold amusement. "I haven't seen the minstrel since you left your father's tent so dramatically."

If all things were as they should be, the suggestion couldn't be more blatantly insulting to her, nor to him more dangerous. Khalidah tried again to pull free, but the man wrenched her around, slamming her against the pole supporting the stable wall. She cried out, but the night returned only silence.

"How dare you?" she spat, wavering between fear and fury.

"I?" the man laughed. "How dare *I*, you ask, after your scene tonight? Numair is a fool! Another man would have stoned his wife for such behavior!"

"I am not his wife," Khalidah cried, "and I never will be!"

She knew even as she said it that it was a mistake, but she couldn't stop herself: the insult of his hands on her drove the words out. As she watched them disappear into the sinkholes of his eyes, she knew that he was going to kill her. And then someone called her name.

She turned toward the sound and saw Bilal. She had barely time to register him stumbling toward them before the retainer caught him on the head with a clublike arm and sent him sprawling. He lay where he fell, ominously still.

"Bilal!" Khalidah cried, but the man had turned back to her and she was pinned, helpless against his rocklike strength. Time seemed to stretch as he drew the knife from his sash, to wash like slow water over stone. Nothing seemed real but the cruel sickle of the knife as he raised it to her throat. Yet as it touched her skin, Khalidah snapped from her torpor. Forcing a smile and a seductive tone, she looked up at the man from beneath her eyelashes and said, "Isn't there anything I can do to change your mind?"

He paused, momentarily relaxing in his surprise. It wasn't much, but it was enough. Khalidah pulled her arm free, grabbed his knife hand, and twisted it away from her. With a grunt, he kicked her legs out from under her. She fell, winded, and he pinned her to the ground. She fought him, managing to keep the knife away from her face and neck, but she couldn't shift him off her.

"If you kill me," she said desperately, "Numair's plans will come to nothing."

"What do you know about that?" he snarled, but once again he had been thrown, giving Khalidah time to wriggle away. He reached for her, grabbing the hem of her dress. She jerked it away, and as he struggled to his feet, she tripped him. He fell forward heavily. Khalidah brought her knee down hard on the wrist of his knife hand and felt something snap. The man screamed such that she thought he must wake the camp, but the supine figures around her didn't stir. She snatched the knife and as he tried to throw her off, she plunged it into his back. He flailed for a moment, trying to reach the knife with his useless hand, and then he fell forward again with a grunt and lay twitching.

Khalidah sank to her knees, shaking. For some reason, all she could think of was her shawl, which had slipped away during the fight: her head felt light and strange without it. But after a moment she remembered Bilal and turned, only to find Sulayman standing behind her, her shawl in his hands and, in his eyes, cautious respect.

"How long have you—" she began.

"Long enough."

"Bilal! He—"

"—will be fine, aside from a few days' headache. I already checked. He's a brave one. So are you." He considered the dead man for a moment, then said, "I can't say I'm sorry for the loss, but this will make more work for us. We'll have to move quickly."

"What are we going to do with him?" Khalidah asked, rewrapping her shawl.

Sulayman smiled, and from the breast of his waistcoat he drew a folded sheet of vellum stamped with a broken red seal. He handed it to Khalidah. She opened it and found a page of writing. Like the rest of her tribe, Khalidah couldn't read, but she knew enough to recognize that this was not Arabic script.

"Is it Franj writing?"

"It is," he said, taking it back.

"Can you read it?" she asked, impressed despite herself.

"I wrote it," he answered, and seeing her puzzled look, he flipped the letter closed, matching up the halves of the broken seal. It showed two knights riding a single horse.

"The Templar seal?" Khalidah said, more puzzled than before.

Sulayman nodded. "Your alibi. Hopefully, it will buy us enough time to get away. It's allegedly a letter from a Templar staying at Kerak to the Grand Master, discussing trouble with the local tribes and asking for help to subdue them. It doesn't mention you, but it's enough—that is, if anyone in this camp can read it."

"A Bedu has no need of written language," Khalidah bristled.

He sighed. "Nevertheless, when your father sees the seal, he'll assume that the Templars killed him"—he prodded the dead man with a toe—"and kidnapped you as a barter piece. With any luck, they'll all race off toward Kerak." He considered the dead man for a moment, then added, "Unfortunately, it makes *him* look like a hero." He thought for another moment, then smiled. "Unless, of course, I make him a conspirator." Sulayman took a small pouch from his sash and tucked it into the dead man's own.

"What was that?" Khalidah asked.

"The rest of the opium," he answered, then pulled the knife from the man's back, laid the letter over the wound, and drove the blade through the parchment and back into the flesh.

Khalidah didn't flinch.

"This isn't the first time you've killed a man," he said, observing her composure.

In fact, it was; but Khalidah still preferred that Sulayman not know too much about that aspect of her education.

"We need to leave now," he continued. "We've already waited too long."

Khalidah nodded and turned to the stable. Sure enough, Zahirah stood inside with her father's favorites, looking at her with wide, calm eyes and long ears pitched forward. Khalidah picked up a saddle and began to ready the horse for riding. She stood as docile as a lamb while Khalidah tightened the girth and slipped on the nose-chain and reins, but underneath the stillness she could sense the horse's taut energy. When Zahirah was ready she looked up to find that Sulayman had tacked Numair's own horse, a gray mare called Aasifa. In contrast to Zahirah's calm, she was dancing and tossing her head against the reins, and her dark eyes showed a rim of white.

"Are you sure about her?" Khalidah asked. "She looks like a handful."

"A horse is only a handful when her master doesn't know how to hold her." He laid a hand on the mare's shoulder and her movements became less frantic, though she still quivered with fear.

"You hate him," Khalidah said as she handed him a water bag and parcels of cracked wheat and dates and dried camel's milk.

Sulayman's face hardened for a moment as he stored the provisions in a saddlebag. "Hatred is a base emotion, but it's difficult to think of a better one to attach to a man who rapes his retainers' wives and then has them stoned for adultery."

Khalidah looked at him in shocked silence, then away. They said nothing more until the horses were loaded and they'd led them outside, beyond the tents.

"Are you ready?" Sulayman asked then.

Khalidah nodded and climbed onto Zahirah's back. Now the golden mare began to dance like the gray. Khalidah took one last look around the sleeping camp, and then she touched her heels to Zahirah's sides. The horse leapt forward like an arrow from a bow, picking up speed as she reached even ground, but Khalidah held her to a canter. She looked over her shoulder. Aasifa was there on Zahirah's heels, throwing her head about, fighting the reins, but it was too late to change horses now. Khalidah turned back to the empty desert unrolling before her and gave the mare her head. Zahirah looked around at her, as if to make sure she meant it, and then she hurtled off across the sand toward the starlit horizon like a spent night's memory of flame, shadowed by the storm-gray mare.

Hidden in the shadows at the edge of camp, Bilal watched them go.

Five

A bald sun rose over Wadi Tawil, bringing wind with it, a sirocco full of grit and heat from the Sahara. Its blasts and lulls rattled the tents like husks, foretelling a dry season. *To add insult to injury*, thought Bilal, looking toward the grazing land where the tender shoots of the new season's grass were already withering. He felt as if he were one of them. His head pounded and his eyes still wouldn't focus properly, though he couldn't tell whether this was a result of the drug or the retainer's fist; not that it mattered much.

"All right, Bilal," Abd al-Aziz sighed. "Let us hear this one more time."

Bilal regarded the solemn group gathered in the men's quarters: Abd al-Aziz, looking gray faced and ill; his brother, pinched and for once, contrite; Numair, whose stony circumspection was now tainted by wounded pride; his mother, Zaynab, whose eyes above her half veil were oddly serene; and at the center, the bloodstained letter, the presence that subdued them all with its implications.

"I've told you everything I know," the boy answered.

"What you have told us is primarily conjecture," the sheikh corrected mildly. "And I am trying to ascertain the facts."

"The facts!" cried Bilal, whose anger had had time enough to grow an offshoot of doubt that fed right back into it, stoking it higher than ever. "What fact is there, but that Khalidah ran away with that rogue like a—"

"Bilal!" Zaynab interrupted sharply.

Bilal shut his eyes for a moment, wishing that he could as eas-

ily shut out his memories of the past night; for whatever the letter with the Templar seal might mean, it did not change the fact
that Khalidah had abandoned family and honor to run away with
a man no better than a servant. *No better*, Bilal's heart whispered
to him, *than you are*. He had tried to tell himself that it changed
nothing—that Khalidah would never have been his anyway, that
he had always known that she didn't love him—but it didn't lessen
his pain. For though she would have been another man's wife had
she stayed, it would not have been her choice and would have taken
nothing from him. What she had done left him not even the sanctity of his impossible love for her to sustain him in her absence.

Still, Bilal agreed with Abd al-Aziz: it was the facts that were
important, and the facts were, in his mind, incontrovertible. Drawing a breath, he said, "I was asleep, drugged like the rest of you,
though not so heavily. I'd only had part of a cup of wine, since my
mother forbade me to have more."

"Wise woman," Abd al-Hadi muttered. The others remained
pointedly silent. Zaynab had, after all, slept through the entire
incident.

"Something wakened me," Bilal continued. "A woman screaming. When I went to look, I saw Khalidah with Abd al-Hadi's
retainer—the dead man. She was saying that she would never
marry her cousin." His eyes flickered apprehensively to Numair,
whose own look remained impassive. "The retainer saw me then,
and he hit me. When I wakened again, it was just in time to see
Khalidah and that—the minstrel, riding away. I followed them to
the edge of camp, but when the horses began to run . . . well, what
could I do?"

There was a moment of taut silence, and then Numair spoke,
his voice as grave as his uncle's but devoid of empathy. "You could
have roused someone who might have been able to catch them."

Bilal looked as though he had been struck. "I tried to, Sayyid,"
he answered tremulously, "but no one would wake."

Abd al-Aziz fingered his beard contemplatively. "And the letter? You have no idea where it came from?"

Bilal shook his head. "The first I knew of it was this morning, when it was found."

"Ah, what I would give for a man in this camp who knows his letters," the sheikh said in a bitter undertone.

"It would not help," Zaynab said dryly, "unless he knew Franj letters too. Besides, what does it matter? The seal tells us everything." She glanced at Abd al-Hadi as she said this. Abd al-Aziz, too, was looking at his brother.

"You cannot blame me if one of my men defected to the Franj!" he cried.

Abd al-Aziz gave him a long look full of conjecture, but in the end he said only, "What we need to determine is whether the Templars had a hand in my daughter's disappearance, or if she left simply because . . ."

Here, for the first time, the sheikh's composure failed him. Though the question had been addressed to Bilal, he looked at Zaynab, who looked back with unflinching eyes. Her silence had a distinct cast of indictment.

"Therefore," Abd al-Aziz continued at last, "although I would never normally ask anyone to betray a confidence, I ask you now, Bilal, whether Khalidah ever said anything to you that might give a clue, a reason why she might have run away. Something, perhaps, about the Templars?"

The sheikh could not keep the hope out of his voice with the last statement, which irritated Bilal. He answered shortly, "The only thing she said to me was that she did not wish to marry her cousin."

Abd al-Aziz scrutinized him for another long moment. Then he said, "Thank you, Bilal. Your faithfulness will not go unrewarded. You are dismissed."

"But . . ." Bilal began.

"You have something else to tell us?"

Bilal shook his head and retreated, avoiding his mother's eyes.

Once outside he circled the tent, ducked past the kitchen with its sharp-eyed serving girls, and then slipped into the stable from the back. When he put his ear to the tapestry, he heard his mother's voice, low and angry: ". . . don't know any more than you do!"

"Forgive me, Zaynab, if I find that difficult to believe," Abd al-Aziz answered.

Zaynab snorted. "Which is precisely why you are sitting here wondering what to do."

"Meaning?"

"You fail to accept what you *do* know."

"What is there to accept?" interjected Abd al-Hadi. "If you ask me, the two events are unrelated. My retainer was deceiving me, and my niece ran off with my good-for-nothing minstrel. The former seems to me to be a closed case, as the man is dead. As for the latter, your daughter's intentions are obvious, particularly in light of her scene last night. No father should be asked to accept such dishonor."

"As I recall, Khalidah offered a legitimate explanation for that 'scene,'" said Zaynab.

"What," scoffed Abd al-Hadi, "that silly story about her mother?"

The silence stretched and sagged. At last Abd al-Aziz broke it. "I would like to believe that Khalidah has gone to look for her mother," he said wearily. "I would rather believe that she was kidnapped by Brins Arnat than what appears to be the case. But I do not think that either Arnat or the Templars could have much interest in a Bedu's daughter, and a sudden longing for Brekhna does not explain the drugged wine, the murdered retainer, the stolen horses, and least of all the presence of the man with the *qanun* in all three." Abd al-Aziz's voice had risen toward the end of this speech, its frayed edges betraying his struggle to resist anger. "Particularly when my wife is long since dead."

"Dead to *you*," Zaynab said stonily, and on the other side of the tapestry Bilal found himself suddenly attending her words.

"What are you saying?" asked Abd al-Hadi, warily.

"Tell them, Sayyid," Zaynab said, in a tone Bilal could not believe his mother would take with the sheikh, and still less that the sheikh would endure. "Tell them that you have lied to your daughter—to all of them—about her mother's fate."

"Don't tell me that you told her so," Abd al-Aziz replied, the anger flowing forth now.

"I kept my promise to you," she said bitterly. "Whatever Khalidah knows, she figured out on her own."

"Indeed?" Abd al-Aziz's tone was cold, mocking, not unlike Numair's. "And what clues did you let slip, out of spite for me?"

"Spite for you?" she answered, equally furious. "Ah, Sayyid, I would never have taken you for so great a fool! Do you not realize that this is your own doing? You might have been able to banish Brekhna from your own heart, but the living cannot be buried. Khalidah could not stop being half her mother's, just because it hurt you; and yet she tried out of love for you, and is it any wonder that you don't like the results? Did you really think that Brekhna's daughter could submit to a marriage of convenience? She tried to tell you—even last night she tried—but the only one who listened was the minstrel. So follow her if you like, but do not underestimate her."

A sweep of fabric, a tinkle of coined anklets, followed by a hush. Bilal sat as stunned as he knew the men on the other side of the tapestry must be, his mother's words echoing through the long silence. Once again it was Abd al-Aziz who broke it, and though the fury in his voice was gone, it remained cold and sardonic.

"You have said very little about any of this, Numair. She was, after all, your betrothed. What, in your opinion, should we do?"

"Let her go," Numair answered without pause or emotion. "She is no longer worth the sweat of our horses."

"And if the letter is not a coincidence? If the Templars had some hand in this?" It was difficult for Bilal to tell from his tone whether Abd al-Aziz himself was advocating the idea.

Numair shrugged. "I will go into Oultrejourdain if you like, and see if I can find her."

"You do not sound particularly keen."

"That is because I do not believe that I will succeed," Numair answered.

"Very well," the sheikh answered, "but I am not so quick to dismiss my daughter. Therefore, I will accept your offer and I will send scouts east."

Numair smiled wryly. "Do not bother, Uncle. I have already sent my own men east."

"You are very certain of her guilt," said Abd al-Aziz, his voice frigid.

A pause, during which Bilal would have given anything to see the expressions on the three men's faces. Then Numair answered with distinct irony, "Allah metes out justice in the few places you cannot reach, Uncle. And now, if you'll excuse me, I will choose two of your horses to replace the ones your daughter has stolen—no, make it three, as I have never seen the horse that could match Zahirah—and then I will be on my way to Oultrejourdain . . . if that's really what you wish."

But his nonquestion was to remain forever unanswered, for there was a sudden clamor of hooves, a horse galloping up to the sheikh's tent.

"Forgive my interruption, Sidi," gasped a man's voice, which, after a moment, Bilal matched to Abdullah, one of Abd al-Aziz's retainers. "I thought that you would want to know immediately—the Sultan has declared war upon the Franj!"

Exclamations of surprise from the adjoining room, and then Abd al-Aziz's voice cut through the commotion like a cool blade: "Please, be seated and explain your message. You, girl—bring the man a drink."

Another pause and shuffle, and then the messenger spoke again, hardly less breathlessly for sitting. "I have just heard it from one of the Sultan's official messengers. No doubt you were aware that the Sultan had appealed to King Guy for the release of the prisoners Arnat has been holding from the caravan. Well, when the king petitioned Arnat, he refused to let them go. And when the prisoners reminded Arnat of the truce and demanded their release upon its terms, he said to them, 'Let your Muhammad come and save you!'"

There was a moment of silence while this sank in, which extended as the serving girl returned with a drink for the messenger and he slurped and gulped. At last he continued, "When he heard Arnat's words, they say the Sultan swore to kill the infidel with his own hands. His army is already mustering in Damascus."

"And so, the time has come at last," said Abd al-Aziz, with what seemed to Bilal to be a cast of anticipation.

"Indeed," Abd al-Hadi answered faintly.

"Will we go to join the army, Sidi?" Abdullah asked, with barely suppressed excitement.

There was a pause, and then the sheikh answered, "Let it be known, Abdullah, that any man of this tribe who wishes to join the Sultan's army is free to go; and may Allah go with them."

"You cannot speak for the tribe!" Abd al-Hadi gasped in disbelief.

"The terms of our agreement, Brother," Abd al-Aziz answered coldly, "state that the two branches of the Hassan remain autonomous until such time as our children should marry. Based upon your reaction to this decree, I cannot help but view my daughter's disappearance as partly propitious."

"This is outrageous—" Abd al-Hadi began, but Numair cut him off, his voice silky-smooth.

"No, Father," he said. "It may be, as my uncle suggests, for the best. And perhaps, after all, we should not be too quick to dismiss the Sultan's call to arms."

"But—but you cannot mean—"

"Come, Father. We can discuss it elsewhere at our leisure. There is no reason to stay here any longer."

As the men bid their stilted farewells, Bilal sat back against a tent post to consider all he had overheard. He had just begun to relax when the stable's flap opened. A barb of light struck the darkness. Numair stood within it, gesturing to Bilal, who approached reluctantly.

"I suppose you have been listening all this time?"

Bilal nodded, waiting for the reprimand, but instead Numair gave him a faint, reptilian smile.

"Good. I need not go through all of that tedium again." He paused, then said, "Tell me—do you love your mother?"

Bilal was so surprised by the question that he thought he must have imagined it. But Numair was looking at him expectantly, so at last he said, "Of course I do."

"There was an unspoken *but* in that statement," Numair observed.

Bilal sighed. "There is not much upon which she and I see eye to eye. There has never been."

Numair nodded as if none of this surprised him. "And your father?"

"I never knew my father," Bilal answered, unable now to meet Numair's eyes. "He died before I was born."

"What if I told you that he did not—that your mother has lied to you all these years, as Khalidah's father lied to her about her mother's death?" Bilal could only stare at him, stunned. Numair smiled. "It's true, Bilal. Your father is alive and well and a mere day's ride from here. Do you wish to meet him?"

Bilal finally found his voice. "Even if this is true—" he began.

"Do you doubt my word?"

"No, Sayyid, of course not . . . only, it is so strange. Who is my father, that he might be so near and I do not know him?"

Numair's eyebrows flew upward in surprise. "Do you mean that your mother denied you even that knowledge?"

"Tell me, Sayyid," Bilal answered softly.

Numair studied him for a long moment and then said, "No. It is far too dangerous to speak of him here. But I will say that he is a man of high position, and he may well see fit to do something for you. If you can be ready in half an hour, I will take you to him. Pack your essentials and meet me at the edge of camp; I'll have a horse ready for you. Tell no one what you are doing."

Bilal was reeling; he half shook his head. "But it is so sudden—"

All at once, Numair's calm turned to menace. He stepped even closer to Bilal and took him by the shoulders. "Usually I do not make an offer twice; but because you are young, Bilal, and because

I understand that this news must come as a shock, I will put it to you again in the clearest possible terms. I am leaving in half an hour to keep a meeting with your father. You can come with me and have a chance at significance, or stay here and rot in oblivion. Those are your choices."

Even then, Bilal knew that this was not quite true, that there were in fact a number of choices before him then and that Numair's offer could not be without strings. However, Numair was correct about one thing: to remain in Wadi Tawil would be to consign himself to a life of oblivion. After a moment he nodded, and Numair smiled.

Six

BILAL'S ride to the castle of Kerak was a nightmare come true. As the Hassan's seasonal migration took them close to Brins Arnat's stronghold, their children grew up on stories of his brutality and their mothers' congruent threats: "If you slap your sister again, I'll leave you at Kerak the next time we pass!" Or: "Quiet down, or you'll wake Arnat, and I hear he is looking for meat for his spit!"

Zaynab's threats had been particularly grim, possessing a chill ring of truth in that she offered them only as a rebuttal to others. For instance, when Khalidah, age six, told Bilal that he'd better give back her toy horse because Brins Arnat came in the night and took bad children away to be roasted for dinner like game birds, Zaynab replied, "Nonsense! But he has been known to take them from his dungeons and throw them from the battlements to entertain his dinner guests." This put a decided end to their squabbling.

Likewise, when Bilal, age nine, told Khalidah that Arnat cut out the tongues of children who contradicted their mothers, Zaynab informed him calmly that she had never heard anything of the sort. "However," she continued, arresting Khalidah's incipient gloat, "once, when a man refused to give him money, he sliced up his bald head, smeared it with honey, and tied him up on the roof of a tower until the swarms of insects drove him mad."

Bilal had not forgotten any of these stories, and the only thing that kept him moving toward that dreaded castle now was Numair's promise that his father was to be found within—though the prospect looked rather different in the bleak light of the desert dawn than it had in Abd al-Aziz's stable the previous day. Numair had refused to tell Bilal anything more about the man they went to meet than that he was to be found at Kerak. He had also admonished the boy to let him do all the talking and to keep his eyes down. Therefore, Bilal didn't look at the knights who guarded the gate at the mouth of the wadi that led up to the castle, nor at the grooms who took their horses in the forecourt. However, he stole glances when Numair was not looking, and they did little to bolster his confidence, for all the people he passed wore the same pinched, haunted expression.

Bilal followed Numair into the keep, where Numair stopped to speak in broken French to a man in a red-crossed white tunic. Following the man's directions, he led Bilal to a chamber no bigger than a closet and nearly filled by a wooden table. At the table a man sat writing in a ledger. As he looked up, Bilal's heart bloomed with sudden hope, for if this was the father Numair had promised, he was worth all that Bilal had forsaken to meet him. He wore a knight's mail and a plain, dark mantle. He looked to be in his early thirties, with dark hair, a high, intelligent forehead, and soft, slate-blue eyes that seemed to look out on something divine. His skin was very white, but his features were warmed by that rare natural kindness that shines from a man like a light and makes others want to befriend and submit to him at once.

"Are you—" Bilal began, in French, but Numair interrupted him with a sharp Arabic "No! Now shut up!" followed by a glower.

Bilal's burgeoning hope disintegrated, and the knight, seeing his dejection if not understanding it, gave him a brief, sympathetic smile. When he looked at Numair it was with a good deal more circumspection. "We had not expected you again so soon, al-Hassani," the knight said to him in Arabic. His grasp of the language was excellent, and his accent made it into a song full of rests and cadences, further charming Bilal, and adding to his disappointment.

"I must see your master at once," Numair said curtly.

"It is very early," the knight answered. "The Master is not yet awake."

"Then wake him," Numair growled. "This cannot wait."

The knight sighed. "And what shall I say is your business?"

Numair looked speculatively at Bilal for a moment, then said, "Tell him that I have brought someone to meet him who will interest him greatly."

With a curious glance at Bilal, the knight closed his ledger and left the room. As soon as he was gone, Bilal said, "Who was that man?"

"Jakelin de Mailly," Numair answered tersely. "Marshal of the Templars, and no concern of yours."

As they waited for de Mailly to return, Bilal mulled over Numair's reference to de Mailly's "master" and his own mother's apparently intimate knowledge of Brins Arnat's personal habits, and a terrible suspicion began to take shape. By the time de Mailly returned and told them that his master would see them, it had solidified to certainty. He followed de Mailly through the corridors in a daze, and when the knight stopped at an iron-studded door, Bilal was shaking uncontrollably. De Mailly nodded and left them. Numair rapped on the door.

"*Entrez*," a man called from within.

Numair pushed the door open. Inside, a man sat by a brazier poking gloomily at the coals. He looked up when Numair and Bilal entered. The light from the window behind him obscured his face, but there was no mistaking the hostility in his voice when he said, "Shut the door."

Numair ignored him, so Bilal shut it.

"I thought I told you never to bring anyone with you!" the man spat.

Numair was smiling again—his hard, glittering smile. "Forgive me, Master, only I thought you would want to meet this particular young man."

The Franji turned toward them, leaning forward out of the light, so that his face came into view. He was handsome, but the quality of his features seemed an afterthought to their intimidating cast, and they were marred now by a great twisted tree root of a vein that had come out on his forehead as Numair spoke. To Bilal, though, all of this was incidental to his eyes. They were the illusory blue of the sea through heat-shimmer, the kind of rare color that marks men unequivocally as kin.

"I consider it an honor, Messire, to present Bilal, son of Zaynab al-Qabbani."

De Ridefort, apparently stifling a rampant fury, barely glanced at Bilal. "What is the meaning of this?" He spoke Arabic as confidently as de Mailly, but with a very different accent: harsh and choppy and overly full of vowels.

"I would think that that would be obvious," Numair answered coolly, taking a seat he had not been offered. "You and I were at an impasse in our negotiations. I have, unless I am greatly mistaken, discovered its antidote." He paused, smirking. "What—have you no words of greeting for your long-lost son?"

De Ridefort smiled coldly. "Blackmail," he said. "How original. But unfortunately for you, I have no son."

Numair leaned his elbow on the desk, rested his cheek languidly on his palm, and studied de Ridefort. If it was an attempt at intimidation, it failed, for the Master met his eyes squarely. Clicking his tongue in irritation, Numair said, "A number of years ago—I'd say about seventeen—you spent some time in Antioch. While you were there, the Sultan Salah ad-Din gave his niece—a girl who had been raised in his household, and of whom he was very fond—in marriage to one of his emirs. She was fourteen years old and, by all accounts, a beauty. Her name was Zaynab."

De Ridefort could not quite hide his flinch. Numair smiled. "I see you remember her. You will recall as well that Zaynab's marriage was a troubled one. Her husband was much older than she was, and he beat her out of jealousy, as old husbands of young wives will. I hear he was rather merciless. Well, she was crying over her bruises one day in her garden when she chanced to look up and see a Franj knight watching her. He had come to her home for a meeting with her husband, he told her, and had lost his way in the corridors. He asked her why she was crying, and she was so miserable that she found herself telling him. To make a long story short, when he offered to rescue her from her predicament, she accepted.

"She wasn't stupid, Zaynab. She knew what the knight's white mantle meant. But she was young, and I suppose like any young girl she thought that love would win the day. She was wrong. Within a week her knight had left her with a bag of silver and an admonition never to speak of their affair or come looking for him. If she did, he said, he would immediately have her returned to her husband, who would of course have her stoned to death."

Numair stopped to observe the effect of his story on the listeners. De Ridefort was staring at him, hostility bristling from him like spears from a martyr. Bilal was white with shock.

"Zaynab did just about the only thing she could do," Numair continued at last. "She disappeared: went south to the wilds of Oultrejourdain and lost herself in a tribe of nomads with whom she passed herself off as a widow. Her son was born nine months later, and the two of them have lived with the Hassan ever since."

"And I suppose you'd have me believe your Sultan has been calling for the head of this errant knight?" said de Ridefort at last.

"Oh, no doubt he's long since forgotten about the affair," Numair answered. "But that's not to say he couldn't be reminded. I am certain he would find the information quite interesting in light of your recent dealings with him. And as for your Order—"

De Ridefort laughed wryly. "The Sultan I will grant you, but the brothers would never accept the word of a Saracen against mine."

"Probably not," Numair agreed, "which is why it's so very fortunate that your son has inherited your most striking feature." He pulled the still-stunned Bilal into the light. Startled, the boy looked up at the Master. "Even among the Franj, one seldom sees eyes of quite that shade of blue. In a Bedu, it is unheard of."

The Master gave Bilal a long, inscrutable look, and then he turned back to Numair. "What do you want, al-Hassani?"

On any other face, Numair's smile would have been beatific. On his, it was diabolical. "I want twice what you're paying me now to carry your information," he said. "And you can forget Ayla. If the Sultan wins, I want Kerak."

WHAT Bilal learned as the men bickered over the next few hours was enough to make the discovery that he was the son of the Master of an order of Franj warrior-monks seem almost prosaic. De Ridefort had decided several months earlier to pave his way with the Sultan against what he considered the likely event of the Muslims winning the coming war by supplying him with the kind of information to which few other Franks had access. But since a man of his position could not be seen to be consorting with the enemy, de Ridefort had hired what he considered a suit-ably insignificant go-between to carry his information: Numair al-Hassani.

De Ridefort's reward for his efforts was the principality of Oultrejourdain—or it would be, Salah ad-Din promised, as soon as Jerusalem was back in Muslim hands. Numair, in turn, was well paid by de Ridefort out of the Templar coffers for carrying his information to the Sultan. At first, this arrangement had suited Numair well enough. But when his father began to speak of his marrying his cousin and consolidating the tribal lands, Numair in turn began to consider power as well as money. To rise, he needed more than a nomad's tent. He needed something permanent, something that signaled his significance to anybody who passed. He told de Ridefort that he would no longer work for him unless he could expect a town after the Muslim victory. To his surprise and delight, the Master had promised him Ayla.

But informing was dangerous and difficult business, requiring long hours of travel, and Numair was essentially lazy. After a run-in with a group of Templars on the way back from one of his mis-sions, he demanded more money. This time, de Ridefort refused and threatened to cut him out of the deal altogether if he continued his demands. So Numair went looking for something he could use to coerce de Ridefort. He found Bilal.

As the men debated the borders of countries that did not yet exist, Bilal's mind drifted. He knew that he was embroiled now in this strange business, and as such, he felt a sudden sympathy for Khalidah. It was clear to him that she had only ever been fodder to Numair's insatiable lust for significance, as he was now, and he wondered if she had known it. Perhaps it was the reason why she had run away—and at that, Bilal felt a pang of guilt that he had not tried to help her, even if it was only to deflect everyone's suspicion for a little while.

All at once, Bilal realized that the two men had stopped talking. Both were looking at him with similarly cold surmise. For a moment he wondered if they were about to kill him. But of course, that made no sense: whatever de Ridefort's thoughts on the subject, Numair still needed him as a barter piece.

"No," said de Ridefort at last, as if in response to a question of Numair's, "I think I will send him north, where he cannot cause trouble." His eyes lit with a sudden inspiration. "Indeed, yes—I will send him north, into the Sultan's army, where he can perhaps be useful to me as an *informateur.* For, of course, it is to my advantage to know what the Sultan is up to, as long as he knows what we are . . ."

Informateur. Bilal understood the word well enough; he understood a good deal of the Franj tongue, if it was spoken slowly and clearly. It seemed ludicrous to him that nobody asked him whether he wished to be a spy, but then, he supposed, it was better than a knife in the back.

"He has no military training to speak of, beyond a raider's," Numair said.

"That must be remedied, if he is to have any hope of getting close to the Sultan," de Ridefort answered. "I will send him to one of our garrisons to train. We will tell them he is to spy for us in the Sultan's army. Nobody will question it, if the order comes from me."

"Do you really think that I intend to let him out of my sight?" Numair scoffed.

De Ridefort gave him a cold smile. "Pack your sword then, al-Hassani. You're about to become the Sultan's newest volunteer."

"But—"

"No *buts*!" de Ridefort roared. "You're useful to me, but you're not irreplaceable, and right now a word from me would land you in Kerak's dungeon. You do know what Kerak does with his prisoners?"

At last, Numair looked chastened. De Ridefort smiled. "It appears then that we have terms."

Seven

The Syrian Desert
Late February

UNDER the full moon the desert was almost as bright as morning, and for a long time they let the horses run. When at last they began to flag, the moon was nearing the far horizon, and Khalidah too was beginning to feel the effects of the tumultuous day and sleepless night. She loosened her hold on the reins and let Zahirah stretch her neck, then looked across at Sulayman, whose eyes were on the east.

"Are you expecting someone?" she asked.

"No one, in fact," he answered. "But I need to be certain the expectation is justified."

"Where are we going, Sulayman?"

"There is a cave southeast of here, with a spring nearby. We'll reach it by daybreak."

Khalidah shook her head in exasperation. "And then what? We will live in this cave until my father forgets that he ever had a daughter?"

"All in good time, Sayyida."

Khalidah sighed. Part of her wanted to push him for the truth; the rest couldn't bear to hear it. So she let the silence carry them over the streaming sand, past towers of stone, wind-hewn and mutable. Her thoughts drifted from her mother's ghost to Zaynab's words to Bilal's motionless body, fetching up at last against the snap of bone, the viscid resistance of flesh to metal. This troubled her mainly in how little it seemed to matter. She suspected that she ought to be appalled at having killed a man; likewise, that she ought to feel the loss of her home and her name. But as she watched the constellations turn on their slow wheel across the sky, Khalidah could find no space in them for grief, only the offer of a wild, glorious freedom.

At last the sky ahead began to brighten, then to glow with light streaks the color of butter and spring grass. Aasifa and Sulayman had taken the lead, and Khalidah, half-asleep in the saddle, nearly tumbled when Zahirah drew up short behind them. They stood at the top of a long, gentle slope, the bank of a shallow wadi. At the bottom a stream trickled with the remnant of the winter rains. Sulayman dismounted and led Aasifa down to the water. When all of them had drunk, he pointed upstream.

"The cave is there."

"Surely this stream is known to the tribes in the area, and the cave too."

Sulayman said nothing, only smiled and led his tired horse off toward a cluster of rocks. Sighing, Khalidah followed him. When they reached the rocks she expected to find them cracked and fissured, as rocks were in that desert when they concealed caves, but instead they walked along a smooth wall almost twice her height. Khalidah could see nothing in it that looked like an opening, and with a sinking heart she realized that Sulayman had been mistaken. *Well*, she asked herself, *what did you expect?* Obviously he was a madman, and she must be mad herself to have followed him.

As Sulayman studied the stone, she leaned miserably on Zahirah's shoulder, burying her face for a moment in the horse's silvery mane. Rather than shy or toss her head, Zahirah stood still and blew softly onto Khalidah's neck. The familiar, sweet smell of horse and the warmth of her breath were comforting. *At least I have her*, Khalidah thought, *and the Franji doesn't*. She looked up again, and then blinked. Sulayman was gone. She tugged Zahirah forward, her heart quickening with fear. She had nearly passed a stand of dead tamarisk trees when a whistle stopped her. Looking more closely at the trees, she saw what had seemed before to be a snip of shadow, except that now, Sulayman's grinning face was peering out of it. She thrashed angrily through the trees and found him standing within an envelope of rock just wide enough to accommodate a saddled horse. Behind him, a passage led into darkness.

"This is no time for games!" she snapped.

"Of course not," Sulayman said demurely. "I am sorry, Sayyida."

Though she doubted it, Khalidah was too tired to protest. Leading Zahirah, she followed him along the stone passage and into a rough chamber just big enough for the four of them to lie down. The crevice narrowed again above their heads, but it ran right up through the rock. High above, she could see a strip of brightening blue.

"We must eat," said Sulayman, "and then sleep. We'll ride all night again."

Khalidah pulled off Zahirah's saddle and bridle, spreading the saddle blanket on the sand to dry. She gave both horses barley and dates and a measure of dried camel's milk, taking some of each for herself and Sulayman. They ate in silence, then lay down on their blankets with their backs to each other.

"I truly am sorry if I frightened you," said Sulayman.

Sighing, Khalidah pulled her blanket over her head and fell into deep, exhausted sleep.

SHE opened her eyes on a mist like a fine veil, full of half-formed faces that shifted as soon as she tried to make them out. The air she breathed was cool and damp and thin, the ground beneath her feet thick with grass. Nearby a figure stood, dressed in a long, white robe with embroidery at the hems and, beneath it, loose trousers like a man's. But she was a woman, of that Khalidah had no doubt, nor of her identity. She turned, revealing golden eyes as deep as wells, dark patterns on her forehead and cheeks, a smile full of tears, and it was no wonder then to Khalidah that they said she had gathered hearts like wildflowers, though she was no beauty.

"I thought I had forgotten you," Khalidah told her, admitting her most shameful secret. "I didn't remember your face, I didn't even dream of you anymore . . ." But that wasn't quite right, because she recalled a tapestry from which this same face had emerged not so long ago, to the bidding of a plucked string. Time pitched and whirled, flagged with images: vines on her hands, blood on parchment, the snap of bone, a smile in a sunlit nimbus. "Were you there? Are you here?"

Little girl . . . life of my soul . . .

The words brushed Khalidah's mind with the insubstantial delicacy of the ghost-ridden mist. "Mother, please," she whispered. Brekhna smiled again, but she was fading, and Khalidah had the sensation of duality that comes at the end of a vivid dream, when the dream world and the visceral one run momentarily parallel. "Wait!" she cried. "Tell me where to find you!"

Again the sad smile, the words like phantom fingers stroking her mind: *First find Qaf . . .*

Qaf. At the sound of the word, fragments of the imam's teachings toppled through her mind: the edge of the world, land of the Jinn, mountains of emeralds and beings of smokeless fire . . . and while she paused to capture them, her mother slipped away like sand through spread fingers.

In her wake, though, the mist cleared. Khalidah stood on a hill above a valley ringed by mountains, the nearer ones green with grass and trees, the farther blue and violet and tipped with snow. On the valley floor a river flowed clear over golden stone and a herd of horses grazed the lush grass of its banks: fine horses, perhaps even finer than the tribes'. There were rows of buildings on a hill to her right—dwellings, she thought, made of wood and stone, each a perfection of carving and care, stacked so that the roof of one formed the terrace of the one above. At the far end of the valley, at the foot of a hill, was a larger building with what seemed to be a minaret rising at its center. A gallery ran along the upper story, and tucked back into its shadows was a seated figure, also dressed in white. The figure looked up and seemed to see Khalidah, seemed about to gesture. Then the mist closed down again, and the dream disintegrated.

At first, Khalidah couldn't remember where she was. Above her was a jagged strip of blue-green twilight, behind her the solid warmth of a sleeping horse. She sat up. Zahirah whickered softly and nibbled the ends of her hair, and everything came flooding back. She looked across at Sulayman, who was still sleeping soundly. Aasifa was standing near the passageway, her head stretched toward freedom.

"All right, let's go," Khalidah said. Grabbing her saddlebags, she led the horses outside to drink.

As they sucked greedily at the little stream, Khalidah did her best to wash her face, wiping it dry on the inside of her dress, which was still relatively clean. Then she knelt and performed the evening prayer, wondering whether Allah was still listening to a woman who had done as much wickedness as she had over the past day and night. She looked down at her broken reflection in the last of the twilight to see if it had changed her face, but she found herself searching instead for her mother in her own features. She didn't find much beyond the golden eyes. Her skin was darker than Brekhna's, her hair resolutely black, and her face was softer, heart shaped, with her father's features.

All at once another face wavered beside hers. She jumped, then whirled angrily on Sulayman. "Don't do that!"

He smiled benignly and knelt beside her, cupping his hands to drink before he answered, "I'm sorry if I startled you."

"No, you aren't," Khalidah said. "It's just like earlier—you were trying."

"Honestly, I wasn't. It's the force of habit."

"What kind of habit requires you to move so silently?"

He tilted his head, looking at her reflection rather than her face. "That is a story in itself, and right now we must be going. Here, put these on."

He laid a bundle of pale fabric beside her. She picked it up and shook it out. It was a man's short, linen robe and baggy trousers, like Sulayman's own. A red sash and *kufiyya* fluttered to the ground. She saw then that he had changed his embroidered cap for a similar headdress, but his was black.

"Where are we going that I am required to dress as a man?" Khalidah asked warily.

"It's not the destination that requires it, but the journey. We'll keep to the desert as we can, but sooner or later we're going to meet other people. Believe me, it's better that they think you a boy."

Sulayman tactfully walked downstream toward the horses while she stripped off her gown and shift and replaced them with the trousers and robe. She plaited her hair and dropped it down inside the robe, then tied on the *kufiyya*. With her dress and shift under her arm, she went down to Sulayman, who had already tacked Zahirah and was working on Aasifa. Khalidah thought that the gray mare looked less skittish than she had the previous night. Sulayman's hands on her were as delicate as they had been on his *qanun*, and though she danced while he tightened the girth and shied when he approached her head with the bridle, the horse no longer trembled. All the time he spoke to her in a low, gentle voice.

"You have a way with a horse," Khalidah observed.

"And you with a pair of trousers. You make a very convincing boy." She scowled at him and he added, "Though an uncommonly pretty one. I wouldn't like to answer for your fate if we meet a troop of lonely soldiers. Better say you're studying to be a dervish."

"Will that really stop a rapist?"

"No. But it will deter him long enough for you to draw your knife." Sulayman laughed at her expression. "Have no fear, Sayyida. I won't let anyone touch you."

She let him give her a leg up into the saddle, but she couldn't repress a smile of satisfaction as she nudged Zahirah's sides and the golden mare shot off, leaving the gray far behind.

Eight

As on the previous night, they let the horses run as long as the ground was good. Khalidah found that she enjoyed this ride much more than the last, whether for sleep or acceptance of the situation or the dreamed reassurance, or all of them. When at last the horses slowed, she drew Zahirah back to walk beside Aasifa. The chestnut mare reached out to sniff the gray's nose. Aasifa snorted, but her ears stayed forward. Sulayman took a packet of almonds from his saddlebag, poured out a handful, then handed the bag to Khalidah. She looked across at him as they chewed. His face was placid in the moonlight, but his eyes showed a mind intricately at work.

"It's time to tell me where we are going, Sulayman."

He rode on in silence for a time before he said, "Qaf."

"What did you say?" she demanded.

"You heard me. And I would have thought that you, of all people, would not give me that look."

"What look?"

"As if I were mad. I have heard the stories about your mother, Khalidah: that she fought like a man and had an uncanny eye for a horse. That she was no beauty, but she conquered hearts as easily as the Queen of Sheba. That your father's good fortune began when he married her, and ended when she died. That she did not come from the tribes, but called herself a Jinni."

Little girl . . . Khalidah shut her eyes against tears. The next moment, though, bitterness blazed to anger. "If you believe that rumor, then perhaps you should heed the others: that she was a succubus with eyes of fire and a voice like honeyed poison, sent to destroy my tribe. That she bewitched my father such that he would never marry again, never produce a son to succeed him. That she left him with nothing more than a witch-child, no better than a curse. Did you think I didn't know? Every jealous slave girl and superstitious old man has whispered it behind my back since I was old enough to realize that they meant me to hear." She looked at him with sharp defiance. "If that is why you wanted me, then I prefer Numair as a fate!"

Sulayman sighed with a note of tolerance that would have riled her further, if it had been possible. "Did I say that I wanted you, Sayyida? I've told you I came to help you, but if you choose to believe otherwise there is little I can do."

They rode in silence for a long time, until at last Khalidah's curiosity got the better of her anger. "You spoke of Qaf," she said, "as if it were a real place."

"It *is* a real place," he answered with good grace, "which I have witnessed with my own eyes. Like most legends, Qaf has its roots in truth. Its mountains are not made of emerald, nor do they lie at the end of the world, but they are both greener and more distant than you can imagine. I know that this must sound like madness to you. In time, *Inshallah*, you will accept that it is not. For now, all you need to know is that Qaf is real, as are the Jinn. They are neither demons nor fallen angels, but a tribe of flesh-and-blood warriors. In fact, they are quite possibly the best warriors in the world, and your mother, Brekhna, was at one time in succession to lead them."

"A woman, heiress to a tribe of warriors?" Khalidah said dryly. "Now *that* is madness."

"You will understand when you meet them."

"When I meet them," she repeated dazedly. "And that will be . . . ?"

"The moon will wax twice more at least before we reach Qaf."

Khalidah looked up at the sky: the moon was just waning from full. She wanted to laugh, but instead she said, "Who are you, Sulayman?"

"I told you already, I don't know."

"You're a grown man. You didn't spring into being as Abd al-Hadi's minstrel. Somebody bore you and raised you. Somebody taught you music, and French, and how to move like a thief."

"Many different people, actually," he said, then paused, looking off over the moon-tinged sand. "But that's something different. I cannot tell you who fathered me, nor what woman carried me, nor even where I was born."

There was bitterness in the words. Khalidah wondered what it was for. Plenty of people knew as little about their origins but did not live in the shadow of that ignorance.

"Then tell me what you do know," she said.

"Well . . . the first place I recall is Cairo. I lived there with a stonemason and his wife. They had no children of their own, and by the time they found me wandering in their street they were too old to hope for any. Luckily for me, they were also softhearted and devout. They accepted me as a gift from Allah.

"I was happy with them. They weren't wealthy, but we were never hungry, and they loved me. My father began to teach me his trade. Then, when I was seven, he and my mother died in a plague. They had no relatives to take me in, so I went back to the streets. But I had forgotten how to survive there. I was starving by the time I found the troupe. They were traveling musicians, and one had a *qanun*. I had never heard anything like it before; it called to me. I tagged along with them while they were in the city, and they ignored me. I became more difficult to ignore when I followed them back onto the road.

"Once again, I was lucky. Rather than send me away, their leader, Umar, gave me a drum and asked me to repeat a string of rhythms. I can only imagine that the result pleased him, because the drum became mine and I became his apprentice. One by one, the musicians taught me to play their instruments, beginning with the drum and culminating in the *qanun*. I grew up with them, traveling the lands of the Prophet, peace and blessings be upon him. By the end of it I had mastered every instrument they owned and learned to read and write in several tongues. I'd learned also to move like a thief, as you say."

"Why?" Khalidah asked, fascinated despite herself.

Sulayman shrugged. "The life of a traveling musician is a string of obstacles. Sometimes to stay alive we had to take advantage of our wealthier patrons, and the dangerous jobs usually fell to me, being the youngest and the quickest. And then of course a musician, by nature of his work, sometimes hears and sees things his employer would rather he hadn't. Then his survival is a matter of outwitting his host . . ."

"So the troupe took you to Qaf?" she asked.

"No. By then I had left the troupe. I was tired of the danger and uncertainty of that life. I bought a *qanun* of my own and set off to find a permanent patron. I went east because the Persians are by far the most generous benefactors of the arts in these lands. But once there, I could not find a place I wanted to settle. Something drove me onward. Eastward."

He shook his head and smiled ruefully. "It was only an idea when it began, little more than a daydream. I never imagined how it would take hold of me. Before I knew it I wanted to go farther east than I had ever gone before; farther than anyone had ever gone. By the time I saw the mountains of Khorasan it had become an obsession. I could not stop. My daydream had been burned away by a compulsion I didn't understand, to keep moving east, always east.

"Winter closed in as I moved from village to village, growing colder and hungrier all the time. At some point I became ill, but still I pushed onward. When I finally collapsed I was days from the last village, deep in a mountain pass in heavy snow. I knew then that I had been bewitched, that some evil Jinni had led me to die in that bleak place." Again he smiled, and again there was more regret in it than humor. "I was right about the Jinni, if not about his intention. For I lay down in the snow, hoping that death would be quick and painless, and awakened in Qaf.

"At first I thought that I had died and awakened in the interworld. That delusion didn't last long, though. I was all too obviously connected to my body, which ached and burned with fever, rejected the broth that some patient soul kept trying to feed me, and made me wish that I had died in the snow rather than suffer this version of living.

"For many days I lay like that. Delirium reached and receded like a tide. People came to me now and again, to feed me or make me drink infusions of herbs or change the bedding. Some were men, some were women. The women had marks on their faces like henna tattoos, and they all dressed strangely, in heavy woolen clothing with thick embroidery. I couldn't understand this. It seemed to me as hot as a summer desert. That is why, on the morning I awakened shivering, I knew that I was getting better."

Sulayman lapsed into silence, and Khalidah waited impatiently for him to continue. Then, when she thought he had said all that he meant to, he began again. "A woman was kneeling on the ground beside me, watching me. She had strange eyes—golden, like yours. Her hair, too, was golden." He paused. "When she saw that I was awake, she got up and came back with a bowl of soup. She put it down beside me and helped me sit up. I asked her where I was, and she told me, 'Qaf.'

"Of course I thought that she was lying, or mad, or perhaps the fever had burned away my senses and my own damaged mind had supplied the word, and for all I knew the speaker too. It didn't much matter. She helped me eat the soup, saying nothing the whole time, and by the end of it I was exhausted again. I went back to sleep and didn't awaken again until the next morning.

"For a long time, that was my life. Sometimes that woman fed me, sometimes one of several girls. All of them had golden eyes, and though they spoke Arabic to me, to each other they spoke a language I had never heard before. I began to pick up pieces of it, but even when I could ask them questions, their answers told me little." He shook his head. "I began to walk again, though only within the house. The place where I had lain ill seemed to be a kind of common living area, with several closed doors leading off it, and a large one that I knew led outside. I couldn't try the doors—I was always watched—and the windows were high up in the walls by the ceiling. A gallery ran around the top of the room, underneath the windows.

"When I asked to go outdoors, they looked at each other in a way that I had seen certain patrons look in my days with the troupe; a look that meant they did not intend to allow me to leave. Then one morning when my requests to go out had become more habit than anything else, Batoor—that was the name of the man of the house—gave a nod and told me to follow him. I wondered if it would be to my death, but he handed me a coat like the one he was wearing, a pair of thick felt boots, and a rolled woolen hat, and that reassured me. Why would he bother giving me warm clothing if he only meant to kill me?

"Then he opened that big door, and I saw paradise. Of course I knew that it couldn't be paradise, any more than it could be Qaf . . . but at the same time, I could see the bones of the legend in it." Sulayman's voice had taken on a wistful tone, and Khalidah knew what she was going to hear next. "There before me was a wide valley covered in lush grass. It was ringed by mountains, the nearer ones green—like emeralds, I suppose—and the farther ones blue with distance and snow. And along the valley floor—"

"Runs a river," Khalidah interrupted, "clear as glass over the stones at its bed. Beautiful horses graze there, and at the far side of the valley, under a mountain, is a wooden building, a mosque I think, with someone in a white robe sitting on the gallery."

Sulayman was staring at her in incredulity. "How did you know?"

Khalidah sighed. "While we slept, I dreamed. My mother came to me, and showed me this place you're describing. She called it Qaf."

"It seems, then, that it was more than a dream," he said after a moment's reflection. "Did she say anything else to you?"

Life of my soul . . . To hide the looming tears, Khalidah said, "Not really." Sulayman's disappointment was obvious, and she told herself guiltily that the words she withheld could mean nothing to him. "Well," she asked, "did you go into the mosque? Did you meet the man in the white robe?"

"Yes," he said slowly, "but it is not a mosque. It is a hermitage of sorts, but the Jinn are not Muslims."

Khalidah turned to him in surprise. "They are Christians?"

He laughed. "Hardly. They follow a religion that was already ancient when Christianity was founded. It is . . ." He stopped, shook his head. "I do not think that I can do it justice. Let it suffice to say that it is a religion of great beauty. As for the person in the white robe, he is your grandfather, Tor Gul, and he is the Jinn's Khan—their spiritual leader as well as their chief. I suppose he is a kind of a Sufi."

"A Sufi is chief of a tribe of warriors?" Khalidah asked. "A tribe of infidel demon warriors, no less!"

"I've already told you, the Jinn are not demons. They are perfectly human, though they have skills and talents that might make them seem more than that at times. And if they are infidels, they still manage to conduct their lives in a manner far more worthy of respect than those of many Muslims I have known."

The moon slipped behind a cloud, rimming it with silver. "Well," Khalidah sighed, "what did you do there?"

"Listened to Tor Gul Khan, mostly. He is a great teacher as well as a great thinker. He gave me peace and purpose while my body healed. When I was strong enough, he sent me to exercise with the warriors. He wanted me to learn their skills, but I fear that I failed him miserably, for just as the roots of the mythical Qaf were there in its reality, it was clear when watching the Jinn's mock battles why they are called demons. They move with a grace and silence that would be the envy of any thief. They seem to come from nowhere: a whirlwind, a blur, and suddenly the straw man is headless, with no swordsman in sight. Even on horseback it's like that. Their horses obey them entirely. They can stand so still they seem to fade into the landscape, and a moment later they're off like comets."

He shook his head, sighed. "Those days passed like minutes, and at night I slept soundly on the floor of Batoor's house. The woman who had tended me was his wife, Warda, and the girls their daughters. There were six of them, and once they knew that Tor Gul Khan had accepted me, they treated me as one of them. I wanted to stay there forever, but on the evening that marked a month from our meeting, Tor Gul Khan called me to him. We sat on the hermitage gallery, and he spoke the words I had been dreading all along.

"I begged to be allowed to stay, to serve him, and he smiled—a kind smile, like yours—and told me that I would serve him best by leaving Qaf. He told me then about his daughter, Brekhna. She had been his pride and joy, one of those charmed creatures who excel at anything she turns her hand to. She had been set to succeed him—'to be our salvation,' those were his words."

"Salvation from what?" Khalidah asked.

"I don't know. The Jinn did not seem to me to need saving, but he did not explain his statement, nor what it was that went wrong between himself and his daughter. I know only what you know yourself: that she left the tribe and never came back. But he must have known more than he said, for he knew about you."

"About me," Khalidah repeated. It gave her an odd, disjointed feeling.

Sulayman nodded. "And that, he said, was why he was sending me away. To find you."

"But what does he want with me?"

"Again, I did not ask, and he did not say; but it seems likely that he intends for you to replace your mother."

Khalidah gave him an incredulous look. "And lead a tribe I know nothing of, except that they are heathens?"

Sulayman shrugged. "He was adamant that I find you. It was the only way I would return to Qaf, he said—and that was the last thing he said to me. He embraced me and gave me a glass of wine. Next I knew it was morning, and I was asleep under a cannabis bush at the edge of a village. I got up and started walking west."

"And now we are going back to Qaf, as you always wanted."

"It was what I wanted then."

"And now?"

Sulayman sighed. "Part of me wants nothing so much as to see that place again. Another part of me dreads it, because I know that I am not one of them, and so it can never be mine."

He looked at Khalidah, and this time she understood his bitterness. She wished that she could offer him some consolation, but she couldn't think of anything adequate. So they rode on in silence until dawn streaked the sky ahead, and they stopped to say their prayers, and Sulayman located another hiding place where they would wait out another day.

Nine

KHALIDAH grew used to traveling at night. The cold no longer bit so sharply, and her eyes had become accustomed to the dark. On the third day they crossed out of the rocky Syrian Desert and into the beginnings of the Nafud, the great sand desert of northern Arabia. Khalidah had traveled the western edge of the Nafud many times with her tribe, but they had never crossed it. No one crossed it, given the choice.

She and Sulayman stopped their horses by the last of the rocky mounds on the shore of the great sand sea. The cold wind of the coming night pulled at their *kufiyya*s and the horses' tails, and their sunset shadows reached eastward across sand like a shimmering expanse of apricot silk. But Khalidah knew that morning would change the soft ripples to a white-hot iron, easily capable of killing them.

"We will not be able to hide out there," she said, turning to look at Sulayman.

He squinted into the east wind with its scouring sand, still as the stones beside them. A herd of oryx crossed the sunset like revenants, pursued by something too far off to see, and were gone as quickly. At last Sulayman turned to her, face inscrutable, eyes hidden in shadow.

"We will not have to," he said. "An-Nafud keeps its secrets."

With that, he kicked Aasifa forward. Khalidah couldn't help feeling that this was the moment of truth: once Zahirah's delicate feet touched the sand of the great desert, her last ties to her home and her old life would snap. A pang went through her—of regret or

nostalgia or simple fear, she didn't know. But Sulayman was looking back, a dark form in a nimbus of sunset linen, his face erased
by the last sear of light. She nudged Zahirah on.

THEY rode through the night and the early part of the next morning. When the sun grew too fierce, they rigged a shelter with their
blankets and crawled inside to wait out the heat. Though Khalidah was tired she couldn't sleep. Her mind kept leaping from one
fruitless thought to the next. Finally she sat up, and a moment
later Sulayman joined her. He opened the bag of dates and set it
down between them. They sat chewing on the fruit in silence,
watching the horses doze in the sliver of shade cast by the make-
shift tent. The animals stood nose to tail, a haze of wind-lifted
sand swirling like smoke around their fetlocks, reminding Khalidah of a question that had haunted her since Sulayman first told
her about Qaf.

"If the Jinn are human," she said at last, "then where have all
the stories come from? The bottles of smoke that take the form
of giants when they're unstopped, the shape changing, and all the
rest?"

"I never asked," Sulayman answered, "but I assume that they
came from the Jinn themselves."

"They invented their own legends and spread them through
the bazaars?"

"I don't imagine that they had to. If you came on one of them
here, for instance—that is, if you survived the encounter, since
you'd be unlikely to come on one unless he intended to kill you—
then the most you'd know of it would be a cloud of dust about the
height of a man on horseback. By the time it settled, he'd be gone;
and by the time you made it to the next town, memory might well
have made him into a demon of smoke, which would grow with the
telling. And who would disabuse you of this idea? Certainly not the
Jinn themselves. They prefer that people hold them in awe."

"To what end? You say they're great warriors, but what do they fight for? Surely not for the protection of Qaf, if it's as remote as you say it is."

Sulayman shook his head. "Qaf is their refuge, and they have made certain that it will stay that way. No; the Jinn are essentially *mujahiddin*."

"But they are infidels!"

"Infidels perhaps, but they are faithful to their own gods, and they fight only those battles that they believe their gods require of them." Seeing Khalidah's dubious look, he added, "All I can say is that in their way, they are devout, and whomever or whatever they fight for, it generally ends up being for the good."

"What good?" Sulayman's eyes shifted away, but Khalidah looked at him levelly. "Whose good is it serving to bring me to them?"

"Whose good was it serving for you to submit to marriage to your cousin?"

"That is an evasion if ever I heard one."

Sulayman looked at her with eyes that were tired and a little sad. "In all that's happened to me since I first saw Qaf," he answered at last, "there has been much possibility and very little certainty. I too find this very strange, Khalidah, and in the end, I know little more than you do. But what I *do* know is that your grandfather is a good and kind man, and he is desperate to find you."

Khalidah sighed. "Very well." She paused for a moment, then said, "How did you know that I would listen to you?"

"What?"

"The other morning, when you told me to say yes—how did you know that I would do what you asked, instead of accusing you of harassing me?"

He smiled and shook his head. "I didn't. It was, at best, a guess; at worst, pure idiocy. After all, you might have accused me . . . or screamed, or fainted."

"I don't scream," Khalidah said, appalled. "And I've only fainted once, and then only because Bilal and I bet each other that we couldn't ride all day without a drink . . ."

Sulayman laughed. "Well then, you might have cried witchery and demanded my head on a platter."

"So, why did you try?"

"As I told you, it was life or death."

And if I had died, you'd have lost Qaf, Khalidah thought, with a trace of disappointment she couldn't quite account for. She was annoyed with herself, and with him. To take her mind off it, she said, "Sulayman, I would like to ask you a favor."

He raised his eyebrows, with the faintest quirk of a smile. "Anything for you, Sayyida, if it is in my power."

Khalidah scowled at him, but she continued, "I would like you to teach me to read."

Sulayman looked at her in surprise. "Now, that is not what I expected."

Wondering what he had expected, Khalidah said, "Well? Will you teach me?"

"If you like."

Khalidah waited for him to begin. When he didn't, she sighed, exasperated, and gestured to the blazing desert. "Did you have other plans for the afternoon?"

Sulayman's eyes rested thoughtfully on her face. "All right," he said at last, and broke two sticks from a desiccated bush. He kept one, handed the other to her, and then settled himself cross-legged beside her. He smoothed the sand in front of them with his hand, and then, with his stick, he drew a symbol. "That is *alif*"—he drew another—"and this is *ba'a*."

He made her draw them several times, repeating their names and the sounds they made. In this way, they went through the entire alphabet, and then again, twice more. At the end of it Khalidah's mind was jumbled and reeling, and she was quite certain that she would never make sense of all the symbols and sounds.

As if sensing her discouragement, Sulayman smoothed the sand again and wrote a string of symbols. "That is your name."

Khalidah looked at her name in the sand for a long moment. It was a strange feeling, to see herself marked on the surface of the earth, if only temporarily. She copied out the characters again, sounding out each one as she went.

"And you?" she asked when she'd finished.

Sulayman wrote in the sand again, this time his own name. Khalidah copied those, too. "Sulayman," she said. "Khalidah, Sulayman." She looked up at him, beaming. In return, Sulayman's ghost-smile lit his face. The sun was behind him, well down the afternoon sky. She had not realized how much time had passed.

"What about 'Zahirah'? 'Aasifa'? And 'Bilal' and 'Zaynab' and 'Abd al-Aziz' . . . ?"

Sulayman laughed. "I need to rest now, Khalidah, even if you do not. Teaching is hard work!" Seeing her crestfallen look, he said, "Don't worry. You are a natural. By the time we reach Domat al-Jandal, I promise you, you'll be able to spell it."

"The fortress city?" she asked. "Do you plan to stop there?"

"We'll need water by then, and other supplies for Jazirah."

At any other time, Khalidah would have inundated him with questions, for she had never been to Jazirah, though she had always longed to see Baghdad, the seat of the Caliph. But at the moment the wonder of her name in the sand precluded anything else.

"Thank you, Sulayman," she said, gesturing to it. "You don't know how much this means to me."

Sulayman's smile blossomed, and Khalidah found that she could not look at him.

SHE dreamed she slept in Sulayman's arms. In her mind they clung to each other, not like lovers so much as twins in the womb: two souls that belonged to one another beyond desire, beyond need. For a moment between sleeping and waking, Khalidah felt a peace unlike any she had ever known. Then she opened her eyes. Through the slate-blue twilight, she saw Sulayman looking back at her. He didn't say a word, but she knew that he read that dream on her face as if it were an open book. For a moment they looked at each other, Sulayman's eyes wide with possibility, Khalidah's with shock. Then she rolled away from him.

Shaking from head to foot, Khalidah went blindly to Zahirah, poured her some water and mixed in dried camel's milk, then leaned with her face in the mare's mane as she drank. She and Sulayman had not touched each other, but she could not have felt more humiliation if they had. Her head swam with rote-learned recriminations, and in her gut was a deep ache, as if she had torn herself when she turned from him. She wanted to say something to him, but there were no words. So they saddled their horses in silence, and in silence, rode toward the night.

It was only much later that Khalidah realized she had forgotten to pray.

Ten

ON the third day after her disturbing dream, Khalidah spotted turrets on the horizon, shimmering in the afternoon heat.

"Qasr Marid," Sulayman said when she pointed them out. "The fortress at Domat al-Jandal. We should reach the town by evening."

The fortress grew larger by increments as the afternoon wore on, and soon Khalidah could see the smaller buildings of the town around it, as well as a pointed stone tower, not quite a minaret, which Sulayman told her belonged to the Mosque of Omar.

"It looks old," she said.

"Seven hundred years old," he replied, "and it began as a Christian church."

Khalidah reflected on this. It was easy to forget that Islam and Christianity had shared the same cradle; that they had, for a time, shared it in peace. Seven hundred years seemed much less when it measured the time it took for a religion founded on love and compassion to become a viper gnawing its own tail.

The guards at the gates barely glanced at them as they rode through. Once they were inside, the town lost the monastical air afforded by the high walls and sandstone hill, its stately solitude dissolving into the manic flurry of an isolated trading post. After so many days in the desert's vast silence, Khalidah found the sudden bustle of tight-packed humanity slightly unreal.

"We'll need to find an inn," Sulayman said, casting a critical eye over her. "You should pass, as long as you keep your mouth shut. Let me do the negotiating."

Khalidah nodded. They rode slowly through the streets. Domat al-Jandal seemed, at first, like any town of its kind. The houses were small and neat. Veiled women in dark gowns collected dried laundry from walls and bushes, children and animals played in the streets, groups of men sat smoking in dooryards and tea houses. And yet it seemed to Khalidah that there was an extra note to the town's purposeful song, like an oud with one string too many. This feeling intensified as Sulayman was turned away at inn after inn, all of them filled to capacity.

"Why are they all full?"

He shook his head. "I don't know, but I suspect something significant has happened since we left."

"Why?"

"Because they aren't just full—they're full of soldiers," he said. "Or those who would be. Men from southern Arabia and Jazirah— some even from Persia."

"They would come so far to fight for the Sultan?"

"If you met him, you wouldn't be surprised."

This startled Khalidah into meeting his eyes for the first time since her unsettling dream. In them, as she had known she would, she saw the awareness of it. Taking a deep breath, she pushed past it: "Do you mean to say that you have met him?"

Sulayman's eyes moved back to the space between Aasifa's ears. "On my way back from Qaf," he said, "I stumbled onto a soldiers' camp and was taken to their emir. I didn't realize who he was until afterward."

"What was he like?"

Sulayman smiled briefly. "Plain. Quiet. Entirely undistinguished. If the others had not so clearly deferred to him, I would have taken him for a servant. He asked me a few questions that all seemed irrelevant, and then he asked me to play for him. In the morning he gave me a few coins and sent me on my way. It was only later that I realized whom I had played for—and how much I had told him, without having been aware of it."

"That doesn't inspire my confidence."

Sulayman shrugged. "On the contrary. I would have every confidence in a man like that, as long as we draw swords for the same side. You could see it in his men: they loved and respected him, yet at the same time they weren't distanced by that respect. He found a way to make each of them feel equal to him, even as they aspired to be like him. That's a rare quality in a leader."

Khalidah wondered whether he realized he was describing the very quality of which she kept seeing glimmers and flashes in him.

By the time they found a room, night had fallen, and the horses were hanging their heads in exhaustion. The inn was on the outskirts of town, where the houses were poorer, the streets shadowed and seedy. It was clean, though, and the innkeeper seemed honest.

"The rooms have all been taken," he said, leading them around the back of the house, then across a small courtyard littered with broken bricks and rubbish from the collapsing building next door. A veiled woman sat by a fire, humming tunelessly and stirring something in a large pot. Khalidah twitched her *kufiyya* across her face as she passed, fearful that another woman would see through her disguise more easily than a man.

"But you can sleep here," the innkeeper said, opening a door onto what seemed to be a disused animal shed. There was a single small window high up on the wall and a couple of old straw mats on the floor. Khalidah heard the whine of mosquitoes and resigned herself to a sleepless night. "And the horses—"

"Will stay with us," Sulayman said firmly. Khalidah could see the man looking over their dusty clothes and sand-crusted shoes, and knew what he was thinking. She had long been aware of the contempt with which city dwellers viewed the nomadic tribes. It would be no different if this man knew that she was the daughter of one of the wealthiest sheikhs in Arabia. But to his credit, the innkeeper only nodded and, after collecting his money, handed them a bucket of water and a towel and left them alone.

After washing off some of the dust and letting the horses drink, they went back out to the courtyard, where the old woman handed them steaming bowls of curried beans and one small flatbread between them. Taking these, they went to join a group of men seated on the rubble from the ruined house. The men were dressed for colder weather, in heavy woolens woven in somber colors. A big man with creases around his eyes and a smattering of white in his beard gestured to Khalidah and Sulayman to sit down with them.

"*As-salaamu alaikum*," Sulayman said.

"*Wa alaikum as-salaam*," the man answered in a heavy Kurdish accent.

Tearing the bread in half, Sulayman gave a piece to Khalidah along with a warning look. "You are far from home," he said to the man who had invited them. "You must be on your way to join Salah ad-Din?"

The man looked warily at him. "Who's asking?"

"I'm sorry," Sulayman said, casting his eyes demurely downward, "I didn't mean to presume. It does seem, though, that all the men of Islam are migrating west at the moment . . . and unfortunately for us, they've all chosen to stop here for the night." He gave a self-deprecating smile. "That is why my cousin and I have the honor of sleeping in a goat shed. I suppose it's little enough hardship for him, though," he added, gesturing to Khalidah.

"How so?" asked the man, interest glimmering through the suspicion.

"Well," said Sulayman with a conversational shrug, "he will endure worse hardships than the smell of musty goat in his quest for divinity."

"A dervish?" The man's tone had softened, and he looked more closely at Khalidah. "He's young for it."

She kept her eyes resolutely on her food, but she couldn't help noticing Sulayman's smile, the one she had begun to think of as his thief's smile—slight as the moon's first waxing sliver and as covert, more of a dare than a promise. Inwardly she cursed him, hoping that he knew some Persian prayers, because she certainly didn't.

"Oh no, he's not a dervish yet," Sulayman answered. "But he was our imam's top student. The man has run out of things to teach him, so he is sending the boy to a group of holy brothers to continue his education. My uncle asked me to escort him. He is, after all, very young, and the roads aren't safe for a boy so delicate . . ." Sulayman raised his eyebrows. Khalidah rolled her eyes at her beans.

"Nor are most monasteries," the man said dryly. "I hope that you are not headed to Persia. It is said that the Sufis there take on beardless boys for no other purpose than—"

"We are not going to Persia," Sulayman interrupted quickly, to Khalidah's disappointment. "Our destination is Jazirah—an-Najaf." He said this with studied nonchalance, and as if on cue, the older man's look changed from sympathy to rapture.

"An-Najaf! Oh, you are blessed indeed! There is no more beautiful city in Jazirah—no, nor in all the lands of the followers of the Prophet, peace and blessings be upon him!"

Sulayman raised his eyebrows as if in surprise. "You aren't from an-Najaf?"

"Near as," said another man, whose reticence appeared to have dropped away as quickly as his companion's at the idea of somebody seeking religious enlightenment in their hometown.

The older man shook his head. "Not so near—we are from the mountains—but we do go regularly to the city to trade. And to answer your original question, yes, we are indeed going to join Salah ad-Din. Ours may be a small village of no consequence, but the news does reach us. When we heard about the incident, we knew that we could no longer lie like dogs for the invaders to kick as they please."

"So we go to fight for Allah," another man said.

"And Salah ad-Din. Who better to lead the jihad than a fellow Kurd? My wife's cousin saw him once, and he said . . ."

Sulayman allowed them to boast for a few minutes before he interrupted, with apparently little interest, "This incident you speak of—you refer to the business with Arnat?"

"What else?" said the older man, whose name, he had informed them, was Birzu Yalik.

"We have been in the desert a long time," Sulayman said. "We heard rumors, of course, but perhaps you could give us an accurate version of events . . . ?"

Birzu nodded vigorously. "Surely you know about the caravan that he attacked?"

"Yes, we heard just before we left. To think of all those poor pilgrims taken prisoner . . ."

Birzu put his plate aside, lit a pipe of *banj*, and drew on it, shrugging. "I suppose it would tempt a better man than Arnat, all that unguarded wealth passing right under his nose. But it doesn't excuse what he did." He shook his head, expelling smoke through his nostrils like a dragon as he passed the pipe to his son. "Yes, he went too far this time. Some say the Sultan's aunt was among those imprisoned—"

"His sister," Birzu's son interrupted.

"My guess is, neither of them was within sight of that caravan, but they have been added to the story for effect. Either way, that wasn't the true offense. Salah ad-Din asked the Franj king to make Arnat release the prisoners. Of course the king had no effect. Then the Sultan sent his own emissaries to plead with Kerak on behalf of the innocent pilgrims." Raising his eyebrows and his voice, Birzu quoted, " 'Let your Muhammad come and save them.' That's what he said. Can you imagine it?" He spat, and the others followed suit, then lapsed into darkly brooding silence as the pipe made its way around the circle.

"And so, Salah ad-Din heard about it," Sulayman prompted.

Birzu shrugged. "Of course. And now he's sworn to kill Arnat with his own hands . . . and we intend to help him do it, *Inshallah*."

"How long ago did he make this pledge?" Sulayman asked.

"A week, more or less."

Sulayman nodded and drew contemplatively on the pipe. Khalidah watched with interest to see whether he would pass it to her, but he handed it over her head to the next man, saying apologetically to Birzu, "My cousin has foresworn smoke as part of his devotions." Birzu shrugged again. "Tell me," Sulayman continued after a moment, "where is the army gathering?"

"Damascus. That's where we are headed, at any rate. You ought to join us, once you have delivered your cousin to the brothers."

"Perhaps I will. Do you have any idea when the Sultan plans to attack?"

"No," Birzu answered, "but it will take him some time to assemble his army, and of course, the battle season is still a few months off . . ."

Sulayman's eyes had lost no intensity to the drug, making Khalidah wonder if he had actually taken any at all. They glittered with thought for a few moments before he said, "Thank you, Birzu Yalik. Your story has inspired me, as it should inspire all men of the Faith, to resist the infidel. I hope that we will meet again. But my cousin and I have a long way to travel yet, and if I am to return in time to join the Sultan's jihad, then we must make an early start. Good night, and may Allah have mercy upon you."

The men wished Sulayman and Khalidah farewell, and the two of them returned to their goat shed for the night.

Eleven

KHALIDAH and Sulayman rose early the next morning and were given bread and cups of thick, murderous coffee by the veiled woman at the fire, who seemed not to have moved since the previous night.

"Thank you," Khalidah said to her as they made ready to leave.

"Take care," the woman said in a voice like wind among sandstone canyons. "The sand cat is close."

"What?" Khalidah asked, turning cold.

"In the night his men came creeping." The woman nodded to herself and chuckled, a gap-toothed grin. "But they could not find the sand daughter, for she too has a wildcat's heart." She began to sing:

> *Though you might see me*
> *sun-beaten as a sand daughter,*
> *ragged, shoeless,*
> *with worn feet,*
>
> *Still am I the master of patience,*
> *wearing its armor*
> *over the heart of a sand cat,*
> *shod with resolution . . .*

They didn't wait to hear the rest, but nodded to her and rode out of the courtyard. When at last the woman's song was lost in the winding of the alleys, Khalidah asked, "Do you think that we have been followed?"

"I think the woman was mad."

"Still, to sing those words—"

"It was Shánfara," Sulayman said.

"I know that," Khalidah snapped. "The 'Ode in L.'"

"It's a common enough poem."

"But what brought it to her tongue? And the sand cat . . . *Numair* means 'panther.' Could she have meant—"

"She could have meant anything," Sulayman answered. "But there's little we can do about it, other than hope that she's only mad. We'll buy our provisions, then put this town behind us. If what those men told us last night is true, then Numair is the least of our worries."

Khalidah considered this. "So you think that Salah ad-Din really means to attack the Franj?"

"I think he means to make a bid for Jerusalem."

Khalidah turned to him in surprise. "That would be madness! The Franj won't let that city go while a soul is left standing to defend it."

"I imagine the Sultan is well aware of that."

She considered this. "Is he really strong enough to defeat them?"

"If he's careful in his alliances, he will be."

They rode through the souk, which had been crowded with would-be soldiers the previous evening and was now deserted but for a few eager merchants unlocking shop doors and unrolling awnings. Sulayman, producing money Khalidah hadn't known he carried, bought more dates and powdered camel's milk, plus dried meat, fruit, and lentils. They stowed the packages with the water bags they had filled at a well the previous day.

"This will do for now," said Sulayman, "but we'll need a packhorse for the mountains."

"And where will we get a packhorse?" Khalidah asked.

"Something will turn up," he answered with irritating assurance, and rode on toward the eastern gate.

Khalidah looked curiously into the shops they passed. Then, abruptly, she pulled Zahirah up. Sulayman saw at once what had caught her eye. In a dirty shop window, among tangles of cheap prayer beads, cracked hookahs, and tarnished candlesticks, was a sword. It wasn't particularly impressive to look at: just an unembellished blade, rather short, neither old nor new enough to be of much value, with a plain leather sheath and belt. There was, however, a stone set in the hilt, dull with dirt but still recognizably golden.

A twinge of foreboding went through Sulayman. "Khalidah—" he began, but she was already scrambling down from Zahirah's back and tying her reins to the window bars. Frowning, Sulayman dismounted and followed her into the shop.

As their eyes adjusted to the sudden dimness, they saw that the shop actually contained very little. There was some broken furniture, a pile of dented pots and pans, a few battered rugs hanging from the walls, and at the center, on a pile of dingy cushions, a small, wizened man. His round face was like a walnut shell, inert and riddled with creases around black, slanted eyes. He looked at them with little interest, drawing contemplatively on a hookah. The mouthpiece was made of bone, carved into the shape of a serpent with garnets for eyes, and the smoke it exhaled had the sinuous sweetness of poppy.

"May I help you?" the shopkeeper asked in Arabic, though his accent was Persian.

"How much for the sword in the window?" Khalidah asked, uneasiness making her voice shrill.

The man studied her. "You do not come from here," he said at last. Khalidah did not answer. "You are at the beginning of a long journey."

Unease growing apace with the conviction that she needed that sword, Khalidah answered, "As is every man in this town. How much for the sword?"

The man set the pipe down, the snake still trailing smoke through its grinning mouth, and hobbled over to the window. He rummaged around and finally returned with the sword. He laid it next to the pipe and resumed his seat on the cushions, studying it with an odd glint in his eyes. He rubbed his thumb over the stone on the hilt. "This could be topaz. And even if it's glass, it's a sturdy weapon, and will no doubt fetch a good price with so many soldiers traveling through town. All you young men running after a piece of glory . . ." The tone with which he said *young men* deepened Khalidah's unease. She waited, not daring to look at Sulayman.

"But you are traveling east, not west," the shopkeeper continued. Khalidah looked up at him in surprise, but his face told her nothing. He paused, still scrutinizing her, and then said, "I do not have long left in this world, and a good story is worth as much to me as a few coins. Tell me where you plan to take the sword, and perhaps I will make you a deal." He sat back, arms crossed.

Khalidah looked at him through the smoke. Her head swam, and it was becoming more and more difficult to focus her eyes. She didn't mean to say it, but the words slipped out, as if the grinning snake had charmed them from her: "It goes with me to Qaf."

The little man smiled without pleasure or irony. "Unlikely," he said, and the room erupted. The hanging rugs fell, revealing three armed men. They wore Bedu robes with *kufiyya*s pulled up to their eyes, and they closed in on Khalidah and Sulayman as the shopkeeper melted back into the shadows. In one fluid move Khalidah had the sword in her hand and perfunctorily slit the throat of one of the Bedu. Then she looked around. Sulayman had drawn his dagger and turned his back to Khalidah's as they faced the two remaining men.

The Bedu circled for a moment, then attacked. They were well trained, but the space was tight and Khalidah was smaller and quicker. She slashed the other Bedu across the face and as his *kufiyya* split, she recognized one of Numair's retainers. The skin of his right cheek hung open, and his left eye poured blood. He stumbled in pain and confusion, lurching into the other man, who lost his footing. As the Bedu struggled to disentangle themselves, Sulayman grabbed Khalidah's arm and pulled her out the door.

The uninjured Bedu freed himself and came after them. Sulayman wrenched the sword from Khalidah's hand and pushed his dagger into it, then turned, putting himself between Khalidah and the Bedu. The Bedu seemed very young, and above his *kufiyya*, his eyes were full of fear. His sword arm trembled. He slashed out at Sulayman, but he had little skill, and fear made him clumsy. He stepped too far forward, Sulayman raised his sword with a look of grim determination, and then the boy's head was rolling in the dust.

It fetched up at Khalidah's feet. She turned and vomited by the side of the wall. She had barely stopped heaving before Sulayman was shoving her into the saddle. He slapped Zahirah's flank with the flat of the sword, and the horse took off at a gallop. Khalidah hadn't had time to get her feet into the stirrups, and her legs were still too weak with shock and sickness to have much grip, so she leaned over the horse's neck and clung to the reins for all she was worth, whispering to herself over and over again, "I will not fall off . . . *I will not* . . ."

At last the horses slowed, and Khalidah realized that they had reached the city gate. "Bedu raiders," Sulayman said to the guards, pointing in the direction they had come from. "They attacked us in a shop on the main road—the Persian's. Go, before they escape!"

They left the guard staring stupidly after them as they kicked their horses into a gallop once again. They rode flat out for as long as the horses could keep it up. When at last they slowed to a walk, Sulayman turned to Khalidah with furious eyes.

"Was it worth it?" he demanded, waving the bloodstained sword at her.

"You can't begin to imagine," Khalidah said.

"Imagine!" he cried. "It was quite clearly bait, laid by your honorable cousin and his Franj allies!"

Khalidah looked at him coolly. "Maybe; but I could not leave without it."

"And why not?"

"Look at the blade," she said. "There, by the hilt."

Grudgingly, Sulayman looked at it. And then he looked more carefully. Underneath the dried blood, he could make out an inscription. Scratching at it, he uncovered the words: *Life of My Soul*. Despite himself, his heart skipped. When he looked up, Khalidah's golden eyes were there already, waiting for him.

"So what?" he said at last, but without the outraged certainty. "It's a common endearment."

"It's what my mother called me," she answered stonily.

He sighed. "Khalidah, anyone could have had a soldier's sword inscribed . . ."

"That is no common soldier's sword. It was my mother's."

"You have decided this because of the inscription?" he asked incredulously.

"No," she answered, "because I remember it. She kept it under her bed, wrapped in old clothes. The only time she ever slapped me was the day she found me playing with it."

"And what good does it do you now?" he snapped.

"I don't think that's really why you're angry."

They rode on in silence that grew increasingly strained. Finally, Sulayman burst out, "All right then: when were you planning to tell me that you trained as a warrior?"

Khalidah's eyes flashed at him. "When you needed to know."

"I see. Well, is there anything else that I might need to know about you?"

"Well, what about you?" she demanded. "You never told me you could fight like a . . . like a—"

"Thief?"

In fact, the word that had tripped her was *archangel*; the one he supplied deflated her anger. Sighing, she said, "I didn't keep it from you out of spite, Sulayman. Remember my position. I have only known you for seven days, after all." He kept grimly silent. "All right, ask me anything—I promise you the truth."

He was silent for a while longer, then he said, "I want to hear it all."

"What?"

"You've had my life story. Let's have yours."

"I wouldn't know where to begin."

"Begin at the beginning. Where were you born?"

Khalidah paused, then said, "Wadi Tawil. The tribe had just arrived for the summer grazing when my mother's time came."

"Do you remember her?"

"Very little. She di— I mean, she left when I wasn't yet three."

"And your father?"

She paused, then said, "I suppose my father never recovered from losing her. He'd married her for love . . . and she too, I suppose. She must have. They brought each other little else."

"They had you."

Khalidah smiled ruefully. "Indeed. An only child, and a daughter."

"And yet, your father thought enough of you to raise you like a son."

"At times, I question the wisdom of that decision."

"It just saved your life."

"That is true, but still, it was a strange decision. Perhaps it was some kind of promise to my mother. Or perhaps it was despair of ever having a son."

"Does it matter?" he asked.

This time, Khalidah didn't answer.

"So you learned the sword and the scriptures, poetry and music. What else?"

"What else?" Khalidah shook her head. "I learned that though a tribe might forgive their chief for marrying a nameless foreigner, they will never forgive his child for bearing her blood. I learned that people don't trust a girl who has learned too much, or whose talents outshine their own. I learned that in the end, a father's primary concern for his daughter is to be rid of her . . . that the truest love is an animal's . . . that real freedom exists only on a horse's back . . ."

Sulayman waited for her to continue, and when she did not, he said, "Should I pity you?"

"That's your decision."

Sulayman thought for a while. Then he said, "And Zaynab? What is she to you?"

Khalidah sighed. "When I was a child, she was everything to me. Now, she's the only thing I regret. I suppose she is my true mother."

"Where did she come from?"

"What makes you think she's not of the tribe?"

Sulayman shrugged. "Just a feeling. Well?"

"You're right. I don't know where she came from, nor when— only that it was sometime before my mother left."

"Haven't you asked her?"

"Of course. But she always put me off. She never talked about her past at all, or Bilal's father, or why she was no longer with him. But she used to cry sometimes in the night, when she thought that I couldn't hear."

"And you love her," Sulayman said. "And she loves you."

"Yes," Khalidah said softly, and then again, "yes."

"And her son?"

"Bilal, too. We were brought up together, like twins. He was my best friend—my only friend, truth be told, given how the Bedu feel about foreign blood . . ."

"But?"

Khalidah sighed. "Bilal is complicated. Laughing and melancholy by turns, and you never know which it's going to be, or why. Discontented too, I think because he's ambitious, and yet he has nowhere to go with it. And lately . . ."

"Your relationship has become difficult," Sulayman filled in. "His love for you took on a shape that yours for him did not."

Khalidah nodded. After a moment she asked, "Why do you want to know about Zaynab and Bilal?"

But he only shook his head, lapsing into silence as the climbing sun slitted their eyes, the fickle sands shifted, and their shadows reached for home as their bodies moved ever farther away.

Twelve

Oultrejourdain
Early March

BILAL looked up at the crumbling façade of a pagan god's palace. All around him the red cliffs rose, their improbable carved columns and porticoes fading into the weirder handiwork of wind and water. Even before it became Franj territory, the tribes had avoided the ruined city of Petra. They believed it haunted by the spirits of the heathens who had cut it from the rock in a past so distant their name was lost.

Turning from the empty-eyed ruins, Bilal's gaze settled on the back of the man who rode ahead of him, and his sense of unreality deepened further. Less than a week ago, Bilal had been a boy certain of, if beset by, his lot in life. Now he followed a man who ought to have been a mortal enemy toward a destiny he had never imagined in his wildest dreams. Strangest of all was the fact that he felt no discomfort with this Franj knight, but rather an unnerving affection and a desire to please him.

As if he'd heard Bilal's thoughts the Franji turned, his warrior's face softening when his eyes lit on the boy. "Not much farther now," de Mailly said in his beautiful Arabic. "You have done well."

Bilal flushed with pride at the praise, and his eyes flickered shyly away from the knight's as they left the ruined city and headed toward a high sandstone hill. To its right was a lower hill, its smooth face pitted by the vacuous cavities of looted tombs. Around the top ran a modern wall, encircling a keep and a tower that reached into the dazzling morning sky.

"Jebal Habis," said de Mailly, pointing to it. "Your home, until your master summons you."

Bilal wanted to answer him, but the words would not come. The mention of Numair, reminding him of his terrible duplicity, had silenced him. For de Mailly believed he was bringing Bilal to Jebal Habis to teach him to spy for the Franj, and though this was nominally true, in the end, of course, Bilal would in fact be helping de Ridefort undermine the Franj. Bilal didn't spare much pity for the Franj as a whole—they were the invaders, after all—but he hated deceiving de Mailly.

The horses broke into a canter as they reached the hill, momentarily scattering his obsessive ruminations. Bilal had to admit that Numair had given him a good horse. She was a dark bay with four white socks and a white star on her forehead, plus three little starlike marks on her right flank, for which she had been named Anjum. She was a tribesman's horse, far better suited to the desert than de Mailly's destrier. He had to hold her tightly to keep her from flying past the Franji.

They entered the castle's forecourt through a gate guarded by two armored knights, who gave Bilal no more than a cursory glance but greeted the Marshal warmly as he rode past. Once inside, de Mailly dismounted and handed his reins to a waiting groom. Bilal followed suit.

"Come," the Marshal said.

Bilal could hear in his voice that de Mailly was already thinking of something else. He tried to stifle his disappointment. After all, he told himself, he had never been more than a chore assigned to the Marshal.

The castle was equally disappointing. Jebal Habis was little more than an afterthought, a poor frontier fortress serving little purpose beyond its signal tower. After Kerak, it seemed tenuous: a child's toy perched on a sand hill. Bilal followed de Mailly through another gate and down a flight of stone steps into a wide yard. The signal tower stood just ahead, its beacon smoldering, ready to be stoked at a moment's notice. To the left, an inner wall enclosed the keep, a mute block of stone with slit windows and faded banners fluttering from the roof.

Early as it was, the castle was already buzzing with activity. Servants ran back and forth on their errands, and knights called to one another on their way to their morning exercise, followed by little squires struggling under their armloads of gear. The few women carried bundles of linen or pails of water; the servants, slops to be emptied somewhere away from the living quarters. De Mailly strode across the yard with an air of authority, nodding to those who stopped to greet him. Most of them bowed to him, and all called him *Messire*.

They descended another set of stairs into a smaller yard with a stone cistern at the far side, half-filled with murky water. To the left, a narrow doorway opened in the inner wall, guarded by two more knights, both wearing Kerak's black-and-red livery. De Mailly ducked through the doorway, Bilal doggedly following. He stopped and gave Bilal a brief, intense look.

"Remember, you represent the Templars here," he said.

If only you knew, Bilal thought; but he said nothing, only stood meekly looking at his feet as de Mailly turned to one of the knights and began speaking to him in French too rapid for Bilal to follow.

"*Oui*, Messire," the knight answered when de Mailly finally finished.

De Mailly looked at Bilal with a shade of pity and a fugitive smile. "This is Thibaut," he said in Arabic. "He will help you settle in."

"Will I see you again?" Bilal asked, trying to keep his voice neutral.

Again the pity, and the smile. "I will do what I can."

Thibaut regarded Bilal as de Mailly disappeared into the keep. He said something to Bilal in French, to which Bilal replied with a shrug: de Ridefort had told him before he left Kerak that it would be better to be seen not to understand much of the language.

Thibaut tried again in broken Arabic: "You Kerak's new spy?" Bilal said nothing, only stared at the man. After a moment, the Franji shrugged his mailed shoulders and turned back toward the stairway. "Come. I to show where sleeps."

He walked off across the dusty courtyard, his mail rattling and clanking like a camp kitchen at mealtime. Sighing, Bilal followed the man toward a ramshackle timber building that leaned against the far wall, his spirits sinking further with every step. He ducked through the low doorway into a dark room that stank of unwashed bedding and forgotten chamber pots. The long row of narrow bunks was empty, but the rank smell of the inhabitants' sweat lingered like a presence. Thibaut seemed to have exhausted his knowledge of Arabic and was speaking to Bilal in a long, impenetrable flow of French. At last Bilal discerned that the man was directing him to an unmade bunk. He nodded and said, *"Merci,"* though he could not bring himself to smile.

The knight studied him for a moment with a cold eye, then said in French: "I hope that you will be quite miserable here, you filthy little heathen. I'd give my horse to know whose bastard you are."

Bilal had to smile. "It would cost you more than your horse," he answered in Arabic, "and even then, you would not believe it."

The knight couldn't have understood, but he was clearly shaken by the idea that Bilal might have. He left quickly, his mail percussing away into the half silence of the morning.

Bilal lay back on the stale straw mattress, thinking about the tortuous path of betrayals that had landed him there, beginning with de Ridefort and ending with Khalidah. Or did it? he wondered now. For with the passing of his infatuation, an idea had suggested itself, becoming more solid each day: that his love for her had never been any more than a figment of his imagination.

In fact, when Bilal thought of love now, a single image came to mind—that of Jakelin de Mailly. The idea of a Muslim boy falling in love with a Christian knight was as ridiculous as it was blasphemous, and yet, when he was perfectly honest with himself, it wasn't really surprising. Once the initial shock had passed, it seemed that this aspect of himself had always been there in plain sight, and its realization had only ever been a matter of time.

Thirteen

INFORMATEUR. The word had a ring of sordid significance when he heard it whispered behind his back, but Bilal quickly found that the reality was merely sordid. The men with whom he shared the stinking barracks were ordinary foot soldiers, a rough and ragged lot as universally despised as their Muslim counterparts. De Mailly had gone back to Kerak the day after delivering Bilal, and when the other knights looked at him at all, it was with much the same expression worn by the servants emptying the morning chamber pots.

And so Bilal's life became one of populated exile. In the mornings he joined the infantry in their exercises, in order to learn the sword. The drills were tedious, and the unmitigated company of the big, stupid men left him far too much time to second-guess his situation. Day after tedious day on that scorched hilltop in Petra, Bilal labored over the convolutions of his situation in his mind, trying to make sense of them and inevitably failing. Most of all, he wished to see de Mailly again, though he knew that this was as likely as a private audience with the king.

Then, when he had nearly succeeded in driving himself mad, his wish came true. Bilal had returned to the barracks while the soldiers went to their midday meal, too tired and dispirited to think of food. He was sitting on his bunk staring at nothing when the light from the doorway suddenly died. Bilal turned, his heart already beating in anticipation of reprimand, but the man filling the doorway was not the drillmaster or any of his soldiers.

"It's you!" he cried, delighted.

De Mailly smiled and said, "Come," then turned and strode out across the bright yard. The boy, still half-stunned, leapt from the bunk and ran after him.

As they mounted the steps to the upper yard, de Mailly said, "How have you enjoyed your infantry training?"

Bilal drew a breath. "It has been . . . informative."

De Mailly gave him an odd, sideways glance and then, abruptly, burst into laughter. "You Arabs are natural diplomats. Sometimes I wonder why we are still at war."

Bilal saw then that they were headed for the stables. Anjum and de Mailly's horse were outside, tacked and ready, their reins held by an Arab groom who would not meet Bilal's eyes.

"Am I finished, then?" Bilal asked, trying not to show too much eagerness. "Are we leaving?"

"We're leaving," de Mailly said equivocally, vaulting into the saddle, "but you are not finished."

"Where are we going?"

"Back to Kerak," De Mailly said.

"Why there?" Bilal asked, unable to disguise his apprehension.

De Mailly sighed. "Because de Ridefort is asking for you."

"De Ridefort?" Bilal repeated, with a slight tremor in his voice. "Why?"

De Mailly's face cracked into a bitter smile. "For good or ill, my master keeps his own council."

The contempt in his voice was so clear that Bilal looked around to see if anyone else had heard. Except for the dour groom, they were alone in the courtyard. He could feel de Mailly's eyes on him, turned to meet them.

"Bilal," the knight said, scorn turned suddenly to supplication, "forgive me if I am speaking out of turn, but I think that I understand your situation, at least a little, and . . . well, I want you to know that you are not alone. You are very young to be involved with men so powerful. If ever you find yourself in need of help, please know that you can call on me."

"Thank you," Bilal said softly, wishing with all his heart that he could wrap his arms around the knight with the saint's face. Instead, he put his hand over his heart and bowed.

"In working with us, you work God's will," de Mailly said with soft fervor. "Remember that."

Bilal smiled, thinking bitterly that he could hardly remember whose will he was working anymore, and wondering if he would ever really know.

Fourteen

In the light of the morning sun, the town of Ras al-Mai looked like an afterthought. Throughout its history it had languished in the shadow of Damascus, less than a day's ride away on a good horse, and would no doubt have continued to do so if the keen eye of Salah ad-Din had not fallen upon it. Where others saw arid plains and dust, the Sultan saw space for twelve thousand cavalry to maneuver unimpeded in their mock battles. Where his emirs saw other towns with the same proximity to training grounds and more in the way of creature comforts, the Sultan saw a water supply that would withstand the demands of an army that he knew, despite the gloomy canting of his advisors, would soon be the largest ever raised against the Franj.

Volunteers began to arrive before half of the recruiting letters had even been delivered. They flowed in from every corner of the Sultan's empire and beyond—Muslims, Jews, and Christians, men from every walk of life and every level of skill, united by the dream of freeing their lands from the invaders and their faith in the Ayyubid Sultan's power to make the dream a reality.

From the beginning, Salah ad-Din was determined that this would be a jihad unlike any that had gone before. Famously pious and fair, he demanded the same qualities of his soldiers. Hundreds of cooks were brought in to ensure that every soul in the army ate the same food; huge, clay-lined baths were dug for communal use; and though no man was allowed to keep a wife at camp, their absence was assuaged by the ministrations of a subarmy of prostitutes, available to anyone with money, and toward whom Salah ad-Din turned a charitable blind eye.

Everybody followed the same schedule as well. Trumpets and drums sounded at dawn, followed by the cry of the muezzin calling the faithful to prayer. Though the Christians and Jews were exempted from these prayers, the army rose as one body. Following prayer was breakfast, and then a visit to the latrines: long trenches dug for the purpose well outside the boundaries of the camp. The day was filled with training—sword fighting and archery, cavalry and infantry maneuvers—until the drums and trumpets declared an end to work and the beginning of the evening meal.

The Sultan's bid for solidarity worked. From bowing to Mecca as a body, dipping their bread into communal stew pots, squatting over the same stinking latrines, and sharing the same whores, the lines between emir and foot soldier, follower of Jesus or Moses or Muhammad, soon faded. The men of Salah ad-Din's army became, first and foremost, precisely that, and as such they treated one another as equals.

To the advisors who had told him it would never happen, the Sultan merely said, "You see, in jihad, all men become equal in the eyes of Allah; why not in each other's eyes, too? For every man of this army recognizes the Righteousness of the Faith." And smiling at the play he'd made on his own name, he threw his arms wide, as if to embrace as one all the men gathered to his beacon.

Fifteen

By the time Bilal and Numair arrived at the Sultan's camp, it dwarfed the town. Banners of every color slapped the lucid springtime sky, and below them ranged tents of every kind, from the rank infantry's humble camel-skin shelters to the brilliant silk pavilions of the nobles, adorned with Quranic verses and classical poetry in flowing calligraphy.

Anyone looking at Bilal would have taken him for a nobleman himself: the younger brother or cousin of the Bedu cavalryman at his side. Like Numair, he wore a lamellar cuirass covered by a robe of fine linen and a peaked helmet wrapped in a silk turban. A bright new saber curved from his sash, and a long spear and round shield were lashed to Anjum's saddle. But whatever his appearance to others, Bilal couldn't fool himself. His guts were a twist of nausea, his head a bee swarm of anxiety. He was terrified of making a mistake and giving away his duplicitous position. He wished that Anjum would wheel and run, but his horse was well bred and impeccably trained, and she carried him into camp with her tail high and her ears forward, as if the chaos of noise and color were a quiet green oasis.

When they arrived at the tent that had been set up by the servants sent on ahead, Numair leapt from his horse, thrust her reins at a groom, and retreated inside without a backward glance at Bilal. After a moment the boy dismounted as well. "Sidi," said a servant at his elbow, with an obsequious nod of the head and, Bilal thought, a flash of mockery. But before he could be sure of it, the man was leading his horse away.

Inside the tent Bilal found a bright rug laid with platters of grilled meat and flatbread and fruit. Numair was already eating, tearing at the food with a ravenous appetite.

"I am surprised you did not starve to death at Petra," he said, causing Bilal to glance nervously over his shoulder. "Oh, don't worry; the men are paid to hear nothing, and too stupid to know what it means if they did."

Thinking of the groom's sly irony, Bilal wondered whether Numair was as mistaken about this as he suspected he was about de Ridefort's ability to keep a promise, but he kept silent. The past weeks, aside from the time he was with de Mailly, had been one long lesson in keeping silent.

"How those fools could have conquered anybody," Numair continued, "let alone a people as superior as ours, on such appalling sustenance, is truly one of Allah's mysteries." He looked up at Bilal's anxious face and frowned. "Stop fretting, and have something decent to eat while you still can. We'll be on army rations soon, and they are only slightly better than Franj slops."

Sighing, Bilal sat down on the carpet with Numair. He was chewing halfheartedly on a tough piece of meat when the servant who had taken Anjum returned and said, "A messenger, Sidi."

"Who from?" Numair asked irritably.

"From the Sultan." Bilal jumped as if he'd been touched with a hot poker. The servant gave him a disdainful glance and then turned back to Numair. "Shall I show him in?"

Numair grunted. Taking this as affirmative, the man retreated, and in a moment he returned with a boy dressed in a silk robe of deep yellow—the Sultan's color. He was about Bilal's age, with delicate, even features; bright, dark eyes; curling hair worn long in the style of the Ayyubids; and a slender grace reminiscent of a Bedu sight hound. The boy glanced at Numair, seeming to appraise and dismiss him in a moment, then turned to Bilal. He gave him a longer look. For a moment, Bilal had the absurd notion that the other boy had seen straight through him to his duplicity. Then that look broke open with the abruptness of a desert sunrise, into the most beautiful smile Bilal had ever seen: warm, enveloping, clearly intended to put its recipient at ease.

"*As-salaamu alaikum*," the boy said, inclining his head.

Instead of wishing him peace in return, Numair looked the boy over with a dubious eye and asked, "Who are you?"

"I am Salim ibn Yusuf al-Ayyubi," the boy answered mildly, but with a glimmer of derision in his eyes. "The Sultan's son."

He should have apologized and made some gesture of respect, but instead Numair demanded, "Why have I not heard of you?"

Bilal wanted to sink into the ground, but the prince did not appear to be offended. Instead, with a ghost of that wonderful smile, he said, "Most likely because I am not Al-Afdhal, the eldest; nor Al-Zahir, the favorite; or even Al-Aziz, who, despite an entire lack of humor or wit, makes a swordfight look like a dance. Hence I am my father's messenger, and as such, I am here to invite you to wait upon him tomorrow morning."

"For what purpose?" Numair asked, with slightly more interest.

"My father seldom takes me into his confidence," the prince evaded politely. "In the meantime, he has asked me to acquaint you with the layout of the camp."

Numair spat out a mouthful of gristle. "One army camp is the same as the next," he said.

Burning with shame and desperate to salvage something from his master's effrontery, Bilal said, "I am not as familiar with such things as my cousin. I would be grateful of a tour, Your Grace."

Numair gave him a black look, but the prince was smiling again, and the glimmer in his eyes now was one of complicity. To Bilal, after a lifetime of superfluity, this was irresistible. He smiled back. "Very good, Sayyid . . . ?"

"Bilal, Your Grace," he answered.

"Bilal. And please, call me Salim. I am not my father." He inclined his head again, then turned toward the door. "I shall return when you have finished eating."

"I'm finished now," Bilal said.

"Let us go, then." To Numair he said, *"Ma'as salaama."* Numair only glowered.

Once outside, Bilal was suddenly reticent. For all the grand names he'd heard bandied about in de Ridefort's meetings with Numair, he had never quite imagined himself in the presence of a prince. He could only think of one thing to say: "I . . . I apologize for my cousin's rudeness . . ."

Salim burst out laughing. Bilal would have been offended if it hadn't been so wonderful: a sound like the morning desert, when all the birds wake at once. "Let me tell you what I have learned as the undistinguished sixth son of a great king," he said. "Apologize to no one but Allah: not for your own actions, certainly not for anybody else's. There is nothing to be gained from it but guilt, which is too often appropriated and always pointless."

Bilal wondered how anybody with such a smile, such an agile turn of phrase, could consider himself undistinguished. "Thank you," he said, glancing shyly at Salim, who smiled back at him.

"Do you know," the prince said, "you have the most extraordinary eyes I've ever seen?" Bilal looked away in confusion. "I'm sorry," Salim added quickly. "I did not mean to embarrass you."

"You didn't," Bilal answered. "It's only . . ." He flailed a hand uselessly, as if trying to capture the words to explain.

"Yes, I know," said Salim, and oddly, Bilal felt quite certain that he did. Then, with another inexplicable, golden laugh, the prince put an arm around Bilal's shoulders and said, "Come. Let me show you this stinking heap my father has raised to the glory of Allah."

Shocked and delighted by his words, Bilal followed him, and for a while he forgot his worries in the chaos of the camp and Salim's glib commentary: "There is the pavilion of our best Kurdish cavalry archer. I cannot fathom why he has allowed it to be erected so close to that group of common foot soldiers; they smell like a pack of swine. There are my father's racing camels. He houses them here better than he does my mother at home; I wonder what they do for him that she does not? There is the pavilion of a paltry emir from Jazirah—purple silk, does he think that he is the Caliph?"

But slowly, as they wove in and out of the rows of fluttering tents, Bilal's anxieties crept back. He thought of the dawn just past, when he'd lain shivering as Numair snored on, impervious to the cold in his drunken stupor. It had not been materially different from any other morning since they left Kerak, but though Bilal had met those with dazed acceptance, this time he'd awakened to murderous rage.

Perhaps it had been the knowledge that they would reach the Sultan's camp that day; perhaps the string of betrayals that had landed him there had faded enough for him to see at last the depth of his folly. Whatever the cause, he had thought to himself: *Now, today, I will stop this. I will kill Numair as he sleeps. I will take Anjum, turn east, and leave all of it behind.* He'd gone as far as to draw his dagger when a hand shot out of Numair's bedroll and closed over his wrist. He'd looked across the dead campfire into Numair's eyes, sardonic and coldly sober.

"Do you take me for such a fool?" he'd said, plucking the knife away. "Before we left Kerak, I entrusted your mother's little secret to one of my retainers. Oh, don't worry—he is a trustworthy man. As long as you are loyal, he'll keep his silence. But if any kind of 'accident' were to befall me, in which you were unfortunate enough to be involved, he would make your mother's story known far and wide, and nothing then would save her from the stones." He'd waved the blade at Bilal's face. "Am I clear?"

"Watch!"

Bilal blinked, and Salim caught him just before he stumbled into the ditch in front of them. They had reached the edge of the camp. Stretching before him were row upon row of trenches buzzing with flies.

"And here are the latrines," Salim said, lips twitching upward toward eyes already laughing, "with which you have very nearly become intimately acquainted. Are you a traitor?"

"What?" Bilal asked, horrified.

But Salim was still smiling, and Bilal saw that it was only another joke. "Shoveling the shit of the faithful is the particular commission of prisoners and lesser traitors." Salim nearly laughed, but a reflective look passed over his face instead, making it more beautiful still. "Or, on occasion, lesser sons."

"Your father makes you clean latrines?" Bilal asked, shocked at last out of his morbid reverie.

"Not literally."

"Then what do you mean?"

Salim raised his eyebrows, graceful as birds' wings. "Ask me that again when we know each other better." And despite the darkness of his previous thoughts, Bilal felt sudden elation at the prospect that Salim intended to know him better.

Sixteen

BILAL was not surprised when Salim arrived at their pavilion the next morning with his father's apologies, asking to reschedule their meeting as other matters had detained him. He was, however, stunned by the prince's invitation to join him in exercising his horse. Bilal accepted, though his suspicion matched his pleasure. He had never in his life been courted as a friend, and despite what Salim had said to him the day before, he could not quite believe that there was not an ulterior motive to the prince's solicitude.

However, over the next few days Salim continued to extend gestures of friendship, and gradually Bilal's wariness dissipated. His disbelief, however, was more tenacious. The only true friend he'd ever had was Khalidah, and though he had genuinely loved her, their relationship had been fraught from the beginning with inequalities that made it increasingly difficult to maintain. Yet it seemed never to occur to Salim, who was so much further separated from him by rank and experience, to treat him as anything but an equal.

Bilal spent a good deal of the early days of their friendship puzzling over this. Much later, he would be equally puzzled that he'd ever wondered why the two of them found such easy respite in each other's company. Different as their lives might have been, both had been shaped by the burden of futile ambition.

Numair, meanwhile, gave himself over to the dissipation he had been unable to embrace under his father's watchful eye. On the afternoon appointed for their rescheduled meeting with the Sultan,

Bilal returned from a ride with Salim to find his "cousin" snoring beside an empty flagon of wine and a redheaded whore, both of them naked as newborns. Salim grinned, but Bilal trembled with shame. When he tried to rouse Numair, the man looked at him blearily and said, "Fuck off," then lapsed again into oblivion. So Salim led Bilal alone to a simple white tent half the size of Numair's, which bore more of a likeness to those he had left behind at Wadi Tawil than the bright pavilions of the nobility.

"Aren't you coming with me?" Bilal asked, alarmed, as Salim turned to leave.

Salim shrugged. "I was not invited."

"But—" Bilal began.

Salim put a long finger to his lips. "He may growl, Bilal, but he will not bite. Besides, I might still find a way inside." His smile flashed brighter than the afternoon sun, and then he was gone.

Bilal turned to face the tent. Two Mamluk bodyguards barred the entrance, magnificent in their green brocade tunics and stiff, fur-lined caps. They kept their eyes fixed straight ahead, long spears at the ready. Bilal was wondering what he was supposed to do next when a little man emerged from beneath the tent flap. He was slight, almost frail, with skin as fair as Bilal's and small, intelligent eyes the color of strong tea. Though his long hair was streaked with gray, his beard was still full and dark. He wore no armor, just the plain black robe and turban of a scribe or holy man.

They exchanged *salaam*s, and then, in a warm, cultured tenor, the man said, "You are not Numair al-Hassani."

"No," answered Bilal around the sudden lump in his throat, "I am his cousin, Bilal. My cousin humbly begs your pardon for his absence. He is . . . indisposed."

"Then I welcome you, Bilal al-Hassani. Please," he added, holding back the tent flap with one arm and extending the other in a gesture of invitation.

Bilal entered the tent, the scribe at his heels. The interior was as spare as the exterior, with somber tapestries, sparse furnishings, and a narrow soldier's bed just showing behind a curtain. The only marks of wealth were a large, finely woven carpet covering the sand, and a pile of brilliantly colored silk cushions. Reclining on the cushions was a large man dressed in fine yellow robes, with a jeweled brooch in his turban and the mouthpiece of an ornate hookah in his hand. Though he was clearly in his later years—his skin was creased and his beard liberally speckled with gray—he retained an air of great strength and vitality. Bilal was comforted to find the Sultan such an imposing figure, despite his austere surroundings.

He bowed low to him and said, "Your Grace, I am honored by your request for my humble presence."

To Bilal's consternation, both the Sultan and the scribe erupted into laughter. Flushing, he looked from one to the other, alternating between anger and uncertainty lest he had made some gross mistake in etiquette that would betray himself and Numair. And then he saw that the scribe's face was lit with a smile that was a replica of Salim's, except that it did not quite erase the sadness in his eyes.

Bilal's face burned; he fell to his knees before the little man. "Forgive me, Your Highness, for my mistake."

Still smiling his wonderful smile, the Sultan took Bilal's hands and coaxed him upright. "No, you must forgive us." He placed a hand over his heart. "This is not, as it seems, a joke at your expense; only a joke on the pretensions of two old men. Your assumptions were entirely justified. But, so as to set the record straight, allow me to introduce my friend, the great chronicler and historian and my most trusted scribe, Imad ad-Din al-Isfahani. And I am Salah ad-Din al-Ayyubi, at your service."

"Sultan . . ." Bilal murmured, bowing again.

"Now, please, make yourself comfortable." Salah ad-Din indicated a few cushions that Imad ad-Din had extricated from his pile and placed on the floor near him.

His head swimming, Bilal sat down. The Sultan sat directly on the carpet, his legs crossed and his back straight as a minaret. He seemed about to speak when the tent flap opened again and Salim entered, bearing a silver tray with a teapot, glasses with gold-leaf filigree, and a plate of almond cakes. He flashed Bilal a wry look as he arranged the tea and cakes neatly on the carpet before the seated men, bowed low to his father, and then turned to retreat.

Without looking at him, the Sultan said, "Stay." Obediently, the boy knelt at the edge of the silk carpet, directly across from Bilal. To Bilal, the Sultan said, "I understand that you have already met my son Salim. He has spoken highly of you." Though it should have been a compliment, the tone with which the Sultan said this left a good deal of doubt as to its meaning. "I hope that his presence at this meeting will not disturb you," he continued, "and that yours might teach him something." This time there was no mistaking the recrimination. Bilal wondered what Salim could have done to earn his father's displeasure; but the Sultan was speaking again, and reluctantly, Bilal turned his attention away from the other boy.

"I am honored that you have decided to join us," the Sultan said, pouring tea into the glasses. The steam curled up from the amber liquid, pungent with mint. Bilal accepted one, though his throat was so tight that he did not think he could swallow it. "Of course, your cousin's services in relating certain delicate information to us have so far been invaluable and will no doubt continue to prove so, but his presence here, and yours, are valuable to me in other ways as well."

Salah ad-Din paused, indicating that Bilal was supposed to say something.

"Your Grace?"

The Sultan shrugged, sipped his tea. "As of yet, few of the Arab tribes have joined our numbers. But it is of your people we may well come to have the most need."

"You flatter us, Sire," said Bilal. "I do not think that the best of our horsemen can match the least of your own."

"I have often remarked that there is no match in speed or zeal for the Bedu warriors. But it was not to your horsemen that I referred. The men of my army are, for the most part, men of towns and cities. If Jerusalem is to be won back at all, it will not be at its gates but here in the desert, and nobody knows the desert as well as your people do."

Bilal sipped his tea automatically, then wished he hadn't. Forcing himself to swallow, he answered, "Again, you flatter us, Your Highness."

"How so?" the Sultan asked, his keen eyes steady on Bilal's face. Involuntarily, Bilal glanced at Imad ad-Din, who looked back with black eyes almost hidden in the folds of his heavy lids. His air was of preoccupation, even vacancy, but Bilal had the sense that the man was absorbing their words like a sponge, to be squeezed out later and considered at his leisure.

"My tribe seldom travels this far north," Bilal said cautiously. "Surely there are others who know this country better than we do."

Salah ad-Din clicked his tongue. "As a sailor knows the sea, the nomad knows the desert." He paused. "Do you know, several of your tribesmen have joined us already."

It was decidedly not a question. Bilal set his glass down, his mind whirling. "With all respect, Your Grace, you must be mistaken," he said. "When we left them, our tribe was preparing to move south. Our affairs being what they are following . . . some difficult family matters . . . none of Abd al-Hadi's men intended to enlist."

"Not Abd al-Hadi's," the Sultan said in the same affable, conversational tone, but Bilal knew by the taut pause that followed that he was being interrogated. "Abd al-Aziz's. You will wish to meet with them, no doubt. I shall have them directed immediately to your tent."

Before he could stop himself Bilal had cried, "No!"

The Sultan regarded Bilal with interest rather than effrontery, and Imad ad-Din's eyes settled on him with the weight of stone. Even Salim frowned. "No?" the Sultan repeated.

Bilal tried to steady his mind. He had forgotten that Abd al-Aziz had given leave for his men to enlist. If Numair had remembered and planned for it, he had not shared those plans with Bilal. He knew only that if he were to meet Abd al-Aziz's men, everything would come to pieces, and so he must not let it happen.

"The two branches of the Hassan have long been at war," Bilal floundered at last, knowing that he had been silent too long. "Though we all hoped that this situation was soon to be rectified, the circumstances under which we last parted were . . . less than happy. Numair was to marry our cousin and unite our clan. But she saw fit to abandon him, to run away with Abd al-Hadi's minstrel." He knew that he was acquitting himself well enough, if not brilliantly. Still, he wished that Salim were not there to witness his stumbling prevarication. Taking a deep breath, he continued: "You will understand that relations between our people and theirs are not entirely friendly at present."

"And yet here, you are all my men," the Sultan said, looking at Bilal with the same unruffled tranquility. "Does that count for nothing?"

"Your Highness, I can only speak for myself."

"He's right," Imad ad-Din said, the first words he had spoken during Bilal's interview. "Quite right, you know . . ." His voice was deep and rich, and he drew the final word out as though he were about to make it the beginning of a diatribe. Instead, he lapsed back into silence.

"Very well," Salah ad-Din said to Bilal, glancing at the scribe. "But tell me: what is the name of your errant cousin?"

"Khalidah."

"And who is her mother?"

"She is dead," Bilal answered, "but she was called Brekhna."

The Sultan narrowed his eyes. "Of what tribe?"

"She was not of the Bedu tribes," he answered, reluctant to look ridiculous in front of this great man by repeating the rumors about Brekhna. "She was from the east—Khorasan, I believe."

But this seemed to be enough of an answer for the Sultan. He drew a breath and then let it slide away, the single indication of how much the information had been worth. "A woman from

Khorasan . . ." he said to himself. He was silent for a long moment, his eyes somewhere far away. At last, recalling himself with a slight shake of the head, he said, "One more request, if you do not mind, Sayyid Bilal. Do you happen to know the name of the minstrel with whom your cousin ran away?"

"I do not know his family name," he said at last, "but he called himself Sulayman."

"And his instrument?"

"The *qanun*," he said.

The Sultan and the scholar exchanged a look too complex for Bilal to decipher, and then Salah ad-Din smiled at his young guest and said, "Thank you, Bilal al-Hassani. This has been a most interesting conversation. And fear not: I will respect your wishes with regard to meeting your rival tribesmen." He paused, then said, "But remember, we are one army here, gathered to serve Allah. Though I might respect your wishes, I cannot speak for Him."

The warning in the words was clear. Bilal was glad that etiquette required him to bow deeply, so that neither the Sultan nor his son could see his fear.

Seventeen

Jazirah
Mid-March

At first, Jazirah differed little from Arabia. Khalidah and Sulayman crossed a wide desert of monotonous regularity, its flat sands broken only by small settlements around the occasional well or oasis, and distant herds of ibex or gazelle, crawling like lines of ants across the horizon. They had abandoned the idea of night travel after the incident at Domat al-Jandal, since it seemed to have made little difference. Now they rose with the first streaks of dawn, rested in the middle of the day, and then rode again until they were too tired to go farther.

After a few such days, green began to encroach on the unmitigated sand. First it was in the form of tough scrub grasses and plants around small, isolated pools or streams, but soon the air grew humid and the desert capitulated to wheat fields and orchards and great stands of date palms, irrigated by well-maintained canals running among neat farms and villages.

"We're in Mesopotamia now," Sulayman explained, when Khalidah commented on the change. "You can see why some scholars believe this was Eden." She looked at the fertile land in silence. Sulayman continued, "We'll reach Basrah tomorrow. We can cross the river there, if it hasn't burst its banks with the spring floods."

"What river?" Khalidah asked.

Sulayman gave her a strange look. "The Shatt al-Arab." Seeing that she still didn't understand, he added, "The river that joins the Tigris and Euphrates."

Khalidah said nothing. Until that moment, Mesopotamia and

its great delineating rivers had been as much a myth to her as Qaf, not because she did not believe in them, but because she had never imagined that she would witness them. But she would witness them; she would cross them, and leave them behind like the familiar deserts of Arabia. To hide her bewilderment, she looked toward the indeterminate horizon, feeling every step of her distance from home.

KHALIDAH slept badly that night. They were camped in a grove of date palms by a small, silty pond. It wasn't hot, but the air was thick with moisture that clung to her skin and hair, making her long for the pure, dry cold of the desert. Flies plagued the horses, and they fidgeted, tails swishing. Khalidah sympathized as she slapped yet another mosquito. She pulled her blanket more tightly around her, thinking of cool wind across sand.

When she finally slept, she had a strange dream. She was back at Wadi Tawil, standing at the top of the hill overlooking the camp. The sun had set, leaving a clear, lazuline sky stamped with a waxing crescent moon. A cloud lay on the horizon opposite the moon, bruised purple with edges of fire. As she watched, the cloud deepened to black and its edges flared crimson. It unfurled into the shape of a lion that leapt across the sky, strewing darkness in its wake, until at last it caught the moon in its jaws and swallowed it. As darkness closed in, Khalidah felt her limbs freezing, her breath sucked from her lungs.

She awakened gasping and shivering. Several minutes of panic passed before she became aware of Sulayman's hand on her head, soothing without words. She was too grateful to protest. Soon afterward, she fell into a deep, dreamless sleep.

THE sun rose red the next morning behind high, broken clouds, like bloodied arrowheads. Khalidah felt better, but Sulayman was acting strangely. His movements were sluggish, and when she offered him food he declined, taking only a few sips of water, then went to Aasifa and fumbled with her bridle until at last Khalidah took it from him and fastened it herself.

"What is wrong with you?" she asked, searching his sallow face for clues. He only shook his head and hoisted himself into the saddle with far too much effort.

They found a narrow track running roughly east across marshy ground. When they had been riding for a while, Sulayman finally spoke. "What frightened you last night?" His voice was thin and apprehensive.

Khalidah related the dream. "Do you think it was like that dream of Brekhna? Does it mean something?"

Sulayman looked ill now as well as troubled. "I don't know. On the face of it, I'd say it was only a nightmare. But then, the images . . . the Franj lion swallowing the crescent of Islam, perhaps?"

"Or perhaps it was only my own fears taking form."

They rode on in silence, Khalidah leading on the straight path across land that became ever wetter. They forded irrigation canals and saw peasants working their fields with water buffalo or plying the waterways with long, graceful canoes they propelled with poles. The day grew grayer and hotter, threatening rain as the jagged skyline of Basrah emerged beneath the low clouds.

"Stop, Khalidah," Sulayman said midway through the morning. "I think I must rest for a moment."

Khalidah looked over her shoulder at him, then wished she'd looked sooner. His face had drained of color, leaving bruised rings under his eyes, and he slumped in the saddle as if he were in pain. She drew Zahirah to a halt and dismounted. Sulayman slid down to the ground and leaned against Aasifa's leg. "I'm sorry, Khalidah . . ."

She reached out and laid her hand on his forehead. His skin burned like the deserts they had left behind. "How long have you been like this?" she demanded.

Sulayman shook his head. "I suppose it began last night. I thought it was only the change in the air . . ."

The clouds opened abruptly, pelting them with the heaviest rain Khalidah had ever seen. Sulayman huddled against Aasifa's flank, looking ill and miserable. Fighting down a wave of panic, Khalidah said, "We cannot stop here. It can't be far to Basrah—"

"No!" he cried. "It is not safe there. There is a place in the marshes on the other side of the city, where I have a friend . . ." He trailed off as though he'd forgotten what he meant to say, or the words he was speaking had suddenly lost their meaning.

"Can you make it that far?"

"Yes," he said, but he had begun to shake, his teeth chattering uncontrollably.

At that, Khalidah realized what was wrong with Sulayman: quartan fever. She'd seen it often enough among the tribe, had even had it herself once. But with no medicine to give him and no choice other than to continue on, the knowledge did her little good. She made him drink, then helped him back into the saddle. They rode side by side, Khalidah keeping a sharp eye on Sulayman's rapidly deteriorating condition, Sulayman himself apparently lost in the rhythmic suck-and-drag of the horses' hooves in the mud, the steady drench of rain, and the hypnotic quality of the monotonous, watery landscape. His silence soon gave way to a rambling commentary that became less and less coherent: he spoke of a searing headache, of lights he claimed he could see beneath the water that encroached steadily on the fields around them, of someone called Ghassan.

When he began to cry out for help to Ghassan, Khalidah finally allowed herself to realize what she had known since that morning: wherever they were headed, she was going to have to get them there alone. So, before Sulayman lost consciousness, she took him by the shoulders and forced him to focus his bloodshot eyes on her.

"Tell me how to get there," she said. "To your friend in the marshes."

"The river . . ." he gasped. "Must . . . cross the river . . . the Ma'dan . . . the floating village. Ask for Ghassan . . ." And having uttered these dubious instructions, he slumped into her arms, unconscious.

"Most merciful Allah . . ." she began, but having no idea what to pray for, or indeed if Allah had forgiven her enough to hear it, she left the request unfinished. She managed to pull Sulayman from Aasifa's saddle onto hers, but when she tried to lead Aasifa, the mare plunged and pulled and refused to follow. Nearly weeping with exhaustion and frustration, Khalidah pushed and pulled herself and Sulayman onto Aasifa's back, and thanked Allah and all of His angels that the skittish mare did not throw them in the process. Tethering Zahirah to Aasifa's saddle, she started forward again, the horses stumbling on across the thickening mire until she saw the lights of a ramshackle settlement at the edge of a swift, swollen river.

The dialect the villagers spoke was so different from her own that she had to resort to pointing and acting to make herself understood, and even then her trial was not finished. Sulayman was shivering so violently that the ferryman was convinced that he was possessed by a Jinni and flat-out refused to carry him in his boat. It cost her both of the silver cheek pieces from Aasifa's bridle to change his mind, and even then he would not touch the sick man or their horses. She had no choice but to dismount, lash Sulayman like a grain sack to Aasifa's saddle, and then lead the horses aboard herself.

But the desert-bred mares had never seen so much water, let alone been expected to step onto a heaving platform atop it, and they thrashed and reared as if the boat contained an army of devils. Coaxing and shouting by turns, while the ferryman and several of his friends looked balefully on, Khalidah managed at last to drive the animals on board, and then stood holding them as firmly as she could with hands that shook as violently now as Sulayman's. At last the ferryman boarded and moved the boat into the pitching stream.

By the time they regained dry land, Khalidah didn't have the strength left to hold Sulayman in the saddle, so she left him lashed to his horse and drove the frightened mare before her, praying with the little will she had left that Aasifa wouldn't bolt. The ferryman had understood the word *Ma'dan* even if Khalidah did not, and he pointed to what might have been a path across the boggy land before he turned his boat and left her.

With no idea where she was headed, except that it might or might not resemble a floating village, Khalidah pushed onward. Sulayman drooped over Aasifa's back like a dead man, his face gray, his breathing sharp and shallow. *At least he is breathing*, she told herself, though it was little comfort. All the time the rain poured down, and soon the day faded into darkness, so that Khalidah had no idea whether she followed the path anymore, if it had ever been a path at all.

When she had almost given up caring whether either of them lived or died, she saw a glimmer of light. At first she wondered if these were the phantom lights Sulayman had seen that morning, if she too was growing ill. But as she rode toward it, it grew more distinct, until she found herself looking across a short expanse of water at a little domed house. Once again she felt close to weeping, but this time it was for relief because the house was floating.

It appeared to have been built on a thick layer of reed mats, which floated like a boat on the water. The mats were tied off to several palm trees with thick ropes. Other, similar houses spread out behind it, their windows glowing with promised warmth, some floating on similar reed mats, some sitting on islands hardly bigger than the houses they supported. Each house had a lithe canoe tied up outside, and some of the bigger ones had outbuildings Khalidah assumed were for stabling animals.

She caught hold of Aasifa's bridle and guided the two horses through the shallow water to the nearest house. Summoning her courage, she rapped on the plaited-reed door. It opened almost immediately. A small, wiry man stood in silhouette against the warm glow. He was about her father's age, with a dark, weathered face, a beard like sheep's wool, and eyes that tended toward kindness but were presently full of suspicion.

"Yes?" he said.

"I am looking for a man called Ghassan. I am sorry, I do not know his name beyond that, but I believe that he is acquainted with a friend of mine—a minstrel called Sulayman."

Now puzzlement joined the suspicion on the man's face. "In that case, you have found him—I am Ghassan al-Feraigati. But who are you, and what brings you here on such a night, asking for me?"

Khalidah said nothing, only stepped aside, revealing Aasifa and her senseless burden. Ghassan's puzzlement deepened for a moment and then shattered into fear.

"What have you done to him?" he cried. "What have you done?"

And Khalidah, to her mortification, burst into tears.

Eighteen

BY the time Ghassan al-Feraigati had untied Sulayman and brought him inside the reed house, Khalidah had managed to convince him that she was not responsible for Sulayman's condition. Ghassan laid him on a rug by a little glowing brazier.

"What happened?" he asked, pressing Sulayman's limp wrist for a pulse.

Bewildered and teary, Khalidah answered, "He got sick . . . it began this morning, I think, though it might have been earlier . . . I believe it is quartan fever."

Ghassan sighed. "I believe that you are right. You did well to bring him here—whoever you are. But we will discuss that, and what is to be done with him, after I see to your horses. Take off his clothes and dry his hair." He tossed her a linen towel. "I will be back in a moment." Without waiting for a reply, he disappeared into the night.

Khalidah sat staring dumbly at the towel in her hands, and was sitting there still when Ghassan returned. His speculative look turned to one of anger.

"Are you an idiot, boy? Did I not tell you to undress him?"

"I . . ." Khalidah began and then, realizing that she was about to cry again, she did something she had not done since the first morning in the desert, when she put aside her dress: she pulled off her *kufiyya*. Her long, wet hair tumbled down her back.

"Ah," Ghassan said, frowning, but the anger had left his face. "Well, child, it seems you have a lot to tell me. Turn your back, and

I will undress him while you explain . . . and please, be assured that I am a friend. You need not lie to me."

Khalidah had little choice but to believe him. She handed him the towel and turned her back, and then, drawing a deep breath, she began, "My name is Khalidah al-Hassani, and I first met Sulayman three weeks ago . . ."

As she told her story, she took stock of Ghassan's house. The walls were woven of reeds in latticed patterns and riddled with shelves and compartments holding vials and jars and bowls, fishing equipment, and drying herbs. The only furnishings were a low wooden table cluttered with more herbs and utensils for their preparation, the bright woolen rug by the brazier, and a neat bed on the floor in one corner. Three cats—one black, one white, and one patched various colors—were curled up on the bed.

When she finished her story, she looked toward Ghassan, who had moved to the table and was busy concocting something in a bowl. "Well?" she asked.

"Well, what?"

"Are you not going to tell me that I'm mad, to be talking of Qaf and the Jinn?"

He looked up at her with mild surprise. "Why should I? Do you not think that I have heard all of this already from Sulayman himself? The fact is he stopped here on his way back from Qaf, to ask my advice about finding you."

She was too surprised to know what to say. Instead, she turned to Sulayman, who was wrapped now in a clean linen sheet and covered by a blanket, his color returning in the warmth from the brazier.

"Can you save him?" she asked quietly.

Ghassan frowned at the pungent mess in the bowl and poured heated water into it. Then he folded his gnarled hands and looked up at her. "You do not seem like the kind of woman who asks a question hoping for a lie. Therefore, I can only say that I will try. But I can also tell you that I have a good medicine on my side. It comes from the Orient, if you believe the trader who brings it. He certainly charges enough for the tale to be true. But in a village where the fever strikes so many, I suppose any price is justified."

"I will pay you back," Khalidah said.

"His survival will be payment enough for me," Ghassan said grimly, then strained the infusion and, picking up the bowl and a spoon, went to Sulayman and began the thankless task of trying to get the medicine into him.

Khalidah gave him a long look of her own, then said, "Who are you to him?"

Ghassan sighed. "Only he could tell you that. But as for who he is to me . . . well, I suppose that he is the son I never had."

"How did you meet him?"

There was a long pause, during which Khalidah knew that he was censoring his answer. At last he said, "I've known him since he was a child—the troupe he once traveled with stayed here when they crossed the marshes."

"And where is here?" she asked.

"One of the many villages of the Feraigat tribe, which in turn is one of the ancient tribes of the Ma'dan, the people of the marshes." He looked carefully at Khalidah's face. It was pallid even in the coals' warm glow, her eyes ringed with exhaustion. "I know that you have questions for me, Khalidah, and I have as many for you. But our friend will get worse before he gets better. There will be time enough to ask and answer in the days ahead. Rest, now. Take my bed. And here, put this on. Your clothes are soaked through, and the last thing I need is for you to fall ill, too." He handed her a long linen robe from a peg on the wall, which she accepted gratefully. "I'll wake you if there is any change."

Khalidah was too tired to protest. She dropped her wet clothes as soon as Ghassan turned his back and put on the robe, which, if far too large, was at least warm and dry. Clearing a space among the grudging cats, she lay down and was asleep instantly.

Nineteen

THE next day brought little change to Sulayman's condition, nor to the weather. Ghassan patiently spooned infusions into his patient, and Khalidah mooned about, restless and desolate by turns. In the clear light of day her situation seemed even stranger, and the silence between herself and the healer became increasingly awkward, as all of her attempts to draw him into conversation were met with monosyllabic rebuffs.

At last, driven by discomfort and frustration, she burst out: "What is it that you are not telling me?"

She had expected another curt evasion, but instead Ghassan set down his bowl and spoon, looked her in the eye, and said, "If you see enough to ask that question, then I suppose you deserve to know the answer. It is not only for myself that I desire Sulayman's recovery. Long ago I made a promise to his mother that I would not let him die, and I'd rather die myself than break it."

Khalidah stared at him in stunned silence, for this was the last thing she had expected to hear. At last she said, "But Sulayman told me that he never knew his mother."

"And so he did not," Ghassan answered, passing a hand over his weary eyes. "Nor does he know what I am about to tell you."

Khalidah shook her head. "Why . . . ?"

"Because I realize now that I was wrong to have kept this from him, though I did it to spare him grief . . . because he might very well die here without knowing that he had a mother who loved him. And though you have not told me what you and he are to each other, I think that he would want you to know his story, if he himself could not. So, Khalidah, do you have the strength to bear it?"

Half certain that he was mad, Khalidah nodded, and for the first time since her arrival, Ghassan rewarded her with a faint smile. "Twenty-three years ago," he began, without ceremony, "my father died. I regretted his death, but my true tragedy was that as a result, I was called home from Baghdad, where I had been sent to study medicine.

"My father, you see, was the village healer, and suffered all his life under the burden of his failures. Of course they weren't his fault. The marshes are a difficult place to live—the damp breeds fever and dysentery, and those who cannot afford outbuildings bring their beasts into their houses, so sickness and injury are rife. But he always felt that a man with more education would have been proof against these hazards, and so he was determined that his only son would be a 'real' physician.

"He saved all through my childhood to educate me, depriving my mother and sisters of far more than I realized at the time, and stoking me with dreams of glory. Because of this, and because I was certain that my mother had called me home out of spite, I came back to the marshes in a wallow of self-obsessed misery, in which I was still firmly entrenched on the night that they found Haya.

"It was winter, a bitter evening alternating between sleet and rain. Radwan, the father of our current clan chief, was still our leader then, and we were gathered in his hall when two of his retainers brought her in. She sagged between them like a sack of wet flour, obviously ill and heavily pregnant, but so beautiful: hair like a rook's wing, eyes like spearheads, smooth skin the color of honey . . ."

There were bitterness and longing in his tone, and Khalidah realized that Ghassan had both loved this woman and lost her. She listened with deepening pity. "They had found her unconscious at the edge of the marsh. A young woman like that, with child, traveling alone so close to her time—there were few conclusions one could draw that left her honor intact. Many villages would have turned her away. Perhaps many already had. But Radwan had a great weakness for feminine beauty, and so he had the men bring her in.

"To her credit, she knelt before him with all the composure of a princess. He questioned her in Arabic, but she answered in Hebrew and in Persian, saying that she did not understand. Of course she thought that no one would understand her, either. But in Baghdad I had studied with a Jewish doctor who had taught me his tongue. I told her in Hebrew that I would help her. She looked at me, a look of such despair . . . I have never seen anything like it since and I hope I never do. No doubt she thought that I intended to take advantage of her." He shook his head.

"But she was in labor; she had little choice. She fought all that night and the next day to bring the child forth. In the end she was raving, and so I learned a good deal more about her than she had intended to tell. The child, of course, was illegitimate. She was on her way from Cairo to her family in Shiraz, hoping that they would accept her back. She never said what her business had been in Egypt, nor why she was unable to apply to the child's father for help.

"When he finally came, the child wasn't breathing. She looked at me and said, 'Save the child, or cut my throat.' So I did something that I had heard about but never quite believed was possible—I put my mouth over the child's and sucked the fluid from his lungs, and then I breathed into them. Five times I gave him my breath, and then, the miracle: he screwed up his face and started to scream."

Ghassan paused, his eyes deep in the past. "Haya refused to tell me anything about the child's father," he said at last, "but when I gave the baby to her, I could see that she had loved him. She named the child Sulayman, and that was when she made me promise: that if she should not survive, I would not let him die." Ghassan paused to look at Sulayman's feverish face, and a shadow crossed his own. "She stayed for a week," he said, "and then she vanished. I looked for her, of course. Youth craves romance, and I imagined myself saving her from disgrace and the child from illegitimacy, bringing them back to live in the marshes as my own wife and son." Ghassan smiled sadly. "I never found her, but I never forgot her either, nor that little boy I had brought back from the dead. I imagined him growing up somewhere, dirty and starving no doubt, but loved at least.

"I know what you must think, Khalidah. Sulayman is a common name, and a city the size of Cairo produces plenty of orphans. I don't suppose that I can ever prove it, but I was certain the very first time I laid eyes on him that Sulayman was Haya's son. He is the image of her."

"Why did you never tell him this?" Khalidah cried. "Do you know what it has cost him, to believe that he belonged to no one?"

"Oh, yes," Ghassan answered, "I know. I have heard him speak the words himself."

"Then why did you keep silent?"

Ghassan looked at her, his eyes sad but calm. "Because knowing would not have changed anything. Yes, I met his mother, but I never knew her. I do not know who she was or who she became. I do not know what man she loved to produce that child I saved, nor why she left him, nor even why she returned to Cairo." He nodded at Sulayman, whose face rippled as if the words cast stones into the pool of his feverish sleep. "As I said, I wish now that I had told him; but I still believe that telling him would not have brought him anything but grief."

Khalidah glared at Ghassan, but as his eyes remained steady on hers, gradually she began to forgive him. At last she sighed and nodded, and Ghassan too seemed to release a breath he had been holding.

"You have a sweet voice," he said after a moment, and once again his own voice had turned speculative, "which could pass well enough for a young boy's . . . You sing?" Warily, Khalidah nodded. "And can you play?"

"On the oud, well enough," she answered.

"In that case," said Ghassan, "bind your hair again and come with me. We both need a break. The boy will be all right by himself for a few hours."

Reluctantly, Khalidah donned her *kufiyya* and followed him out into the rainy night.

Twenty

THE house of Radwan ibn Radwan al-Feraigati was as beautiful as any palace Khalidah could imagine. The latticed walls had been woven in long, continuous strips of striking intricacy, no two the same. Huge pillars of bound reeds supported the walls, and small, round windows were set in a row under the eaves of the reed-matting roof. Even through the driving rain, she could hear animated chatter from inside, and someone playing a reed flute.

Pulling her *kufiyya* lower over her forehead, she followed Ghassan inside. The room was lit by flickering oil lamps and a few smoking braziers with coffeepots warming on top. It appeared that most of the men of the village were gathered there. They sat on reed mats and woven rugs, some holding little earthenware cups of coffee, some sharing pipes of *banj*. Reclining on a pile of cushions against the far wall was a heavy, middle-aged man with deeply lined skin, a prominent nose, thick, fleshy lips, and small eyes already heavy from the hookah. He glanced up at Khalidah with marked disinterest and said, "Who are you?"

"His name is Khalid," Ghassan said with an ingratiating smile, "and he is my guest. His traveling companion is ill, and they will be staying with me for a few days."

The chief grunted. "Can he do anything?"

Khalidah looked apprehensively at Ghassan, who smiled at her and then answered, "He can sing and play the oud."

"Well, let's hear him," Radwan said, as if he didn't expect to be impressed. He snapped his fingers and someone handed Khalidah an oud, and then he settled back into his pile of cushions and apparently forgot about her.

Sighing, Khalidah sat down on a rug and began to tune the instrument, which was badly in need of it. When at last she had put it right, she settled it on her lap and ran through a series of scales, finding her fingers tight and clumsy from lack of practice and long hours wrapped in the reins. She widened the scales to arpeggios and finally felt the muscles begin to loosen. Almost unconsciously, the exercises diverged into a soft, haunting melody that had been germinating in her head since the morning they left Domat al-Jandal.

Khalidah rarely composed, and never tried to. She had found long ago that it didn't work that way. When music came to her, it came by grace, a thousand fragments filtering through her unconscious over weeks and months until they emerged almost whole. Even then, the new song remained a mystery until she touched finger to string, as a child is a mystery to its mother until the moment their bodies separate. So Khalidah had no solid idea of what would emerge that night in Radwan's house until she found herself singing, the words fitting the music as if she had planned it meticulously:

Thin as the new moon,
ashen-faced, like arrow shafts
rattling around
in the hand of a gambler . . .
He howls in the empty spaces,
they howl,
as if they and he were bereaved women
on the high ridge, wailing.
His eyelids sag. He grows silent.
They follow his lead.
They, he, forlorn,
take heart from one another . . .
surging, hard pressed,
keeping composure
over what they hide . . .

She sang on, oblivious to the men who listened now with rapt attention as Shánfara's ancient words twined seamlessly with music that had begun as the chant of a mad old woman, endlessly stirring her stew pot at the edge of a desert town. But when Khalidah reached the lines about the sand daughter, she faltered.

"Nobody told you to stop," Radwan barked.

"Forgive me," she answered, unnecessarily retuning the instrument. "The oud does not like the rain."

The chief studied her from beneath his heavy lids. "You're no street busker, and no mere child, either." Radwan raised the hookah's mouthpiece, sucked, and then lowered it again in a cloud of pungent smoke. "Come here, boy," he said in a low, rasping voice. "Let me look at you."

Many of the men had fallen silent against the music, and now they watched the scene with keen interest. Khalidah had the feeling that they all knew something that she didn't. Ghassan looked suddenly apprehensive, but she had little choice other than to lay down the oud and approach the lumpish clan chief of the Feraigat. She knelt before him, her eyes on the floor, but he reached out and lifted her chin, forcing her to look at him.

"Such unusual eyes," he said speculatively, "and such smooth skin . . . almost like a girl's . . ." Her heart fluttered in panic, and she thought, *He knows.* The thought seemed confirmed when she saw the spark of lust in his eyes. "Tell me—where is it that you are going?"

"Yazd," she whispered, confirming their direction, but naming a city she hoped was far enough away he wouldn't want to accompany them. For all of her quick plotting, Khalidah was barely aware of what she was saying. "I am going to be a dervish."

"Are you?" Radwan said. "A pity."

She saw that the glint in his eyes had turned to one of disappointment. All at once she understood, and was both relieved and mortified. To her irritation, she saw out of the corner of her eye that many of the men were laughing into their sleeves.

"And how long will you be staying with Ghassan?" he continued.

"I do not know," she stammered. "My—my cousin has quartan fever, and I cannot leave until he recovers."

Radwan scrutinized her for a moment, and then sighed. "Ah, well," he said resignedly, "at least your voice is sweet. You will play for me every night that you remain in my village."

"As you wish, Sayyid," Khalidah said.

"I trust that you haven't forsworn all the pleasures of the flesh?" Radwan asked, and Khalidah was confused until she saw that he was proffering her the mouthpiece of the hookah. She looked at Ghassan, who only shrugged. Reluctantly, she accepted it. The chief watched as she drew on it, then exhaled in a gasping cough. Apparently, this was a satisfactory response. He gave her a bleary, gap-toothed smile and a whack on the shoulder and then cried, "Now, boy, get back to your oud and play!"

THE rain had slackened by the time Ghassan and Khalidah finally stumbled back into his canoe. After her unwitting rebuff, Radwan had warmed to Khalidah, demanding song after song and plying her with harsh grain liquor and *banj*. The liquor she managed to pour into the floor's matting when no one was looking, but the air was soon so thick with smoke that she could not have avoided its effects if she had ignored the passed pipe entirely.

Khalidah's prior experience with *banj* consisted of a single afternoon five years previous, spent with Bilal and a lump of cannabis resin that one of the retainers had dropped under Bilal's sharp gaze.

"Are you sure?" she had asked him, doubtfully examining the lump he held out on his palm, which resembled nothing so much as the petrified lumps of undigested rodent the hunting hawks periodically vomited.

"It's hashish, all right," Bilal had said with a withering look that told her he was even more uncertain than she was, but determined not to show it. "Only, it does not look like very much . . ."

In fact, it was enough hashish to stun a horse. They'd smoked it with a will, neither having to tell the other that their honor depended on reducing the lot of it to ash, no matter what the consequences. The consequences were a brief euphoria followed by mind-crushing paranoia, which ended with them running to Zaynab in terror and tearfully confessing everything to her as they vomited their stomachs dry. Khalidah had not touched *banj* since that day, and as a result, she was now more intoxicated than she had ever imagined possible. She hoped that this would not become the norm of her stay with the Feraigat. If it did, she had as little chance of surviving it as Sulayman.

But seeing Sulayman sobered her again. The coals in the brazier had burned down almost to nothing. She knelt by him as Ghassan added more, and low red tongues of flame lapped the edges of the new coals like the crimson lines around dark clouds. He felt Sulayman's forehead, gave him another dose of medicine, then turned to Khalidah.

"I am sorry about Radwan," Ghassan said. "I did not think he would take to you in quite so . . . immediate a fashion."

She waved his apology aside and said, "I will stay up with him tonight."

But Ghassan was already shaking his head. "Sleep now," he said, "and let Sulayman sleep. The morning will bring change one way or the other, and I'll need you rested."

Khalidah tried to protest, but she was too sapped to argue for long. She lay down with guilty gratitude on her blanket on the opposite side of the brazier from Sulayman and fell asleep to the tide of his breathing.

Twenty-one

KHALIDAH awakened the next morning to a stabbing brightness, feeling as if she'd been dragged for miles by a fast horse over hard ground. Her mind swam with the sound of lapping water and the sense that something was not as it should be. When she finally managed to turn over, she realized what it was: after so many days of unmitigated rain, the sun was shining. It shot like a knife strike through the chinks in the reed walls, sparked from the myriad vessels of glass and glazed pottery, and filled the doorway in a searing, sickening block. Slowly, she remembered: Ghassan, Radwan, the oud, and the plangent sound of her own voice rendering Shánfara's words into something other than what they had been. And then, strange dreams of an endless desert unrolling to the whine of mosquitoes that slowly became a voice hissing her name, a scorched wind that blasted her until she shook and burned with it by turns, a dark fissure in the earth full of red eyes and teeth like sabers, with which she fought for Sulayman's limp body. She sat up abruptly, gripped by the fear of the half-remembered nightmares as the room reeled around her. And then her eyes caught on Sulayman's. They were open, and fixed on her.

The pitching room stilled. She leapt to her feet, crying, "You're better!"

"But still not well," Ghassan said from the shadows by his work table. "I imagine the two of you need to talk—but Khalidah, don't tire him. I'll be back soon." He stood and disappeared through the bright doorway.

Sulayman pushed himself up slowly as Khalidah sat down by his bed, and then they sat looking at each other, neither knowing quite what to say. She wondered whether he was repressing a powerful urge to embrace her, as she was him. She felt near tears again, and fought them angrily.

"I'm sorry—" she began.

"*You're* sorry?" he interrupted. "The blame for this is mine. I've been so wrapped up in reaching Qaf, I haven't thought about much else. I ignored the symptoms when I started to be ill, and so I left you to drag my carcass across half of Jazirah—"

"And I'd do it again, to save you," she said, with a level look.

He smiled weakly. "Brave words, Sayyida; let us hope you will never have to make good on them." Then the smile died, and he shook his head. "Quartan fever—honestly! I know better. The first thing the troupe taught me was never to camp in a damp place with bad air."

"There was a Berber herbalist who traveled with my tribe for a time," Khalidah said, "who claimed that quartan fever isn't caused by bad air but by mosquitoes."

"Well then, he was a fraud."

Khalidah smiled. "That's what my father said when he dismissed him. Still, we have seen a lot of mosquitoes in the last few weeks . . ."

Sulayman shook his head. "If I am ill, it is because Allah wills it . . . and let us hope that He wills me a quick recovery, too." They sat in the not-quite-silence of wind on reeds and water. Finally, he asked, "What do you think of Ghassan?"

"He is hard work."

Sulayman laughed. "Yes, he is; but name me something worthwhile that isn't." *You, most of the time*, Khalidah thought. "Did he tell you how long it will be until we can leave?"

Khalidah sighed. "Ghassan tells me very little. I do not think that he likes me overly much."

"Ghassan does not suffer fools. If he didn't like you, you would not be here."

With eyes fixed on the sliver of bright water visible through the doorway, Khalidah said, "I think that he would suffer more than a fool for you."

Sulayman considered this, his lips pressed into a ruminative line. "Did he tell you how we met?" he asked at last.

The image of a laboring woman flashed into Khalidah's mind. She stifled it quickly, but Sulayman had read the distress on her face. "What?" he asked, his voice suddenly tense and low. "What did he tell you?"

"You will have to ask him that yourself."

He looked at her with eyes stripped bare. When he nodded, she could not help feeling that it was less in agreement than in acquiescence to something he knew already.

DUSK came in a slow glide over the watery village. As the sun set in a quicksilver sky, mothers called their children home, water buffalo slopped heavily back to their stables, men plied canoes full of fish or fodder collected during the day, and the smoke of fifty cookfires drifted skyward. Sulayman and Khalidah sat outside with Ghassan before his own little fire as he cooked flatbread and grilled fish, then set the food down in front of them.

"Working cures sharpens the appetite," he said, tearing into the food and gesturing to his guests to join him.

Sulayman picked at a bit of bread, but Khalidah only gave Ghassan a long, incisive look. "Yes, I know that you want me to tell him," Ghassan replied, waving a hand dismissively. "All in good time."

"I do not like to have a secret divide us," she answered.

"And if you can keep to that, you'll be better off than most couples," he answered dryly.

Sulayman and Khalidah looked at each other, then away again, blushing. "You presume too much," she said in a low voice.

"Oh, I don't think so," Ghassan answered. His voice was curiously harsh, and cut by a resonant note of longing. He chewed reflectively for a long moment, then he said, "But, if you will . . ."

He proceeded to tell Sulayman the story he had told Khalidah the previous day. Sulayman listened to the whole of it with his eyes on his hands. The silence stretched out after Ghassan finished, until at last Sulayman asked, not quite bitterly, but without warmth: "Do you tell me this now because I am dying?"

"I am telling you because you are mortal."

"That is no answer!" Sulayman retorted.

Ghassan looked at him calmly, then said, "We are all dying, Sulayman, from the day that we are born. I accept that I should not have kept Haya's secret as long as I did. Please, let the rest of it lie."

Sulayman looked at Khalidah. "And you? Do you believe I am this Jewish woman's son?"

Khalidah drew a breath of the watery air, then said, "I believe that what I believe does not matter. Just as I must construct the truth of my past from the pieces I am given, so must you."

Sulayman looked at her for a moment, then retreated back inside.

Twenty-two

Ras al-Mai
Early April

"SANCTIMONIOUS bastard," Numair grumbled, pulling his pillow over his head as the drums and trumpets shattered his stupor, followed by the high wail of the muezzin. Bilal made no attempt to rouse him. After the first few days in Salah ad-Din's camp he had learned that it was generally a futile effort, and his life was invariably more pleasant if his "cousin" was allowed to sleep late.

He dressed quickly and left the tent. The world around him was full of indistinct movement. Dark figures with rolled prayer rugs over their shoulders shuffled toward the infantry's practice ground like a herd of small, misshapen pachyderms. For a moment he stood watching them. Overhead the sky was still dark and strewn with stars, but a rim of brightness ran along the horizon, as if night were a lid on the world and day fought to break the seal. For a moment he thought of the open desert, of other dawns when he and Khalidah had crept away from the sleeping camp to race her father's horses toward the rising sun. They'd generally been whipped for it later, but no pain could match the ecstasy of that moment when all four hooves left the ground and two earthbound creatures grew the hearts of angels.

Bilal blinked. A solitary figure had broken from the herd and moved toward him. A smile materialized from the shifting wash of shadow; a slender hand touched him. "*As-salaamu alaikum,*" Salim said, but Bilal could not answer him. He was too busy trying to stem the ensuing thought: that perhaps there was one feeling to match the divinity of flight, and it came in the shape of the five mortal fingers now resting on his arm. For if it was true, then there was no peace for him, no destiny but despair. He saw it stretched before him like his mother's loom lying warped and ready, the fabric not yet woven.

Stop it, he ordered himself, and forcing a smile, he answered the prince's *salaam*s. Salim slipped his arm through the curve of Bilal's, and they walked together to the dawn prayer, bowing to Mecca as the sun tore the heart out of night.

When the prayers were finished and the rugs rolled up, Salim sat back on his heels and said, "I have a secret."

With a flutter of anxiety, Bilal asked, "What is it?"

"If I told you, it would not be a secret." Salim laughed at Bilal's frown. "But I will show you," he relented, then paused, giving Bilal a long, speculative look. The rising sun turned his eyes to the color of strong tea. "My father is leaving," he said at last.

"Is that the secret?"

"Ha! He has given my brother Al-Afdhal command of the army, and Al-Afdhal will have wasted no time in letting everyone know it. I will not drill with you today," he added abruptly. "I am to sit with my father and observe a Sultan's preparations for war. Meet me after supper."

"I do not know whether my cousin—"

"I will send a whore with a bottle of wine," Salim interrupted, his eyes laughing. "Your cousin will not even realize you are missing. I will wait for you—don't be late." And he slipped away, a slight figure swallowed by the bright blood of day.

SALIM had been correct in his prediction: by noon, every soul in the army had heard of the Sultan's imminent departure. Rumors flew about a private meeting with a Franj leader—Count Tripoli, Gerard de Ridefort, even King Guy himself. The truth, as usual, was a good deal more mundane. The month of Muharram was nearly two weeks old, and it was in this month that the greatest number of pilgrims was on the road home from

Mecca. The first caravans would already have reached Oultre-jourdain, and Salah ad-Din knew how great the temptation to Brins Arnat would be. Fearing another raid, he was leaving the gathering army in order to take his elite guard to police the pilgrim road.

As the surge of excitement was dampened by the truth, camp life returned to normal. After breakfast came the cavalry drills, at which Bilal acquitted himself far better than he did at the following exercises in swordsmanship. These were purely voluntary on his part, for as a Bedu cavalryman, he was expected to use the long spear, which he had been taught to wield since he could sit a horse. He told himself that he practiced the sword out of personal interest, but deep down he knew that he did it for Salim. The prince, like all boys of his class, used a sword as if it were an extension of himself, and Bilal could not bear for his friend to see his own awkwardness. So he hacked away with his unwieldy blade, pouring sweat into the ravenous sand, and wondered about Salim's secret.

By the time he arrived back at the tent in the late afternoon, mild curiosity had grown into a fever of anticipation, so it was with a good deal of dismay that he found Numair neither drunk nor tangled in the embrace of the promised whore, but washed and sober and obviously waiting for him.

"Change your clothes," Numair said. "And arm yourself. I have an errand for you."

Bilal shook his head. "What errand?"

"Do you question me?" Numair replied, giving Bilal the hard, metallic look that he'd seen him cast on Khalidah during their doomed henna ceremony. Bilal shivered, feeling a prickle of empathy for her. "If I tell you I have an errand, you do it with a smile on your face."

"This time, I cannot," Bilal heard himself say, with partial disbelief.

Numair stilled, that alien look sharpening. "You cannot?" He spoke in a tone of gentle mockery with an edge like a dagger's.

"Have you forgotten why we are here? What is it, precisely, that would keep you from your duty?"

"A meeting," Bilal faltered, already regretting his defiance.

"With the Sultan's runt, no doubt," Numair answered. Bilal said nothing, but felt his face burning, with anger or with shame he no longer knew. "Did you think that I had not noticed all the time that you spend with him? What are you playing at, little cousin?"

Hating himself for the lie, but hating Numair more, Bilal answered coldly, "I have not forgotten why we are here. And given your master's desire for information on the Sultan's plans, I would have thought that you would be pleased that I have befriended his son."

"I did not take you for a schemer." Still those eyes glittered at him, dissecting his purpose. Bilal said nothing. "Watch your step, little cousin. Princes make dangerous lovers."

"What?" Bilal cried. "We are not—"

Numair cut him off with a chuckle. "Save your breath, Bilal. I don't care what you do with him—just don't cross me. Remember that your mother's life is in my hands."

Of course he remembered. Remembering poisoned every moment of his own life. Numair watched him squirm, smiling faintly. Then he said, "Now listen carefully, and remember everything . . ."

De Mailly's face was like marble in the light of the full moon, the cross on his mantle the color of ash. He stood by his horse's withers, one hand absently toying with its mane as he listened to Bilal's message.

"Is it bad news?" Bilal ventured when, several moments after he finished, de Mailly had still said nothing.

De Mailly looked at him with a weary smile. "I do not know. You say Salah ad-Din intends to send a detachment of troops to Tiberias, to bolster Count Tripoli's garrison there—are you absolutely certain that that is correct?"

"That is what I was told. Why, Messire? What does it mean?"

De Mailly looked closely at him, frowning. "Does your cousin explain nothing to you?"

"Only when it suits him," Bilal answered.

"Which I take it is not very often," de Mailly said, his contempt obvious. "Very well, then: our nobles are currently divided between supporters of King Guy and those of Count Tripoli. Wherever the right of it lies, a divided kingdom cannot stand against Salah ad-Din, and just now the nobles of Jerusalem can talk of nothing but how to make Tripoli recognize Guy and thereby reunite the kingdom."

De Mailly paused, then said, "Kerak and my master de Ridefort favor military action to force Tripoli's submission. The barons prefer diplomacy. But whichever they choose, if they fail, we stand to lose Jerusalem. And if Tripoli has the Sultan's help, as your information suggests he will, then they will quite likely fail."

"And what do you think, Messire?"

De Mailly sighed. "It does not matter. Nobody asks the opinion of the Marshal of the Temple—only of its Master."

"I am asking."

De Mailly looked startled, then rewarded Bilal with a sweet smile. "Indeed, you are. Well, then: I think that Tripoli is far and away the best statesman in Outremer, but he is also an idealist. His wish to reconcile with the Saracens is noble, but I believe that it is misguided."

Bilal looked at the knight's solicitous face, sick with the thought that this man didn't realize he was being double-crossed by the very Master he served so honestly. Softly, he said, "Do you think that it is possible for our two races to live at peace with one another?"

De Mailly's smile saddened, and he touched Bilal's cheek. "Perhaps it is possible. But we must first learn to live in peace with our own kind. In that, your Sultan appears to have succeeded where our kings have so far failed. I only hope that we will not need to spill our own people's blood to achieve solidarity."

Bilal said, half to himself, "I wish it were not like this."

"I wish that too."

"If only there were something that I could do . . ."

De Mailly smiled, mistaking his meaning. "Brave boy . . . I fear this is beyond you. Your master, on the other hand, ought to have seen this truce coming and sent word. I hear that he failed to keep the meeting de Ridefort arranged for him with the Sultan. Tell me, what is distracting him?"

"What isn't?" Bilal muttered. Then, thinking that he had been too flippant, he added, "Perhaps I have not tried hard enough to keep him from temptation. I will do better."

"Do not blame yourself, *petit*. You are not responsible for the failings of your master." He sighed. "And yet, I worry about you here, with only your cousin to protect you. Perhaps I should apply to de Ridefort to find a better position for you."

"No!" Bilal said sharply.

"But why not?"

Bilal looked away. "It is complicated . . ."

He thought that de Mailly would push him, but the knight only said, "Very well. But my offer still stands, Bilal: if ever you find yourself in need of help, do not hesitate to call on me."

Bilal nodded. "Is there a message to take back?"

"There wasn't," de Mailly said grimly, "but given what you have told me about your cousin's attitude, I think that you had better stress to him the importance of undermining the Sultan's mission to Tiberias. If he cannot stop it, then he must at least be among the forces that go to Tripoli's aid, the better to inform de Ridefort of his interactions with the Sultan."

And de Ridefort will tell him exactly the opposite, at the first opportunity, Bilal thought with disgust. "He will not like that," he said out loud.

This time, de Mailly's smile was cold. "I don't care."

Twenty-three

SALIM reclined in the shade of a fluttering pavilion at the edge of camp, eating a pomegranate, while Bilal watched him intently. The fruit was long out of season, but this wasn't the reason for his interest, for over the weeks of their friendship the prince's apparent command of the miraculous had come to seem more or less ordinary to Bilal. What fascinated him was Salim's method of eating it. Rather than pushing the leathery skin inward and consuming the fleshy seeds in greedy bites (as Bilal had done with his own half) he held it like a cup in his left hand, while with the right he picked out each individual red-cased seed with the delicacy of a musician plucking an oud's strings.

Besides, watching Salim was preferable to acknowledging the column of horsemen snaking away from camp to the southwest, toward Tiberias. Tripoli's agreement with the Sultan was sure to tip the scales in favor of a military action against him, and ridiculous as he knew it to be, Bilal could not bear the thought of de Mailly going into battle. However, one distinct advantage to the situation was that de Ridefort had ordered Numair to volunteer for the detachment and Bilal—whose friendship with Salim had not been lost on him—to remain behind. The possibility of Numair being run through with a Templar lance was enough to bring a smile to Bilal's anxious face.

"What amuses you?" Salim asked, sucking a seed from his fingers, inky eyes intent on his friend. Bilal's smile leveled. "Ah—I would not have marked it, had I known that marking it would crush it! Sayyid's smiles are rare enough. Is civilization proving too comfortable? Does your nomad's heart pine for the bare, blowing sands?" Bilal could not help smiling again at that. "That's an improvement . . . and here is your reward."

A pomegranate seed balanced on the tip of Salim's outstretched finger. There was a hint of a smile in his eyes, a challenge perhaps, and in a moment of liminal radiance, Bilal saw himself leaning forward, taking the seed with his tongue. The image was so vivid that he could even taste the salt of Salim's skin. He shut his eyes for a moment, and when he opened them the seed still quivered before him like a songbird's heart. Shaken to the core, he took it between his thumb and forefinger and crushed it, but he could not stop himself from licking the juice. Its bittersweet spark mocked him.

Salim's eyes narrowed for a moment, showing perhaps a tinge of disappointment; then he went back to picking at the fruit. "You have not asked me, you know," he said, with the shade of petulance that sometimes crept into his tone, the only affectation that ever belied his rank.

"Asked you what?" Bilal asked, with ignorance as disingenuous as Salim's peevishness.

"What I was going to tell you the other night, when you did not come."

Bilal sighed. "I've told you I'm sorry about that. Numair wouldn't let me leave. My cousin has suddenly embraced sobriety, and it has not left me time to think of much beyond his demands."

Salim was looking down at the pomegranate husk, his long hair half obscuring his face. "So you have said." The petulance was more overt now, and with it the genuine disappointment.

"I am sorry . . ." Bilal repeated.

For a moment Salim kept his silence; then, crushing the empty husk in his hand, he looked up with one of his cloudburst smiles. "It doesn't matter. Soon you won't have to worry about your cousin, sober or not."

"What do you mean?" Bilal asked warily.

"It's what I wanted to tell you the other night. My father has asked me to go south with him, and he is giving me command of a cavalry unit. Thirty horsemen of my choosing, to be used for reconnaissance. And he has told me to be certain to include you!"

For a moment elation surged through Bilal. Then he recalled that the hajj road ran past Kerak and de Ridefort's watchful eye, and he knew who had been behind this command. Neither the Sultan nor de Ridefort could be without his informer, after all. He watched as the last of the Tiberias detachment were subsumed in the dust of their departure, unable to find words to answer Salim.

"I had thought that you would be pleased," the prince said, and this time there was no petulance in his voice, only bewilderment and hurt.

"I *am* pleased," Bilal said. "It is only that . . . so much has changed so quickly. Two months ago I was nobody, and now I ride in a prince's cavalry unit." He shook his head. "But please don't think that I am not grateful. I am, Salim—for everything."

"Do not thank me," Salim said, taking Bilal's hand in his, still sticky with red juice. "Allah looks after the faithful."

His smile flashed out like a flaying knife.

THEY left Ras al-Mai at dawn, the Sultan solemnly entrusting his army to the eager Al-Afdhal—all pride and adolescent arrogance beneath his sparse black beard—before wrapping his heir in a fatherly embrace. Salim, watching from horseback at the fringes of the crowd, rolled his eyes, grinned at Bilal, then gave his mare a sharp kick. She reared and then plunged into a gallop, abruptly cutting short the ceremonial farewells. Salim and his men were gone before his father's frown could catch him.

By midmorning, however, even Salim's enthusiasm was flagging. A brisk wind had risen with the light, filling the air with the road's powdery dust so that even those at the front of the march found it difficult to breathe.

"Imad ad-Din would call this an omen," Salim said to Bilal,

who rode at his side. Like the others, Salim had pulled a corner of his turban across his nose and mouth, but the bare parts of his face and the black waves of his hair were caked with the pale dust, making him into the parody of a Franji.

"And you?" Bilal asked.

Salim's eyes narrowed, and Bilal knew that under the dusty linen he was smiling. "I think that omens are the props of old men who prefer wine and women to Allah's call."

"Don't let your father hear you say that," Bilal said.

"Indeed . . . and yet, I do not count the great chronicler amid our company."

Which was true enough, though Salim knew as well as Bilal did that it had more to do with the Sultan's practicality than the scribe's preference for the comforts of home. Though Salah ad-Din was fond of his records, he also knew that it was a risk to leave the main body of his army behind, and that he must be ready, if the need arose, to drop everything and return to the north. So: no scribes, no whores, not even a pretty serving boy who might distract the soldiers from their duty.

The men of this miniature army were professionals, heavy cavalry and Mamluk archers led by the Sultan's favorite emirs. Bilal's gut ground in a now-familiar twist of anxiety when he imagined drawing his sword alongside them, and the only comfort he could offer himself was the very real possibility that he would die before it ever came to that. In fact, a timely death in Allah's name would solve most of his problems. Sighing, he tried to lose himself in the rhythm of Anjum's falling hooves.

At nightfall they reached the city of Busra, where they planned to camp. Lying on a fertile plain almost due south of Damascus, the town had been in existence for at least twenty-five centuries. An old story claimed that a Nestorian monk had met the young Muhammad here, passing through with his caravan, and predicted that he would be a great prophet. It was for this reason that Salah ad-Din had chosen the city as their outpost.

Bilal was too exhausted when they arrived to care about any of this. He could think of nothing but raising his tent and crawling into it. Salim, however, appeared to have left his weariness in the saddle. Bilal looked up from the jumble of ropes and pegs to see the prince walking toward him, carrying a lantern whose latticed sides threw stars on the sand.

"Leave that," Salim said. "There is something we must see."

Bilal looked wearily up at him. "The only thing I want to see is the backs of my eyelids, and I cannot do that until this tent is raised."

"Then share mine tonight, and tomorrow I'll send servants to raise yours . . . but only if you come with me now."

Bilal sighed. "What can we possibly see in the dark, anyway?"

Salim only smiled. Inwardly cursing his friend's cheerful energy, Bilal turned his back on the tangled tent and followed Salim toward the town wall. At the gate, the prince slipped a gold coin to each of the guards, who let the boys pass without comment. They wandered the quiet streets, Salim seeming more or less assured of his direction, until at last they came to a high wall of black stone that rose against the star-tacked sky.

"What is this?" Bilal asked.

"The citadel," Salim answered, and led him to a gate in the high wall, where he bribed another guard to let them inside. Once past the guard, Salim took Bilal's hand and led him into the shadows of an arched doorway, along corridors of closed doors lit by flickering torches, and finally out again into the open. They stood facing a crescent of stone. Behind them, curved benches soared upward in widening arcs to the height of several houses. Before them spread a vast platform, with an elaborately linteled doorway at its center and columned galleries on either side.

"What is this?" Bilal repeated, this time in a reverential whisper.

"A theater," Salim answered, setting his flickering lantern on the stone bench nearest him and sitting down, pulling his legs up underneath him.

"I thought you said this was the citadel."

"It is both," Salim answered. His face was rapt as he surveyed the structure. "The Romans built the theater a thousand years ago, when this city was theirs. It could hold fifteen thousand spectators. The greatest actors of their time performed the greatest plays on that stage. Then, when the Umayyids had power, they built walls around it and made it into their stronghold, and that's what it's been ever since—a castle with a theater at its heart. Can you imagine anything stranger?" Salim shook his head. "My father said that soon there will not be enough room for the garrison. He plans to enlarge it."

"You have been here before."

"No. I have only heard and read about it. But I have always wanted to come, and I wanted you to see it with me."

The simple, straightforward kindness of the gesture overwhelmed Bilal. Much later he would wonder why it was this, and not the countless previous kindnesses, that broke him. At the time he felt only a sudden, acute awareness of the ancient stonework hovering like a mountain slope above him, and the hopeless wish that it would let go and crush him in this moment when he was as near to happiness as he had ever been. But the stone held, offering neither judgment nor release, and Bilal collapsed beside Salim, head in his hands and shaking with sobs.

"But—what is the matter?" Salim asked in surprise.

"I don't . . ." Bilal faltered, "I cannot . . ." He paused, then looked up at Salim, who looked back, bewildered. "Why, *why*, Salim, did you choose me?"

Salim looked at him for a long moment, then answered, "Because my father is waiting for me to fail." His voice wavered, suddenly fragile. "He gave me this command to prove to me that I am incapable of it, and I, being selfish, and no doubt as weak as he supposes me, could not face the failure without a friend beside me. But if you would rather leave—"

"No!" Bilal cried, dismayed both by the confession and by the thought of separation. "No, that isn't what I meant. I didn't know about this, about your father . . . I only wanted to know, why did you choose me as your friend?"

"Do you wish that I had not?" Salim asked, obviously hurt.

"That's not what I mean either . . . Allah have mercy on me, I cannot seem to make right of anything!" Bilal looked miserably at Salim, who waited with soft, patient eyes for his explanation. Bilal knew that he could not continue to deceive him. "You have been the truest friend of my life," Bilal said, "and yet I have not been true to you."

"You have accepted my friendship and given your own in return," Salim answered, puzzled. "I see nothing false in that."

"But if you could see into my heart, if you only knew—"

"Ah, but I think I do," Salim interrupted. To Bilal's bewilderment, he had begun to smile, and beneath the smile was something beyond forgiveness, beyond affection or even affinity. "Why didn't you speak earlier?" Salim continued, reaching toward him with one tentative hand. "I cannot bear the thought of you suffering, thinking . . . well, I know well enough what you were thinking." There was steely defiance beneath the smile and the soft words.

"No . . ." Bilal whispered, but Salim's hand had come to rest on his cheek, and he could not deny the warmth that kindled in his cold heart in response.

"I know what the imams say, Bilal, but I cannot believe that love is a sin—not even when it looks like this."

Salim lifted Bilal's right hand and touched his lips to his palm, then leaned forward to kiss his forehead, and finally his mouth, silencing the truth Bilal had not been able to speak. Bilal suspected then that he was damned, but he didn't care: everything he had ever worried or longed for had shattered against the sudden miracle of Salim's lips against his own. The world ebbed with their embrace. For a little while, all that mattered fit into the lantern's pool of stars.

Twenty-four

Western Persia
Early April

Though Sulayman continued to regain his strength, Ghassan still insisted on coming with them into the mountains. "Whatever he says to us, his health is still fragile," he told Khalidah in a tone that suggested there was a good deal more that he was not saying. "I'd like to keep an eye on him for a few more days. Besides, the Zagros are the fiercest mountains in Persia, and I know them well."

Khalidah left him sorting herbs and went to the stable to see to the horses. She found Sulayman there already, slumped against the wall with his head between his legs.

"All better, are you?" she said, looking down at him reprovingly.

He looked up, bleary-eyed. "Don't start," he said through clenched teeth.

Khalidah shook her head, but offered a hand and helped him stand.

Aasifa whinnied a greeting when she saw her master, looking up from the manger where she grazed between Zahirah and a water buffalo, who glanced balefully at her as she danced with two weeks' pent-up energy. Despite the rest and the plentiful fodder, the horses still looked slightly out of condition. As she saddled Zahirah, Khalidah tried not to feel the nearness of rib to skin, nor to see the frequency of Sulayman's pauses in his own preparations.

As she was stowing her saddlebags, Khalidah looked up to see Ghassan splashing across the marsh on a tall bay gelding, leading a gray pony with a pack saddle. The bay had a long, straight nose and a rangy body that gave him the look of a hunting hound.

"That's an Akhal-Teke," Khalidah said admiringly. "Who does he belong to?"

"To me," Ghassan told her with a proud smile. "He stays in Radwan's stable—mine is too small. He was a gift from a Turcoman noble whom I cured of an embarrassing condition a few years ago. He'd heard of me in Basrah and came out here to avoid gossip in the town . . . anyway, I believe that in Wasim, I had the better end of the bargain. I do not know what Wasim thinks."

He dismounted and handed Wasim's reins to Khalidah while he loaded the rest of their gear onto the pack pony. The horse pranced and shook the fly tassels on his bridle, looking playfully around at his master with a smile in his eyes, and Khalidah knew exactly what Wasim thought.

The weather was fair as they set out, so clear after the days of rain that they could see the foothills of the Zagros on the horizon. Ghassan knew the best routes through the marshes, and the water seldom reached higher than Zahirah's knees. Still, it meant a slow, steady gait, for which Sulayman was grateful. As the sun moved across the sky, the marshes became shallower and the grassy patches wider, until at last the water dispersed into damp meadowland studded with well-tended orchards of fruit trees and date palms. At midday they stopped, and Ghassan prepared a bowl of medicine for Sulayman. He drank it and nibbled a piece of flatbread while Ghassan and Khalidah ate a more substantial lunch and the horses cropped the long grass.

"And now, Sulayman, you must rest," said Ghassan when the younger man had drunk the last of the foul liquid from the bowl.

"I don't need to rest," he protested.

"Yes, you do," the healer said sternly. "It will take all your strength to cross the mountains, and at the moment you have little to spare. Rest, now."

Sighing, Sulayman unrolled his blanket and lay down under a tree. He was asleep almost immediately. Looking at him, Khalidah wondered how he had managed to convince them that he was better. His face was sallow as parchment, and the fingers resting on the blanket by his cheek were slender as river reeds with the weight he had lost.

"He's not really recovered, is he?" she said.

"Perceptive girl," Ghassan answered dryly.

Khalidah frowned at Ghassan, whose lined, almond-shaped face remained impassive. "Then what are we doing?"

"We are going to the Zagros."

"Of course—just the place for an invalid. Or do you have some plan that you aren't telling me?"

"If I do," he answered with an infuriating smile, "why would I tell you merely for asking?"

Khalidah gave him a long look, then said, "Why do you disapprove of me?"

Ghassan shook his head. "The arrogance of youth! My silence has nothing to do with you. But if it will save me two days' dose of a young woman's petulance, then you might as well know that I have heard of someone in the mountains who might be able to help him . . . and perhaps you, too."

"Help me?" Khalidah demanded. "With what do I need help?"

"Tell me," he said, "what is it you hope to find in Qaf?"

Khalidah's mouth collapsed into an obstinate line, and Ghassan smiled wryly.

"Very well, then; you keep your secrets, and I'll keep mine." And with that, he lay back on Wasim's saddle, drew the end of his turban over his face, and gave a pointed snore. Sighing, Khalidah leaned against a palm trunk to wait.

It was late afternoon by the time they started off again, and the nap seemed to have erased their earlier altercation from Ghassan's mind. "Tell me, Khalidah," he said, "do the tribes intend to join the Sultan if he makes a move for Jerusalem?"

"I can only speak for my own," she said, "and even that has no straight answer, for we are a divided tribe, half following my father, and the other half my uncle. My father supports the Sultan, but my uncle . . ." Khalidah looked at Sulayman.

Sulayman smiled wryly. "Abd al-Hadi wants little beyond a plateful of delicacies, a bedful of slave girls, and a peaceful death in the shade of a palm tree . . . or so he would have you think. With him, it is often difficult to tell."

"Do you, too, intend to join the jihad?" Ghassan asked Sulayman.

"If you don't kill us in the mountains first," Sulayman answered neutrally. "And if we return from Qaf in time."

Ghassan gave him a shrewd look. "Somehow, I do not think that will be a problem."

"What do you mean?" Khalidah asked.

"Does the timing of all of this strike neither of you as odd?" When they looked blank, he added, "The heiress to the greatest warriors of the Oriental world is called to their leader just as the Islamic world is about to engage in one of the most important battles of its history. I think the two were meant to converge."

"It would be a neat theory," Sulayman answered, "except that the Jinn have no stake in Jerusalem. They are not even Muslims."

"That does not preclude a common cause."

"Perhaps not. But either way, Tor Gul Khan does not approve of Salah ad-Din."

"Does he know him?" Ghassan asked with interest.

"No, but he certainly knows of him. I believe he called the Sultan 'that arrogant, overreaching son of a goatherder.'"

Ghassan chuckled. "Well, kings seldom have a high opinion of each other. But none of it convinces me that the Jinn have no place in Salah ad-Din's jihad." He paused, then turned to Khalidah and said, "And you, Khalidah—what will you do if you find that the Muslims and the Jinn do indeed have a common cause?"

"Fight with them," she said, "to cast the infidels from Jerusalem."

"You are so certain of your righteousness." Ghassan sighed. "Yet one must never forget that the Franj are here because they, too, believe in the righteousness of their cause. Like our *mujahid-din*, they believe that they are God's warriors."

"And you think that this makes them worthy of respect?" Khalidah demanded. "Have you never heard that the Franj slaughtered and ate Muslim children when they first took Jerusalem?"

"Do you think that the people of Islam have never committed atrocities?" Ghassan returned.

"Then you suggest giving the Franj free rein of our lands."

"I suggest nothing of the sort! But we are all people of the Book . . . surely, if our only quarrel is over prophets, there must be a way for us to live together in peace?"

"But it is not just about prophets!" Khalidah cried. "It is about the sanctity of Jerusalem, and the lands they have taken from us—"

"Ah," Ghassan interrupted, "and there we have it. In the end, all wars are about the ownership of a scrap of earth. I'd have thought a nomad's daughter would have known better." Khalidah glared at him, but Ghassan only continued mildly: "Take Jerusalem, then. Is our claim to it any greater than theirs?" He didn't give them a chance to answer before he continued, "Who founded the city?"

"King David," Khalidah answered, "one thousand years before the birth of the prophet Iesu."

"Someone's taught you well," Ghassan smiled, "but not the whole truth. Jerusalem was already two thousand years old when King David 'founded' it. He took it from the Jebusites, who had no doubt taken it from someone else. And after him it passed to the Assyrians, then the Babylonians, Alexander of Macedon, Ptolemy, the Seleucids, the Maccabees, the Romans, the Byzantines, and then—only *then*—the Muslims. We are a mere scratch on the surface of that great city: a scratch no longer or deeper perhaps than the Franj, in Allah's grand scheme. For if Allah has willed our existence, then He has willed theirs, too."

"What, then," Khalidah asked with somewhat dampened defiance, "do *you* think we should do about the Franj?"

"First, consider them," he said, ignoring the dark look that passed between Khalidah and Sulayman. "Perhaps they are here to teach us something about ourselves."

"And what do you think the Franj have to teach us?" Sulayman asked, preempting Khalidah's retort.

Ghassan shrugged. "I'm a physician, not a philosopher. But it seems to me that we ought to take heed of their mistakes. Their jihad has sown hatred and misery, not least among their own people. They have all but forgotten the word of Christ in their struggles for power. If we are to wage war in Allah's name, then perhaps, rather than acquisition and repression, its object should be to spread His word. After all, what place is there among peace, enlightenment, and fulfillment for avarice and greed?"

Sulayman shook his head. "You are describing the Sultan: a man devoted to Allah and to his people, whose generosity and mercy are an example to us all. Isn't it better to follow a man like him into battle than to grovel at the feet of a race of invaders determined to subjugate us?"

Ghassan smiled sadly. "Do you think that the Sultan is really all that the rumors tell us he is? Chivalrous he may be, Sulayman, but he is a man nevertheless, subject to weakness like any other; and, more to the point, his army is made of men. They'll loot and rape despite him and call it Allah's will, and then not faith nor mercy, not our God nor the Franj's, can save this land from the damnation of war."

"War may be inevitable," said Khalidah, her eyes fixed on the deepening sky, "but I don't think that it is necessarily damnation. As you say, you are a physician: you know that sometimes salvation can be bought only by violence. A suppurating limb must be removed to save the rest of the body from infection; a living child cut from the belly of its dying mother so that two lives are not lost. You do these things because you believe in the sanctity of life." At last she looked at him, and the softness of her eyes after her earlier anger surprised him. "Well, could this not be the same? Could a sword not be our salvation, if the one who wields it believes strongly enough in faith, or mercy, or God . . . believes beyond his own strength or weakness, for the good of all who will succeed him?"

"Perhaps," he said after a long pause. "And so may you raise your sword only in that belief, Khalidah; and I pray that you prove me wrong."

There was pain on his face, and he turned away from her look of surprise. They rode on in silence through the dying light, toward the purple mountains looming like fate.

Twenty-five

SULAYMAN ate almost nothing the next morning, but all of Khalidah's inquiries about his health were met with the same defiant glare. Before they left, Ghassan handed him another draught of medicine. He gulped it down and then paled, looking bilious, but he did not throw it back up.

They had camped in the Zagros foothills the night before, and they spent that day climbing. The long, plodding hours passed for Khalidah in a string of images that surfaced like islands from the abstraction of worry and aching muscles that had overtaken her: dry, rocky hills occasionally split by meadows of sparse grass, rivers quick with meltwater the color of stone, gullies and plateaus and a few white peaks in the somnolent distance. At last they reached a high, windy ridge, and for a moment Khalidah's mind cleared as she took in the magnitude of the scene before her. From the ridge the mountain plunged steeply into a valley of yellow-green grass spotted with wildflowers. At the far side of the valley the mountains rose again, their slopes crosshatched with the remnants of ancient stone walls, the higher ones dusted with snow, on up to a ridge higher than the one on which they stood. Behind that was another higher still, and so on they marched to the horizon, their icy crowns bloodshot with the setting sun.

"These are the lands of Asag," said Ghassan, "who took the mountains as brides and had boulders for children, and was finally slain by Ninurta in the Battle of the Gods . . ."

Sulayman smiled. "Your head should roll for blasphemy."

"What is it, really?" Khalidah asked. "This place?"

"The Zagros mountains are the territory of the Grand Lur clan," Ghassan answered. "This part traditionally belongs to the Bakhtiari."

"And who are they?"

"A tribe of nomads not unlike your own. They live in black tents and migrate with the seasons over their traditional grazing lands, but they keep goats rather than horses. At any rate, they are not here now, and I doubt that they would grudge us a night on their grasslands if they were. Come, before the sun sets, or make your bed on these stones." He nudged Wasim with his heels and tugged the pony's lead rein, and the horses began picking their way downward through the gathering dark.

THAT night, Khalidah saw Sulayman's dreams. She did not look for them, but they were there when she closed her eyes. A sword of fire flayed him slowly; red wolves chased him through a labyrinth of dark volcanic stone. He screamed then and she woke; he screamed again when she and Ghassan tried to pull the blankets from his burning body, for he saw them as leering Franj with naked swords. By the next morning the delirium had passed, but it took the last of his strength with it. He could not even make himself swallow his medicine. As he shook on his blanket, Khalidah asked Ghassan:

"How much longer until we reach this place?"

"A day, if we can keep this pace and I can remember the path."

"Will he last that long?"

He sighed. "It is in Allah's hands."

It took both of their strength to get Sulayman into the saddle, but Aasifa pitched him out again immediately, smelling sickness on him; or so Khalidah told herself, unwilling to face what else the animal might have sensed. So they put him on the stalwart pony, but when they tried to load the packs onto Aasifa, she reared and screamed. In the end the pack saddle went onto Zahirah, who bore it with a bemused look, while Khalidah rode Aasifa, who made her feelings about this known by shying and swerving at every blowing leaf. Khalidah clung grimly to the horse, wishing that she had insisted rather than suggested that Sulayman choose another.

They crossed the meadow and then began climbing again. Sulayman's instinct for the saddle went deeper than his illness, and he shifted his weight automatically with the shifting terrain, though he seemed to sense little else. Khalidah was so intent upon him and the battling horse beneath her that she recalled no images from that day, just the sharpness of the wind, the searing brilliance of the sun, the air so thin and cold she felt that she could not make it fill her lungs. She heard Sulayman gasping, too. The sound seemed to come from far away.

In the afternoon he lost consciousness. Like that terrible rainy day when the fever first took him, he began to slump in the saddle, and finally to slide. Following a quick, curt negotiation, Ghassan and Khalidah agreed that if one of the horses was to bear a second rider, it had best be the slighter rider. And so once again she found herself sitting behind Sulayman, holding his sloppy weight with one arm while she guided the patient pony with the other. Behind her, Ghassan struggled to hold on to both Zahirah and Aasifa as they picked their way up the stony path.

And Sulayman, trapped now in the deadly current of his dreams, clung to a thread of consciousness like a drowning man clings to a floating log. In his delirium he raved about it—a sound, disembodied, like the steady beat of a horse's hooves hitting sand. Somehow, Khalidah felt that she should know what he meant. It haunted her for hours before at last she realized that the sound he clung to was the beating of her own heart.

THEY forded the Pasitigris late in the afternoon and stopped briefly to let the horses drink. A vast plain stretched out beyond the riverbank, rippling with long grass, but Khalidah looked past it to the place where the ground began to rise again. When Ghassan turned

Wasim toward the mountains, Khalidah followed without protest. She knew that it was madness to go back into the mountains so close to nightfall, but she also knew that Sulayman might not live until morning. He shook and burned in her arms, and that alone would have driven her on.

As luck would have it the sky remained clear, and though the moon was a waning sliver the stars were bright, and it wasn't difficult to follow the paths once Ghassan found them. But finding them was something else again. The assurance with which he had led them previously was gone, and at each split in the track he paused, deliberating. Khalidah tried to keep her temper, but at last she burst out:

"Why do you hesitate, when he is dying?"

Ghassan gave her a bleak look. "Because his only chance—and, indeed, ours—is to find the right path. But if you'd prefer to go galloping off the nearest cliff—"

"All right," she conceded. "Just tell me one thing: have you ever actually been to this place you are taking us?"

Ghassan's look was all the reply she needed. Khalidah nudged the weary pony forward again.

They climbed through the night, the air growing thinner and colder and the path ever more treacherous, until they were forced to dismount and lead the horses. With instinct born of exhaustion, Khalidah made Ghassan shift Sulayman onto Wasim's back, and the tall horse proved his worth. Although Sulayman slumped lifelessly over his neck, Wasim shifted his gait carefully with the terrain so that Khalidah only needed to help on the steepest slopes to keep Sulayman in the saddle. After the crescent of moon had set, taking with it what little light they had, they had reached another ridge, this one covered with a thin layer of snow. Glittering peaks stretched around them like waves on a frozen sea. Khalidah could no longer feel her hands and feet. The bitter wind cut through her clothes. And then she caught an incongruous whiff of wood smoke.

"There!" Ghassan cried.

With the last of the moonlight, Khalidah followed his pointing finger. At the very edge of the ridge, just before it fell away to nothingness, was what appeared to be a pile of stones, with a thin curl of smoke rising from its center. They made their way toward this, and soon they could make out a dull flicker of light: a doorway, with just enough headroom for the horses.

Inside, the stone hut was surprisingly spacious, encompassing a natural hollowing of the rock. In the center a fire burned, the smoke rising up through a hole in the roof, but the smell that permeated the room was of cultivated earth, for it was filled with living plants. They appeared to grow straight out of the rock, from the tiniest alpine flowers to huge tropical trees. The floor was strewn with rushes and sweet herbs, and the horses immediately fell to munching.

It took Khalidah a few moments to make out the tiny woman kneeling by the fire amid this bizarre profusion of foliage. The woman gave the impression of beauty, though her features were in fact unremarkable, beyond a pair of clear green eyes. Likewise she exuded a sense of youth and vitality, although her face was wrinkled and her long hair tangled and gray. When she smiled at them, Khalidah had the sudden and utter conviction that Sulayman would live.

Ghassan said, "Sayyida," and knelt before the old woman.

She smiled slightly, looking not at him but at Khalidah. She laid a hand on his head. Instantly, he fell asleep. She beckoned to Khalidah then with a gnarled hand. With the last of her strength, Khalidah dragged Sulayman toward the fire. The old woman smiled and nodded as she laid him before her.

"Poor little thing, so lost," said the woman, in a voice like the wind among palm fronds, and though in fact Sulayman dwarfed the woman, the statement did not strike Khalidah as odd. The woman laid a hand on Sulayman's burning forehead.

"Can you save him?" Khalidah asked.

The woman looked up at her again, her eyes deep with compassion. "I can divert death," she answered, with an equivocal look.

"Please, do it."

"In good time," the woman answered, and continued to stroke Sulayman's face as she might a favorite pet's. Her eyes were intent on Khalidah, boring deep into her. "What about you?" she asked. "Why have you come here?"

"I came for his sake," Khalidah answered resolutely.

"That is not all," the woman said, "and it will do you no good to deny it. Every longing means something, Khalidah. Would it comfort you to know a bit of your destiny?"

Khalidah looked at her, confused, anxious, and desperately tired. "Should it?"

The woman gave her a smile of surprising sweetness. "You ask the right questions. In youth, that's rarer than gold. Very well, then, I'll tell you only this: in choosing Shambhala, you chose correctly."

"Shambhala?"

"Shambhala . . . Eden . . . Qaf . . ." The woman shrugged. "But choosing correctly does not guarantee ease. Your road will have many turnings. Some lead to battles, others to peace; some to loss, and some to joy. You will be mourned by many when you are gone." She paused, her green eyes glinting. "Do you want to know more?"

Khalidah shook her head. The woman smiled again, perhaps in approval. "You have carried him a long way," she said, "but he is safe now. Sleep."

Khalidah wanted to argue, but she found that she could no longer keep her eyes open. She lay down where she was, and it seemed there was a pillow beneath her head and a blanket covering her, though she was certain they had not been there a moment ago. The last thing she saw before sleep took her was the old woman crumbling herbs into a copper basin, as she hummed Khalidah's own tune to Shánfara's ode.

KHALIDAH dreamed that she fell through time, lighting now and then on scenes that flared with a crystalline clarity. She saw people in furs on a land of ice, then the young green of new gardens. Black-haired riders with slanted eyes galloped westward over vast plains of grass. Three little ships like walnut shells, their sails crossed with red like the Templars' mantles, battled a wide, stormy sea. In one vision she stood in a sandstone room with a long window in one wall. Light poured through the window, and a woman sat haloed in its brightness, sewing. She had thick, black hair that nearly reached the floor, black eyes with a slight eastern tilt. She sang in a foreign tongue with a voice of such sweetness that it made Khalidah's eyes sting with tears.

The darkness opened beneath her, seared suddenly with light. Two armies faced each other, darkening the bright sands of a valley. On either side were wooded hills and, far off in the distance, a vastness of water. Their standards waved in the morning breeze, on one side the red-crossed white of the Templars and white-crossed black of the Hospitallers, the colorful banners of the great houses of the Franj; on the other the warrior houses of Islam, yellow for the Ayyubids and Mamluks, green and white for the Fatimids, black for the Seljuqs. The armies came together with a roar like thunder, the ground shook, and they were lost in the great clouds of dust they raised. Khalidah heard her own voice crying, "Now!" and then she pitched downward toward the storm of flesh and steel.

Just before she entered it, she jerked awake. Her pounding heart slowed gradually as she took in her surroundings, though at first she could not think where she was. She lay on an old reed mat on the floor of a cave, covered with her blanket. Beside her were the cold remains of a fire, touched here and there by sunlight streaming through chinks in the rocky roof. A battered copper bowl sat beside it, with what looked like the residue of an herbal decoction scumming the bottom.

Sulayman and Ghassan lay on the other side of the spent fire. Khalidah scrambled to Sulayman's side, fearing the worst, but found that he breathed easily. When she touched his cheek, it was cool. She sat back and looked around at the bare stone walls, her mind tumbling with confused images of flowers and foliage and a woman with an old face and young eyes who spoke in riddles, before sending her to sleep. But it all tangled up with her dreams, until she could not be sure that any of it had really happened.

She awakened Ghassan first. "Was she real?" she demanded. "Was any of it real?"

Ghassan nodded toward Sulayman. "You tell me."

Khalidah sighed, dropping her head into her hands. "Who was she?"

"Ameretat," Ghassan answered.

Khalidah looked at him incredulously. "You expect me to believe that we've slept in the home of a Persian goddess?"

"I don't expect you to believe anything, except that we have slept in the home of someone called Ameretat, and she has saved the life of our friend."

Khalidah sighed again. "Well, what now?"

"Now," said Ghassan, reaching for Wasim's tack, "you must be on your way, and I on mine."

"Aren't you coming with us?"

Ghassan smiled and shook his head. "This is your journey, Khalidah; yours and his." He nodded to Sulayman. "But stop by my way when you return, if you can, and tell me how you have fared." He looked at her, and his eyes softened. "Say good-bye to him for me."

"Don't you want to say it yourself?"

Ghassan shook his head. "He won't remember any of this, and that's probably just as well. Let him think that you left me in the marshes and he recovered on his own."

Khalidah looked at the man; then she knelt before him, taking his hands in hers and touching them to her forehead. "Thank you, Ghassan. And I'm sorry—"

"Don't be sorry," Ghassan said. "Live truly." He kissed her forehead, then led his horse toward the door, disappearing into the rising sun.

Twenty-six

Busra
Mid-April

"**Hush**!" Bilal whispered, putting his hand over Salim's mouth. "You will be heard."

The prince lifted his hand away, lacing his fingers through Bilal's. "'The secret of love,'" he said, eyes glinting with mischief in the light of the hanging oil lamp, "'how can it be contained?'"

"I don't know, but you must learn to contain it, unless you'd like your guards to join us."

"Who knows? Perhaps that would be amusing."

"You're hopeless!" Bilal said, and rolled away from him.

But after a moment he felt Salim's fingers on his back, gentle as water, and when he spoke again he had lowered his voice. "'Beloved like a hart, with the heart of a panther . . . if you desire to slay, my heart is in your hand as clay.'"

"A poem?" asked Bilal, who could never maintain exasperation with Salim for long. "Is it yours?"

Salim laughed softly. "A poem. Certainly not mine." He kissed Bilal's shoulder. "'Beloved, like a scarlet cord his lips, burning like fire for they are his censer, and in them is the work of his signs . . .'"

"The poet is speaking of Allah."

"Yahweh, in fact. His name is Isaac ibn Abraham. He is a Jew from Al-Andalus."

Bilal said nothing, though inwardly he burned for his ignorance.

"But what does it matter?" Salim continued, oblivious to Bilal's shame. "Don't the Sufis tell us that Allah resides in the love one being feels for another?"

"Do they?" Bilal asked quietly.

"'To watch and listen to those two is to understand how, as it's written, sometimes when two beings come together, Allah becomes visible.'"

Bilal shivered with the beauty of the words, of the passion with which Salim spoke them, wishing that he could match them. Sometimes it seemed that regret made up the better part of his love for Salim, regret that deepened when Salim misread it, as he did now.

"Do you still believe that what we do is wrong?" he asked.

"No," Bilal said, finally turning to face him. Salim's eyes were black wings in the lamplight, his mouth a split plum. "I never did. It's only that sometimes I am reminded that I'm unworthy of you."

"How can you say that?" Salim asked, genuinely incredulous.

If only you knew, Bilal thought. He said, "I do not know any poems, nor half of what you take for granted."

"You have only to ask. I'll send to Damascus for books—"

"Books I cannot read," Bilal said with quiet bitterness.

"Then I will teach you," Salim said, without hesitation.

If Bilal had not already loved him, he would have then for those words alone, and so he spoke before he thought: "Khalidah always said that one day she would ask her father for a tutor who could teach us to read—" He stopped abruptly, but it was too late.

"Khalidah?" Salim repeated with sudden interest. "Is she not the woman your cousin Numair was to marry?"

"She is," Bilal said after a pause.

"But if the clans of your tribe were at war, how is it that you were in a position to be taught by her tutors?"

There was no accusation in his tone, only curiosity. Bilal drew a deep breath and answered, "Because I grew up in Abd al-Aziz's camp, not Abd al-Hadi's. My mother looked after Khalidah after her own mother died. I ended up with Numair because . . ." Bilal sighed, wondering how to lie without quite lying. At last he said, "I suppose, indirectly, because of Khalidah. When she disappeared, it confused everything. No one even knew whether we were still at war. Then word came that your father had called for jihad, and the debate about whether to go after Khalidah turned into a debate about whether to join the Sultan's army. Numair was the first to go north, I'd been thinking of joining anyway, and . . . well, I suppose events just threw us together."

It sounded ridiculous even to him, yet when he ventured a look at Salim he found the prince's eyes deep with thought, not suspicion. Salim said, "That's all very interesting—really, I had no idea Bedu politics were so complicated—but you must realize that what I really want to know is whether this woman, Khalidah, was your lover."

Bilal stared at him for a moment and then burst into laughter, as much for relief as for the absurdity of the idea. "Khalidah was my best friend—almost a sister, since we were the same age and brought up together. As for love . . ." He shook his head.

"What? Is she very ugly?"

Once again, Bilal laughed. "No, she is not ugly. But she was the sheikh's daughter, and I was only another boy from the tribe."

"You are not only another boy," Salim answered. "And besides, she ran away with a minstrel. Class can't have figured much into her choice of men." Bilal only shrugged, and after a moment Salim continued, clearly enjoying himself, "So, we have a headstrong desert princess who is not ugly, with a wild Khorasani mother . . . I suppose she can ride like the wind, fight like a warrior, and look fetching covered in a day's sweat and dust?"

"Often all three at once," Bilal answered, grinning.

Salim rolled his eyes and shook his head. "You loved her. You cannot tell me you didn't."

"Yes, I loved her," Bilal said, suddenly serious, "but that is not what you asked. I loved her as a friend—as one lonely child loves another. We were both outcasts in our tribe, she because of her mother's blood and I . . . well, for my own reasons. Yes, there was a time when I thought that I wanted more from her than friendship . . ."

"But?"

"It wasn't Allah's will." Bilal looked shyly up at Salim, his pale eyes prismatic in the lamplight. "And now, I am glad of it. Now I know that she never lived in my heart."

Salim blinked, then smiled in pleased surprise. He touched Bilal's cheek. Bolstered by this, and the courage of confession, Bilal put words to something he had kept close for a long time: "And you, Salim? Have there been others before me . . . others, I mean, like this?" He gestured to their shared bed, its storm of tumbled blankets.

Salim gave him an arch smile. "I did not think that the stoic nomad would succumb to jealousy." Bilal frowned, and he relented. "There have been girls like your Khalidah—and a couple of boys—whom I thought I loved and were far beyond my reach; and there have been others whom I knew I didn't, and who weren't." He paused, then said, "I may not have been a virgin when we met, Bilal, but what went before was merely the satisfaction of lust. You alone are the heart of my heart."

Bilal shivered at the words, both for their sweetness and their implicit challenge to all the impossibilities of this love. Salim, mistaking it for cold, slipped his arms around him, and Bilal shut his eyes, curled his fingers in Salim's hair, and let himself believe, for a little while, that love could vanquish threat as easily as it could the freezing desert night.

Twenty-seven

"A full week we have been here," Salah ad-Din said as he poured the tea, first into Bilal's glass, then into Salim's, and finally into his own, "with all as quiet as a Franj monastery."

He paused, looking out at the camp's morning bustle with narrowed eyes. The front of his pavilion had been rolled up. Sunlight glinted on the ruby on his turban and the golden embroidery on his red robes. Bilal wondered what had made him decide to dress like a king here—which was more or less the middle of nowhere—when his clothing had been so self-effacing at the courtlike Ras al-Mai. But then, he had long since given up trying to understand the Sultan's motivations, finding the man's mind as labyrinthine as the sandstone wadis of his home.

"The men are getting fat," the Sultan concluded, frowning.

"I hardly think it likely, on our rations," Salim answered dryly.

"Save your wit for the bedroom," the Sultan retorted, at which Bilal flushed. "I am telling you that we must have action before these men forget entirely what the word means." He drank, then said, "That is why I am sending you south: to find us someone who requires salvation, protection, or whatever else might provide occupation for an elite band of soldiers."

"Shall I go to Kerak?" Salim asked with palpable hope.

"Absolutely not!"

"But it would be useful to know what Arnat is up to."

"I know what he is up to," said Salah ad-Din. "He is in Jerusalem with the other nobles, trying to prod their king into some kind of action against Raymond of Tripoli . . . Of course, they will not be expecting Tripoli's new Muslim guard." A shade of a smile crossed his face.

When it faded, he focused his avid eyes once again on his son. "At any rate, as Arnat is currently occupied, this is the ideal time for reconnaissance. If possible, we must find out exactly how strong Kerak is—which of his family are in residence, how many knights in the garrison, the state of their supplies, water—"

"You intend to besiege them?" Salim asked, sipping his tea and then setting the glass aside. Bilal could not help watching him; the prince's grace was mesmerizing. The Sultan too was watching his son, and Bilal thought that there was a glint of approval in that look, however deeply buried. He wondered why the man wanted to hide it.

"I would rather it didn't come to that," Salah ad-Din said at last. "Not yet, anyway. I cannot waste the time or the men right now. On the other hand, if Arnat's forces can be contained, then Jerusalem's army is significantly weakened. Let us leave further speculation until such time as we are equipped with facts."

Abruptly he turned to Bilal. "You say the clans of your tribe have a long-standing feud. Did you yourself ever take part in their raids?"

Surprised, Bilal answered, "Only as a scout, Your Highness."

The Sultan studied him for a moment, then said, "The Bedu are without a doubt the finest raiders I have ever seen. I am hoping that you can teach my son something about your people's tactics. You will accompany him south." He turned back to Salim. "You will leave this evening. Go now and prepare your men."

The two boys bowed to the Sultan and left him looking thoughtfully after them.

SALIM laughed when Bilal asked him if he thought that his father suspected the nature of their relationship. "Do you think that my father does not know of everything that happens in his camp?" He laughed again at Bilal's look of horror. "I assure you, he knew the exact moment that you came to my bed, and he doesn't care. Why should he? You are not a maiden with a bride price or gold-digging father to threaten his honor; nor are you a married woman who could ruin mine. Besides, we are not the only lovers here. It is a part of life in a mobile army, when men are far from their wives and whores forbidden."

Daunted nevertheless, Bilal threw himself gladly into the preparations for their departure. They rode out at dusk with little ceremony. The Sultan and his son nodded to each other, but exchanged no words. All that they might have said was gathered in the look they gave each other before Salim wheeled his horse and his father turned back toward his tent: love tempered by disappointment, pride by doubt. Bilal knew that Salim ached with them. He had never lamented so bitterly that the nature of their love made it impossible to take Salim in his arms right then and hold him until the pain had passed.

Instead, he gave Anjum her head and tried to lose himself in the visceral perfection of her speed. The unit rode throughout that night and finally stopped in the lee of a low hill that had once housed a fortress, covered in the sand of many years' abandonment. They did not bother to set up tents, but lay down on their blankets wherever they could find a blank bit of sand and waited for dawn.

Twenty-eight

※

THOUGH it was as old as Busra and had once been as great a city, Amman was no more than a desert outpost by the time it fell to the Franj. As such, they had not bothered to build more than a squat hill tower, ringed by a ditch and castrum, to defend it. At full strength it could not have housed more than thirty men, but Salim's scouts estimated that the garrison currently numbered half that.

"And they do not look like knights to me," Salim concluded, moving away from the window of the ruined house from which he was studying the village.

Bilal took his place. De Ridefort had taught him enough to recognize the two guards stationed at the gate as infantry. Though logic had told him that this paltry outpost would never be manned by Templars, he could not contain a sigh of relief.

"Indeed," Salim said, misreading it, "they should not give us too much trouble, assuming we can lure them out . . . though I wonder if it is even worth the effort. Those men do not look the sort to possess the kind of information that would interest us. Perhaps we should try farther south."

But they were already closer than Bilal had ever wanted to come to Kerak, and so he said, "I would not be too ready to dismiss it."

Salim turned to him with a quick, birdlike intensity.

"I know the country to the south of here. It's terrible for raids—barren desert, flat as a platter. But we'd take easy prisoners from this garrison. In fact, if it came to it, we'd probably have a good chance of taking the entire fortress."

"Do you think so?" Salim asked, a sparkle of inspiration beginning in his eyes.

"I did not mean to suggest that we should," Bilal said quickly, "only that we might."

Salim's returned to the window. "Think what my father would say if I won him a Franj castle."

"Salim."

"Bilal?" Salim's mouth twitched into the beginnings of the smile Bilal had come to fear, for in the face of it, he could not deny Salim anything. "After all, we can only fail, and my father expects that already."

He touched his fingers to Bilal's own. The contact was slight, but like lightning grazing a tent pole it seared straight through him. "Are you with me?"

Bilal was with him; it had never been in question. But he could not disentangle consent from the desperate relief at having avoided Kerak. He closed his fingers around Salim's to shut out the doubt, but as Salim's smile blossomed, sweet with trust, Bilal wondered if there would ever be a day when he did not despise himself.

BILAL had thought that the emirs would talk Salim out of an attempt at the fortress, but he had underestimated the effects of so many months of boredom on soldiers used to action. They supported the idea unanimously, clamoring at once to devise a plan of attack.

"I have no doubt that we can cut them down like so many stalks of wheat," said Salim, who sat before a map of the area, "if we can only draw them out. This, you see, is our problem. We are cavalry, they are foot soldiers, but even if we were fairly matched, the Franj would still be fools to leave the safety of their fortress without good reason."

"We could give them reason," said a tall, mournful Turk. "There are, after all, women and children in the town."

Salim resolutely shook his head. "I will not use the weak and the innocent to reach my ends. That is for the likes of Arnat.

Besides, you know what my father would say to it, and my father must not find fault with this mission."

They nodded agreement, even the Turk, but Bilal knew that they didn't begin to understand. Of all of them, he was the only one who knew exactly what hung for Salim in the balance of his father's approval. He was ruminating on this when he realized that they were all looking at him.

"You are asking my opinion?" he asked incredulously.

Salim gave him a quizzical half smile. "Did you not tell my father that you had participated in your tribe's raids?"

Bilal shook his head. "Against other tribes, yes. But a Bedu camp is not a Franj garrison."

The emirs stole anxious looks at one another, but Salim held his eyes. "My father sent you with us for a reason, Bilal. I know that you will not fail him."

And please do not fail me: the words were there in Salim's eyes, as clear as if he'd spoken them. "All right," Bilal said reluctantly. "Well . . . a Bedu raid is about stealth and speed: engaging the enemy when he does not expect it, killing him quickly, carrying away the prize before he even suspects that you desire it . . ."

His heart beat suddenly with the memory, and he ached with a sharp, unexpected nostalgia. Salim's smile widened. "Go on."

"I suppose," he said, "that although this is a fortress, and the prize is information rather than gold or livestock, the same principles could be applied here to draw out the garrison in a way that endangers none but those who raise their swords against us."

He glanced up. Every set of eyes was fixed on him. Looking quickly away he continued, "Though the Franj see 'Saracens' as infidels, they respect us in their way because we adhere to codes of honor that they recognize. But to them, Bedu are not Saracens. In their eyes we are lawless devils, and perhaps in some ways their view is justified, for a band of Bedu raiders would not be discussing how best to draw the soldiers forth and spare the women. To a Bedu raider, the women would be part of the prize. So if the men of the garrison can be made to believe that we are Bedu raiders . . ."

Bilal stopped, confounded by the weight of all the eyes on him. Many of them were now cold with jealousy, but Salim paid them no attention.

"Tell me," he said, "how many raiders would be required to rouse the garrison?"

Bilal shrugged. "If we time it right, then only enough to be identified as such. Just before dawn, for instance, the soldiers will be sleepy and confused, unable to assess our numbers properly. If we are very lucky, and enough of them are drawn into the fight, we might even take the fortress before they realize what has happened . . ."

Bilal broke off again, still not quite believing that this idea was his. But Salim's delighted smile convinced him. He reached for the map. "These are wadis? And these are hills and ruins? Good. It is the best kind of country for a raid. We will begin here."

Twenty-nine

BEFORE daybreak the next morning they were all in position. Salim and the main body of the unit hid behind a hill at the back of the fortress. Bilal and four other horsemen, dressed in their best approximation of nomads' robes, waited in the desert bordering the most populated portion of the town. They watched the sky for Salim's naphtha flare, their signal to move.

When it came Bilal gave a wordless cry, and Anjum leapt forward. They swept through the straggling town like revenants, the horses' shoes striking sparks from the paving stones, their torches streaming comet tails behind, leaving flames and tattered screams in their wake. Though they touched no woman or child—Salim had been clear that anyone who broke this rule would pay with his life—more than one townsman tried to engage them, and more than one fell. They were old men and boys, unsuitable for service in the fortress or the king's army, and none of them should have been out of their beds, let alone engaging professional cavalry. In his heart Bilal cursed them for fighting; but they did fight, and so he had no choice but to cut them down.

It didn't take long to reach the fortress against such slight resistance, but still the news of their presence had preceded them. The garrison poured from the open gates as Bilal's band approached, the Franj soldiers half dressed and wild-eyed and numbering not more than a dozen. They realized their mistake almost immediately, but it was too late. As if by magic, the little band of Bedu raiders had become a ring of professional cavalry closing in on them from all sides. For a moment there was total, taut silence; then, with an anonymous cry, the cavalry and the foot soldiers fell upon each other.

Bilal hovered at the edge of the fray, watching with morbid fascination as Salim's horsemen decimated the Franj with apparent effortlessness. He had always felt that a pitched battle had a certain bleak integrity to it, but this was not a battle. It didn't even have a Bedu raid's structure of honor to rationalize it. The Franj had never had a chance, yet they fought bravely, and Bilal could not help feeling for them, as he always felt for the vanquished.

He caught a glimpse of Salim as his horse reared, yellow tunic lashed with blood and face ablaze with violent rapture. For a moment he hated him for his very righteousness, and then he looked down. By his knee was a Franji, one of a few civilians who had come to the aid of the floundering garrison. He was about Bilal's age, with colorless hair and a pockmarked face that was almost nondescript, except for the conviction that shone from it with the brilliance of sunrise. Bilal faltered, and nearly paid with his life. But Anjum was not troubled by human sentiment, and with her breed's innate good sense and her own meticulous training, she wheeled as the little Franji raised his sword and struck, taking the blow on her own flank and saving her master.

In that moment Bilal surfaced from the torpor that had subsumed him when Numair and de Ridefort co-opted him for their plot. He was filled with a sudden, overwhelming rage at the Franj—for forcing his lies, for daring to fight his people, for being here at all. He turned Anjum back then and dropped the boy with a slash to the neck, and felt nothing but triumph as he watched him die.

"So Amman surrendered," the Sultan said as they sat in his tent that evening. He looked at his son with eyes in which speculation had replaced censure. "You took no prisoners?"

Salim shook his head. "There were none to take. But we did take this." He reached into his bloodstained tunic and pulled out a piece of parchment with a broken red seal, which depicted a running wolf. He could not conceal the flush of pride as he handed it to his father, nor the vulnerability. Bilal kept his eyes cast down, but he stole glances at the Sultan as he read the letter.

"So, it is as I had hoped," Salah ad-Din said at last, his thin lips now curved in a faint smile of his own. "Better, even—every one of the southern lords in Jerusalem trying to bend the king's ear on the issue of Tripoli, and now a frontier town taken from under their noses . . . indeed, it could not be better. You have done well, my son." The prince flushed more deeply still and smiled at his hands.

"And you, al-Hassani." The Sultan turned to Bilal. "I hear that this success is due in large part to your inspiration." He paused, fixing Bilal with his golden-brown eyes, more intent than ever. "I admit that I had my doubts about you and your cousin when you joined us. I had heard rumors to suggest . . ." He trailed off, his look turning inward. "At any rate, I am glad to find that you have vindicated yourself." It was not lost on Bilal that he said nothing about Numair. "I hope that you will join us in our next venture."

Bilal inclined his head, wishing that etiquette allowed him to ask what that would be. But the next moment Salim voiced the thought for him.

The Sultan raised a quizzical eyebrow. "You tell me."

"Kerak!" Salim answered, his eyes bright with anticipation.

This time, the cloudbreak smile. "Good boy. Now go and tell your men we ride at dawn."

Thirty

Eastern Persia
Mid-April

SULAYMAN didn't ask any questions, either when he awakened in the cave or in the following days. Perhaps he knew the answers already, or else he was too grateful for his sudden, blooming health to question it. Either way, Khalidah was content to allow the story of their strange night in the cave to remain unspoken.

Ghassan had left them the pony, and they traveled more quickly now that the horses carried less weight, winding their way through the mountains on paths almost as familiar to Sulayman as they had been to Ghassan. At last the hills grew gentler and the air warmer. They descended toward a desert of searing brightness, patched in wide, glittering mosaics of austere beauty. Khalidah was wild with joy at the thought of letting Zahirah run again, but when she said so to Sulayman, he shook his head grimly.

"What you see down there is not sand," he said. "It is a *kavir*—a salt desert. This part of Persia is covered with them. Once they were marshes, and beneath the salt crust there is still a layer of silt that would devour you like quicksand if you broke through. There are safe passages across them, if you know how to find them. But there will be no running."

"And once we cross it? What then?"

"We'll head southeast, past Yazd."

"We should stop there. We're running low on supplies."

"Yes, and we'll also need warmer clothes for Khorasan. But we cannot stop at Yazd; we've told too many people that story. We can make it a bit farther on the supplies we have left, if we're careful. Let's try for Ravar."

Khalidah had no idea where Ravar was. She sighed, resigning herself to further days of subsistence on stale almonds and camel's milk. Still, she was glad enough of Sulayman's health that even these hardships didn't dampen her spirits for long. That afternoon they descended into a sun-seared, rocky valley that gradually gave way to the *kavir.* A hot wind blasted across the salt flats. Sulayman moved carefully along a tortuous path among them, which to Khalidah was indiscernible.

However, any doubt she had in his judgment disappeared when, in a moment of carelessness, she allowed the pony to step to the left of the invisible path, and the animal plunged screaming into the salty sand up to her shoulder. By dumb luck Khalidah had kept hold of the lead rein. Sulayman eased the pack saddle off the struggling pony. Her rear end was free but floundering, and it took all of them, humans and horses, to pull her back to solid ground. It was a long time before she was calm enough to accept the saddle again, longer still before Khalidah stopped shaking.

After several more grueling hours the ground began to rise again, and at last the treacherous sand became stone beneath the horses' feet. They had come into a wide valley fenced on both sides by jagged peaks. For the first time in days, the horses could move with ease. Tossing her head, Zahirah broke into a canter, but Khalidah, still shaken by their near miss, pulled her back to a walk. As the sun sank behind them, a mountain emerged ahead, its peak thrusting free of the others around it.

"It's called the Lion's Mountain," said Sulayman, squinting through the horizontal rays of the dying sun. "There's a good place to camp near here."

They made camp in the brief twilight, in a wide, rocky cave in the shadow of the great mountain. But when she lay down on her blanket, despite the distance they had traveled that day, Khalidah couldn't sleep.

"What are you thinking of?" Sulayman asked across the dying fire.

"Home," she answered, but there was no wistfulness in her voice. After a moment she continued, "I wonder what has happened to the tribe—whether they have joined the Sultan as my father wished, or run like cowards with my uncle."

"I imagine the answer is a good deal more complicated than either one."

Khalidah was silent for a moment; then she said, "I can't stop thinking about what Ghassan said . . . that the timing of all of this is Allah's work. Do you think . . . I mean, could it be that the Jinn might fight for Salah ad-Din? That that is the purpose of our journey?"

Sulayman sighed. "Again, I think only that the answer will prove more complicated than we can imagine."

"If they did mean to join the jihad," Khalidah persisted, "would we even make it back in time?"

"Salah ad-Din keeps to the traditional battle season," Sulayman answered. "He won't challenge the Franj until summer. If we go on as we did today, we will make it to Qaf in time to be home by midsummer. But that assumes that we do not plan to stay there long."

If, Khalidah thought. "Sulayman?"

"Yes?"

"Thank you."

"For what?"

She had intended a simple answer, a gesture of gratitude for all he had shown her she was capable of. But all that came was the memory of his fever, of the tremulous tide of his breathing. There were no words for that, but he must have seen some of it in the look on her face. He extended his hand to her through the ember-red light. She met it with her own, clutched it as she had when she had thought he was dying. It was only now, though, that she realized why.

Spreading her fingers like the petals of a lotus, he kissed her palm.

JUST before dawn, the earth buckled. At first it was gentle, and Khalidah only half awakened. Then rocks began falling, and Sulayman was dragging her out of the cave as its stones began to shift and finally to topple. All around them the earth was tearing itself apart in screeches and groans, drowning out the terrified screams of the horses. They only managed to catch them because the animals were too afraid to know where to run; Khalidah wrapped her sash around Zahirah's neck and held on grimly as the horse reared and plunged. She knew well enough that if they lost the horses, they were finished.

The earthquake seemed to last forever, but in fact it could have been only a few seconds. When it was over Khalidah stood shaking, trying to calm her horse and calling for Sulayman. "Here!" he cried at last, and leading Zahirah toward his voice, Khalidah found him far down the valley, holding the pony's rein with one hand and trying to soothe Aasifa with the other.

"Are you all right?" he asked.

"Yes," Khalidah said. They both stood for a moment, listening to the last falling pebbles settle. "Will it come back?"

"Not like that," Sulayman answered. "But sometimes there are smaller ones for a few days afterward."

"What will we do?"

He sighed. "Sleep in the open tonight. Even if the cave is not covered, it will not be safe. Tomorrow, we'll see if any of our things have survived."

When the horses were finally calm, they lay down in the lee of a boulder that sheltered them from the wind. Despite it, and Sulayman's body close against hers, Khalidah never shut her eyes again that night. When the sun rose and she looked at him, she knew that he hadn't either. He ran a hand over her rough hair, then got up to check the horses.

Aasifa and the pony were unscathed, though Aasifa had relapsed into her old skittishness, and she wouldn't let Sulayman touch her head. Zahirah had a long cut on her back right leg. There was no heat in it, but it was deep.

"I would know what to do if I were back home," Khalidah said, "but here . . ."

"We can do nothing but wrap it and go on," Sulayman finished. "Come, let's see if there's anything left for bandages."

They picked their way through the rubble of shattered stone until they saw the corner of Sulayman's saddle blanket protruding from a pile of sand and scree. Digging around, they gradually uncovered the rest of their belongings. Two of their three skins of water had burst, but miraculously, Sulayman's *qanun* had survived. Khalidah picked it up and plucked a string.

"Some angel watches over you, Sulayman," she said.

He smiled, but his eyes were sober. "Don't say that until we've made it to the next well on one skin of water."

As she handed the instrument back to him, she asked what she had been too shy to ask before: "Will you teach me to play it?"

The question didn't appear to surprise him. "If we find ourselves in favorable circumstances," he answered, wrapping it up again.

They reburied what was damaged beyond repair, in case they were still being followed, and then they bound Zahirah's leg and set off again. They hadn't ridden long, however, when they found their path blocked by two boulders apparently shifted by the earthquake. As Khalidah led Zahirah around them onto the slope where they had lain, she found herself walking on a monster's trail: five footprints stamped into the stone, the tracks of a three-toed beast, each as long as her forearm from toe to heel.

"Must we face dragons now, too?" she asked Sulayman, who had come up behind her.

He studied the prints, then answered, "Once in these mountains I broke a stone while trying to light a fire. When the two halves came apart I found between them the imprint of a fish's bones. I took it to Yazd to sell it, thinking that such a wonder would fetch a fortune, but I was promptly directed to a man in the marketplace with a table full of such stones. He paid me a pittance for mine, and told me that the mountains of Persia yield many such wonders, and far greater ones, too. He said these hills are the graveyard of creatures that roamed the earth before men—giant lizards and birds without feathers and long-toothed fishes such as we cannot imagine—and that time turned their bones to stone. Perhaps the same has happened to their footprints."

"The Quran says nothing of giant birds and lizards," Khalidah said skeptically.

"And the Quran tells us that the Jinn are made of fire."

Khalidah sighed. "A world ruled by monsters," she said, and a chilling image flashed through her mind: that on the other side of these mountains they would find not the city of Yazd or the town of Ravar, but a desolate plain where great scaled creatures roared and clashed. "I am tired of Persia," she said.

Sulayman laughed. "You have not seen Persia. Someday I hope to show it to you, for you would not find a more splendid country if you traveled the world from one end to the other."

"Not even Qaf?" Khalidah asked.

"Qaf . . ." Sulayman said after a pause. "Sometimes I think it is a world unto itself." He stood and led Aasifa forward, and they left the monster's trail to the mercy of time.

On the sixth day after the earthquake, Sulayman and Khalidah finally saw the minarets of Yazd thrusting into the hazy morning sky. But their food ran out well before Ravar, and they were forced to stop at a nameless town in the foothills preceding the Dasht-e-Lut, the vast salt desert at Persia's heart. The town was inhabited by a flock of fat-tailed sheep and their minders, seminomads with bright, finely woven clothing and cutthroats' eyes. They did, however, have a well, plus ample stores of dried meat and apricots, and they were willing to trade. They spoke a quick, guttural dialect of Persian, and since Khalidah's grasp of the language had been gleaned from classical poetry, she had little sense of what was being bartered. But she understood well enough when the tribe's chief demanded Zahirah's silver bridle pendant as payment.

"It seems a lot to pay for a few bits of desiccated mutton," she said to Sulayman.

"On the contrary, it is a bargain," he answered. When she opened her mouth to argue, he said, "A useless scrap of metal in exchange for a chance of surviving the Dasht-e-Lut—or do you prefer to eat sand tonight?"

She pulled the pendant off the bridle and handed it to the chief, who looked at it, tested its authenticity with teeth the color of dried palm leaves, and then pocketed it. Negotiations complete, the people turned suddenly hospitable, urging Khalidah and Sulayman to spend the night with them. Sulayman finally managed to decline, but they did sit down for a glass of tea in a black tent very like those of Khalidah's tribe. She sipped the strong brew in a wallow of homesickness, then helped Sulayman fill the water skins and load the new supplies onto the pony, and they set off again.

That night they reached the fringes of the Dasht-e-Lut. It was an eerie place, gray and empty, the sand a strange, coarse mixture of grit and salt and pebbles that ran before a fierce north wind. The upper layers visibly undulated like ocean waves, shattering against dunes as high as the foothills Khalidah and Sulayman had just left behind. They stopped in the lee of one of these great hills. There was no fuel for a fire, nothing for them to do but huddle together against the stinging wind and listen to its keening as the sky grew dark.

"I'm afraid that the *qanun* lesson will have to wait again," Sulayman said at last. "We can't even work on your reading in this wind."

"It's all right," Khalidah answered. "There's time for both."

There was a long pause. Then he reached out, took her hand, and said, "Khalidah, there is something I have wanted to say to you for many days."

She could just make out the features of his face in the last of the twilight. "What is it?" she asked, working to keep her voice steady.

He drew a breath. "When we reach Qaf," he said, "I intend to ask your grandfather to marry us. If you consent to it, that is—I would rather have no wife at all than a bitter one."

Khalidah sat for a moment in stunned silence. At last she said, "I cannot agree to marry you at Qaf."

Though it was too dark now to see him, Khalidah could feel Sulayman recoil, and then bristle. "I suppose it was presumptuous to imagine that a sheikh's daughter would have a worthless minstrel," he said bitterly, letting go of her hand, "but I am sure you can see why I thought you felt differently."

His sudden coldness stung her like the wind-flung pebbles. "What fools you men can be!" she cried. "If you had listened beyond your pride, you would have heard me say not that I do not wish to marry you, only that I do not wish to do so at Qaf."

"Why not, then?" he said, chastened.

She sighed, the quick anger dissipating. "Because I know nothing of it, nor of what path my life or yours will take when we reach it. Because, however many moral laws I have broken by coming with you, I am still a Muslim, and if I am to marry I do not intend to do it among infidels. But mostly because if we were to lie together, we might start a child, and I do not intend to bring a child into the world unless I can offer him—or her—a secure place in it. My actions have made me an outcast among the only people I know, and you—forgive me for saying it, Sulayman, but it is the truth—have no people at all. Where would we live? How would we keep ourselves and our children?" She shook her head. "No; I will not marry you nor anyone, if I have the choice, until I know where I stand myself."

Khalidah lapsed into silence that grew more painful with every moment that Sulayman did not break it. She wondered if she had damaged their friendship irreparably. Then he said, "You are right, Khalidah—I am a fool." He touched her cheek with the tips of his fingers. "No promises, then. But if—when—we find solid ground, perhaps then I may hope for an answer?"

Khalidah took his face between her hands, glad that he could not see the tears in her eyes, and said, "I have answered already." And with a boldness gleaned from the fireless dark, she kissed him. As always, they lay down at a chaste distance from one another, but they awakened at dawn to find their limbs tangled and Sulayman's desire quite obvious. Khalidah lay for a moment barely breathing, knowing that for all the clothing between them, she was as bare to him then as she would ever be to anyone. Then she pulled away and sat up, shedding the sand that had drifted over them in the night. The dunes were the color of an old wound, the rising sun cauterized by a wind full of salt and the dust of dead armies. She bowed her head and felt Sulayman behind her, but she didn't know whether it was his fingers in her hair or the wind, moving with the inexorable hunger of a vine toward the light.

WATER determines the course of life, and in the vast central wastes of Persia they saw none of either. They rode for days across the shifting dunes, and except for the steady passage of the sun from their faces to their backs, they might never have moved at all. Near dark on one of the first days, they came to the ruins of what must once have been an oasis. There was a single, shallow pool of water in the parched stream bed, which the horses drank dry in minutes.

"What happened here?" Khalidah asked, looking around at the dilapidated wooden shelters and a series of curious walls, also made of wood, with the wasted remains of shrubs and vines and a few twisted fruit trees still clinging to the sand behind them.

"Wind," Sulayman said, trying the door of one of the huts, which promptly came away in his hands. "The oases in the Dasht-e-Lut are fickle. For a few years the spring meltwater or an underground canal keeps one going, and people are able to grow a bit, to graze their animals. Then a sandstorm fills the stream or the source of the aqueduct and, overnight, the oasis dies."

"And the people?" Khalidah asked.

Sulayman shrugged. "They move on. That's why they don't build to last." He nudged the fallen door with his foot and then, sighing, he put the horses in the most solid-looking shelter and chose the next best for himself and Khalidah. Its wood was bone dry and had shrunk so much that large gaps showed between the boards of the walls. The whole structure shuddered in each gust of wind. "At least there is a good supply of firewood," he said, dropping an armful of wind-blasted boards on the sand floor. "Listen—the wind is rising."

Khalidah listened and shivered, longing for a goat-hair tent. She hated this dead place, and she knew that if the wind thrashed itself into a full sandstorm, they might be here for days. At least the horses had shelter, she reflected, and they were doing reasonably well for provisions.

Sulayman managed to light the fire, and they boiled water for tea. "This is a good night for the *qanun*," he said, and so, when they had eaten, he unwrapped the instrument from its blankets. He tuned it, explained the rudiments of the technique, showed her how to place the plectra, and then set her some exercises. She repeated them dutifully, glad of the distraction from the shrieking gale outside until Sulayman—who turned out to be a strict teacher—declared them passable.

"Will you play something now?" she asked.

Sulayman took the instrument and held it for a moment. Then he began to pluck the strings in a kind of musical rumination until a melody emerged, slow and wistful, turning and twisting around one note like a banner on its staff in a fluctuating breeze. The mastery was in the nuance, the delicate shifts of the variations, and the words, when he began to sing, mirrored the pattern of the music: no linear narrative but a series of scenes, joined like jewels by a repeated phrase that gradually disclosed the story of a tragic love.

Even now,
My thought is all of this gold-tinted king's daughter
With garlands, tissue and golden buds,
Smoke tangles of her hair, and sleeping or waking
Feet trembling in love, full of pale languor;
My thought is clinging as to a lost learning
Slipped down out of the minds of men,
Laboring to bring her back into my soul . . .

Even now,
When all my heavy heart is broken up
I seem to see my prison walls breaking
And then a light, and in that light a girl
Her fingers busied about her hair, her cool white arms
Faint rosy at the elbows, raised in the sunlight,
And temperate eyes that wander far away . . .

The wind raged through the darkness, seeking the walls' rifts, and the words drove into Khalidah like a burning arrow bearing an image: a woman hardly beyond girlhood, fluttering silk the color of young leaves, tawny skin and a sweep of black hair that looked too heavy for her slender frame. She raised her arms in a flash and tumble of glass bangles, with a smile as sudden as desire.

Even now,
Though I am so far separate, a flight of birds
Swinging from side to side over the valley trees,
Passing my prison with their calling and crying,
Bring me to see my girl . . .
Even now,
Only one dawn shall rise for me. The stars
Revolve tomorrow's night and I not heed . . .

The bright girl faded to a guttering lamp on a prison wall. The *qanun* exalted, Sulayman's voice mourned on and on, each line more beautiful than the last.

. . . Upon a day
I saw strange eyes and hands like butterflies;
For me at morning larks flew from the thyme
And children came to bathe in little streams . . .
Even now,
I know that I have savored the hot taste of life
Lifting green cups and gold at the great feast.

Just for a small and a forgotten time
I have had full in my eyes from off my girl
The whitest pouring of eternal light . . .

The music trailed off into a half cadence, fading into the moaning of the wind. Sulayman sat with his head bowed over his instrument, his forefingers still ringed by the plectra and hands resting on the strings. Khalidah watched him silently, tears streaming down her cheeks. At last he raised his head and set the *qanun* aside.

"Did you write it?" she asked.

"The music, yes; the words, I think, are Allah's."

"He spoke them to you?"

He smiled ruefully, shaking his head. "It's a very old poem. I first heard it from a blind bard from Hindustan. We were caught by snow in a Kurdish inn and passed the time exchanging poems. I am no scholar of Sanskrit, but the little I understood of this poem caught at me. I hounded him until he agreed to help me write it out. It was no easy task. Persian was our only common tongue, and neither of us fluent in it. But I put down the bones of it, and over the years it has become a bit of an obsession. I have sought out other versions and gradually pieced together an Arabic translation, though I don't think that I have done the original any justice."

"And who wrote the original?"

Sulayman began to wrap the *qanun* carefully in its blanket again. "A poet called Chauras," he said. "He fell in love with a king's daughter, Vidya, and when their affair was discovered Chauras was sentenced to death. In the last few hours of his life he composed the poem, and when he was called upon before his execution to account for his actions, he recited it as his answer. Some say that the execution was carried out anyway; others, that the king was moved by the poet's words and spared him. Some even say that he was allowed to marry the princess."

"Which do you believe?" asked Khalidah.

Sulayman sighed. "I would like to believe that it ended happily, but I have known too many kings."

And no doubt some wanton princesses whom you've wooed with this sad story, Khalidah thought dismally, never imagining that Sulayman had not sung that poem aloud from the day he wrote down the blind man's translation until this night; still less that he had intended never to do so.

"Anyway, does it matter?" he continued. "Life is fragile, but truth is immortal. Chauras's words tell a truth that time can never erode. Few men can claim that."

"Perhaps one day you will teach it to me," she said.

In the dying firelight her eyes were a dark tide, her heart-shaped face a cipher. Sulayman knew that the poet's words rendered in her siren's voice would flay him. He said, "We will start tomorrow."

Thirty-three

FOR two days the sandstorm vented its wrath on the ruined village, and at times Khalidah was convinced that the flimsy hut would finally collapse around them. At last, though, it blew itself out in a violent but short-lived squall of rain. They filled their water skins before the sun dried the puddles and set off again under a brilliant sky.

Though the salt desert was monotonous, it was not actually very big—not, at any rate, compared with the vast deserts of Arabia—and within a couple of days another clutch of mountains rose on the horizon. "Say good-bye to the sand," Sulayman said, and then, pointing to the mountains, "we'll see little but that until we reach Qaf."

They passed from the desert into the province of Sistan, which, according to Sulayman, had once been a vast garden of a country housing a refined and peaceful civilization. But peaceful civilizations never fare well in a world wedded to war, and over long years of ravage by invading armies, Sistan became a no-man's-land between Persia and Khorasan. It was still a fertile place, though, its mountains interspersed with tilled valleys where wheat, melons, and sesame grew in abundance.

The farmers of these valley fields belonged to a tribe called the Baluchi, who lived in wicker huts with roofs of cloth and spoke a language even Sulayman could not decipher. They rode curious horses with fine heads on long necks, bodies somewhat heavier than the Arab horses', and long ears that curved toward each other to touch at the tips. Despite the language barrier, the Baluchi understood trade as well as any tribe and appeared to have goods to spare for it. Sulayman and Khalidah replenished their supplies and found ample grazing for the horses when they stopped at night.

After the lands of the Baluchi, they crossed dry steppes dotted with crumbling ruins, and once an entire abandoned city, its broken columns thrusting skyward like the ribs of some ancient slain beast. They climbed hills and came down again into a marshy region bisected by the Hirmand River, which flowed from the heart of Khorasan. Its water was pure and freezing cold, and welcome to them after days of warm water tainted with the taste of the skins.

On what Sulayman said would be their final day in Persia, they stopped at a small city called Zabol. It was a collection of low mud buildings baked to the dull, dun color of the mountains at its back. But it was also green: behind its walls were gardens fed by the same great river. They had not stopped at a town of any size since Domat al-Jandal—a place that now seemed the provenance of dream—and Khalidah felt a strong reluctance to enter the city.

"Is it really necessary to stop here?" she asked.

"Unless you want to freeze in the mountains," Sulayman answered. "There are things we need to buy here before we can go on."

Sighing, Khalidah nudged Zahirah onward. Once they were inside it wasn't so bad. Many of the townspeople spoke Persian, especially in the souk, where Sulayman bought men's clothing for them both.

"The hills are rife with bandits," he answered, when Khalidah questioned the need to maintain the disguise. "Better they believe you are a boy."

He handed her a porridge-colored woolen hat, tubular in shape and rolled to sit as high or low on the head as the wearer desired. Next he bought long woolen coats woven in somber stripes, and generous woolen shawls, a red one for himself and a blue one for Khalidah. They also bought a new load of provisions, paying for it all with the last of the silver from the horses' bridles.

"And now we are as ready as we can be," he said to Khalidah as they packed their food and new clothes onto the pony. They rode away from the souk, and the chaos of the streets dissipated. Now the houses they passed dreamed within walled gardens full of shade trees and the muted sounds of moneyed life.

"This is not the way to the mountains," Khalidah observed.

"No," Sulayman answered. He hesitated, then said, "We may have reached the last stage of our journey, but it will be by far the most difficult. Tonight we should have a proper meal, and sleep in real beds."

"We have no money for an inn."

"We do not need it. I have a friend here."

"You have a friend everywhere," Khalidah said.

"Are you angry?"

"No; only, why did you not tell me this before?"

"I didn't know whether our road would take us here, and I didn't want to raise your hopes."

It was a strange thing for him to say. Nomad's daughter that she was, Khalidah was indifferent to the charms of a stuffed mattress, and though a hot meal would be welcome, she hardly pined for it. She was about to question him further when he pulled Aasifa up outside the largest house on the street, a sprawling two-story place surrounded by the ubiquitous wall and date palms. Somewhere beyond the wall Khalidah could hear children's laughter and the subtle harmonics of falling water. Their interlacing tones and rhythms filled her with an unfathomable longing.

"How will you explain me to this friend?" she asked as they dismounted by the gate.

"There will be no need," answered Sulayman. "Sandara knows your story already."

"How?" Khalidah asked sharply.

"This is not the place to discuss it," Sulayman answered, then rapped on the door. It was opened by a boy of about six, a skinny child in fine clothing that had clearly been clean that morning. He was unremarkable except for a pair of huge, black-fringed eyes the color of the palms' shade. At the sight of Sulayman his sharp little face broke into a grin of delight, and he launched himself into the man's arms.

"You've come back!" he cried.

"I promised you I would," Sulayman answered, kissing both of his cheeks and then setting him down again. "Daoud al-Tamuri, may I introduce Khalidah al-Hassani."

The child said his *salaam*s, and then, "I thought you were a boy."

Khalidah smiled. "That is what I wished you to think."

"Is your mother at home?" Sulayman asked.

"I will fetch her," Daoud said. "Come in and let your horses drink."

He indicated a fountain set at the convergence of four pebbled paths and surrounded with well-tended apricot trees. Two little girls a year or two younger than Daoud leaned over the stone rim of the fountain, dropping pebbles into the water. As Khalidah and Sulayman led the horses toward the fountain, they looked up with smoky green eyes like Daoud's. Their pretty oval faces were so alike that if they had not worn different-colored headscarves, Khalidah would not have been able to tell them apart.

"Sulayman!" they cried together, and flew at him as the boy had done. He caught one in each arm and kissed them both.

"What have you done to charm these children?" Khalidah asked him as she stripped off the horses' tack.

"It's they who charmed me," Sulayman said, collapsing back onto the rim of the fountain with a little girl on each knee. "These are Daoud's sisters, Madiha and Maliya." To the girls he said, "This is Khalidah."

Khalidah nodded to the twins and then cupped her hands to drink from the fountain. She was swallowing water as greedily as the horses when a shadow fell over her. She turned to find a woman standing between herself and Sulayman. She was tall and slim and clad head to toe in black, including a crepe veil over her face that admitted no glimpse of her features except for a faint, sporadic glint that could have been an eye. The woman bent down and took the wriggling girls from Sulayman, then regarded him silently. Or she seemed to: it was impossible to tell, through the veil, where her eyes fell.

In a sweet, retiring voice she said, "I am so glad that you have returned, Sulayman." As she spoke, the veil fluttered like the apricot leaves in the evening breeze. "And you, child," she said, turning to Khalidah. Her voice wavered between wonder and tears. "Can you be Brekhna's daughter?"

Khalidah had a powerful sense of ingenerate nobility in this veiled woman, not unlike what she had felt when she first met Sulayman.

"By all accounts, I am," she answered.

A nod; the veil fluttered over the glint of a shadow-green eye. Sandara set the twins down, and to Khalidah's shock and mortification, she knelt before her in a graceful sweep of black robes. "Welcome, daughter of Brekhna, granddaughter of Tor Gul Khan. You will always find welcome in the home of your most humble servant, Sandara bint Arzou al-Jinni."

Thirty-four

OVER the lavish dinner she laid out under the apricot trees, Sandara told Khalidah of her childhood in Qaf, which she had left for the first and final time as part of a small battalion hired by a Persian emir to settle a land dispute.

"I did not know it then," she said, her voice like softly falling water, "but I would never return to my childhood home. Like your own mother, I married an outsider and was thereby exiled."

"Where is your husband now?" Khalidah asked.

"Dead," Sandara answered, with a sudden hardening of her tone. It only lasted for a moment, but when she continued with her story, Khalidah could not help hearing its echo. Sandara spoke of the cloth business that kept her family in comfort; the gardens she took pride in tending; the children who were her greatest joy. Yet like her voice when she had pronounced her husband deceased, her account of her life grasped at wholeness while it circled a jagged rent as black as her widow's weeds. Khalidah longed to know the cause of it, and did not dare ask.

When they finished eating, Sandara left to put the children to bed. As soon as she was gone, Khalidah demanded, "What is she hiding?"

"That is for her to tell you, not me," Sulayman answered, tuning his *qanun*.

"I do not like prevarication," she said, though in fact what she did not like was the reverence with which Sulayman seemed to regard the older woman.

"You will like the truth even less," he said bleakly.

Khalidah sipped her tea, watching the stars come out between the apricot leaves and contemplating this response until Sandara returned, carrying a lantern and a coffeepot. "You are good for them, Sulayman," the woman said as she set the light by Sulayman's knee and knelt to pour the coffee. "They have little contact with men, now; they have little contact with anyone but me. It is a sad life for them. Sometimes I wonder if I should return to Qaf . . . I think that my parents would take the children in." She paused, then sighed. "I should do it, and yet I cannot bear to be without them." A laugh that sounded very near to a sob. "What a terrible mother I am. A selfish, weak woman . . ."

Moved past jealousy by the wretchedness of her voice, Khalidah reached out through the darkness for Sandara's hand. The older woman took it and clutched it with desperate strength. "Play something, Sulayman," she said. "Play something before I drown us all with my self-pity."

"I will play," he said, "and I hope Khalidah will sing." Khalidah nodded.

They performed Chauras's lament, and whether it was Sandara's clinging grief, the serenity of the garden night, or simply the specter of the journey's end, Khalidah's voice had a soulful sweetness, Sulayman's strings a tenderness that they hadn't before. By the time they finished nightfall was complete, the garden a sea of shadow challenged only by the oil lamp that had lit Sulayman's path across the strings.

Sandara said, "I sincerely thank you both. I know that you have given something of yourselves to ease my pain, and in return, Khalidah, I will tell you what you wish to know, though I doubt that you will thank me for it." She paused, then continued, "I have shared with you most of my history, but there is one thing that I have not told you. As a girl, as well as being a promising warrior, I was a beauty. So I was told, anyway—I didn't think much of it. Well, I told myself I didn't, but perhaps I did . . . perhaps flouting my beauty was a greater vanity than accepting it as the gift it was." She shook her head.

"It was my beauty that caught Aslam's eye. I knew that, but I was too young, too naïve, to realize that for him, it was also the whole of my worth. He was the only son of a wealthy family. He could have any beautiful thing that caught his eye, and that was the problem. However dutiful, a woman is still a living being with a will of her own, and I was not just a woman but a Jinni—duty means something different to the Jinn. But though I knew this, and all the other reasons why Jinn should never marry outside our own kind, I was young, and love in youth does not suffer reason.

"We had not been married long before I realized my mistake. Aslam did not like the way that other men looked at me. First he forbade me to go out. Then he insisted that I go veiled even within the house. Later I was forbidden to show myself to visitors, even family, veiled or not. But even that was not enough. He was convinced that someone would take me from him. I could do nothing but watch as jealousy drove him mad."

She paused, and then slowly she put back her veil, revealing a profile so exquisite that Khalidah caught her breath: a cheek pale as dawn, a long gold-green eye, a delicate aquiline nose and black eyebrow like a bird's wing. But something was wrong: Sulayman, seated on her other side, was looking at her with tortured pity. For a moment Khalidah did not understand. Then Sandara turned to her with the terrible truth. The other half of her face was a monster's, a livid mess of slabby scars: the eyelid melted into the surrounding skin, leaving the milky, unseeing eye exposed; the lips peeling back from the teeth in a permanent snarl.

"He got drunk and poured burning oil on my face as I slept," she said, her voice at last capitulating to bitterness. "You see, he had convinced himself that it was better to obliterate my beauty than to live with the knowledge that he could not possess it entirely." She smiled a rueful, hideous smile, then dropped her veil. "He succeeded, and yet he failed, for when he was told that I would live he impaled himself on his own sword. And so I am a widow, rich but unmarriageable, and if it were not for the children I would have followed Aslam in his fate long since."

When she spoke next it was to Khalidah, who had not yet begun to recover from her shock. "I have heard every denigration of your mother," she said gently. "I grew up with her as a chastisement, a threat: 'See what will happen if you deny the tribe? Even our princess was not spared exile and humiliation.' But I for one will never condemn her, and whatever the Jinn may tell you, nor should you; for we who give up Qaf pay for it every day of our lives thereafter, each in our own way."

She paused, and then she said slowly, "It is futile to wish that I had not left the Jinn, since I do not think that it was in my power to resist Aslam, and what I took for love. But this"—she gestured to her face—"is my own doing. He began to erase me as soon as I gave myself into his keeping, and for pride—for weak and willful pride—I allowed him to do it. No Jinn woman should ever have submitted to the treatment he gave me, but it seemed easier to forget that than to admit that I had been wrong; and so it reached its obvious conclusion.

"Go to Qaf, Khalidah. Meet your grandfather and hear what he has to say. Learn what it means to be a Jinni, see if there is a life there for you. But never, never forget who you are." Sandara stood abruptly and retreated into the shadows, leaving the echo of her words to dissolve slowly into the sound of falling water.

Thirty-five

Oultrejourdain
Late April

LATE afternoon, and the black king was faltering. The white knight's path ran clear to the black knight; taking him would open the black king to checkmate—and Bilal's first victory since Salim had taught him to play chess. They'd spent that day and most of the previous one trapped by a violent wind in a narrow, nameless wadi in the wastes between Amman and Kerak. It had been long enough for Bilal to get a good sense of the nuances of the game, but not long enough for him to be able to beat Salim so completely.

He looked up at his friend. Salim leaned on hip and elbow, legs bent like a knight's hooked path behind him, face flitting in and out of shadow as tattered clouds tore the sky above. He wore a look of calm surmise and a hint of the smile that had been there on the afternoon he offered Bilal his heart in the shape of a pomegranate seed. For a moment Bilal hesitated; then he took a black fortress with a pawn.

"I've taught you better than that," Salim said.

"You were letting me win."

"You don't know that."

Bilal didn't answer. For a moment the sun carved a fickle script on the wadi's sandstone walls, and then it retreated again. Salim sat up and cleared the board with a sweep of his hand. "Tell me why you fear Kerak," he demanded.

"What?"

"You heard me. And please, spare me the lie: there's been nothing but trouble in your eyes these last three days, and I do not think that it comes from my beating you at chess."

Bilal paused, then said, "Kerak is very near to Wadi Tawil."

"So?" Salim answered. "If we meet any of your tribe—which at any rate seems unlikely—do you really think they would still blame you for leaving? Even if they did, you're my father's soldier now. He would never let them harm you."

"It's not that," Bilal said slowly, "but the thought of being there again . . . it reminds me of all that I am not, and what I cannot be to you."

Salim's face set, his lips thinned to a ruthless line. Bilal had never seen him angry before. It gave his face an unnerving look of his father's. He watched silently as Salim collected the chess pieces, laying each of them in their box with cold precision.

At last he said, "You keep telling me this, and yet it tells me nothing but that when you lie with me, you lie indeed."

The words hit Bilal like the flat of a hand. "How can you say that?" he cried.

"How can I not?" Salim answered bleakly; and then, in a motion of violent despair, he hurled the box of chess pieces into the tent, where it burst and they scattered. But more shocking than this were the tears in his eyes. For all that had passed between them, Bilal had never quite believed that he'd touched Salim in any lasting way, and the proof of it stunned him.

As if to drive home this miserable epiphany, Salim continued, "Do you think that I feel only lust for you? Do you know that I stay awake to watch you when you sleep, just to see your face without the doubt?" His hands clutched convulsively, but the sand they met slipped through his fingers. "When you touch me, Bilal, you touch the quick of me. There is nothing that I would not do for you . . . and yet you don't even consider me worthy of the truth."

"As if it were so simple!" Bilal cried, glad now of the wind that tore their words away, shattered them before they could reach other ears. "You've never known a brutal truth."

"Oh yes, I have," Salim answered bitterly. "I know it every time I let you fuck me, knowing that you don't love me."

Bilal was appalled, not by the ugliness of the words but by the knowledge that he had earned them. In the wake of their devastation he looked truly at Salim for the first time. Instead of grace and beauty he saw a stained robe and a face smeared with grit and tears; instead of a king's son, a boy trying to be a man in a world that didn't need him.

Sick to the soul, Bilal said, "All right." He paused, trying to still his whirling thoughts, and then he said, "The truth, Salim, is that I am not Numair's cousin—"

"You've told me that already."

"I know; but I have not told you that I'm no blood kin to the Hassan at all. I'm the bastard son of a serving woman and a Templar knight . . . no, not just any Templar knight, but their Master, Gerard de Ridefort." He stopped, waiting for a reaction.

Salim wiped a filthy sleeve across his face, drew a shuddering breath, and said, "Is that all?"

Bilal uttered something between a laugh and a sob. "I would give my soul that it was. My father is a traitor, Salim, and so am I. I am here as a spy."

Salim looked at him incredulously. "As my father knows very well. I did not think it was a secret."

Bilal shook his head. "You do not understand. Yes, Numair and I carry de Ridefort's information to your father, but we also carry information about your father to de Ridefort. I do not know for certain, but I believe that he does not intend to keep the deal he has made with your father. He cares only to secure his place no matter who wins the war for Jerusalem." He'd intended to leave it there, but he found that having begun to unburden himself, he could not stop. "And you're wrong, you know. I *do* love you, and I've lied to you only because I wanted you to love me for a little while longer. And now you can take me to your father, it's what I deserve, but please, Salim, if you ever cared for me at all, then tell him to be quick—"

He broke off then because Salim had begun to laugh. There wasn't much joy in it, and when Salim reached for him Bilal didn't know whether it was to throttle or embrace him, until he found himself enfolded. "I am taking you nowhere," Salim said, "except perhaps to bed, if you'll still have me after the things I said."

Bilal pushed him away with a look of abject incredulity. "I've betrayed you, Salim!"

"And who but yourself accuses you of it?"

"Didn't I just tell you—"

"Yes," he said, "and once was enough." He sighed. "I do not doubt your words, Bilal, but nor can I deny the witness of my eyes. You have fought by my side for my father's cause and Allah's, and it is by this that I choose to judge you, if you will make me judge."

"I have carried information intended to betray your father to his enemies!"

"And did you supply it?" Salim asked. "Or was it fed to you by your 'cousin'?"

Bilal shrugged, but Salim took his meaning.

"Very well, then; you have done nothing but transport words from one man to another. That makes you a pawn, but not a traitor." He studied Bilal for a moment, then said, "And that is what I do not understand. If you bear no love for your father or Numair, then why is it that you do their bidding at all? If you fear that you would be implicated by accusing them, then I could speak to my father—"

"No," Bilal said wearily, "it is not that, nor anything to do with me at all. It's my mother I fear for."

"They've threatened to reveal her infidelity if you defy them? Hardly original. Are you even certain that it's true?"

Bilal nodded miserably. "But Salim, I cannot ask you to endanger your own father for my sake. You must tell him what I have told you."

Salim rested his chin on his knee. "And if I tell you that my father has never trusted Numair, nor believed de Ridefort anything but duplicitous, will it clear your conscience?"

Bilal sighed. "For the moment, perhaps. But it does not change the basic problem."

"Ah, Bilal," said Salim, smiling sadly, "are you not content with the trouble you are given, that you must seek out more?" He shook his head. "Even the Templars charge with the conviction that it is God's will. Well, so is this. However you came to be here, Allah's hand was behind it. Now you *are* here, and Numair and de Ridefort are not. You answer to no one but the Sultan. So ride with me to Kerak and fight for your people. If we live through that battle, then we'll worry about the next. And if we live through them all, then I think we'll have earned the right to live unbeholden to anybody."

Dusk had fallen, sinking Salim's eyes into shadow, but Bilal could imagine their expression of gentleness and wisdom and, however inexplicable, love. "Salim," he said, "how can I possibly—"

"By not finishing that sentence," Salim interrupted, "not ever. I do not want gratitude from you, Bilal. I do not want to question your worth. I only want to love you for the length of God's patience."

Inshallah, Bilal thought, reaching for him as the first stars pierced the night.

Thirty-six

MUCH later, Bilal lay awake listening as the wind screamed around the tent like a damned soul, his few hours' tenuous peace in tatters. For in the intermittent lulls of the storm, he heard something that he could not have heard: the whistling cry of a peregrine. It was a sound that snaked back to his time in the wadi by Kerak, waiting for word to go north, where it had been his father's secret summons. At last he gave up trying to ignore it and slipped from Salim's arms: a murmur, a crease of the forehead like a hand across water, and fingers that clutched once at nothing before capitulating to sleep. Expelling a breath he had not known he held, Bilal tucked the covers around Salim, then pulled on a tunic, picked up the lamp left burning by the tent flap, and went out into the night.

A few steps into the darkness he found him, standing like a tombstone while the storm broke around him, his white mantle a whipping flag. They stood looking at each other until at last de Ridefort turned and began to walk toward a black stand of rock, where his horse waited in a shallow cave beyond the reach of the wind. Bilal followed at a wary distance.

"You have grown," de Ridefort said speculatively, as soon as he could make himself heard.

"I have grown?" Bilal repeated, incredulous. "You came here to tell me that? Do you not know that this is the Sultan's own camp? His guard never sleeps, and if they had found you—"

"What, Bilal? Do you forget that I am the Sultan's ally? Or do you know something that I do not?"

Every word of the Master's was barbed with irony and challenge. Bilal opened his mouth to answer, then closed it again and shook his head. They passed a few moments in silence. De Ridefort was ruminating once again on his son's face, and Bilal had the disquieting feeling that there was something specific he looked for there.

Abruptly, the knight said, "Why do you share the prince's tent?"

"How do you know about that?" Bilal demanded, and immediately wished that he hadn't. But there was no taking the words back.

De Ridefort smiled derisively. "I 'know about that' because I have had your detachment followed for many days . . . and I must say that what I have heard about your conduct worries me, not least your relationship with the Sultan's son."

"If you know about it already, then why did you ask?"

"To hear what you would answer."

"And what do you make of my answer?" Bilal asked, with a defiant courage he had not realized he possessed until that moment.

"That you are treading on dangerous ground. What exactly is that boy to you?"

Bilal's first instinct was to tell him that it was none of his business, but somehow that answer felt like a slight to Salim, as if he, Bilal, were ashamed of the truth. So he answered with Salim's own words: "He is the heart of my heart."

The look on de Ridefort's face was enough to make a brave man blanch, but Bilal stood before him unflinching. "Filthy heathen," de Ridefort muttered at last, at which Bilal smiled.

"If you think so, Father, I will happily take your leave, and we can both pretend that we never laid eyes on each other."

De Ridefort laughed wryly. "And leave you free to poison the Sultan against me? Do you really think so great a fool would have risen as high as I have done?" He shook his head. "No, Bilal, I am not here to sever ties with you. 'Keep your friends close, hold your enemies closer'—that is an Arab proverb, is it not? Well, you have become a liability, and it cannot continue. I do not intend to let you out of my sight again. I have not yet decided exactly what to do with you, but I think some time with a holy order—a Christian order—would be beneficial. Once you have learned the error of your ways, you may yet be of some use to me."

It was clear that de Ridefort expected anger and defiance, but Bilal nodded calmly, his eyes never leaving his father's. "Perhaps you are right," he said. "Perhaps it is time that I repent of my . . . many sins." As Bilal had intended, de Ridefort was unbalanced by this response, and while the knight stared at him, trying to find the trick in his words, Bilal whipped the sword from his father's belt.

De Ridefort was furious, but he was also a military man, and he knew when he was beaten. He looked at his son down the length of his sword, now pointed at his own throat, and said, "It seems that I taught you better than I realized."

"No, Father," Bilal answered. "What I have learned, I have learned from Salim."

De Ridefort's jaw worked for a moment. Then he said, "Very well. I am at your mercy; what do you want?"

"I want you to leave me alone," Bilal answered, "and for that promise, I am willing to spare your life. However," he added, as de Ridefort began to reply, "I know very well that your word alone is worth little. And so, remember this: I serve the Sultan, and he knows it. If you ever try to coerce me again, I'll go straight to him and tell him that you are a traitor."

"He would not take your word over mine," de Ridefort scoffed.

"I have fought loyally for him," Bilal answered. "One might even say that I gave him the victory at Amman. What have you given him but empty promises?"

De Ridefort pinned him with a long, icy look and said, "If you ever attempt to shame me among my own people, you will not live to tell about it."

Bilal smiled bitterly. "Believe me, de Ridefort, I have no more desire to be known as your son than you have to be known as my father." He lowered the sword. De Ridefort reached for it, but Bilal only laughed. "As you say, Messire, you taught me well."

With a last, bitter glance at his son, de Ridefort mounted his horse and gave him a vicious kick. When Bilal was certain that he was gone, he slumped down against the wall of stone, shaking and filled with elation. He knew that there would be a price to pay for that night's work, but at the moment, he could not think beyond his victory. For although he had walked the earth for sixteen years, he had not until that night realized that the reins of his destiny were his for the taking.

IN the following days Bilal came as close to happiness as he'd ever been. The windstorm raged on with tenacious ferocity, and he prayed to Allah to preserve it, if it meant that he could stay forever in that dusty wadi with Salim and their chessboard and their pipe of *banj*. But as his mother had been fond of saying, the only certainty in life is change, and with gritty inevitability the storm finally blew itself out. Once again the Sultan's small army set off south.

A day's steady riding would have brought them to Kerak, but instead Salah ad-Din led his band in a zigzag course along the King's Highway, sending raid after raid across the border into Franj territory. It maddened Salim, who after his success at Amman was itching for a proper battle. As the days wore on even Bilal began to long for Kerak as an end to the monotony of the raids, though he did not entirely share Salim's enthusiasm for bloodshed. But Salah ad-Din met his son's pestering with a calm, indulgent smile.

"To take back Jerusalem," he said, "we must engage the Franj; to do that, we must first draw them forth. And, as Amman taught you, the Franj do not like to come forth from a fortress. This will be truer still when their fortress is their Holy City." He paused, his eyes rambling the horizon where sand hazed to sky. "Yet my biggest problem by far is how to occupy my own army in the meantime."

"So you send them on raids to keep them busy?" Salim asked incredulously.

"Precisely."

The Sultan had caught sight of a far-off wisp of dust, no bigger than the plume from a spent lamp, but he knew that it spelled another victory. He turned at last to his son, who stood waiting with tremulous eagerness to oblige him, and was struck all at once by Salim's resemblance to his mother. The only child of a Persian emir, she should never have been a harem wife. She was too used to autonomy and also to significance, all spit and fire over a deep and devastating need to please. Though for a brief time he had loved her with a consuming passion, Salah ad-Din wished now that he had never touched her. He ought to have known that a son of hers would break his heart.

"Yet like the best tactics," he said at last, "it serves more than one purpose. Our successes here keep the public in our favor and bolster the morale of the army waiting for us in the north. But the primary reason why we do not make straight for Kerak is that I have had word from Al-Adil."

At the mention of his father's brother, the governor of Egypt, Salim perked up. "Does he mean to bring his army to join us?"

The Sultan gave him a smile of circumspect approval. "They are on the road already, and should reach Ayla in the next few days. With his help and Allah's grace, we stand to gain not only a castle, but a province. Now, does that not seem a fair trade for a few days' patience?"

This delighted Salim beyond further questioning, and the Sultan watched with troubled eyes as he ran off, no doubt to repeat it all to the Bedu boy. He had his doubts about their intimacy—not for its nature, but because he was not yet certain that the boy was trustworthy. However, he had more pressing worries than his son's love affairs. He had not been entirely honest with Salim about the reasons for delaying the march on Kerak. There were many good ones, but the most significant was also the most shameful: doubt. For Salah ad-Din had challenged Kerak before, and however his chroniclers might choose to apotheosize his efforts, the simple truth was that he had failed. And so he rode south slowly, to buy time to think.

When the castle rose at last like a wart on the wavering horizon, he was no nearer believing he could take it. Yet knowing that this must remain his own guilty secret, he gathered his emirs and said: "The Franj have learned much over their hundred years in our land. They do not come out from cover without cause, nor, more to the point, unless the circumstances are favorable. Our raids will have given them cause; now we must convince them of favorability. Therefore I will go myself to challenge them, and I will take only my own guard and my son's."

He silenced the ensuing clamor of protest with a raised hand and continued, "The rest of the division will wait until the Franj come forth, and then you will strike as you have struck all down the backbone of Oultrejourdain—quickly and ruthlessly."

And so it was. Salah ad-Din rode forth at first light, flanked by his own guard and Salim's. Bilal rode near the front of the detachment, watching the castle as they drew closer to it with a disconnected vigilance. There were the tower and the wall he knew so well, there the great gate that had once admitted him as an ally. But now the portcullis was drawn, and daylight sharpened the walls' arrow slits to bared fangs, the crenellated battlements to broken teeth. All along the walls the garrison ranged with their wives and their whores, to jeer at this paltry party come to challenge them.

The master of the garrison, a blunt-bodied man with a face like a pale, stubbled pudding, rode forth with a handful of cavalry to meet them. To the Sultan's *salaam*s, he replied, through a translator, "What do you want?" in a voice that suggested he would far rather be back in the keep, drinking his absent master's wine.

"Must you ask?" Salah ad-Din answered contemptuously. "Can you not see the smoke of your burning villages? Have your people not yet come to you for refuge?"

"We have seen it, and they have." This time, his voice was coldly serious.

"Well, then: I come to offer terms."

The Franji uttered a low chuckle. "And who has asked for terms?"

The Sultan held the knight in his gold-brown gaze until the knight looked away. Then he said in a calm, conversational tone, "News of your master's outrages travels farther than perhaps you realize: as far, in fact, as Cairo. My brother commands the army there. You might have heard of him. He is called Al-Adil—that is, 'The Just'—and it is not without reason. He is waiting at Ayla to extract justice from Arnat, if he will not give it freely."

"Arnat is not at home," the Franji said.

"Do you think that this is news to me?" Salah ad-Din asked in a low, merciless voice. The Franji didn't answer. "Believe me, I know all that you know about your present circumstances, and a good deal that you don't. Now, will you hear my terms?"

"There will be no terms!" the officer roared at the Sultan's tranquil face. The stunned translator paused for a moment and then relayed his message.

"Very well," said Salah ad-Din. There was a brief, lucid moment as the Sultan raised his blade, in which the Franj knight realized that there had never been any terms at all.

It was easy after that. The whey-faced officer's rolling head goaded a band of cavalry from the castle keep, and the Mamluk horse archers and auxiliary cavalry fell on them like lightning. Deep in their midst Bilal fought with a will, and when he found himself looking too closely at the faces of the men he slew, he looked instead at Salim, whose own face beneath his helmet glowed with the ephemeral joy of proving his worth. In little more than minutes the field was reduced to a mire of bloody mud and broken Franj bodies, soon battered further by the riderless horses that plunged among them in terrified confusion.

The Sultan's men turned back to the gates then, beating their shields and calling out for further contest, but no one came to meet them. The castle was still and silent, the battlements empty, for the garrison and all their retinue had retreated into the keep. It wasn't quite the victory Salah ad-Din had longed for, but then, it would serve his purpose well enough. Plunging his sword into its sheath, he divided his detachment and set them in a ring around the castle.

"Contain the garrison," he said to the emirs, and then, gesturing to his son, he wheeled his horse to the west.

"Where are we going?" Salim asked.

"To meet my brother," he said, "and teach Arnat a lesson he won't forget."

FOR a week Salah ad-Din and the Egyptian army razed the province of Oultrejourdain, their earlier exploits paling in comparison to the earthly hell they now made of Arnat's lands. They burned the fields where the first crops were ripening and slaughtered livestock and anyone who raised so much as a hand against them. To begin with, Bilal was ambivalent about the wanton destruction; many of these people hated and feared Arnat as much as he did. But a human heart can absorb only so much brutality before hardening to it. Soon enough he rode to the slaughter as avidly as the rest, screaming praises of Allah and of the Sultan who worked His will.

Yet at night when he lay in Salim's arms, he knew that his battle cries were empty. He did not fight for the Sultan or even for Allah, but for the human boy he loved. As successive victories fired them with a passion beyond anything either of them had imagined on that first moonlit night in Busra, Bilal realized too that he had no people but Salim, nor did he want any. He knew that someday the wars would end, that for all their brave promises life would in reality demand things of both of them that might make their love impossible. But for the moment at least, he preferred to do as Salim had told him in the narrow, windy wadi: survive the following day, and then consider the next.

Thirty-eight

※

Khorasan
Late April

SANDARA was distant when Khalidah and Sulayman said good-bye the next morning, and her children crestfallen. But she sent them away loaded with still more food and water and warm clothing. As Khalidah leaned down to embrace her from Zahirah's saddle, Sandara whispered in her ear, "Do not forget me, Khalidah. I will not forget you." She said something to Sulayman that Khalidah couldn't hear, but which caused his eyes to flicker inadvertently toward her. And then they were leaving, and with one last, yearning look at them, Daoud shut the door on that hushed, haunted garden.

They rode in silence out of the city. Only when they reached the arid foothills did either of them dare to break it. From a rocky precipice they looked out across a vista of undulating red hills that marched ever taller toward the horizon, where they could just make out snow-capped peaks.

"This is Khorasan," Sulayman said at last. He looked at Khalidah, who looked into the distance with troubled eyes. "And Sandara has made you wonder whether you should have come at all."

She didn't answer, but by the sudden downward cast of those eyes, Sulayman knew that he had guessed correctly. He sighed. "Sandara is a good woman," he said, "and I thought that meeting her might help you understand your mother, also perhaps protect you from some of the things you will hear about her in Qaf. But you must also remember that Sandara views the world through a lens of loss and regret, and that is at best a skewed view. I have met her father. He has long since forgiven her, and would help her if she would only ask."

"And you have not told her so?" Khalidah cried.

Sulayman answered with a rueful laugh. "I told her so when I returned from Qaf, and I told her again this morning, before you awakened. You might even say that I begged her to hear reason, for the sake of her children and her aging father if not herself. But Aslam's fire burned away more than her beauty. She is lost in a labyrinth of remorse, and without being able to forgive herself she can allow no one else to forgive her. It is killing her. I only hope that she loves her children enough to save them before she succumbs."

Once again, the silence spun out across the empty hills.

As time shifted her perspective on Sandara, Khalidah's apprehension for Qaf faded. Once again she looked eastward with anticipation, though it was more circumspect now. To keep her mind from dwelling on her worries, Sulayman filled their evenings with lessons in writing or the *qanun*, and their days relating what he knew of this barely tamed frontier of Islam. He worked through Khorasan's history until he reached the Ghaznavid Turks, whose King Mahmoud had plucked the country from the Persians like a ripe apricot. But Mahmoud had no sooner secured Khorasan than he was off again eastward on a mission to convert the subcontinent to Islam.

"And it's from his bloody conquest that the Jinn's part of the Himalaya takes its name," Sulayman concluded. "*Hindu Kush* means 'Slaughter of Hindus.' And it's not just the Hindus who have been slaughtered. When Mahmoud died—not fifty years ago—the country dissolved once again into a chaos of battling dynasties, and that is how it has been ever since. Therefore you must be vigilant on this road. The mountains are full of bandits looking to kill or co-opt you, depending which side you're on."

Khalidah had nothing to say to this, though now she rode with the decided sensation of hostile eyes, if not arrows, trained on her back.

For some days they followed the river Khash, with a snowy peak towering to their left, rendered a searing violet by the lucent air. After that they turned their backs to the mountain and rode down into the valley of the Helmand, a green hurtle of meltwater cold as a knife strike. They followed this river for several days, and all the time the mountains surrounding them grew in stature.

"There," said Sulayman one morning as Khalidah shook off the dew that had frozen over their blankets in the night. He pointed north through the blazing sunrise to the faint plicae of a mountain range, higher still than anything they had yet encountered. "That is the Hindu Kush. Somewhere in those mountains . . ."

You will discover whether it is me you love, Khalidah thought as he trailed off, *or my connection to the land you long for*. She was immediately ashamed of the thought, yet she could not quite banish it. She gulped her tea, shivering even as it burned her mouth. They had camped in a place where the river was narrow and its valley deep. The sunlight would not reach it until midday, and then only for an hour or two. Khalidah looked sadly at the horses, which were growing thin despite the now-abundant grazing: they could not eat the grass as fast as the cold and exertion ate their flesh.

"Soon it will be better," she whispered to Zahirah, and indeed, for a few days the conditions grew gentler. They turned away from the river somewhere south and west of Kabul and crossed the Shomali Plain, a vast, fertile expanse of vineyards and fruit trees with little baked-mud villages rising from their midst like anthills. When they passed through these settlements, children smiled and women offered them tea and dried apricots and mulberries, the new season's fruit being still green and hard.

The respite didn't last long, though. From the gardens of Shomali their path rose into the Baba mountains—the first bony fingers of the Hindu Kush—growing narrow and rutted with the violent rains and searing sun that continually battered the land.

The road clung to the sides of the mountains, at times covered with ice, at others overhanging sheer drops of thousands of feet down to desolate valleys of reddish stone and dust.

Despite the inhospitable nature of the road, there was a steady stream of other travelers, particularly as they neared the Khyber Pass, which was the only route from Kabul to the Orient. When they met travelers moving west, Khalidah would shut her eyes and pray that Zahirah's feet not betray her as they maneuvered a passing on a path barely wide enough for one. Sometimes they came upon little villages clinging to the sides of the mountains like fungi on the trunks of great trees. Women and children would squat in front of their mud huts, watching the travelers with a look of abject longing.

After two grueling days of climbing, they reached the pass and crossed into the Bamiyan range. From the giddy air of that towering gateway they began to descend: Sulayman with a look of mild expectation, Khalidah trying not to faint with the altitude. Down and down they went, until the muscles of Khalidah's thighs, so long used to climbing, seized from all the hours of riding with her weight pushed back. But when she asked to stop, Sulayman said, "Not yet."

She was angry with him—angrier than she had yet been—for what she thought was wanton stubbornness. For an hour she imagined all the imprecations she wanted to hurl at him and then, abruptly, she understood. They had arrived in a sandstone valley, still high enough that the air was dilute but low enough that the snow-crusted peaks beyond the surrounding foothills looked every *farsakh* of their dizzying height. The floor of the valley was green with meadow grass and the cultivated fields of the farms scattered across it. Beyond the farms, at the base of the foothills, huddled a small town, and soaring high above the town were three great arched niches carved into the sandstone cliffs. They contained stone carvings of human figures. The westernmost one was the largest, the central one was the smallest, but Khalidah was still too far away to make out any more detail than that.

"What is this place?" she asked as they rode toward the town between fields of ripening wheat.

"Bamiyan," he said. "Once it was the most important city in Khorasan, and the hub of the Silk Route. It didn't matter whether you were traveling from Beijing to Rome or Samarqand to Jaipur, you passed through Bamiyan."

"Are the statues idols of infidel gods?"

"The statues represent Buddha," Sulayman answered, "a prophet who lived—"

"Yes," Khalidah said testily, "I know about Buddha. But what are his statues doing in a Muslim country?"

"This was not always a Muslim country." They were close enough now to the cliffs to see that they were honeycombed with caves. Indicating them, Sulayman continued, "You see those? They were Buddhist chapels and monasteries. Once, thousands of monks lived there, and they would put up travelers and pilgrims. They're empty now, but you can still see the paintings and statues the monks made while they were there—the monks, and others too. In those caves you'll see Chinese calligraphy and Tibetan mandalas side by side with paintings of Ganesha and Zeus and the prophet Iesu."

As they approached, the features of the Buddhas became clear in the sunset light, their heavy-lidded eyes and tranquil smiles cast to the valley below. The largest of them stood as high as the cave above the camp at Wadi Tawil.

"Once, I am told, they were colored," Sulayman said. "Painted and gilded and covered in jewels. I suppose time and thieves have taken care of that."

"Let's go up there," Khalidah said. "Let's sleep tonight in the Buddhists' caves."

Sulayman smiled. "That was my plan. They have done for countless travelers in the past, and at any rate, we have no money left to stay in town."

So they rode around what was left of the town of Bamiyan—huddling, it seemed, in the shadow of its own glorious past—and then led the horses up onto the cliffs, over narrow paths and crumbling stone staircases. They found a cave that was deep enough to give shelter from the evening wind and high enough for the horses to stand. Sulayman lit a fire, and by its flickering light Khalidah examined the walls, covered with frescoes as Sulayman had promised. In one, men with long Oriental eyes and blood-colored robes drifted through a field of flowers. Another showed a golden chariot drawn by moon-white horses, driven by a man with magnificent hair that flowed across an azure sky. She turned from them at last to find Sulayman lying on the floor, looking up at the paintings on the ceiling, eyes half lidded like the Buddhas'.

"How far now to Qaf?" she asked.

Sulayman was silent for a few long moments. At last he said, "I don't know."

Khalidah came and looked down on him. "What do you mean?"

He sat up. "Remember when I told you about my first journey to Qaf? I arrived there and left it in oblivion. We could be one *farsakh* away or one hundred. But the village where I awakened under the cannabis bush was only a couple of *farsakh*s from here. The best we can do now is ride that way, and hope."

Khalidah looked out into the blackness beyond the cave's mouth, wondering what it was she hoped for.

Thirty-nine

THEY reached the village with Sulayman's cannabis bush and passed it without incident, except for the contemptuous stare of a nanny goat munching the resinous leaves. Soon they were climbing again, this time into hills as inviolate as they were fearsome. Not even a mud village broke the monotony. Snow fields and glaciers, meltwater torrents, and lakes all had the unyielding, luminescent beauty of a land untouched and untouchable.

Sulayman no longer knew the names of mountains and rivers. Khalidah doubted that they even had names, beyond what Allah had given them at the beginning of time. The grazing grew thin and finally nonexistent; the horses reluctantly reverted to their rations of camels' milk and dates. At least there was no longer any shortage of water.

Farther and farther they traveled into those mountains, shivering through their nights and stumbling through their days. Early on they abandoned riding, since the footing was so treacherous and Zahirah's leg wound was not healing properly, and led the horses on their winding path between glacier and mountain. Though they were running low on supplies again, they dared not approach the shepherds who occasionally crossed their path with their flocks: ferocious-looking men in dirty woolen clothing with faces like the granite cliffs above and eyes bloodred where they should have been white. When she saw their eyes, Khalidah thought that they were devils, and Sulayman had a hard time convincing her that it was merely a custom of these men to stain their eyes with madder, to make them look fiercer.

"It's hardly necessary," Khalidah said, not quite believing him but even less inclined to test the theory.

"Come, Khalidah," he soothed. "It can't be long now."

But his reassurance was transparent. They had traveled farther east than he had ever been before, yet there was no trace of human habitation of any kind, unless they counted the demon-eyed shepherds and their fat-tailed sheep, which moved across the landscape like filthy caravans on their way, apparently, from nowhere to nowhere. At last Sulayman came to the decision he had been avoiding for days. It was only midday, but the sky to the north looked ugly and the wind was picking up, so they set up camp in the lee of a tumid glacier that offered as much protection as anything could. They huddled together over their smoking fire, having covered the horses with the blankets, for if their sweat froze on them it would kill them.

As Khalidah stirred their meager rations into a kind of stew, which would at least be hot if not particularly appetizing, Sulayman said, "It's over."

Khalidah's eyes flew to his face. "What?"

"We cannot go on," he said in a small, defeated voice. "We have barely enough food to get us back to the last village, assuming that nothing stalls us on the way."

She stirred the stew, saying nothing for several minutes. At last, handing him a spoon, she said, "No."

He looked up at her incredulously. "No? Do you think we can survive on ice and gravel?"

"I think," she said, sipping a spoonful of the noxious concoction, "that we have come too far to give up now."

"Khalidah—"

"Last time you reached Qaf only when you were at the very end of your endurance. Perhaps it is the same now. Perhaps it is a kind of test, a measure of our worth, and the Jinn will come for us when we've proven it."

"I would think they'd tested mine already," he said irritably, "and yours is beyond question."

"Is it?"

"You're a Jinni."

"No—I am the daughter of an exiled Jinni and a foreign sheikh. A half-breed heathen, to them."

"Then why did Tor Gul Khan send me to find you?"

"I imagine because he hoped that the Jinn half of me would prove the stronger. Perhaps this is a way of testing his theory." She paused, then added, "And perhaps he is also testing our faith."

"Our faith in what?" he asked, with hard, bitter eyes.

"In him," she answered calmly.

"How can he expect us to have faith in him when he has offered nothing to sustain it?" he cried. "How can I have faith in something of which I have not the smallest memento to prove that it ever existed outside my own mind?"

"Is that not the meaning of faith?" she asked softly. Her golden eyes rested on him without question or presumption, with little more than a raptor's steady certainty. But Sulayman knew that he would rather die in this nameless, frozen valley than live in a world that would betray such a look. Picking up his spoon, he began to eat.

THAT night a blizzard raged, and they clung together with the horses curved around them, marking a tiny, tenuous circle of life in that vast wilderness of stone and ice. Khalidah was afraid to sleep, knowing that if she did she might never wake up again. But at last she could hold out no longer, and the sting of blowing snow gave way to soft warmth and gentle hands stroking her head. She knew then that she must be dead. She opened her eyes to the flutter of a white shawl embroidered with colorful birds and flowers.

"Mother," she said, struggling to sit up, but the hands pressed her back down. She could see nothing of Brekhna's face except the penetrating golden eyes, and as she looked they dissolved into the blowing sand of a desert evening, where an army raged in battle.

They were Muslims—that she could tell by the fluttering banners with their Quranic inscriptions—and so vast in number that at first she thought they fought each other. Then, gradually, among the flying dust and flashing steel, she began to make out white tunics crossed with red—the Templars. But they were bodies only, torn and broken, trampled beneath the hooves of the Muslim army's horses.

Then, after another moment, she realized that this was not quite right either. In the midst of that vast army of Islam one Christian knight still stood, a man with a face that should never have belonged to a soldier. Tears rolled from his soft, slate-blue eyes into his dark beard as he raised his sword again and again, hacking with doomed determination at the enemies who surrounded him. Behind him, on horseback, another young man watched: a Muslim, wearing a bloody yellow tunic over a prince's armor, his troubled soul written all over his fine face. He watched as the soldiers taunted the Franj knight, drawing out the inevitable, his own bloody sword lying on the pommel of his saddle and his knuckles white on the hilt. Khalidah found herself praying for the prince to deliver the failing knight, and as if he had heard her, he raised his sword. The Franji never saw it coming. With one clean stroke, the prince split his helmet and his skull, and the Franj knight fell. Then he turned his horse away from the bloody field and kicked her into a gallop, but not before Khalidah saw the devastation on his face.

As he rode away, she heard the incongruous voice of a reed flute playing a melody she did not recognize, though it seemed to echo the bitter sorrow in her heart. Gradually the sounds of the battle faded and its image collapsed into darkness, but the flute remained, calm and steady and sweet, and there were arms around her, and a beating heart beneath her ear. She opened her eyes to find that she was lying against Sulayman's chest, clutching his coat in two white fists. She remembered snow and fractured rock, but she could not find them now, nor the ranging army and setting sun. There were only a flickering fire, a soft cushion beneath her, the moon shining through a high window, and perfect, blessed warmth.

"I did not know that you spoke Pashto," Sulayman said, looking down into her face, smiling around the worry.

"I don't," she said.

"And yet you were speaking it a moment ago, in your dream . . . screaming it, really. What was it you dreamed of?"

"Do not ask her yet," said a man's low voice with an accent she could not place. She realized then that the sound of the flute had ceased when the man spoke. She turned and saw him sitting on the floor near them: an old man, but still vital, wearing a white robe and a dark turban, the reed flute resting on his lap. He smiled at her, though it did not quite reach his golden eyes.

"Where are we?"

She had directed the question to Sulayman, but it was the old man who answered: "In my home."

"And you are . . . ?"

"Tor Gul Khan. Your grandfather." He bowed to her, hand over his heart. "*As-salaamu alaikum*, Khalidah al-Hassani. May I be the first to welcome you to Qaf."

Part Two

One

Castle of Tiberias
County of Tripoli, Galilee
Late April

COUNT Tripoli stood on the wall of his castle at Tiberias, watching the dusty glitter of an approaching band of cavalrymen. He suspected that they were an envoy from Jerusalem, come to demand that he pay tribute to Guy as king. But as the horsemen drew near enough to make out their heraldry, he saw that the banners were yellow, with Quranic inscriptions. Salah ad-Din was still away harrying Oultrejourdain; therefore the visitor would be one of the Sultan's sons.

Tripoli frowned. Though he held the Sultan in the highest regard, he had never been able to stomach his heirs. The eldest was an arrogant brat, the second a charmer with a dangerous disrespect for his skill, and the third a prodigy with a sword and no brains to balance it. Still, his terms with the Sultan left him no choice but to welcome his sons. Turning his back on the bright morning, he retreated into the castle.

He descended to the great hall, sent a serving girl after refreshments, and then sat down at the banquet table. The table was made of Lebanese cedar and had borne the elbows of Saracen kings a hundred years before the Franks began their march to Jerusalem. Tripoli was ruminating on the irony of this when a page—some plain little relation of his wife's, whose name he could never recall—appeared with the inevitable announcement: "Th-the Sultan's s-son for you, please, Messire . . ."

Tripoli looked past the page to his visitor, certain that there had been some mistake. The young man who stood before him was none of the three princes he knew, nor anything like them. Whereas all of them had inherited their mother's solid, stocky frame, this one was tall and slender, with a feline grace and quick, intelligent eyes in a face of luminous beauty. He could be no more than sixteen, yet he moved across the echoing hall with the nonchalant assurance of a man certain of his own significance. He stopped at the far end of Tripoli's table, and inclining his silk-turbaned head, he said the *salaam*s.

"*Wa alaikum as-salaam*," Tripoli intoned automatically, and only then realized that he had stood and bowed. "Whom do I have the honor of greeting?" he continued in perfect Arabic.

"Salim ibn Yusuf al-Ayyubi," the young man answered, with another courteous inclination of the head, "the Sultan's son." But he lowered his chin not a fraction more than courtesy demanded.

Sultan's son indeed, Tripoli thought, *and the only one worthy of his father*. But it would not do to let the boy know that he had impressed him. Tripoli sat down again. Leaning back in his chair he said, "What brings you here, Your Grace?"

The faintest of smiles touched the boy's face, and at last Tripoli saw the familial resemblance. "I come on behalf of my brother Al-Afdhal," said Salim, "with a message from our father." He handed him a letter with the Sultan's seal. "He most humbly requests passage across your territory tomorrow, in order to inspect the shores of Lake Galilee and the region of Acre beyond."

There isn't a humble hair on your father's body, nor your own, Tripoli thought. He said, "I understood that your father was still in Oultrejourdain."

"With respect, Messire: does your own king not make a habit of directing his army, even when he is not able to do it personally?"

Touché, thought Tripoli. "How many men will he send?" he asked, breaking the seal on the letter.

"Seven thousand," Salim answered, as if it were the most natural thing in the world for Salah ad-Din to send a quarter of his army on a reconnaissance mission.

Tripoli was forty-five—an age that in those harsh, warring

lands was an achievement in itself—but he had never felt it until that moment. He looked at the Sultan's letter for confirmation of this outrageous request before he continued: "I suppose that this 'reconnaissance party' will be armed."

"As every man goes armed in these troubled times," the prince answered. "But my father holds you in the highest regard, Sayyid, and as you know he is a man of honor. He has no intention of breaking your truce."

Indeed, thought Tripoli; and yet their hasty truce had made no provision for self-defense. All at once he was angry: at the Sultan for forcing his hand; at the boy who stood before him now with wide-eyed insouciance; but most of all at himself, for the stubbornness and pride that had brought this upon him, for he knew already how it would end. By virtue of their truce he could not deny the Sultan's request, but the local Christian garrisons would consider the Muslim presence in their territory an affront. They would fall on them with all their zealots' fervor and they would be destroyed, which in turn would vindicate all the Frankish nobles who'd called Tripoli a traitor. He would have no choice then but to capitulate to Guy, or break from the Frankish states entirely, and that, for all the respect he bore the Muslims, he could not do.

At last he said, "Tell your brother that the Sultan's request is granted—but only on the condition that his men are out of my territory by nightfall, and that they attack neither person nor property subject to me."

In the prince's ensuing smile, Tripoli saw the measure of his ruin.

Two

In fact, disaster was nearer at hand that day than the count realized, for on the previous morning, the court envoy he had expected had left Jerusalem for Tiberias. In the end the moderates had won their plea for diplomacy, but the feeling among the members of the envoy as they rode north was one of distinct uncertainty. In large part, this was due to de Ridefort. Though the bumbling king had been persuaded to stay at home, and Kerak had stomped off in a huff at being denied a battle, de Ridefort would not be dissuaded from joining the mission. Moreover, he insisted on riding at its head, despite the effrontery to the many accompanying nobles who outranked him.

By the time the king's envoy reached Galilee, the news of Tripoli's agreement to the Muslim reconnaissance had spread far and wide, and the vein Bilal had marked on de Ridefort's forehead on their first meeting throbbed visibly. Tripoli had learned that they were headed to the fortress of La Feve, and sent a letter ahead, so that it was waiting for de Ridefort when he arrived. De Ridefort's expression as he read it could not have been fouler if its news had been a complete surprise, and he ended by balling it in his fist with a string of colorful curses he would have whipped one of his knights for uttering.

"Traitorous cowardly son of a Saracen whore!" he concluded, though Tripoli's mother had in fact come from good French stock. De Mailly, waiting at his elbow, kept his silence, certain that the Master wasn't finished. A moment later de Ridefort rewarded his foresight with the demand: "Where is des Moulins?"

De Mailly knew that the Hospitaller Master had slipped away with a serving girl soon after their arrival at the fortress. However, he also knew better than to say this to de Ridefort. So he answered, "I will find him for you."

"You will indeed," de Ridefort said. "And send someone with wine!"

"Messire," said de Mailly, and bowing to his master, he made his escape.

As he reached the courtyard, the exhaustion of two fraught days caught up with him all at once. He would have given anything then to lie down and sleep, rather than roust des Moulins from his bed of sin. As he tried to remember which door he had seen the Hospitaller Master take, his look was as close to grim as it ever came. Though he didn't know what de Ridefort was planning, he was certain that it would end in a good deal of spilled blood.

Sighing, he began knocking on doors until at last he was rewarded with a gruff *"Oui!"* followed by a curse and what sounded very like a body falling out of a bed.

"It's de Mailly," he said. "De Ridefort would like to see you."

"And I would like nothing less," des Moulins grumbled. A moment later he added, "Tell him I'm coming . . ."

There was a pause, then a girl's muffled laughter. De Mailly sighed. It wasn't that he judged des Moulins's lecherous predilections: for one thing, they were far too common within the Orders (no matter what the Rule claimed) to be shocking, and secondly, de Mailly was of the broad-minded opinion that every man is a sinner in one way or another, and to attempt to assign degrees to sin is essentially pointless. He only wished that des Moulins had chosen a manner of transgression that was somewhat less time-consuming.

To his credit, des Moulins was outside and decently dressed within ten minutes, though his face was unnaturally flushed and his exasperation obvious. The Hospitaller Master wore anger to great effect. His gaunt height and black-and-white tunic made him look stern at the best of times, and threw any degree of irritation into impressive relief.

"What does he want with me?" he inquired as they walked across the courtyard.

De Mailly shook his head. "It's about the Muslim reconnaissance."

"Then God help us," des Moulins answered grimly.

When they reached the hall, they found de Ridefort pacing the room. "Tripoli has insulted us!" he cried, waving the letter at des Moulins. "He has agreed to allow this 'mission' to take place on the very day we intended to bring our envoy to Tiberias."

Sighing, des Moulins sat down at the table, on which someone had placed a jug of wine and a bowl of fruit. He poured some for himself and de Mailly. "As far as I know, Tripoli's abilities do not extend to prophecy. We did not send word that we were coming, and therefore he could not have known that his plans interfered with our own until it was too late—a fact that he has demonstrated by sending this letter, which is more than either chivalry or justice required of him."

"Chivalry and justice! To leave the king's people open to attack—"

"The Saracens have promised *not* to attack," des Moulins reminded him, "and the Sultan, for all his sins, has never shown himself to be anything other than a man of his word."

"No reconnaissance mission requires seven thousand men. Mark my words: this is a plot constructed by the Sultan and Tripoli to draw us into a fight, and if it's a fight they want, it's a fight they shall have! How many knights are there in this garrison?"

Des Moulins gave de Ridefort a shrewd look that incorporated, for the first time, a tinge of anxiety. "Not nearly enough for what you are thinking."

De Ridefort began pacing again. "Then we will have to find more. De Mailly, go and rouse the Templar garrison at Qaqun. I will gather the secular knights from Nazareth, and des Moulins—"

"Will not aid you in this madness!" des Moulins roared, his patience spent at last. He looked like death incarnate. "You are talking about a hundred knights, two hundred at most, against seven thousand! You may have cowed the king, but you do not command me, and I will not order my men to certain death!"

"Of course you will not," de Ridefort answered with soft cruelty, "because you are a simpering cowardly fornicator, far more concerned with satisfying your damnable lusts than meting God's justice."

De Mailly caught des Moulins's arm before he could throw the punch he had aimed at de Ridefort's face. "Stop it!" he cried. "We will gain nothing by fighting among ourselves, certainly not God's favor. Now, Messire," he addressed de Ridefort, "the count has shown his loyalty to us by his letter of warning. For the good of the kingdom, let us not respond to his gesture with an insult."

"The only insult here is Tripoli's," de Ridefort replied. "Des Moulins may do as he likes, but I order you, de Mailly, to go now and rouse the garrison, or I shall have you tried before your brethren as a traitor to God!"

De Mailly looked at his master for a long moment, his face cold with fury. The very rarity of the expression made it far more terrible than de Ridefort's foulest rage. "Very well, Messire," he said at last. "But tomorrow when you call the charge, remember that you and you alone have ruined us."

"I ask no more of my knights than I am willing to risk myself," he protested. "I will fight by you tomorrow, and die by you, if God wills it . . ."

But de Mailly was already shaking his head. "Tomorrow *I* will die in battle as a brave man should," he said, "but you, Messire, will flee like a traitor." And as he turned to leave, for the first time in many years, de Ridefort felt the spectral chill of doubt.

Three

❧

"**WHAT** do you mean, you are not going?" Salim cried, trembling with indignation. "It is an insult to your men and to our father!"

From the pile of pillows on which he reclined, his brother Al-Afdhal shrugged and drew on the mouthpiece of his hookah. He offered it to Salim, who waved it away with a look of disgust. "Ah, Salim," he said, letting out a gust of acrid, resinous smoke, "you take yourself far too seriously."

"And so I should be like you, and take nothing seriously at all?"

Al-Afdhal only laughed.

Salim looked closely at his brother. True, Al-Afdhal was intoxicated, but even so, Salim would have expected to see some vestige of irritation at the blatant insult. Yet he saw nothing in his brother's face but a heavy-lidded smugness. All at once, he was worried.

"And what is it that you know, Al-Afdhal, that I do not?"

"If I'd meant for you to have the answer to that," his brother said, "then you would not be asking." And he smiled, as if his words had somehow shown great wit.

Salim studied him for a moment longer, then said, "You have been talking to Gerard de Ridefort." Though this was no more than a guess, he spoke it with conviction, and his gamble paid off. His brother's face drained suddenly of color, and he sat up, hookah forgotten.

Gesturing to a servant to close the front of the pavilion, Al-Afdhal drew his brother down until they faced each other, then hissed, "Who has told you? Was it the Bedu boy?"

In fact, Bilal had spoken to Salim quite recently about his fears that de Ridefort would attempt to double-cross the Sultan in his absence. But Salim kept his face blank and said, "What would Bilal know about the Templar Master?" He shook his head. "What I know, Brother, I have taken the trouble to learn for myself. Do not forget that I have been privy to all of our father's negotiations in the south."

Al-Afdhal gave him a narrow-eyed look and said, "That does not mean that you will be privy to mine."

"Very well," Salim answered. "But I cannot in good conscience allow our father's men to ride to Tiberias tomorrow if I suspect that they are riding into a trap." He stood up. "So, if you'll excuse me, I shall go now and call the emirs—"

"Stop!" cried Al-Afdhal. Salim turned and regarded him coldly, though what he felt was cruel delight as he watched defeat and fury fight for purchase on his brother's face. At last Al-Afdhal said, "There is no need to say anything to the emirs. Quite likely it will all come to nothing anyway."

"What will?" Salim asked.

Al-Afdhal sighed. "All I know is this: an envoy from Jerusalem arrived in Al-Fulah today. Since then, the local Templars have been gathering at Nazareth."

"And de Ridefort was among the members of this envoy," Salim said, watching carefully for his brother's reaction.

"He was," he answered, with an odd, wistful note in his voice.

"Has he sent word to you?"

"No." Al-Afdhal sighed. "I do not even know whether he still has an agreement with our father. Do you?"

"If I'd meant for you to have the answer to that," Salim said, smiling coldly, "then you would not be asking."

"Watch your tongue, you little son of a whore. You aren't in the south anymore."

"No, I'm not; and if you'd ever known a whore's son, you'd know better than to threaten him."

Al-Afdhal frowned at him and took up his pipe again.

"Now, there cannot be more than a hundred knights in the local Franj garrisons," Salim continued. "If they are so foolish as to attack us, they will be crushed. Why then do you fear to join the mission?"

Al-Afdhal smoked in silence; he would not meet Salim's eyes.

"I suppose Al-Zahir and Al-Aziz will be going, and of course I will be there with my cavalry unit." He paused, then added, "It would certainly be a neat way of ensuring that nothing interferes with your succession, if all of us were to be so unlucky as to succumb to a Franj attack . . ."

"You insult me!" Al-Afdhal cried.

"No, Brother," Salim said. "You insult yourself and all of the men who follow you. For if this army cannot withstand an attack by a couple hundred Franj knights, then who but you would care to lead it?"

SALIM'S words did nothing to sway Al-Afdhal's decision, so the command of the detachment was given to the Turkish emir Gök-böri. Salim told him about the Franj muster at Nazareth, but in the end they agreed that it was pointless to tell the men. If the Franj attacked, the Sultan's men were well equipped to defend themselves. But if they were expecting something of the sort, they might be tempted into picking a fight with Tripoli's subjects, and that must be avoided at all costs.

Even so, by the time they rode beneath the walls of Tiberias, where the townspeople stood watching them in eerie silence, the tension was palpable. The Muslims moved slowly by virtue of their great number, and the fierce heat made the men irritable. But to their credit, their swords remained sheathed, and at last they reached the lake. After a brief stop to eat and to water their horses, they turned and retraced their path toward Ras al-Mai. Salim was beginning to believe that the mission would actually come off without incident when, in a sparse wood near a watering hole the

Franj called the Springs of Cresson, a band of knights appeared from nowhere, lances couched and mounts at full gallop.

De Ridefort had managed to gather almost four hundred infantry along with the hundred and forty knights supplied by the garrisons, but even so his army was no more than a fluttering scrap against the vast fabric of the Muslim force. Besides that, the suddenness of the charge left the foot soldiers stranded and the mounted ones vulnerable to a countercharge, which Gökböri ordered as soon as the few Franj knights who had not broken themselves against the Muslim defense turned to re-form their line. They didn't get the chance. Within minutes, the Muslim front line had surrounded them.

Back in the ranks, Bilal and Salim hung on to their battle-crazed horses, looking for something to fight. Seemingly from nowhere, a man in a white tunic with blood pouring from a wound in his neck reared up, raised his sword over his head, brought it down, and then fell dead at their feet. The blow had landed on Bilal's own sword arm halfway between elbow and wrist. His armor had kept the limb from being severed, but he knew immediately that something was very wrong. At first he felt only numbness, but when Salim pulled off his gauntlet, Bilal nearly fainted with the pain. The lower half of his arm flopped uselessly onto his thigh.

"It's broken," Salim said, tearing a piece of his tunic to make a sling, "probably both bones. You cannot stay here. Go back to camp; my father's physicians will tend to you. Tell Imad ad-Din what has happened, and have him write immediately to my father and tell him of our victory."

Victory? Bilal thought dumbly, his mind clouded by pain. Looking across the sea of heaving bodies that stretched and writhed to the horizon, he saw not a single red-crossed banner, and the meaning of what had just happened finally dawned on him.

"De Ridefort—" he began.

"I know. I will look for him."

"Do not let him escape!"

"You don't need to tell me. Now go."

"One other thing," Bilal managed to say, though he thought he was about to be sick. "There is a knight called de Mailly . . . the Marshal of the Temple. If you find him alive, spare him."

Salim gave him a puzzled look. "Why?"

Why indeed? Bilal wondered, but he was in no frame of mind for introspection. "Please," he said.

Still puzzled, and inclined now to think that the pain had addled Bilal's mind, Salim nodded. "I promise to spare him if it is in my power," he said, and because Bilal appeared to be considering another request, Salim slapped Anjum's flank with the flat of his sword, sending her streaking toward home.

But as he turned back to the battle—if that was a fair term for the uncontested slaughter unfolding before him—he knew he needn't have bothered with the promise. With seventy *mujahiddin* to every Franj knight, there could be none left to spare.

Four

✦

BILAL was dozing in the grasp of a draught of opium, dreaming of blood-soaked white tunics and slate-blue eyes, when a gust of cold air wakened him. He opened his eyes to a blurred image of Salim standing in the doorway with the tent flap in his hand, looking vaguely around as if he could not remember where he was. After a moment the prince drew a deep, shuddering breath, let it out, and came inside. He was caked in dust and dried blood, and his face looked defeated, years older than it had when they had parted.

Bilal was too stunned to do anything but stare at him as he dropped his sword and helmet in the corner, then took off his tunic with slow, dreamlike movements and held it up, studying the rents and bloodstains before dropping it, too. It drifted to the ground like a shot bird. After that he tore at his clothing, hurling bits of armor and cloth into an indiscriminate pile until he stood naked and shivering. Then he gathered it all into his arms and threw it out into the night. At last he saw Bilal watching and approached him, the night lamp revealing stark tear tracks in the dirt on his face.

"How is your arm?" he asked, so ponderously that Bilal thought the impression must be a result of his own drugged state.

"You were right," he answered. "Both bones are broken, but the physician said they were clean breaks, and they should heal well. Though the setting of them was no pleasure . . ."

"I'm sorry," Salim said in the same strange, detached tone.

"It was not your doing."

"I should have seen it coming."

"And so should I. Now don't tell me that's why you have been crying."

"No," Salim answered softly.

"You cannot have lost the battle, so what is the matter?"

Salim looked at him for a long moment, his lips open but not quite forming the words, and all at once Bilal knew what was coming. "I killed him, Bilal. I killed Jakelin de Mailly."

Bilal drew a deep breath and released it. "Then I am sure that you had no choice," he said.

"Oh, but I did," Salim answered miserably, his voice brave and brittle at once. "He was not even fighting me. Ah, Bilal—I do not know the words for it!"

"Begin at the beginning," said Bilal gently, "and you will find them."

Salim sat on the bed by Bilal, wrapped his arms around himself, and began: "When you left, it was already over. The Franj who hadn't died in the first charge were dying by then, or else they'd surrendered; all except one."

"Him," Bilal said.

Salim nodded. "You did not tell me that he was so beautiful, Bilal. Like those Persian paintings of angels . . ." Salim's look had retreated with memory, and at last Bilal felt the beginnings of grief. "When I saw him, he was trying to fight three men at once, and he was almost spent. He had to have known that his fellows were dead or captured, but he fought as if he had an army of thousands at his back. I told them to stop—those who were fighting him, and the others who were taunting him. They obeyed me, and he swayed there, leaning on his sword, but he nodded to me like the well-bred Franj do. I asked him his name, and he said that it was Jakelin de Mailly." Salim paused, then repeated, "Jakelin de Mailly. Our language flowed from his tongue like water, Bilal—not like the other Franj, who sound as though they've drunk too much wine. I told him that I was taking him prisoner, and he told me that he would rather keep fighting. I answered that he would certainly die if he did not let me help him, and he thanked me, but declined. He did not fear death, he said. The only thing he feared was breaking his vow to God.

"I thought that he was mad, and I told the men to take him prisoner. But he raised his sword when they came near, and so it began again. That was when I realized that he wasn't mad at all. He was, perhaps, the sanest man I've met in all this mad land, because . . ." He paused, his jaw working and eyes filling again. "Bilal, he didn't want to do it! He didn't want to fight us, and he didn't want to die, but he believed that God required it of him and so he did it anyway. He trusted his God beyond even his own heart, and how can a man who believes like that be an infidel? How can he deserve anything but our respect?"

Bilal offered no answer; he had none. After a moment Salim shook his head, casting tears that sparked for a moment in the light before expiring. "I could not bear to watch it. The men were taunting him again, making a game of his death. I saw how they would draw it out, I knew that I would not be able to stop them, and I could not bear it. So I killed him. I cut straight through his helmet when his back was turned to me. I wanted to give him deliverance, but the moment I struck that blow I knew that I had cheated him, for I was not God, nor any better than a heathen to him, and worst of all I had broken my promise to you." At last he capitulated to the tears.

"Come to me, Salim," Bilal said, and he came, curling up beside him and weeping into his lap like a frightened child. Bilal pulled the blanket over him and said, "It will be all right."

"No," Salim answered, his voice full of despair. "Nothing will ever be all right again."

And Bilal could think of no answer to that, because he knew that Salim might very well be right.

Five

Qaf
Early May

WHEN Khalidah awakened, she lay for a few moments without opening her eyes, praying that she wasn't dreaming. She couldn't remember the last time she had awakened to anything but freezing wind and hunger, shivering despite her woolens and Sulayman's body beside her. Rather than receding, however, the warmth and stillness became more apparent as her consciousness increased. At last she opened her eyes, and found herself looking into a girl's face, less than an arm's distance away.

She was about Khalidah's age, but tiny, with a bird's paradoxical look of fragile strength, a round face with a pointed chin, and wide green eyes flecked with gold. Her skin was fairer than Khalidah's, her hair black and tightly plaited in four sections, one looped around her head in a coronet and the other three hanging free to her waist. She wore clothing like what Brekhna had worn in Khalidah's dreams: a long, creamy woolen robe and loose trousers caught in at the waist with a deep red sash, the hems and collar covered in bright, intricate embroidery. There was a gold stud in her nose and delicate patterns inked on her forehead and cheeks—curving, vinelike patterns quite different from the angled henna designs of the west.

When she saw that Khalidah was awake, the girl smiled and said something unintelligible.

Khalidah started up, clutching the blankets around her. "I don't understand."

The girl spoke again, this time in oddly accented Arabic. "I am sorry. They told me that you spoke Pashto."

"Pashto? Where am I? And who are you?"

"My name is Abi Gul," the girl said patiently, "and you are in Qaf. Specifically, in one of the girls' dormitories at the hermitage."

At last, the memories began to creep back. Khalidah looked around her. The bed on which she lay was really no more than a pile of quilts on the floor, much like her bed at home had been. Rows of similar beds stretched along the walls of the room. There were small windows at the roofline, a fire circle full of glowing embers in the center, and little else.

"Is this your bed, in which I have slept?" she asked at last.

"No," Abi Gul answered, "it is yours. It has been ready and awaiting your arrival these last months, Bibi Khalidah—ever since Tor Gul Khan told us that you would come."

"Bibi?"

" 'Lady.' Because you are the khan's granddaughter."

Khalidah sat trying to digest all of this, to make it fit with the little she remembered of the last few days. "How long have I been here?" she asked at last.

"Two nights and a day."

"And I have slept all that time?" she cried, dismayed.

"You were given a draught," Abi Gul said, "on the first night. Tor Gul Khan thought it was for the best. You had a vision; you were distraught."

Khalidah shuddered, remembering the bloody field, the single Franj knight fighting for his life, and the beautiful Muslim boy who had delivered him. "Where is Sulayman?" she asked.

Abi Gul's eyes twinkled; she appeared to be suppressing a smile. "Do not worry—your man is safe."

"*My* man?"

"Do you know," she continued, leaning in confidentially, although they were quite alone, "Zhalai had to drag him out of here last night."

"Zhalai?"

"Our house mother. You spent the first night in Tor Gul Khan's rooms, and then they moved you here. Of course, only women are allowed inside, but Sulayman barged right in, saying that he would not leave you." A bright peal of laughter. "Oh, you should have seen it! He and Zhalai facing off in the middle of the room, and all the girls shrieking and screaming because there was a man in our dormitory." Khalidah marveled that she had slept through it all. "Anyway, Zhalai tossed him out at last, and he's sat outside ever since, never sleeping a wink . . . honestly, I've never seen a man so smitten—wait! You cannot go out like that; you aren't properly dressed!"

Indeed, Khalidah found when she stood that she was wearing nothing but a linen shift. However, she had long since gone beyond modesty where Sulayman was concerned. She flung the door open, and there, against a backdrop of towering peaks and lush grass, his face wan and eyes bloodshot with exhaustion, was Sulayman.

"Khalidah!" he cried as she flung herself into his arms, and they embraced as though they had been parted for years rather than days. He pushed her away after a moment to look at her. "Are you all right? Tor Gul Khan gave you something after that nightmare; he said it would help you sleep, but I did not think he meant an entire day and night through. If I did not trust him so well—"

"Honestly!" cried Abi Gul, who had caught up with them. She stood with her hands on her hips, like an irate nursemaid with recalcitrant children. "Zhalai would have my hide if she knew I'd let you out half dressed! Please, Bibi Khalidah, come back inside and put on some proper clothing before somebody sees you!"

Khalidah looked at Sulayman. "Don't worry," he said. "I won't go anywhere."

Abi Gul shook her head. "Smitten," she pronounced emphatically, though her look was rather wistful. Then she guided Khalidah firmly back into the dormitory.

***

HALF an hour later, Khalidah was dressed in a robe and trousers much like Abi Gul's, a sapphire-blue sash, and soft leather sandals to replace her shoes, which were falling to pieces. Abi Gul combed out her dirty, tangled hair, commenting grimly that there was not time to wash it, then plaited and bound it like her own.

"There," she said when she was finished, and held a small piece of polished metal for Khalidah to look into. Khalidah hardly recognized herself. Her cheeks had hollowed over the course of the journey, lengthening her face, but the change was deeper than that. She couldn't put a finger on it, other than to recognize Brekhna in it. But because Abi Gul was waiting for her verdict, she nodded approval.

Abi Gul smiled. "Let us go, then." She led Khalidah back outside to Sulayman, who was waiting where they had left him.

He blinked in surprise at Khalidah's appearance, and then smiled. "It suits you," he said.

"Tor Gul Khan says that you are free to look around today," Abi Gul told them. "At sundown, the Psarlay festival begins."

"Psarlay?" Khalidah asked.

"What is the word . . . 'spring.' We have a festival to mark each season," she said, "but Psarlay is the most fun. Sulayman can tell you."

Khalidah bridled at the complicity in her tone and shot Sulayman a look.

"My time here last year overlapped Psarlay," he explained.

Abi Gul nodded. "Now, I must leave you. If you need anything, ask anyone—they will all be glad to help."

Khalidah wondered if this was indeed true, or if Abi Gul was merely being polite; surely their feelings for Brekhna's daughter would be mixed at best. But she thanked her, and Abi Gul smiled, dipped her head again, and then left them.

"You're tired, Sulayman," Khalidah said when she was gone. "And I'm quite capable of showing myself around."

He smiled, touched her hand. "I want to come with you."

"Very well."

"If you'd rather I didn't . . ."

"I'm trying to be kind! Haven't you learned yet that I don't lie to appease?"

He laughed. "It seems I haven't, though you've certainly given me ample opportunity. What first?"

"I want to see Zahirah."

Sulayman sighed. "Why did I even ask?"

As they walked down toward the river, Khalidah took in her surroundings for the first time. It was just as she had glimpsed in her long-ago dream: snow peaks shot the distance with shimmering brilliance, and in the foreground the valley's circumscribing foothills were green with grass and trees. There were tilled fields on the valley floor, and some of the hills had been terraced for crops. All were hazed with the soft green of new growth and dotted here and there with people working among them. Orchards of fruit and nut trees extended in orderly rows on the far side of the river, which flowed across the valley floor in its wide, golden bed, ripples glinting in the morning sun. On the near side, a small herd of horses grazed among goats and fat-tailed sheep.

Zahirah broke from the group as soon as she spotted them, galloping toward her mistress with the occasional skip and bunny-hop, as if she'd already forgotten the vast distance they had traveled to reach this horse's paradise. Khalidah kissed her grass-stained nose and then ran a hand along her flank to her bandaged leg. Somebody had taken a good deal of care over her: her coat shone like a new coin, and the bandage was clean. There was no heat or swelling in the leg.

"You needn't worry," said Sulayman, patting Aasifa and Ghassan's gray pony, which had trotted up behind their friend. "The Jinn love their horses at least as much as you love yours."

"Have they been at this grass since we arrived?" Khalidah asked, ignoring him. "They will get colic . . . founder too, if they keep eating like this."

"Don't worry," Sulayman repeated. "They let the horses graze here for a few hours in the morning and then they move them higher up into the hills, where the grass is not so rich."

Satisfied at last that her horse was being properly cared for, Khalidah began to examine the others. Like her tribe's horses, they were mainly solid-colored, with occasional splashes of white on their faces or legs. Their coats were in good condition, though many of them were marked with battle scars. They had wide, deep chests and strong legs, prominent withers, and lean bodies, with the kind of square, well-muscled backs that made it easy to ride without a saddle. Their heads and necks were heavier than Bedu horses', without the distinctive dished profile, but they had similarly large, liquid eyes with a kindly look. This was borne out as Khalidah walked among them, for they nuzzled and whickered to her and didn't protest when she felt their legs and picked up their feet. They wore no irons, and the walls of their hooves were thicker even than those of the desert horses. Khalidah found this strange, given the valley's soft, grassy footing.

"They breed them that way," Sulayman explained when she commented on it, "crossing in the best of the local mountain ponies, which have the hardest feet I've ever seen—for as soon as they leave Qaf, they need them."

"There's more than mountain pony in these," Khalidah said, admiring a particularly fine honey-colored mare. She blew gently into the horse's nostril, and the mare flicked her ears forward, snuffling curiously, then sprinted away, showing off a liquid gallop. The others ran after her, wheeling across the valley floor like the wing of a great, mottled bird.

"Many of the tribes of these mountains claim descent from Alexander the Great," Sulayman said. "Well, the Jinn turn their noses up at the idea of a bloodthirsty Macedonian ancestor, but they insist that their horses bear the blood of Alexander's famous stallion, Bucephalus. Of course, they also claim that the breed was founded on a god's mount."

"Perhaps they are right on both counts," Khalidah answered, "for I've never seen horses quite like these."

They continued on a slow circuit of the valley, during which Khalidah gained an impression of the Jinn as happy, industrious farmers and herdsmen—an impression that increasingly troubled her. Leaving a group of women who had shown her their weaving—

a fine, light silken cloth that, inexplicably, they informed her was to be used for underwear—Khalidah said, "These people do not strike me as fearsome warriors, Sulayman."

"I suppose that is because most of the time, they are not," he answered. "But hand any one of them a bow or a spear"—he gestured to the gossiping women—"put her in front of an enemy, and he would be felled within seconds." Khalidah looked doubtfully at the silk weavers and Sulayman said, "Let me show you something."

He strode off along the valley, away from the temple and hermitage, passing the herds, the fields of turned earth, and the hillsides tumbling with stone and wooden dwellings. When they passed the last of these he led her up a grassy bank. From the top, Khalidah found herself looking down into a wide natural arena, perhaps a *farsakh* long and wide, where forty or fifty horsemen were practicing cavalry maneuvers. Or so she assumed, for they rode and bore arms, yet their methods were unlike anything she had seen before.

The group was split into squadrons ranged loosely across the field. At some indiscernible cue, the rear ranks would spur their horses, which broke from standing into a strange, quick gait, their legs moving laterally in two beats rather than the four beats of a gallop. The smoothness of the gait allowed the riders great precision with their arrows, and they timed the volleys such that one horseman was firing as his neighbor was nocking the bow, making the barrage continuous. When they were within yards of the straw army, the archers split and veered off to the sides, riding parallel to the enemy front line, still firing continuously. As they reached its edges, they veered again to encircle the enemy from behind, and simultaneously the two front ranks charged, changing bows for swords as they met the straw soldiers. Then they re-formed their lines to do it all over again.

"They are very good," Khalidah ventured at last. "Especially with the bow."

"It is probably their greatest skill."

And then something else occurred to her, a discrepancy that

had been niggling all the time she watched the maneuvers. A Bedu raid was underscored by war cries and ululation, prayers and consignments to Allah, but aside from the thumping of their horses' hooves and the whistle of their arrows, the Jinn riders made no sound. Nor were there any apparent visual signals.

"How are they organizing these maneuvers?" she asked.

"By impeccable training and discipline, and their trust in and knowledge of each other."

Khalidah watched a small figure on a steel-gray stallion fire a spurt of arrows at the straw men, then wheel away with the grace of a bird in flight.

"What would a band of Templars do, faced with fighting men like these?"

"Die of shock, most likely," Sulayman answered. His eyes were laughing at her.

She glared at him, baffled.

"Those are no fighting men, Khalidah," he said. "They are mere apprentices. Not one of them is older than sixteen, and every one of them is female."

As if to prove his point, the archer on the gray stallion pulled off her helmet, releasing waist-length black plaits. Abi Gul turned her grinning face up to Khalidah and waved.

Six

"ALL right, Sulayman," Khalidah said as they walked back toward the hermitage late in the afternoon, "you've made your point. But I am lost as to the ultimate purpose of all of this. Qaf is virtually impossible to access, so why the need for an elite army?"

"That is equivalent to asking why the Jinn exist at all."

"You promised me an explanation when we got here," Khalidah reminded him, "and though this day has been nothing if not interesting, I have no better idea of who these people are or what they want with me than I did when we left Wadi Tawil."

"You will tonight."

"Stop being cryptic!"

"I'm not being cryptic. One night of a Jinn festival will tell you more about them than I ever could. You should give them the chance to explain themselves to you in their own way."

Before Khalidah could reply, someone called her name. She turned and saw a group of girls approaching, led by a sweaty, beaming Abi Gul. Their white robes were mud-spattered and the patterns on their faces smudged. All of them carried padded leather armor and metal helmets. They had bows slung over their shoulders and short swords tucked into their sashes. Having witnessed the girls' skill, Khalidah felt shy in their presence, but they looked equally intimidated by her. Only Abi Gul appeared unperturbed.

"You were watching us," she said. "What did you think?"

"I was humbled," Khalidah said. "You put my father's raiders to shame."

The girls looked at each other, blushed, and giggled. There were four of them besides Abi Gul, and she introduced them in a blur of names. Ambrenn was tall and auburn-haired; Hila small, sturdy, with brown hair and dark skin; Afshan rosy and laughing, with fugitive black ringlets escaping her plaits; and Shahascina an unparalleled beauty, with hair as astonishingly yellow as a Franji's. Though the shades varied, every one of them had golden eyes.

"Come with us," said Abi Gul, taking her hand. "It is time to get ready."

"Sulayman?" Khalidah said, suddenly panicked at the thought of surrendering to this group of girls. She had had no female friends among her father's tribe, and after their long months of solitary travel, she couldn't imagine being without him.

"Go with them now," he said. "I will not be far away." He turned before he noticed the looks the girls exchanged, but Khalidah saw them. She turned her own eyes away, mortified.

"Ah, come now," Abi Gul said when she noticed her charge's embarrassment, pulling her firmly toward the dormitory. "Who would not envy you such words, from such a man?" Another peal of giggles.

"You don't understand—" Khalidah began, but seeing Abi Gul's raised eyebrows, she abandoned the denial. After all, what they assumed was likely very near the truth.

Sighing, she followed them into the dormitory, which was heaving with girls ranging roughly in age from twelve to sixteen. Khalidah had counted twenty-five beds that morning, but there had been twice that number on the practice field.

"Where are the others?" she asked Abi Gul, who was hanging her gear in an alcove by the door.

"This is not the only dormitory," she answered, wiping her sword carefully before she sheathed it and hung it with the others, between two long pegs extending from the wall. Khalidah caught a glimpse of her own sword standing in a corner beside her saddle, bags, and travel clothing. All had been cleaned. *By whom?* she wondered. *Was it a chore or an honor?*

"There are four in all," said Abi Gul, "two for the girls, two for the boys. We live with our families until we are twelve, and then we move here." Khalidah followed her to one of the beds, where Abi Gul began to undress. "For four years we live with the other apprentices and do nothing but train. It's the only time in our lives when we do not help with the crops or the herds or anything else."

She tossed aside a long garment of finely woven silk—the underwear, apparently, for which the women had been weaving cloth earlier—and then stood stark naked, to Khalidah's mortification, her finger to her lips as if she were trying to recall what to do next. At last she reached for a woolen robe and tied it around her body with her sash.

"When we turn sixteen," Abi Gul concluded, "we are sent on our first battle. If we fight honorably, and if we return, then we are Jinn."

"What are you until then?" Khalidah asked.

Abi Gul shrugged. "Children."

Khalidah considered this. Though her unmarried state had put her somewhat in limbo, she had been a woman in the eyes of her tribe since she started bleeding at age twelve. When she had left with Sulayman, many of her peers already had two children; if she had been a boy, she would have been a seasoned warrior by now. She tried to imagine what it would be like to live all one's life in a single setting, and to leave it the first time to go to war. She wondered what kind of courage it would take to forsake Qaf for a world one had only glimpsed from an arrow sight. How common were Sandaras or Brekhnas?

"Look, you are still dressed!" Abi Gul cried. She reached for another robe, which hung on a peg by the neighboring bed: her own, Khalidah realized. "Come, or there won't be time to wash your hair."

Looking around, Khalidah saw that the dormitory was nearly deserted. She stripped quickly, wrapped herself in her robe, and joined the exodus. The girls streamed down the hill toward a large wooden building on the banks of the river, with smoke rising from a hole in its roof. Inside, it was filled with steam and chattering girls. Their robes hung from pegs near the entrance, and they shrieked and giggled as they washed themselves or each other's hair. The water, apparently redirected from the river, ran in a trough down the length of the building, and then out again through an opening at the other side. Older women, dressed in shifts, warmed water in massive kettles over a fire at the center, ladling it into the bowls and pitchers the girls brought them.

Khalidah had never bathed with anyone but Zaynab, and she was mortified at the thought, but Abi Gul seemed to understand this, and led her to a quiet corner where Ambrenn and Hila were sharing a bowl of hot water. "I'll get more," said Abi Gul, and left Khalidah with them.

Hila smiled kindly at her, and Ambrenn nodded. Khalidah could not decide whether the latter was haughty or shy, but thought it best to give her the benefit of the doubt. She smiled, and hesitantly, Ambrenn smiled back. Shy, she decided, and this knowledge gave her courage. She untied her robe and hung it by theirs. When she turned back, Ambrenn was proffering a chunk of soap.

"Wash in the cold," she said in Arabic less fluid and more heavily accented than Abi Gul's, "and rinse in the warm."

Khalidah accepted the soap and took it to the trough of running water. She could not remember the last time a bath had constituted more than a quick plunge in an icy river, and soap was a distant dream. She embraced the luxury wholeheartedly, scrubbing herself from head to toe, and was trying unsuccessfully to rinse her hair in the cold trough when Abi Gul joined her.

"Not like that," she said, and filled a pitcher partly from the bowl of hot water she had brought, mixing it with cold before she tipped it over Khalidah's head. She repeated the process until Khalidah's hair was rinsed, the soapy water running away through the slatted wooden boards of the floor.

By the time she was finished, Khalidah had grown less shy of her nakedness, and she listened with interest to Ambrenn and

Hila as she worked a comb through her tangled hair. They were speaking in Pashto, and as she listened, Khalidah felt a kind of déjà vu: not quite understanding, but like the memory of understanding. One or two words seemed to form the basis of the girls' conversation, and when Abi Gul returned, dripping and goose-pimpled from the cold-water trough, Khalidah asked her what they meant.

Abi Gul laughed. She said something to her friends in rapid Pashto, and Hila joined in her laughter as Ambrenn flushed red, and Khalidah wondered what terrible thing she had said.

"I told them that they should watch their mouths around you," Abi Gul told her, "you have a sharp ear for our tongue! *Aghundem* means 'to dress, to put on.' *Meerre* literally means 'warrior,' but in this case it also means 'husband.' My friends are talking about how to dress tonight to best attract a husband."

The other girls objected loudly to this. "She'll think we are featherheaded fools!" Hila cried.

"I have seen evidence that you are anything but," Khalidah answered.

Hila inclined her head, acknowledging the compliment, and continued, "It is true, we were discussing the dresses we will wear tonight. I doubt there is a girl here who is not discussing them—our mothers have spent the past month making them for us."

"Then it seems you would be ungrateful daughters not to boast," Khalidah said, thinking with a pang of the red silk dress Zaynab had made for her wedding. She wondered what had happened to it, and then made herself stop, for to wonder that was to open her heart to a stampede of painful speculation.

"As for attracting husbands," Hila continued, "that is only half the story, as Abi Gul knows full well." She flicked water at her friend. "You see, it is during Psarlay that betrothals are made official. And although everybody pretends that the official betrothal is the first they have heard of an intended union, in reality everybody has known about it for months . . . or in Ambrenn's case, for years." She grinned, and poor Ambrenn blushed still more deeply.

"So, you are to be married?" Khalidah asked her gently, wondering whether congratulations or commiserations were in order.

Ambrenn looked up at her, and by the shining eyes above her flushed cheeks, Khalidah saw that it was the former. "After we both return from our first battle."

"Indeed, poor Ambrenn and Mirzal must eye each other chastely for a while longer," teased Hila.

"How do you know that they are chaste?" Abi Gul asked wickedly.

"Of course they are chaste!" Hila retorted. "Ambrenn is too well behaved to suggest anything else, and Mirzal too dreamy to think of it until she does." She and Abi Gul collapsed into laughter, and Ambrenn stood up, tied her robe on, and stalked away. The other girls sobered immediately.

"Ah, now we'll have to apologize," sighed Abi Gul. "Honestly, she should know that we tease her out of jealousy."

"Then neither of you is betrothed?" Khalidah ventured, hoping that she wasn't overstepping any boundaries by asking.

Abi Gul shook her head. "We are still 'free,' alas . . . though rumor has it Sarbaz means to speak for Shahascina this Psarlay. He has certainly mooned over her long enough, though she plays her cards close . . . we'll have to wait and see. Come now, let's catch Ambrenn before she works herself into a state." They tied their robes, collected their combs, and made their way back up the hill to the dormitory.

Though still crowded, the dormitory was more ordered than it had been when they left. Khalidah suspected that it was due to the presence of an older woman who was stoking the fire in the center of the room. She looked to be in her early twenties, tall and thin with gleaming blue-black plaits and skin like new milk. Abi Gul led Khalidah to the woman and introduced her.

"Zhalai, this is Bibi Khalidah; Bibi Khalidah, Zhalai, our mother."

Zhalai smiled, bowed to Khalidah, and, seeing her confusion, elaborated: "*Mother* being a relative term. I watch over the girls in this dormitory for the years that they live here, taking over where their mothers leave off. I am, therefore, an honorary mother to them all—and honored indeed that you have joined my house, Bibi Khalidah." She bowed again, and this time Khalidah reciprocated. "I trust that Abi Gul is taking good care of you?"

"The best," Khalidah said, smiling. "Thank you."

"Don't thank us," Zhalai said, her look suddenly sober. She drew breath as though she meant to add something, and then appeared to think better of it, but not before the unspoken thought had time to infect Khalidah with a seed of curiosity, and doubt. It was a look she had encountered many times that day among her mother's people. It was not comfortable to know that they expected something of her that they were afraid to ask for outright.

"You had best get ready," Zhalai said then, and turned back to her fire.

Khalidah wanted to ask Abi Gul what it all meant, but the other girl had launched into a chattering tirade, perhaps to preclude just such a question. ". . . dress is on your bed," she was saying when Khalidah tuned back in, "and when you have put it on I will help you with the rest."

Khalidah nodded vaguely, noticing another white woolen robe laid out on her bed, this one more finely woven and intricately embroidered than the last. As she put it on, she wondered who had made these things for her. They didn't look like hand-me-downs, and they fitted perfectly. But before she could think long about that new mystery, Abi Gul produced a comb and made Khalidah sit so that she could replait her hair. This time she wove strings of beads and cowry shells into the plaits, and when she finished she produced a shawl, deep blue and covered with embroidered horses.

"It is beautiful!" Khalidah exclaimed, running a hand over the minute stitches. "Who made it?"

For once, Abi Gul was silent, but by her heightened color and pleased embarrassment, Khalidah knew the answer. Moved, she said, "Thank you, Abi Gul . . . but please don't be offended if I ask you how you knew?"

"We have always known that you would come." She took up a pot of kohl and a brush and indicated to Khalidah to sit so that she could line her eyes. "Does it bother you to hear me say so?"

In fact, it was a bit like the Pashto words: unexpected, yet unsurprising. "How could it," Khalidah answered, "after everything else?"

"Tell me," Abi Gul said, pausing, brush in hand, "how did Sulayman ever persuade you to go with him?"

So Khalidah related the story of her short-lived engagement to her cousin, Sulayman's warning, and their subsequent flight. Abi Gul listened with a mixture of laughter and awe, and when Khalidah had finished, her only comment was, "Well, that's your Jinn blood showing." Then she put away her pot of kohl and brought out another pot and a brush so fine, it seemed to be made of only a few hairs.

"What is that?" Khalidah asked dubiously.

"It is ink made from . . . ah, I cannot remember the word . . . we call it *tut*."

"Mulberry," Khalidah said abruptly.

Abi Gul nodded, surprised. "Yes, mulberry—but how did you know?"

"I have been thinking about this since Sulayman told me that I spoke Pashto during that dream on my first night here. I think that my mother must have spoken it to me, and perhaps, long ago, I spoke it too. Understood it, at least. Now that I'm here, bits of it are coming back."

"That makes sense. Perhaps you will be able to speak it again before too long . . . well, anyway, this is ink made from mulberry, and we use it to paint the *harquus* on our faces. You have seen them on the women?" Khalidah nodded, and Abi Gul began painting something on her forehead, between her eyebrows. "When we return from our first battle," Abi Gul continued, "we are given permanent *harquus*—the mark of the Jinn. Until then, we paint them on."

"What about the men?" she asked.

"They get them too, but theirs are on their backs."

"Why?"

"Why not?"

Khalidah sat in silence, considering the day's many revelations until Abi Gul finished. She held the scrap of mirror for Khalidah's approval. She had painted a delicate, vine-patterned triangle on Khalidah's forehead, and tiny mandalas on both cheeks. To their equal surprise, Khalidah leaned forward and hugged her.

Seven

THE sun had sunk behind the mountains when Khalidah and Abi Gul emerged from the dormitory. The sky was bluish green, scattered with stars and a waning moon. A bonfire had been lit on the riverbank, surrounded by people dancing. She heard drums, a high-pitched flute, and some kind of stringed instrument, its voice louder and more brittle than an oud's, and underscored by a drone. When they reached the fringes of the dancers, the oudlike instrument suddenly picked up a melody, plaintive and beautiful.

"Where is that coming from?" Khalidah asked.

Abi Gul took one look at her rapturous face and rolled her eyes. Khalidah didn't understand until she followed her friend's pointing finger. Seated by the fire was a group of musicians. Sulayman sat at their center, holding a strange, long-necked oud. He played on and on through a series of serpentine variations. Abi Gul wandered away, but Khalidah stayed, fascinated by the music. When at last it ended, it was met by cheers of delight. Sulayman smiled, thanked the other musicians, and then handed the instrument to a woman in the circle of listeners.

"What was that instrument?" she asked Sulayman, when he joined her.

"A *setar*," he said. "I learned it on my last visit here."

"Will you ever run out of surprises?"

He smiled. "If I do, will you tire of me?"

"No," she answered dryly, "it is only then that you will cease to tire me."

He laughed and slipped an arm around her waist. She looked around anxiously, but no one seemed to have noticed. In fact, as she looked, she saw other couples similarly entwined.

"They see things differently here," Sulayman said, picking up on her apprehension. "Do not worry—your honor is quite intact among the Jinn." Khalidah nodded, though she still could not quite believe it. "Come, you must see the dancing."

They moved toward the outskirts of the crowd, where bodies spun and whirled in the darkness. The dancers formed a ring, the men and boys at the center, moving to the music with wild, individual abandon, while the women linked arms across each others' shoulders in small groups and moved together in slow, elegant lines around the periphery.

"What is this all about?" Khalidah asked.

"They are asking the gods and goddesses to bless the herds and crops during the growing season," said Abi Gul, who had returned with cups of wine.

"And who are your gods and goddesses?"

"Soon, someone will recite the creation story. I think it will explain most of what you are wondering."

Khalidah sighed, impatient, but then the girls dragged her into the dances, and she forgot her questions for a time. The night wore on, food and drink were served, and gradually the dancers retired, settling into a ring by the fire. The drums suddenly went silent. A figure emerged from the shadowy throngs and made his way to the center of the circle: Tor Gul Khan.

He wore a plain white robe and, on his head, in place of the other men's rolled woolen caps, a multicolored turban with the glint of golden threads. He had a face the color of tea with a splash of milk, ridged and valleyed with age, eyes as brilliantly golden as an eagle's, a fierce aquiline nose. He regarded them in silence for a moment, and then he cried something in Pashto, his voice rolling across the crowd like an ocean wave.

"What is he saying?" Khalidah asked Abi Gul.

"Hail to Khuday, the creator of all things!" she translated.

"Hail to His creation which sustains us, and to the deities who serve Him, who keep us by their grace! Hail to the consecrated Kings of Hewad, from whom our race descends!"

"Hewad?" Khalidah asked.

"Literally, 'homeland'; the place where our people originated."

The crowd was murmuring something in response to Tor Gul Khan's words, and when they finished, he turned in a slow circle, carefully examining the faces of his rapt spectators. They looked back expectantly, even hopefully. At last Tor Gul Khan's eyes came to rest on a young woman with golden hair—Abi Gul's friend, Shahascina. He nodded to her, and she beamed with pride. Amid the sudden buzz of whispers around her, she stood and approached the leader. Laying one hand on her shoulder, Tor Gul Khan addressed the people again.

"Shahascina is Khuday's voice tonight. Give her all the respect you give Him." With that, he retired into the shadows, and Shahascina knelt at the center of the circle. She looked around at the throngs of people, as had Tor Gul Khan, and with no less composure she began to speak:

"In the beginning, when Khuday formed the earth, He placed the great mountain at the center of the world. On the mountain's peak was the land of Hewad, where the lesser deities made their home. Half were to oversee the west, half the east of the world of men. But both wanted sovereignty over the earth, and so they fought, tearing each other to pieces.

"When the pieces fell to earth they became evil spirits that wreaked havoc on the land. They salted the fields and poisoned the waters, sent pestilence among the herds and plagues among the people. When Khuday saw what was happening, He was furious. He came down to Hewad and put Himself between the warring deities, of whom only twelve remained: six women of the east and six men of the west.

"'Your war ends now,' He said to them, 'and to seal the peace you will each take a spouse from your rivals. The first child born of these unions will be sent to earth to live as a man. He will be a great warrior, and he will deliver the people from the monsters you have created.'

"Within a year the child was born, and he said to his parents: 'I have been born to fight the enemies of men. Take me down the mountain to the valley and give me to the barren woman who lives there.' The child's parents took him to a stone hovel in the shadow of the mountain, with a rag for a door and a sheep's skeleton in the yard. A wizened woman sat on the sheep's skull, watching them. 'This is where you leave me,' said the child, and they had no choice but to leave him in that terrible place of their own making.

"The evil spirits knew that the child had been sent to drive them from the earth, and they thought to destroy him while he was still an infant and helpless. So they set perils upon him; but he met and vanquished each of them. The old woman realized the nature of the child she had been given, and she knew that she could not raise such a child in her barren valley. So she bound him to her back and walked until they came to a place where people still lived in comfort. She took a job in the kitchen of a wealthy family, and there her son grew to a young man.

"He was well built and handsome, and succeeded to such a degree in tests of strength and cleverness that people began to say: 'He is no ordinary man. A warrior of such strength and cleverness must have been sent by the gods!' And they begged him to fight the evil spirits which had plagued them for so long.

"Not knowing what to do, the young man climbed the mountain to Hewad and appealed to the deities. 'If I am truly of your blood,' he said, 'then show me some sign.' When he had spoken, he found at his feet a pool of water. When he looked into the pool he saw not his own face, but the fearsome face of a warrior. When he looked up again he found before him a coal-black warhorse, with hooves so hard they struck sparks from the stone and eyes that flashed like the fire that lives at the hearts of mountains. Lashed to its back were a suit of armor, a sword, and a bow. And so he became Mobarak Khan, our Sacred Leader.

"He said a prayer of thanks, then took up the armor and weapons, mounted the horse, and rode down toward the world he had pledged to deliver from evil. As the horse galloped down the mountain, the thundering of his hooves awakened boulders that became mounted warriors who followed Mobarak Khan until they were a hundred strong. And when they reached earth, men joined him too until he led an army of ten thousand. His army met the army of monsters and evil spirits in the shadow of the sacred mountain, and there they fought until the evil spirits fled. But their battle was so fierce that the mountain crumbled, destroying the stairway to Hewad.

"The people of earth were wild with joy and so they did not notice, but Mobarak Khan silenced them, saying, 'Evil is not vanquished, only driven back, and now your ladder to the gods is lost.'

"'But will you not defend us, should it rise again?' the people asked. And Mobarak Khan answered, 'I will fight for you, but I am a man now and I will not outlive my appointed time.' Then the people asked him to be their king. But he said, 'I am a warrior; for a king, look to your princes.' So they asked him what he would do instead, and Mobarak Khan said, 'I will go in search of a place I have seen in dreams. The mountains protect it, the sun smiles upon it, its soil is fertile and its water clean. It reminds me of Hewad, which is lost to us. My people shall live there in peace, but they shall be trained as warriors worthy of the gods from whom they are descended; and if ever the evil spirits rise again, you will find them at hand with their weapons, ready to serve you.'"

Shahascina looked up and around at her audience, as if surfacing from a dream. "And so Mobarak Khan left with his band of warriors and went in search of the valley of dreams. In good time he found it, and in good time he and his men married and had sons and daughters, who had sons and daughters in turn." Shahascina's voice had grown soft, reverent, and yet the silence of the listeners was so complete that it reached every one of them as distinctly as a cry. "And this is the story of Mobarak Khan, our sacred Father;

of Qaf, our home; and of us, the Jinn, the children of the fallen mountain. Forevermore, we uphold our Father's pledge."

"We uphold his pledge," murmured the Jinn. And Khalidah too found herself speaking the foreign words, with tears in her eyes.

Eight

PSARLAY lasted for a week and continued much as it had begun, with music and dancing and offerings to various gods, to enlist their help for the growing season. There were informal gatherings at which the elders recounted legends of Mobarak Khan's feats, along with those of more recent Jinn heroes. There was almost always music: quick-paced songs that spurred energetic dances and others, long and slow, elegies to former battles or lost loves.

Witnessing their devotion to their gods, Khalidah found it ever more difficult to dismiss the Jinn as heathens. On the last day of the festival, when the girls rose at dawn for their own ceremony, she joined them. They went down to the meadows where the horses grazed, filled baskets with wildflowers and long grasses, and then brought them up to the temple. It was the first time Khalidah had been inside it. She followed Abi Gul through the carved wooden doors and into the vast, echoing space lit by rows of high, narrow windows. The floor was covered with plush, knotted carpets like the Persians', rather than her tribe's flat-woven rugs. Many little altars were set against the walls, covered with wood carvings and tiny, flickering lamps.

The girls moved toward one of the larger altars. As they drew close, Khalidah saw that its carvings were of horses—thousands of individual figurines, spilling from the top of the altar onto the lamp-laden steps and the floor around it. Each was uniquely detailed, carved, and painted, apparently with great care. Some of them looked very old.

"When a warhorse dies, we carve his or her effigy and place it here," Abi Gul told Khalidah. "We honor them as we honor our dead warriors, because without them, we would not be warriors at all."

Khalidah sat down with the other girls. They took up handfuls of grass and flowers and began to plait them into wreaths. After watching for a moment, Khalidah began her own clumsy attempt. While they worked, the girls sang, and Khalidah recognized enough of the words to know that they were singing praises to their horses.

After a while, Abi Gul said to her, "You have an extraordinary voice."

Khalidah had not realized that she had been humming along.

"I have heard that Brekhna did, too," she continued. "You must sing something for us—one of your own tribe's songs."

"I don't think—" Khalidah began, but she was immediately drowned out by protests and urgings.

Sighing, she considered her options, and in the end she chose her own arrangement of Shánfara's "Ode in L." Her voice echoed strangely in the vast hall, taking on an ethereal quality. The girls kept working while she sang, and because they didn't focus on her, Khalidah relaxed. When the song ended the girls thanked her, and she was surprised and pleased to detect neither the discomfort nor the reverence with which she usually met when she performed. Rather, another girl began another song a few moments later. And so they worked on, until all of their grasses and flowers were woven. Then they laid them at the foot of the altar, saying something in Pashto as they did it.

Abi Gul repeated it in Arabic for Khalidah: "May your spirits guide your sons and daughters to glory."

Once they had laid their wreaths, the girls left the temple. "Will it bother anyone if I stay here for a little while?" Khalidah asked Abi Gul, when they had added theirs to the pile.

"Only Sulayman," she grinned.

When Abi Gul left, Khalidah knelt before the horse altar,

searching for the one she could not hope to find, for surely if Brekhna was an outcast then her horse was too. All at once a wizened, white-robed arm reached over her shoulder and plucked a bright chestnut from the ranks. The horse had been carved midtrot, head and tail high and proud. She turned and found herself looking up at Tor Gul Khan.

"Husay," he said, handing her the carving. "It means—"

" 'Falcon,' " she interrupted. "I . . . I remember him." For all at once, she did. She had ridden this horse, or rather she had ridden in a sling on her mother's back as her mother had ridden him, the wind whistling past her ears, drawing her delighted screams like a banner behind them.

Tor Gul Khan gave her a pensive smile. "No doubt, if you remember your mother at all. She loved that horse more than life. Besides, I'd be willing to bet your pretty mare bears some of his blood."

That was a thought stranger even than the memory. Tor Gul Khan knelt beside her, looking at the altar where the wooden horses seemed to leap and gallop in the flickering light. At last he said, "You have borne up well."

Khalidah shook her head. "There has been nothing to bear. Everyone has been very kind to me."

"As I would expect them to be. But I referred to your journey, not to the days you have spent in Qaf." Khalidah wondered how he knew the details of that journey. "Tell me," he said after a moment, with a glimmer of humor, "what do you think of our Abi Gul?"

Khalidah smiled. "She is kind. And she talks like the west wind."

Tor Gul Khan nodded, smiled back. "And yet, if you will believe it, her precision with an arrow is preternatural."

"I know. I saw her practicing."

"She will be one of our best warriors, one day," Tor Gul Khan said ruminatively, "if she does not fall prey to her beliefs."

Khalidah felt a chill of apprehension. "What do you mean?"

Tor Gul Khan scrutinized her as the wind scoured the stone

tower above them, swelled by the distant calls of animals, the far-off cry of a hawk, the beat of a drum, and the droning voice of the *setar*.

"Your mother was my heir," he said, "but that was only incidental to the fact that she was Mobarak Khan's. When Brekhna turned her back on the Jinn, not only the succession but the natural order of Qaf and its people were displaced."

"And you think that I am meant to restore it?"

"The truth, Khalidah," he said with weary sincerity, "is that I have no idea." His eyes were obstinate, unblinking, crowded with questions rather than answers. Before she could respond, he spoke again: "Do you know what a *betaan* is?"

Khalidah shook her head.

"He, or she, is a prophet. Not a prophet like Iesu the Christ or your Muhammad, upon whom a religion is founded, but something rather more mundane, more functional and yet indispensable—a kind of oracle and priest in one. A *betaan* speaks to spirits, who in turn speak to the deities, and so he is in that sense the voice of the gods."

Tor Gul Khan paused, perhaps guessing that she would need a moment to digest this. Then he continued: "Alipsha is our current *betaan*. He lives in the high pastures, where we graze our flocks in summer, to keep his mind pure. I go to him when I am in need of advice. More rarely, he comes to me with messages or warnings. For instance: on the eve of my marriage to your grandmother, he told me that I would have no son, and that after me Mobarak Khan's line would pass to a woman. Naturally, when Brekhna was born, I assumed that she would be this woman. But, you see, I had not listened carefully to Alipsha, as he pointed out when I went to him with my fury and accusations after Brekhna left us. A woman would succeed me, that was all that the spirits had told him, and all that he had told me. Neither they nor he had said anything about her being my daughter, or even of my blood at all."

Tor Gul Khan stopped abruptly, as though the words he needed to continue were too painful to speak.

"You called me here to find out if I am the one to succeed you?" Khalidah asked.

Her grandfather drew a deep breath, but rather than answer her question, he said, "You have heard the story of our origin and of Mobarak Khan's pledge, and you will understand from that, from your days here in Qaf, and from what Sulayman has no doubt told you about us that we devote ourselves to fighting evil and injustice whenever and wherever it shows itself. For we believe these things to be the progeny of the evil spirits that Mobarak Khan conquered. But there is an addendum to the story."

Another pause, coupled, it seemed, with some kind of internal bracing. Then he said: "In Mobarak Khan's time, there was a shepherd among the Jinn named Pamir. Some called him simple, but he was known for having visions that often came true. Today, he would most likely have become a *betaan*. At the time, the Jinn did not recognize any prophet but Mobarak Khan.

"Pamir was in the high pastures with his flocks when Mobarak Khan died, and yet three days after Mobarak Khan's death, on the morning when he was to be laid to rest, Pamir appeared at the gravesite. He showed no surprise to find the leader dead and lying in his coffin, but he *was* surprised at the grief of his people. 'Why do you carry on so?' he asked them. 'Mobarak Khan has not truly died, only left us for a time, like a shepherd gone to the summer pastures.'

"The people dismissed his words as a sign of his madness, but he told them that he had been visited in a dream by the spirit of Mobarak Khan, who had told him that the Jinn would prosper for many generations, winning the battles they were called to fight, making a good life in their valley when they were at peace. But one day, he said, the evil spirits he had scattered would band together again and form an army of great strength. They would come from the west, from over the sea, with swords raised to slaughter. The army of evil would roll across the lands of the east, the cities would drown in blood, and the people who survived would be slaves. But when that day came, Mobarak Khan would once again take human form, to lead the armies of men against the evil spirits."

Khalidah found herself clutching the model of Brekhna's horse so tightly that it hurt. She waited, barely breathing, for Tor Gul Khan to continue.

"Prophecy is seldom so specific as one would like," he said at last. "Mobarak Khan's spirit had told Pamir that he would be reborn to a tribe of local nobility but relative obscurity; that he would not be born a leader of men, but would have to prove himself as such. He would be a child of a new religion and a model of its virtues, while still fulfilling those of the old. But Pamir could not tell his people when this rebirth would come to pass, nor where, nor even whether Mobarak Khan would reincarnate as a man or a woman."

Khalidah drew a deep breath and then let it out. "Please do not tell me that you think I am Mobarak Khan."

Tor Gul Khan turned finally to look at his granddaughter. To her consternation, he smiled. "No, Khalidah, I do not." She felt an unexpected stab of disappointment at this. "I'm afraid that the implications of this story, and your part in it, are a good deal more complicated than that. Religion, as you of all people must be aware, is inherently divisive. Take Iesu: your people, the Jews, and the Christians all believe that he once walked the earth and delivered an important message. But depending on one's viewpoint, he is an outdated prophet, a heretic, or a god. To me, it seems madness to spill blood over the discrepancy, for at the core of it all, was he not a man who preached the sanctity of love and kindness? Yet to the people fighting for control of Jerusalem, it is the difference not only between life and death, but also between salvation and damnation.

"And then there is Islam itself. You all agree on Muhammad as its figurehead. Yet from the moment of his death you have been divided over a matter of succession, and blood pools in the divergence." He sighed again. "Well, our own religion is no different. Though it must seem primitive to you, hardly comparable to the ones you have known, if you scratch the surface you will find that it is at least as complex and contentious as Christianity or Islam. From the moment Pamir spoke his vision, the Jinn have been divided on whether the shepherd was an oracle or a madman spurred by grief at the death of a beloved leader. Some of us, therefore, believe that Mobarak Khan was a messiah, others that he was a man—helped by the gods, perhaps even bearing godly blood, but flesh and blood like you or me, subject to the finality of death.

"If Pamir's prophecy had been the end of it, the rift might have healed. The factions might have softened with the softening of grief. But unfortunately, that was not the end of it. You see, Khalidah, we do not burn nor bury our dead, but place them in wooden coffins in hillside cemeteries, open to the elements. We believe that this is the quickest way for the body to return to its source. But it also means that graves are occasionally attacked by animals or robbers. On the day after Mobarak Khan's burial, a group of women, led by his wife, went to lay bread on the grave—a custom of ours, food for the gods—and when they arrived, they found the coffin empty. The lid had been prized off, and no sign remained that anyone had ever lain there.

"There were plenty of mundane explanations, but of course, to those desperate to believe that he had not truly left us, it was a sign that Mobarak Khan's body had been taken by the gods, to be returned at that time of need Pamir had spoken of. From then on we have been divided by our beliefs. The division has at times been contentious, but we have managed to live with it. That is why the Khan is so important: his job is, first and foremost, to keep the peace.

"Of course, to do this he must remain neutral in the eyes of the tribe, no matter what his personal beliefs, and by luck or by wisdom this has always been possible."

"Until now?" Khalidah asked warily.

"Until now," he agreed. "For now the Franj have come from the west, across the sea with swords raised, drowning cities in blood and vanquishing the native tribes, and the Kurdish prince is raising an army against them."

"Your people think that the Franj are the evil spirits," Khalidah said slowly, "and Salah ad-Din the messiah." She looked closely at Tor Gul Khan. "But you do not."

"In every generation," he answered after a moment, apparently choosing his words with great care, "there are both an evil and an opponent who accepts its challenge. Sometimes it is on a small scale and resolves in little battles whose villains and heroes are quickly forgotten. But sometimes the hero infects others with his zeal, capturing a broader imagination, as when Musa led his people out of slavery in Egypt or when Iesu took on the might of Rome. As a man committed to fighting evil, I can honor these men's ideals and the sacrifices that others make to them. But as a leader I must protect the future of my people, and just now my people are as vulnerable as they have ever been. They know that I am growing old, with no heir in line to replace me; and they know why."

At last, she understood. "Brekhna believed it," Khalidah said wonderingly. "My mother left here to fight the Franj because she believed Salah ad-Din was the messiah."

Tor Gul Khan stiffened, and Khalidah knew that she had hit on a painful truth. Yet when he answered, his voice wasn't angry, only weary and terribly sad. "She met him, you see. It was long ago, before he was Sultan. They fought together against some petty tribe or another, and unlikely as it might seem, they took to each other. He infected her with his ideas about ousting the Franj—and with the fear of what might happen if he couldn't. He asked her to bring the Jinn back to help him when it was time. She came back to Qaf full of fire and asked me to let her lead the believers west."

"And you said no," Khalidah guessed.

Tor Gul Khan's look was one of abject despair. "How could I do otherwise? You are young, Khalidah, like Brekhna was when she first heard of the Franj. I know that they must seem to you the epitome of evil, and indeed, they have wreaked havoc the like of which the lands of Islam have never known. But an army of evil spirits that threaten the world as we know it?" He shook his head. "I have fought evil in many forms, and I tell you, though the Franj are brutal, they are no more brutal than any other power-hungry tribe. More than that, I do not believe they have the strength or the inclination to expand to the east."

"But they could," Khalidah answered. "If they believed their God demanded it of them, they would march from Jerusalem to Qaf as mercilessly as they marched from their homeland to Jerusalem one hundred years ago."

"That was Brekhna's argument," he said, "and it is the argument I fear will be the end of us."

"Why?"

"Because although some of the Jinn revile Brekhna for abandoning us, many more revere her."

"For what?" Her tone was bitter. "Running away and marrying an outsider? Then abandoning him and her only child?"

"They do not see it as you or I do," he said gently. Khalidah saw in his eyes the desire to comfort her and to be comforted. She wished she knew how to accept it. "All legends are the same at their heart: they are built on a few twigs of fact and a good deal of wish and hope. Those of my people who believe that Mobarak Khan was a supernatural being think that Brekhna was called by him, and followed that call."

"So I will tell them that it is not true. That she married an ordinary man and lived an ordinary life."

"It will not matter, any more than the disappearance of Mobarak Khan's body mattered to those who wanted to believe him immortal."

"Which is all well and good, except that nobody knows where she is . . . unless you do?"

He shook his head. "If she is still alive, Brekhna is beyond reach, and certainly beyond helping us."

Sighing, she said, "Where do I come into it?"

"You," he sighed, "are the answer to the prayers of those faithful to Pamir's prophecy. As Brekhna's daughter, you are the obvious choice to lead them to their messiah and their holy war."

"But it would divide the tribe. You cannot want that."

"You're right. I don't."

"Then why in the name of Allah did you send Sulayman to bring me here?"

Tor Gul Khan did not answer, only looked at her, his eyes no longer those of a proud leader but of a feeble old man. Khalidah saw the answer in them and was torn between pity and rage.

"You hoped that I would tell them that Salah ad-Din is not what they think he is," she said. "You want to use me to keep them here."

"I would never use you," he said vehemently, "nor ask you to lie. If you truly believe that the Jinn's place is with Salah ad-Din, then I will not stop you telling them so."

"I do not dictate the actions of others."

He gave her a level look. "Tell me: do you intend to fight for Salah ad-Din?"

"He is not in the habit of taking women into his army. But even if I were to manage it, it does not translate into a suggestion that your people follow me."

"A leader inspires others' actions by his or her own."

"I am not the Jinn's leader!"

"That is not your choice, but theirs," Tor Gul Khan answered with infuriating calm. "Therefore, before you act, be certain that you have chosen the right course."

"How?" Khalidah snapped.

"Live with us for a few weeks. Understand the people whom you would lead. Decide for yourself whether jihad is the answer they seek."

Khalidah considered this. She was little inclined to do anything for Tor Gul Khan, but she could not forget Abi Gul's open-armed friendship, nor the kindness shown her by all of the Jinn over the past week. That, at least, had been sincere. She sighed. "Three weeks. No longer."

Nine

OVER the next few days Khalidah had a good deal of time to consider her discussion with her grandfather and to wonder whether her promise had been folly, for as he had predicted, Psarlay was hardly finished before the questions began. It was the unquenchable Abi Gul who sent out the first tentative feelers, asking Khalidah, as they groomed their horses, whether she had ever met Salah ad-Din.

"I would be lucky if Salah ad-Din allowed me to serve in his kitchen," Khalidah answered warily.

This clearly surprised Abi Gul. "I can see that he might not recognize your Jinn ancestry, but you are still the daughter of an Arab king."

"Hardly," said Khalidah, picking stones ruminatively from Zahirah's hooves. "I'm the daughter of the sheikh of a Bedu tribe. The Bedu may be useful to the landed nobility when it comes to war with a common enemy, but they have little time for us otherwise and still less respect. To them we are little better than your hill bandits." She sat back on her heels, looking at the river. "Though perhaps that is not entirely fair to the Sultan. I have heard that he takes a rather more generous view of us than others of his class."

"And will your people fight for him against the invaders?"

"My father wanted to, but his brother, who controls the other branch of our tribe, was against it. My leaving might have made it impossible for my father to follow his own wishes."

Abi Gul seemed to know better than to press her on this, but the possibilities opened up in Khalidah's mind anyway, each more grim than the last: Abd al-Aziz drawn once again into war with his brother, sacrificed to Numair's greed, victim of a treacherous knife in the back; the tribe scattered or subjugated; Bilal a martyr and Zaynab a slave.

"I hope that he has gone to Salah ad-Din," she said at last. "I pray for it every day."

Abi Gul worked silently for a time, and then she said, "Do you believe that your creator—that is, your Allah—has sent Salah ad-Din to drive out the invaders?"

"I know that the Sultan believes it," she said carefully, "and that his belief infects others, so that perhaps in the end it comes to the same thing: by believing in him, they will believe in themselves enough to ensure his success."

Abi Gul had forgotten her work and her horse wandered away. "We have a story," she said, inevitably, "a prophecy—"

"I know," Khalidah interrupted gently. "Tor Gul Khan told me. Perhaps the Franj are your army of evil spirits, perhaps Salah ad-Din is your messiah . . . but 'perhaps' is the best I can do. For all I know, the Sultan has already fought the Franj and lost."

"He has not," Abi Gul answered with surprising conviction. "Our *betaan* has seen him, and though the time is drawing near, the Sultan has not yet made his move."

This was the last thing Khalidah had expected to hear, and she took a moment to consider it before she answered. "Very well," she said at last, "but you must consider what it would be like if the Jinn really went to fight for the Sultan. His army is huge, his tactics entirely different from yours. You would be made to surrender the skills that make you such perfect warriors."

"Would we?" Abi Gul asked, with the conviction of someone who has pondered something long and hard and already countered all of her own doubts. "Or would we teach his army something that would make the difference for them in this coming war?"

Khalidah sighed. "I suppose anything is possible. But there is something else: we are a long way from Damascus. If you decided to go to Salah ad-Din, how would you reach him in time? And if you did, how would you convince him of your worth and your loyalty, given that he is a devout Muslim and you are a tribe of foreign infidels?"

Abi Gul smiled. "It's why you have come to us, Khalidah. You are the link between Salah ad-Din's people and the Jinn." Khalidah only realized that she was shaking her head when Abi Gul contradicted, "Yes, Khalidah, it is true. Call it the will of Mobarak Khan or Allah; one way or another, there is a reason why you have been sent on this particular journey, at this particular time."

Khalidah wondered how many more times she would have to hear this before she believed it.

"You are heir to two proud races, and right now the future of both hangs in the balance. What is your purpose if not to be the link between them and thereby the foundation for that future?"

Khalidah saw that it would be useless to argue against Abi Gul's passionate certainty. Instead, she asked, "How many of you believe that I am this . . . link?"

Abi Gul's look was answer enough. Khalidah dropped her face into her hands. "You are mistaken," she muttered, "oh, how you are mistaken! I am nothing but a silly girl who ran away because she didn't want to marry her cousin."

She felt Abi Gul's hand on her shoulder. "If you truly believed that," she said, "you would not be here now." She was silent for a moment, giving Khalidah time to compose herself. Then she said, "Come. If you are going to lead us, then you must learn to fight like one of us."

"I did not say that I would lead you," Khalidah answered querulously.

Abi Gul only smiled.

THEY taught her how to shoot with bow and arrow, and ways with the sword that she had never imagined. They bound her hands behind her and put her on one of their own horses and sent her through grueling dressage drills until she could sit the two-beat battle gait with perfect balance, and then they returned her bow and taught her to shoot while she rode. Though she began by hating it, after a few days Khalidah developed a great enthusiasm for that smooth, quick pace and asked why they didn't ride that way all the time.

"It is too taxing on the horse," said Zhalai, who oversaw the training of her dormitory. "Many of them must be taught to pace, but even those that come to it naturally are worn down by it quickly. If you ride a horse too hard at the pace, he will go shoulder-lame. Then he cannot be ridden in battle, for the lameness can reemerge at any time, without warning."

Khalidah nodded, humbled by the realization of how much she had to learn.

Though she hardly saw Sulayman, Khalidah didn't have time to miss him. The days were taken up by training, and at night she wanted nothing more than to fall into bed and sleep. Sometimes this was possible, but on other nights the girls, who seemed to possess boundless reserves of energy, would climb up into the foothills and dance late into the night, singing praises of the stars and the moon and their own youth and happiness. And they were happy: that was what struck Khalidah most profoundly about the Jinn. They seemed secure in their love for their beautiful valley, the simple purpose of their lives, the righteousness of their beliefs. Khalidah quickly came to envy them this, but she feared for them too. Though she knew that they faced it habitually, she couldn't quite believe that they could withstand the outside world, its neuroses and duplicities and its dereliction of faith. Their reverence for life was so different from her world of vengeance and honor, their infidels' faith somehow far more civilized than the warring cosmologies of the west.

As the days passed, Khalidah came grudgingly to agree with her grandfather that to join Salah ad-Din's jihad would be brutally hard on the Jinn. Yet she also saw how deeply the faith in Pamir's prophecy ran among those who had embraced it, and how it colored their view of her. As the days turned into weeks, their unspoken expectations began to fill her with a bleak despair, until at last she couldn't stand it and went looking for Sulayman.

He was too old for the boys' dormitory. Though he joined their training during the day, he had been living with Warda and Batoor—Shahascina's parents—who had kept him during his first stay in Qaf. Theirs was a big house, situated at the end of one of the rows, with clear views to the practice grounds from its rooftop terrace. The wooden door was covered in intricate carvings of scenes from Mobarak Khan's life. An ibex skull hung from the lintel, horns reaching outward like a two-pronged claw.

The door stood half open to the evening breeze when Khalidah approached. A drift of wood smoke enveloped her, heady as incense. Before she could knock, a child appeared in the gap. She was about six years old, with a fairy's face and hair the color of ripe wheat. Like many of the children of Qaf she carried a pet mynah bird on her shoulder, which studied Khalidah with eyes as inquisitive as its mistress's. After a moment the child grinned, showing two missing front teeth, and started hollering for her mother. Warda appeared a moment later, wiping her hands on her apron. She too smiled when she saw Khalidah and immediately invited her inside, scolding the child for neglecting to do so.

"Please, sit," she said, indicating one of the low wooden chairs pulled up around the central hearth. "Sulayman is outside with Batoor—I will fetch him for you."

Khalidah looked around. The room was as Sulayman had described it long ago in the desert: there were the closed doors leading off the central living area, and above them the gallery with the high windows, full of green twilight. The room was silent but for the crackle of the fire and the sigh of the wind through the smokehole and the open doorway.

Khalidah had almost settled into its easy peace when the child returned with a tray of tea and promptly announced, "Ghairat says that you know Mobarak Khan."

She nearly choked on her mouthful of tea. "Who is Ghairat?"

"He is my friend," the child answered, feeding her mynah crumbs from a plate of bread spread with sheep's butter.

Khalidah sighed. "Well, tell Ghairat that he is mistaken."

The child looked up at her with wide-eyed appeal. "But he says that you have come to show us the way to Him. If not you, then who?"

"Mahzala!" Warda said sharply from the doorway. "I am sorry, Bibi Khalidah," she said, but there was a hint of curiosity beneath her mortification. Khalidah was very glad to see Sulayman stooping through the doorway behind Warda. "We will leave you alone to talk," Warda said.

"It is not necessary," Khalidah answered politely, but she was grateful when Warda ignored her words, taking her daughter firmly by the hand and leading her upstairs. Sulayman watched them go, then sat down in another of the chairs by the fire and poured a cup of tea.

"I take it from your expression that you are not keen on your role as intermediary to a messiah," he said with his thief's smile.

But Khalidah dropped her head into her hands. After a moment she felt Sulayman's hand on her hair, stroking and soothing. "Ah, Khalidah—you knew that they would expect something of you."

"I did not think that I would be expected to introduce them to a god."

He laughed wryly. "Has it been that bad?"

She was comforted to find real sympathy on his face along with the humor. "Oh, yes. They are polite about it, but they've made their expectations clear. Do the boys talk about it too?"

"They talk about nothing else."

"What am I going to do, Sulayman?"

"What can you do, but follow the path that Allah has laid out for you?"

"I would like to believe that that is what I am doing; and yet, could Allah really have intended that I lead a tribe of infidels to their false deity?"

"Are you questioning His will?"

Khalidah didn't answer. She didn't know whether he was teasing or serious, or how to account for her own doubt. Sulayman's eyes were gentle, but troubled. "I am afraid for them, Sulayman," she said at last. "I fear that if they follow me, it will be to their doom."

"I know," he said, "but you cannot let fear preclude your faith. It was you who reminded me of that on the night we came here; have you forgotten? Now, as then, you must trust Allah. If He tells you that your destiny is to stay here and do Tor Gul Khan's bidding, then do it. But if you believe that it is to fight for Salah ad-Din, then you must accept that as His calling, and be prepared to lead these people if He calls on them to follow you."

"And yet, who am I to lead them?" she asked bitterly.

"Who else, Khalidah?"

Ten

Tal Ashtara
Late May

IT was several weeks before the full impact of the massacre at the Springs of Cresson made itself felt, and for both sides to realize how fundamentally they had been changed by that short, brutal battle. For the Muslim soldiers who had fought it, it meant instant celebrity. Even those who had not taken part were inspired by it. As news of the victory spread, a whole new wave of would-be soldiers flocked toward Damascus, fired with dreams of the glory to be found fighting in the Sultan's army.

Yet Salah ad-Din himself received the news with mixed feelings. Though he was glad to be rid of so many of the troublesome Templars, he was distinctly put out that he had not been there to witness the event. He considered his situation—the returning hajj caravans slowed to a trickle, the battle season imminent, the Franj of Oultrejourdain beaten and cowering—and decided that it was time to go home. He sent a letter to Al-Afdhal instructing him to find a good mustering point for their ever-expanding army, and then he requisitioned half of the Egyptian troops, sent his brother back to Cairo, and turned his camel north.

The news that Salah ad-Din had finally departed from Oultrejourdain did little to cheer the reeling Franj. The loss of so many of their best knights at Cresson was a disaster, but perhaps the greater disaster was their ensuing loss of faith. Those dead knights had charged the Muslim army with the conviction shared by most of the Christians of Outremer: that it was God's will that they drive the Saracens from their kingdom. As such, they could not believe that He would let them fail. But at Cresson they had failed; there was no possibility of denying it. Of the five hundred men who followed Gerard de Ridefort into battle that day, the Templar Master was the only one to have escaped with his life.

The ensuing whispers of treachery, the suspicion that he had purposely led the knights to their deaths, might have grown into a whole lot more had the kingdom not faced more immediate practical problems. Though the castles of Kerak and Shawbak had not surrendered to Salah ad-Din, little else was left intact in Oultrejourdain. Farms had been abandoned, entire towns deserted as terrified peasants flocked to Muslim-ruled areas to escape the Sultan's wrath. This was exactly as Salah ad-Din had intended, for without peasants to provide food, the castles would be easy prey to sieges the following winter.

There could only be one response to such unmitigated disaster. At the end of May, King Guy sent out the arrière-ban, summoning every able-bodied free Christian man in his lands between ages fifteen and seventy into his army. For once, he acted on no advice but his own, for even the likes of Guy de Lusignan could see that war with Salah ad-Din was now inevitable.

Tal Ashtara had been the favorite campground of Salah ad-Din's predecessor, Nur ad-Din, because of its many springs and the resulting meadows, which could support an army's worth of horses in a good season. Al-Afdhal saw no reason to look any farther for a muster point, so as Salah ad-Din rode north, his son directed the relocation of the army to the new site south of Ras al-Mai. Like some ponderous beast, the city of tents that had grown up around the town began to disperse, until there was nothing left of it but piles of litter, trampled circles where the pavilions had stood, and the feeling of vast abandonment that clings to ancient ruins.

Meanwhile, the soft green meadowland of Tal Ashtara was rapidly disappearing as the old tents and pavilions were pitched anew and then new tents were pitched around them. It was as if the camp had taken nourishment from its new, fertile location. Day after day it swelled as more soldiers streamed in with their gear and their animals, until a man standing on a siege tower at its center would not have been able to mark its limit.

Salim and Bilal pitched their tent by the edge of a trickling spring, in the shade of a sprawling pomegranate bush. Or rather, Bilal pitched the tent while Salim looked listlessly on, going through the barest motions of living as he had every day since Cresson. Over the course of those weeks, Bilal had begun to feel that Salim had somehow departed himself, as lost to the battle as if he'd died there. He passed his days in bruised silence, speaking only perfunctorily. At night, though he permitted himself to be held, he lay like an effigy of himself, steadfastly ignoring Bilal's gentle attempts to break through his torpor.

At first, it seemed the move to Tal Ashtara had made no difference to Salim. But the sound of running water, the days full of heat and tedium, seemed to soothe him, and little by little he began to return. It started with a gradual refocusing of his eyes on the things around him. Then one day, for no apparent reason, he reached for Bilal's hand, his own as tremulous and uncertain as Bilal's had once been. Bilal matched his steps as he'd learned to do long ago when breaking a young horse, careful not to show too much of a reaction one way or another, but to accept each overture as the gift it was.

One stifling afternoon, when they'd been at the new camp for about a week, Salim said abruptly, "What if we are wrong?"

They were sitting with their feet in the spring. Salim did not look at Bilal but at the pomegranate bush, which was dropping scarlet flowers into the water. Bilal didn't have to ask what he meant. It was the only thing he'd thought about since Cresson.

"I don't think that it's a question of right and wrong," he answered carefully, poking around inside his splinted bandage with a stick in an attempt to relieve the itching. "It's about belief. We act according to the dictates of Allah, as the Franj do their God. We each fight for our holy city. Unfortunately, it happens to be the same one . . . Ah, merciful Allah!" The stick had broken off inside his bandage. Now he was casting about for another with which to remove it.

Salim lay back on the grass, resting his head on his outstretched arm and considering Bilal. "That is not quite what I meant. Although in a way, it is . . ." He paused. "As you say, we share the same holy city. Has it never struck you as strange that Islam and Christianity—and Judaism too, to be fair—hold so many of the same places sacred? We speak different languages," he continued slowly, as if he were working out the thoughts as he spoke them, "we and the Franj, and yet we mean the same things. Cut out our hearts and you could not tell one from the other."

Bilal frowned at his broken arm. He'd succeeded at last in removing the stick from the bandage, but it had left shards of wood behind, which would no doubt give him sores and earn him a lecture the next time the physician changed the splint. Giving up, he brought his eyes to rest on Salim's.

"I loved Jakelin de Mailly," he said. "Truth be told, he was the first man I loved. But there are not many Franj like him."

"No, nor many men at all," Salim answered, but his voice was speculative rather than bitter. "Don't mistake me, Bilal. I do not pine for the Templar Marshal. I do not even blame myself anymore for his death. But he haunts me all the same. It isn't that I've found a love for the Franj, but after him, I cannot hate them. Nor can I simply call the things we've done to them the will of Allah, or just retribution, because . . ." He lowered his voice against the blasphemy he was about to speak. "Because, by the Book, our gods are one; and so perhaps these warring prophets in whose names we fight are not opposed at all. What if none of us are infidels, and guilty only of being too human to realize it?"

Bilal studied Salim, and for a moment Salim had the strange sensation that Bilal's eyes were not a part of him at all, but little windows punched out of the corporeal world onto the silent blue beyond.

At last Bilal said, "I think that you may well be right, but I do not think that it would change anything even if all the world knew it. Because in the end, none of it is about our gods or our prophets."

"It's about power," Salim answered bitterly.

"No," Bilal said, "it's about the nature of men. For by our nature we must master others, or be mastered by them."

"Must we?" Salim asked, and the desperation in his voice turned Bilal cold. He pulled his feet from the water and crossed them under his legs. They sat in silence for a long time, watching the flowers swirl on the stream like bits of blood-soaked silk. "What will happen to us, Bilal?"

"I thought that you didn't worry about the future."

"That was before I realized how much can change in a moment," Salim answered.

Bilal considered the drifting flowers. "Well then, it seems to me that there are two choices. We can stay and fight for your father . . . or we can leave all of this and look for a place to live where de Mailly would not have died."

"Do you think that there is such a place?"

Bilal looked at him, thinking that for Salim, he would build it with his own hands. But he knew that this was not the answer that Salim sought. He was silent for a long time, his eyes searching the water, the hazy sky, for the right words.

"Bilal?"

In the end, he could only tell the truth. "I do not know."

Salim gave him a strange, resigned smile that he didn't like at all. Before he could protest, though, Salim had pushed him onto his back and kissed him in a way he had almost forgotten, shattering his anxiety with the sudden sharpness of desire.

Before he lost his will entirely, Bilal caught Salim's chin with his good hand and said, "Promise you won't leave me."

"I could not live without you," Salim answered, and it was so long since Bilal had heard such passionate conviction in his voice that he was willing to ignore the fact that Salim had not really answered at all.

Eleven

LATE in the spring, Salah ad-Din at last rejoined his army. Despite the influx of new soldiers, the first thing he did was to send out another round of recruiting letters. The second thing he did was to call upon his sons and formally congratulate them for the victory at Cresson. Only Al-Afdhal took it as his due. Al-Aziz had his eyes fixed on his elder brother with withering jealousy, and Al-Zahir looked abashed, if pleased. Salim, whom the Sultan had last seen flooded with the sanguine glow of success, and whom he'd expected to be swelled with the pride of having personally executed the Templar Marshal, was wan and distant.

Salah ad-Din wondered momentarily if he'd fallen out with the Bedu boy. Then, deciding that it was probably a good thing if he had, pressed on with the business at hand. "Indeed, you have acquitted yourselves admirably," he said, "but I do not need to tell you that our work has only begun." He sipped his tea, noting that of the four boys, only Salim had not touched his own. "Cresson was a victory, but no victory is without its consequences, and therefore we can consider our truce with Tripoli nullified."

"Has he said so?" asked Al-Zahir, his wide, good-natured face uncomprehending.

Salah ad-Din sighed, wondering how Al-Zahir could possess such a genius for combat, so unmitigated by any other vestige of intelligence. "No, he has not said so," he said patiently, "but the other Franj nobles will blame him for the debacle, as indeed I would do myself in their situation. I believe that Tripoli wants to live in peace with us, but he is a Franji, and I have never met the Franji who would turn his back on his people for the sake of a Saracen."

Al-Zahir appeared to be attempting to follow his reasoning. Al-Aziz's attention was clearly wandering, and Al-Afdhal's had been absent from the start. Only Salim seemed to be taking in what he was saying, but Salah ad-Din was struck by the false note in his interest, a cast to his attention that was too much like antipathy.

Sighing, the Sultan said, "It will not be long before King Guy sends another envoy, and this one will not ask for Tripoli's compliance—they will demand it. Tripoli will have no choice but to acquiesce. Once the Franj states have patched up their differences, they will turn on us. Your men have been lazy while I have been away. It is time to make them start working again. We must be prepared."

"How long?" Salim asked abruptly, and though his voice was as distant as his expression, the Sultan could not conceal a slight smile that encompassed both approval and humility for, once again, the son he had nearly written off was the only one to have asked the right question.

"A few weeks," he answered. "A month, perhaps. I am calling Taqi ad-Din back from Antioch and Lu'lu from the south with the navy. I will meet with the emirs after I have finished speaking with you, to begin our strategy for drawing the Franj into battle."

He paused, looking at each of his sons in turn; at last, he saw with approval, he had their attention. "Before this summer is out, I will raise the crescent over Jerusalem."

Twelve

Tiberias
Early June

ONCE again, Raymond of Tripoli stood on the battlements watching an approaching envoy, but this time he had no doubt about its identity or intentions. He was only surprised that it had taken them so long; more than a month had passed since the debacle at Cresson. Then again, he thought wryly, with so many of their best knights lost on that day, it was no wonder that it had taken time for the court faction to gather enough fighting men to confront him.

He noted the standards of the key nobles, along with those of various priests and knights of the holy orders, and even that of Heraclius, the Patriarch of Jerusalem. The king's was markedly absent. Tripoli could not stem the disgust that rose in him then: the previous king, consumed by leprosy, had led his army until he had to be tied to the saddle to stay in it. When that had failed he had continued to direct his affairs from a litter with clearheaded wisdom, until he drew his final breath.

But even that was not the worst of it. As the envoy drew closer, Tripoli made out a familiar figure in a red-crossed tunic riding at the head of the column. A moment later he confirmed that it was Gerard de Ridefort. That the others could have forgiven his betrayal at Cresson at all, let alone allowed him to lead the envoy, told him more about the state of affairs in Jerusalem than anything could. The count watched as his guards opened the gate and de Ridefort rode through. Then he turned from the window to meet the inevitable.

WHEN de Ridefort's entourage entered the great hall, they found the count seated at the head of his banquet table, perusing a stack of documents. De Ridefort looked Tripoli over for signs of repentance, or at least a knothole in the audacity that had brought him to his present position, but his composure was unruffled. Stifling his fury, de Ridefort approached the table. Tripoli gestured for the nobles to be seated and then paused, surveying them. Another man would have assumed that the count was waiting for one of them to break the silence. De Ridefort knew from experience that Tripoli was waiting until their discomfort peaked before breaking it himself.

"It is kind of you to come so far out of your way on my account," he said at last, the maddening taint of Arabic in his accent more pronounced than ever. "To what do I owe the honor?"

"You know very well why we are here," de Ridefort answered tersely. Tripoli's head snapped upward, accompanied by a click of his tongue: an Arab gesture of negation that infuriated de Ridefort still further. "Well, then," de Ridefort continued, "I shall spell it out. Your refusal to recognize your rightful king, as well as your traitorous alliance with the Saracen leader, has cost me half of my knights. I have come now for recompense."

Tripoli leaned his elbow on the table and rested his head languidly on two extended fingers, looking as though de Ridefort had asked his opinion of the weekend's weather rather than charged him with treason. "It was not I who called the charge," he said.

"You put the infidels there to taunt us!" de Ridefort cried.

"I did no such thing," Tripoli answered with icy composure. "I was honoring my agreement with Salah ad-Din, and he honored his with me. But for you, no blood would have been shed on that day."

This time it was one of the nobles, Balian d'Ibelin, who answered: "This is no time for casting blame. We are here to ask you whether your agreement with the Saracen king still stands."

"I am not a man to break my word," Tripoli answered.

"Not break your word!" de Ridefort began. "You are a traitor and—"

"Silence!" roared Heraclius. He turned from de Ridefort to Tripoli. "Where is your loyalty, Count? Do you honestly mean to tell us that you have given it to an infidel?"

Tripoli smiled bitterly. "Not one year past," he said, "every man here swore his loyalty to a dying king. We all gave our word that his sister would not succeed him, unless it was by decree of the Pope in Rome. I do not recall the Pope being consulted before Sibylla was crowned."

"You know as well as anyone that Princess Sibylla was the rightful heir to the Kingdom of Jerusalem."

"Sibylla," Tripoli mused, drawing the name out, rolling it on his tongue. "More of a man than her husband, when it comes right down to it . . . and yet it's in his name that you come here, not hers."

"Things are as they are, Tripoli," snapped de Ridefort. "If you do not pay homage to King Guy now, you brand yourself a traitor."

"And then?"

"Then?" De Ridefort was florid with rage, the vein in his forehead pulsing to its beat. "Can you really mean to defy us again? You pride yourself on being like the Saracens, and you must surely have converted to Islam or you could not tolerate what happened at Cresson! To allow the infidels to cross your territory, to slaughter Christian knights without ever raising a hand to stop it, you must be a traitor to God Himself!"

Heraclius frowned at de Ridefort's words, but he did not ask him to retract them. Instead, he said to Tripoli, "By continuing to defy your rightful king, you defy God. If you do not repent immediately, I will have you excommunicated and your marriage annulled, for I could not ask a good Christian woman to remain married to a heathen."

The gauntlet had been dropped. Tripoli might despise Guy and all the rotten politics that had set him on the throne, but he loved his wife and children beyond anything. And so he said, the words like sand in his mouth, "My lords, I beg your pardon for any part that I had to play in the tragedy of Cresson, and I am prepared to make reparation to the kingdom as you see fit."

De Ridefort opened his mouth for a sharp retort, but Balian d'Ibelin, whom Tripoli respected for his levelheaded intelligence despite his staunch loyalty to the king, put a restraining hand on his arm. "For that we thank you, Count," he said, "and the only reparation we require is that you pay homage to Guy as your rightful king."

Shaking off d'Ibelin's hand, de Ridefort added, "And you'd best pray that he's still in a mood to receive it!"

D'Ibelin, Heraclius, and several of the barons were looking daggers at the Templar Master, but Tripoli only smiled. "Still in a mood to receive it?" he repeated. "He would fall to his knees and grovel for it if you'd let him or, more likely, send his wife to do it for him. That is precisely why you are here and he is not." He shook his head. "Do not mistake me—I still believe that you are fools to put your faith in King Guy, but for some reason God has set him on the throne of Jerusalem, and for God I will call him king."

He stifled the barons' sighs of relief with a look like a sharpened blade. "However, I must say this: though I may have been the instrument of our defeat at Cresson, I was not its instigator. I will fight Salah ad-Din if God requires it, but I will not follow you on another fools' mission."

Hastily, before de Ridefort could think of a response, d'Ibelin said, "Very well, then. Come with us now to Acre, where your king is waiting, and let us all welcome you back."

Thirteen

✦

A few days after Tripoli's capitulation, Guy's army began to muster at the oasis town of Sephoria. It was a good position, with plenty of water and grazing land and proximity to Salah ad-Din's own growing army. But despite the success of the arrière-ban and the addition of Tripoli's troops, Salah ad-Din's army still outnumbered the Franks' by a good margin.

Salah ad-Din was aware of his advantage, though it would take a full review to know exactly how large it was. New religious volunteers were arriving all the time, the Tiberias detachment had returned a couple of weeks earlier, and the previous day his favorite nephew, Taqi ad-Din, had returned from his campaign in Antioch with another large contingent.

But his satisfaction was not unhampered by anxiety. The change in his son Salim disturbed him, for in their time in the south he had come to rely on the boy more than he had ever meant to. He was also aware that Numair al-Hassani had not returned with the detachment from Tiberias. No doubt there was a connection between the two, but with so many more pressing problems demanding his attention he couldn't pursue it.

Then one night in the middle of June, when a dry wind from the desert shifted the sluggish air of the oasis, he heard a voice outside his tent speaking with the guard. It was only on hearing it that he realized how long he had expected it. A moment later the Bedu boy ducked into the pavilion, said his *salaam*s, and bowed to the Sultan.

"Bilal," he said, "to what do I owe the honor?"

"Please, Your Highness," Bilal faltered, "there is something that I must tell you, only I am afraid . . ."

His eyes looked bluer than ever, transparent as water and deep with sorrow. When he knelt, Salah ad-Din realized that they were brightened by tears. Grief gave his face a soulful beauty, and though he had never felt much of an attraction to boys, for a moment the Sultan understood his son's infatuation completely.

"You have long since proven your loyalty to me," the Sultan said gently. "Speak your heart without fear."

He had expected a confession from Bilal, and had guessed that it would incriminate Numair, but for all his years and experience reading the hearts of men, the Sultan had never imagined that the Bedu boy's could hold such tortuous secrets. It was the eyes, he decided. Like clear water, blue eyes had always seemed to him incapable of dissimulation—which was ludicrous, he realized, given the predominant coloring of the Franj. As Bilal spoke he considered his options carefully, and when the boy at last lapsed into tremulous silence, he asked him the last question Bilal expected:

"Tell me, do you love your father?"

Bilal gave him a terrible, twisted smile. "I would gladly see his head on a pike."

The Sultan raised his eyebrows. "Strong words from a boy who could be coerced to treason by a mere threat."

"I have changed since then," Bilal said defiantly.

"My son, too, has changed." Now there was a flinty note, a hint of accusation, in his voice. "Tell me, how long has he known what you have told me?"

Bilal paused, then said, "It is not the reason for the change in him."

"That is not what I asked," the Sultan replied, irritated that the boy had seen so easily through his words to his intent.

"But with respect, Sire, is it not what you meant?" Bilal gave Salah ad-Din a direct look. The Sultan met it, but said nothing. "He has known since Oultrejourdain—I told him when we were trapped in the wadi by that sandstorm. I have severed ties with de Ridefort since then," he added quickly.

Salah ad-Din nodded, and though he kept his silence, his look told Bilal to continue.

"Your Highness," he said, sighing, "your son is sick at heart. I am not the cause, but sometimes I wish that I were, because then perhaps I could do something about it . . ." He shook his head, then continued, "It was Cresson that changed him. He has become battle-sick."

"That does not make sense," the Sultan said. "I have watched Salim in countless fights. He is no softhearted fool."

"No, he is not," Bilal replied. "But Cresson was different. Up until then, we had always fought men who would kill us given half a chance."

"And at Cresson you fought Templars," the Sultan said, his voice waspish, almost peevish. "Do you think that they would have spared you if the roles had been reversed?"

"No," Bilal answered wearily, "of course not. But there was a reluctance to their actions on that day, as if they knew that they should not be there. For many of us, there was no joy in such a victory. And then, when Salim killed the Templar Marshal . . ." He shook his head. "Did you know Jakelin de Mailly?"

"I do not recall him."

"You would, if you'd met him. He was different from the other Franj. Different from any man I've known. He didn't care about power or politics. He loved his God purely, simply, and he fought from that love. He was, perhaps, divine . . . either way, he should never have been at Cresson. Salim saw what he was, and he killed him to deliver him, and that is the root of his sickness. I don't think that Salim had ever considered before that, that a Franji could be worthy of mercy, and it was very hard that he must realize it in such a way. At Cresson he learned that there is a dark side to our fight . . . that not all of our actions can be righteous. He has been wandering in that darkness ever since."

"I see." The Sultan was clearly angry, and Bilal thought that the anger was for Salim's weakness. He could never have anticipated the truth.

"Would it help him to know that it was Gerard de Ridefort who was responsible for de Mailly's death—in fact, for all of them?"

"He already knows that de Ridefort called the charge."

"Don't be a fool, boy!" Salah ad-Din said sharply. "I mean that he sabotaged his own men. The last time I met with him, I told him that I no longer wished to deal with him. I have never trusted him, and for some time he has been failing to uphold his portion of our agreements. He promised to prove his loyalty to me. I told him that I did not believe he had it in him to turn against the Order that has raised him so high. Apparently," he concluded dryly, "I underestimated him. Or at any rate, his greed."

Bilal blinked at him for a moment, digesting all of this. Then he said, "Forgive my impertinence, Sire, but I think you had best not tell Salim this."

The Sultan raised his eyebrows in surprise. "Why not? Will it not cause him to stop blaming himself?"

"Oh, yes," Bilal said. "Instead, he will blame you."

The Sultan's face flushed with anger. For a moment Bilal thought that the man would strike him. But then his expression changed again, to one of defeat. "I fear you are right, al-Hassani; and you are a wiser man than I."

Bilal smiled sadly. "Hardly, Sire. Only, I do know Salim very well."

The Sultan sighed. "At any rate, we have strayed from the matter at hand. I admit that much of what you have told me about your family has come as a surprise. Where Gerard de Ridefort is concerned, however, you have only confirmed what I have known all along: he is a man whose only true cause is his own ambition. I have always known that for every promise he made me, he made two elsewhere. I see that you are wondering why, then, I have dealt with him at all? Well, even a treacherous egoist has his uses . . ."

He fell to musing, apparently forgetting about Bilal. A moment later, however, he locked eyes with the boy. "As for you, when I said that you had nothing to fear from speaking the truth to me, I meant it. But whatever hand is at work in all of this, it has placed you at the center of a powerful man's quarrel with the world. Any step you take will lead you deeper into danger."

The Sultan's eyes softened, as Bilal had seen them soften a handful of times for Salim. A knot of sadness tightened in his chest.

"Listen to me, Bilal al-Hassani, for I speak to you now not as a king to his subject, but as a father to his son: you must be careful, as you have never been careful before. You were always a liability to Gerard de Ridefort, and now you have spurned and humiliated him as well. He will waste no time in trying to be rid of you, and given what I have told you about Cresson, you can see that doing so will not trouble his conscience in the slightest. As for your 'cousin' Numair, I cannot guess what he is plotting now, but it strikes me that he will take no more kindly to your defection than de Ridefort."

"I am not afraid of them," Bilal answered.

The Sultan smiled. "I am glad to hear it. But if you have no thought for your own safety, then at least consider Salim's."

Bilal froze, then babbled: "Oh, Your Highness, I had never thought—if being with me puts him in danger, then I will—"

"Do nothing, least of all what you were about to suggest!" the Sultan interrupted sharply. Then he sighed, pulling at his beard. "I can think of no one likelier to help him right now than you. He may not be my heir, and I know that I have given him little cause to think that I value him, but I do, more than he knows. So please, be careful for his sake."

Seeing that the Sultan had turned back to his papers, Bilal stood and started to leave. But as he reached for the tent flap, Salah ad-Din said, "Oh, and one more thing: you need not fear for your mother. In fact, that to me is the true travesty in all of this. Her husband was a brutal, worthless scoundrel—yes, was. He was cut to pieces by a moneylender whom he'd cheated a few months after your mother left him. So you see, Numair lied to you, too: whoever told him her story, it was not Zaynab's husband. But even if he had lived, you must rest assured, I would never have allowed any man to cast a stone at my niece on his account. Nor will I willingly allow any man to harm her son. Bilal ibn Zaynab al-Ayyubi . . . it has a certain ring, doesn't it?"

Once again, the Sultan smiled. Bilal nodded, then stumbled out into the night, dazed and euphoric despite everything. For in all the months that he wrestled with the acquisition of a hated father, he had never considered that Numair had also unwittingly bequeathed him a family.

Fourteen

Qaf
Early June

WHEN Khalidah and Sulayman had been in Qaf three weeks, the Jinn received a request for assistance. The scouts brought the supplicant to Tor Gul Khan early one morning, emaciated and half mad from his days wandering in the mountains. As the girls walked back from the practice grounds for their midday meal, they could see the tribal elders gathering at the temple to discuss his request.

"What will happen if they decide in his favor?" Khalidah asked.

"Tor Gul Khan will send him home with twenty or thirty warriors tomorrow morning," Abi Gul answered.

"And will you go with them?"

She laughed ruefully. "I am two months short of sixteen. But Afshan and Shahascina will likely be sent."

The two girls looked both hopeful and uncertain. "Do you fear it?" she asked them. "Leaving Qaf for this first battle?"

"It is how we become what we are," Shahascina answered. "Fear has no place in it."

"And yet," Abi Gul said to Khalidah, slowing her step so that the other girls drew ahead and out of earshot, "it is not quite so simple. We may ride from Qaf toward the same goal, but each of us returns to a separate destiny. My friends both wish to distinguish themselves, to earn their places as adult members of the tribe. But once they are women, Shahascina will marry Sarbaz, move into her own house, and, if her mother's fertility is any indicator, be a mother herself within a year. Her first fight could well be her last.

Afshan, on the other hand, will most likely join the ranks of the regular warriors."

"And you will lose two friends," she said.

Abi Gul shrugged. "For a while, I suppose. Until I fight my own first battle and join the ranks, or . . ." She glanced at Khalidah and then away.

Khalidah sighed. "If you are not sixteen, you will not be allowed to go to Salah ad-Din even if Tor Gul Khan gives his blessing to the others."

"Were you 'allowed' to forsake your marriage and come here?"

"That was different."

"Did you not choose to follow the dictates of your heart rather than those of your people? How is that different from this?" She flung her hands outward in a gesture of exasperation. "Difficult as it may be for you to accept, Bibi Khalidah, I believe that Salah ad-Din is our messiah. I believe it as fundamentally as you believe that Allah is the only God and Muhammad His prophet. Like every Jinni, I am a warrior before anything else. And if I am to give my life in battle, I would rather it be God's battle than that of some petty tribal chief like the one pleading his case up there in the temple."

They had reached the dormitory. Khalidah gave her friend a long, searching look and found only determination in her gold-and-green eyes.

"I will not let you protect me," Abi Gul said, "so please, do not try."

"Very well," Khalidah answered, "but I will promise no more until you have done something for me."

"Name it."

"I need to speak to Alipsha, your *betaan*."

Abi Gul grinned. "I thought you would never ask!"

THE afternoon was warm, the sky strewn with cottony clouds. It was the first time Khalidah had ridden Zahirah since her bandage had come off, but the mare's fitness seemed to have improved rather than deteriorated, and there was no sign of lameness. Abi Gul eyed Zahirah from the back of her own stallion, who was called Tufan, which, like *Aasifa*, meant "storm."

"She's a fine horse," she said. "She'd bear Tufan a lovely foal."

"Don't even think about it!" Khalidah scolded. "She can't very well make the journey west if she's in foal—never mind ride into battle."

"Perhaps someday, when the battles are behind us . . ." Abi Gul said wistfully.

"*Inshallah*," Khalidah agreed.

They rode over soft grass and in and out of sparse forest until, after a couple of hours, they reached the high pastures, where the air was thin and the sun brilliant between the drifting clouds. Some of the shepherds had already brought their herds up for the summer grazing, moving into stone huts built by the trickling springs that fed the river in the valley below. Near the huts were pens into which the sheep were driven at night, to keep them safe from predators. As they approached one of the dwellings, Abi Gul called out in Pashto and a boy emerged, squinted at the riders for a moment, and then ran forward, laughing. Abi Gul jumped down from her horse and embraced him, then turned to Khalidah.

"Bibi Khalidah, may I introduce my brother, Arsalan."

Arsalan bobbed his head to Khalidah, and she did the same in return. The boy was a few years older than Abi Gul. He looked just like her, except for the plaits and the mulberry *harquus*. Abi Gul spoke to him in rapid Pashto and he answered likewise. Khalidah caught the words for *horses* and *snow* and, repeatedly, *betaan*.

At last Abi Gul turned back to her and said, "Forgive us, Bibi Khalidah. Arsalan's Arabic was never very good, and since he opted for a shepherd's life he has forgotten most of what he knew. Anyway, he says that Alipsha is at home and he will take us to him. We will have to leave the horses here, though, and walk. The melting snow has made the paths too treacherous."

Arsalan helped them remove the horses' tack, then shut them in the sheep's pen. "Ready?" he said in Arabic. Without waiting for them to answer, he turned and set off up the mountain.

He moved like an ibex. Abi Gul and Khalidah followed rather less quickly. Khalidah still wasn't used to exertion at such a high altitude, and they had to stop frequently for her to catch her breath. Even Abi Gul seemed glad of the pauses. Soon enough, Khalidah saw why Arsalan had made them leave the horses behind. The grass gradually gave way to rocky soil underlaid by mud. At times, Khalidah could hardly find footing; the horses would have been useless.

At last they reached a stony ridge, where an icy wind whistled from the snow peaks beyond. Khalidah wrapped her shawl around her head and shoulders and tried not to look down as they picked their way along a path by a dizzying drop. Finally they crossed the mountain's backbone and found themselves in a little hollow, just big enough for the shepherd's hut that huddled in the embrace of the ridge. It was sheltered from the wind, giving respite to sparse grass and a few wildflowers. A tethered nanny goat munched on a patch of brilliant blue poppies, and a vein of smoke rose from the hole in the hut's roof.

Arsalan approached first, peering into the hut. He spoke to someone within, his voice muffled by the wind that screamed across the ridge above them. After a moment he reemerged with a man whom, it seemed to Khalidah, life had gnawed to the bone, leaving nothing but sinew and spirit. His threadbare white robe hung off of him like laundry drying on a frame, hands emerging from the sleeves like gnarled roots. His dark skin hung equally loose, battered by the elements, and his hooked nose seemed to engulf his hollow-cheeked face. But his eyes, a brilliant Jinn gold, blazed with a young man's fire. He grinned toothlessly at Khalidah, taking her hands in his own and kissing both of her cheeks in between muttered blessings and exclamations in Pashto.

When at last he let her go, he beckoned to them all to come into the hut. The packed-earth floor was covered with rugs so old they were beginning to disintegrate. The fire pit was no more than a depression in the center of the floor, the fuel dried goat dung. Three flat rocks sat at the edges of the fire pit with a cauldron balanced on them, the simmering liquid within giving off a pungent, not-quite-unpleasant herbal smell. Alipsha gestured to them to sit down. They sat directly on the rugs, as there was no other furnishing in the hut, unless one counted the enormous ibex skull in one corner. Khalidah wondered if the old man slept directly on the floor, wrapped in his moth-eaten carpets, and she was poised to pity him until she recalled that a dervish often embraced equally harsh deprivations in his quest for unity with Allah.

Alipsha disappeared outside and then returned with a wooden bucket. He set it before Khalidah and handed her a ladle. It was full of milk. Certain that she was consuming the man's weekly sustenance, but well aware that refusing it would be an insult, she took a small sip before passing it along to Arsalan. Alipsha settled himself across the fire from Khalidah and studied her for a time before at last addressing her.

"Welcome, Bibi Khalidah," he said slowly, in Pashto. "I have been—"

Khalidah looked at Abi Gul and repeated the end of the sentence, which she had not understood: "*Matale . . . ?*"

"*Mateledal*—'to wait for,' " Abi Gul explained. "Alipsha has been waiting for you to come to him."

"Why?" Khalidah asked the old man.

He gave her a long answer, which she quickly gave up trying to translate. She waited until he had finished and then looked at Abi Gul, who said: "He has been dreaming of you for the past three weeks—that is, since you arrived in Qaf. And before that . . ." She paused uncomfortably.

"Please, just tell me."

"He says that he has been speaking with your mother."

The words sent a shiver down Khalidah's spine. She looked over her shoulder, despite herself.

"She appears to him in dreams," Abi Gul added quickly, "and

she asks him to guide you. But he says that he needs to know how you would be guided. That is, he wants you to ask him."

"But how can I?"

"Speak," said Alipsha, "and you will find that we understand each other."

The smoke in the hut had thickened, and Khalidah could not recall what language the man had just spoken, only that she had understood him.

"How . . ." she began.

"Because I am the *betaan*," he answered, as if this explained everything. "Now, Khalidah, tell me why you are here."

She looked at his kindly, wizened face through the steam rising from the pot. It seemed to shift and blur into a different face—that of a young man, though with similar features. It was like looking at two images, each with one eye, and it sent her head spinning. She found that it was easier to close her eyes.

"My father," she said, "and Bilal and Zaynab . . . What has happened to them?"

"Open your eyes," he said, and she obeyed.

The steam from the pot hazed the shapes of the room to indistinct blotches. Within them, something was moving. Gradually it resolved into a band of galloping horses backed by black-clad riders. The one at the front was her father. The image faded, merged into one of Zaynab stirring a pot in a kitchen—her own kitchen, the one beside the women's quarters where she and Khalidah had lived together. She was singing; happy. Then it shifted again, and Khalidah was looking at two boys—one with long, curling black hair, the other with a bandaged arm and a head shorn like a Bedu's—sitting on a riverbank by a flowering pomegranate bush in their loincloths, their legs in the water.

As she watched, the long-haired one lay back with his head on his outstretched arm, turning his fine-boned face toward her. She knew him at once as the Ayyub warrior who had killed the Templar in her dream that first night in Qaf. But this had barely begun to sink in before the other boy turned and leaned over him, and

Khalidah found herself watching Bilal kiss the beautiful boy with a lover's passion. As their limbs tangled, the image dissolved.

She shut her eyes again, her heart racing. "What are they doing?"

The *betaan* chuckled. "Did your nursemaid teach you nothing?"

"All right; but Bilal, I never . . ."

She stopped, not knowing how to put her thoughts into words, or even what her thoughts were. Despite what the Quran and the hadith had to say about it, and the fact that the staunchly traditional Bedu frowned on the concept, she was well enough educated to know that this kind of love was tolerated—even encouraged, within certain parameters—in other parts of the Islamic world. Moreover, what Bilal had done was no more outrageous than her months traveling alone with Sulayman. In fact, far less so.

"Very well, then; where was my father leading those men?"

"I do not know."

"Do you know who is looking after Zaynab and the rest of the tribe?"

"I saw no more than you did."

"What about the boy, the one Bilal was . . . well . . . I have seen him before. Do you know who he is?"

"That, I can answer. The boy is the son of the Sultan, Salah ad-Din."

Khalidah's head spun. She had assumed that he belonged to the Sultan's retinue by the yellow tunic he had worn in that first terrible vision of him, but Bilal the lover of an Ayyub prince? She could not imagine how it had come to pass, and her reaction was to panic, for if the simple boy whom she had thought she had known inside out could change so radically, what might have happened to the rest of her people in her absence?

But Alipsha had sensed her anxiety. When he spoke, his voice was soothing as fingers stroking her hair. "The world never ceases changing, Khalidah, but the ones you love are alive and apparently well . . . is that not enough?"

Khalidah couldn't argue with this.

"Now," said Alipsha, "if I have put you at ease, then tell me why you are here."

"In Qaf? I suppose because I believed that my mother was calling me here. But now I am not certain, for she is not here herself, and I don't sense her at all."

"The spirit is transient," Alipsha answered, "as is time. Brekhna is here, and not here; but she is not the answer."

"Perhaps not," Khalidah said, "yet Brekhna is the reason why the Jinn believe that I will lead them to their destiny."

"Are you certain of that?"

"If you know something different, I would prefer that you tell me plainly. I have had enough riddles and visions to last a lifetime."

There was a pause, a momentary hollowing between them, like a sigh. Then: "Khalidah, a *betaan* does not see in a linear way. For me, cause and effect do not form a chain but an infinite web, each filament an individual life, and each life a part of the whole. Some threads spin out long and strong, some weaken and break. Some cross others, some gather them. Some hardly touch any at all. I am not omniscient—far from it—but at times I am granted glimpses of the web. For whatever reason, your section of the fabric appears to me more often than most. I cannot tell you much, but I can tell you this: while your thread touches Brekhna's only in places, those of the Jinn, it gathers and binds."

"And what does that tell me?" she cried, exasperated. "It could mean that I am to stay here and take Tor Gul Khan's place, or as easily that I am to lead the Jinn to Salah ad-Din."

"Would it help if I told you that your thread is equally bound to those of your father's tribe?" Khalidah was surprised by how much this affected her, moved her even; but there was no time to question, for Alipsha was speaking again. "It also crosses that of Salah ad-Din. In fact, there is a great convergence of lives upon you, from all sides of this land and beyond. Your tugs on the fabric will be felt for a long time."

"Then I am destined to lead the Jinn to fight the Franj."

He sighed. "Khalidah . . . our religion is perhaps most different from yours in that we believe that nothing is written, nothing predetermined. I see likelihoods, no more. In other words, despite what I have told you, you can still choose your own fate."

"Then really," Khalidah said bitterly, "you have told me nothing."

"Haven't I?" the *betaan* asked. "Or do you simply mean that I have not told you what to do? I know that it is difficult. It is always difficult for the ones like you. You could not be blamed for losing faith, as your mother did."

"What?" Khalidah asked, suddenly, stingingly alert. "What do you mean, as my mother did?"

But Alipsha ignored her question, saying, "If you want advice, I will tell you what I would tell any man or woman who asked: choose your path and then follow it to the end. But it is you alone, Khalidah, who must choose."

Fifteen

TOR Gul Khan sent his supplicant home the following day with twenty Jinn warriors at his back. Shahascina, Afshan, and Sarbaz were among them, their mothers weeping and laughing by turns as they saw them off. The entire village watched as they rode toward the foothills to the south and then disappeared into the rolling green.

When they were gone, Khalidah turned and walked up to the temple. She carried the sword she had found in Domat al-Jandal, wrapped in her shawl, since it was not permitted to bring naked weapons into the temple. She had hoped to find her grandfather there, but there were only a handful of celibates, most of them meditating. Approaching one who was not, Khalidah asked her where she might find her grandfather. The woman indicated the door that led into the hermitage, and Khalidah followed her pointing finger.

She had not been to Tor Gul Khan's living quarters since her first night in Qaf, and she realized now that she had no idea how to find them. She walked down a long, whitewashed corridor lined with open doorways. These were the cells of the celibates. Each revealed a neat little room with a narrow bed, a simple woolen carpet, and a small altar set with carved deities and flickering lamps. At the end of the corridor was a narrow wooden stairway. She followed it up into another corridor, this one with a row of doors on one side that led onto the gallery at the front of the temple and three on the other, one of which stood open. A faint drift of incense came from within.

Khalidah approached it slowly and looked inside. The room was bigger than the cells below, but almost as spare. Tor Gul Khan sat on a plainly woven rug in front of a burning censer, meditating. Khalidah hovered inside the doorway, uncertain what to do, until, abruptly, her grandfather looked up at her, his golden eyes keen as knives.

"Come in," he said.

Khalidah knelt on the rug facing him, still clutching the wrapped sword. Her grandfather glanced at it, but when he spoke it was to say, "You have decided to go to your Sultan." There was regret in his voice, but not anger. Khalidah nodded. "And you will take the believers with you."

"I have kept my promise to you," Khalidah said. "I have not knowingly spoken any word to your people to encourage or discourage them from their beliefs. I have decided for myself; no more. When I leave I will not ask them to follow, but nor will I stop them if they wish to come."

He studied her, saying nothing, the minutes stretching uncomfortably. At last he said, "Very well, Khalidah. But as you are not here to ask my permission to take my people west, why *are* you here?"

She unwrapped the sword and handed it to him. He looked at it for a long moment, his expression unreadable, though he passed his thumb thoughtfully over the golden jewel in the hilt.

"Was it my mother's?" she asked in a voice she had intended to be firm and clear, but which came out rather more tremulously.

He handed it back, sighing. "And *her* mother's, and her mother's mother's, and so on back through time. The jewel is ancient, a yellow diamond from these hills. The inscription is not so old—it was made by an Arab sultan who owed a large debt to your great-great-grandmother. I am glad that Brekhna left it to you."

"She didn't," Khalidah said flatly. "I found it in a junk shop at the edge of Jazirah."

"I see," he answered evenly, though the shock was evident on his face.

Abruptly, Khalidah flooded with rage. "Tell me what happened to her!"

"You know that already."

"Yes," she snapped, "I've been told her story by a hundred different people in a hundred different ways, ever since I was old enough to understand. And yet, none of them ever really told me anything . . . not until I spoke to your *betaan*."

"And what did he tell you?" he asked, his body very still and his voice nearly a whisper.

"He told me that she lost faith."

Now, along with the shock, Tor Gul Khan's face showed fear. "What did he mean?"

He shook his head, the movement barely perceptible.

"I don't believe that you don't know!" Khalidah insisted. "There is something you are keeping from me. You say that she left the Jinn to fight the Franj with Salah ad-Din, and yet she did not join him, but married my father instead. She abandoned this sword, which, if I have understood anything about the Jinn, was like throwing away the purpose of her existence. And then she abandoned her husband and her only child." She ran her finger over the inscription on the sword. "*Life of My Soul*, this says . . . it's what she called me, too. What does it take to make a woman forsake the life of her soul?"

Tor Gul Khan passed his hand over his face. When he looked at her again, he had become the broken old man of their first conversation, who had pleaded with her to keep his people in Qaf.

"It takes betrayal, Khalidah. Sometimes just one, but in the case of a strong woman like Brekhna, it takes many. They chipped away at her soul, little by little, until at last it shattered. That is why she left you, and her Jinn calling. It is why she is not here now and never will return."

Khalidah watched him, willing him to continue, not to lose himself in the remorse and bewilderment now clouding his face. At last he said, "She was such a brilliant girl—talented at everything, it seemed. She was no great beauty, but she had that sparkle that draws the eye despite it. She had many suitors, but there had only ever been one boy for her—Sher Dil. He had a brilliance too, but it came from his kindness. He was sweet-natured, too sweet to make a warrior, really; but still he had the talent for it, and because he knew that it was Brekhna's calling, he pursued it.

"At Psarlay, when they turned sixteen, they were betrothed. But though they had finished their training there was no battle in sight, no chance for them to initiate themselves as adults, no way for them to marry. As the months went by they pleaded with me to marry them anyway, and I refused. How could I make an exception for my daughter and deny all the others in her situation?"

He shook his head. "But Brekhna wore me down. She made me promise that they would both be sent on the next mission, whatever it was, and like a fool I agreed. The next call came from a northern village of Tajiks fighting an insurgence of Mongols. The Mongols are difficult opponents because their methods of fighting are like our own. We had always suffered heavy losses when we fought them, and I did not like to risk Brekhna on such a mission. But what could I do? I had promised. And so Brekhna and Sher Dil rode out together . . ." His look was distant, bitter.

"And he was killed," Khalidah said softly.

"In the first charge. The Mongols use scissor-headed arrows, as we do, and his arm was severed near the shoulder. He was dead by the time Brekhna reached him." He sighed. "Another girl would have grieved until, with time, her heart softened again. But not Brekhna. It was as if she bled her heart out with Sher Dil on that northern steppe. Afterward she was good for nothing but war. She volunteered for any mission going. A few more fights and she had surpassed every warrior in this valley in skill and brutality. It was as if in each enemy she faced, she saw the Mongol archer who had killed her beloved.

"And then, on a mission in Persia, she caught the eye of a Kurdish emir. He asked her to come west with him, for he knew of a man who could use the Jinn's help in fighting a group of invaders he called the Franj."

"And that was when she met Salah ad-Din?"

Tor Gul Khan nodded. "Salah ad-Din, and the Franj, and her battered mind and heart saw in their struggle the bones of our old prophecy. She and her band stayed for many months with him, fighting the invaders. When at last they returned I found Brekhna changed again. I had not thought that anything could be as painful as watching her thwarted love for Sher Dil become such bitter hatred, but now I knew that I was wrong. Now it had changed into religious faith, the kind of burning passion that takes the soul as a flame takes kindling and reduces it to ash. She wanted to lead the believers back to Salah ad-Din."

"And you said no."

"Can you blame me, Khalidah?" he asked, and she saw that a bit of the fire had come back into his eyes. "She was a madwoman by then, without regard for anything but her conviction."

"The same has been said of each of Allah's prophets, in his time."

"Believe me mistaken, if you will," he answered wearily. "There is no changing the past. I told her that I was still the Khan and I would not give her mission my blessing. I suppose in her way she did still respect me, for she didn't take anyone with her, just slipped away one night with her sword and her horse and nothing else. She went back to Salah ad-Din, and for several years she fought for him. I don't know what happened—whether it was a sudden epiphany or a gradual disillusionment. I know only that at some point the fire burned out. She lost her faith, or perhaps simply the strength to pursue it. An Arab chief with whom she had fought had asked her repeatedly to marry him. At last she accepted, and so she became the wife of Abd al-Aziz al-Hassani."

"How do you know all of this?" Khalidah asked, despite a premonition of the answer.

Tor Gul Khan paused. "Because she told me."

Khalidah shut her eyes, as if in doing so she could shut her heart against the terrible truth she was about to hear.

"I suppose that she had hoped to salvage herself by marrying," he continued, as if it were a great effort, "in living a simple life as a wife and a mother. But Brekhna was Jinn, and a Jinni never stops being a Jinni, not even after life has burnt her to a cinder." He paused, giving Khalidah a look of terrible sympathy. "War couldn't save her, nor marriage, nor even motherhood. By the time she realized that, there was a single ember left burning in her, and that was the desire to return to Qaf. That was why she left you, Khalidah: to come here, to ask to be taken back. But she did not intend to abandon you—that, you must understand. She would have brought you with her."

"Would have?" Khalidah repeated.

"Yes," he said softly, bitterly. "I could not forget my own anger and forgive her. I told her that she had made her choice. She would never be welcome here again, nor any half-blooded child."

Khalidah felt the words like a slap; it was only by tremendous effort that she didn't run from him. But she knew that there was still more to come, that she must hear it, and so she kept still, kept listening.

"She accepted it with what I thought was equanimity. I could not see that I had snuffed that last living corner of her heart. With that betrayal, I had killed my only daughter. Oh, she still lives— Alipsha has told me that. She is somewhere far from here; far from anywhere, I suppose. But what her life is like now . . . well, I wish I did not need to imagine.

"As for me, I realized my mistake the moment she left. Since then I have known remorse the like of which you cannot imagine. I spent a few years looking for her, until I realized that she did not want to be found. Then I began looking for you."

"So I am here to soothe your conscience?"

He flinched. "I suppose I deserved that. But if you can find it in yourself, please believe that I wanted you to come here because I wanted you to have the choice that I denied your mother. What else can I do, Khalidah, to begin to atone for what I have taken from you?"

His eyes were pleading. She studied him, imagining the many ways that she could answer this question. But in the end, she cast them all aside in favor of the only one that mattered.

"You can let the believers follow me," she said, "and fight for Salah ad-Din, with your blessing."

He closed his eyes and inclined his head. "And along with my blessing, take this knowledge with you, Khalidah: in my eyes you are Jinn, you are my blood, and nothing will ever change that. If you choose the life of your father's people, I wish you well in it. But if you ever find yourself longing for Qaf, then come back to us. I don't care how long you have been away. You and whomever you choose to bring with you will always find a home here."

When Khalidah nodded, she found her hands spattered with tears.

Sixteen

"**WELL?**" Abi Gul asked eagerly. "What did he say?"

She and Sulayman had waited for Khalidah on a wide, flat rock on the riverbank, near where the horses grazed. Khalidah sat down with them, winding one of her plaits around her hand.

"He said that we are free to go," she answered, "and that we will go with his blessing."

Abi Gul leapt to her feet, clapping her hands like a child, her face aglow with excitement. "May I tell the others?" she asked.

Khalidah could not help smiling at her friend's delight; she only wished that she felt the same. "Of course you can—and hurry. We must leave as soon as possible if we are to catch the Sultan's army in time."

Abi Gul waved away Khalidah's words like flies. "Don't worry about that—we have ways of traveling fast when we need to." And with that cryptic assurance, she was off up the hill to the dormitory to spread the news.

Sulayman had been watching Khalidah carefully throughout this exchange, and once Abi Gul was gone he said, "There was more. A lot more, judging by the look on your face."

Khalidah looked at him. He was almost unrecognizable as the minstrel who had accompanied Abd al-Hadi to her father's camp so many months ago, well fed, bearded, cloaked in the studied obsequiousness of the intelligent servant. Now he was clean-shaven like the Jinn men, his hair shorn close under his rolled cap, and his features had taken on the quality of the Jinn's that marked them as creatures of these remote mountains, as if they had been shaped by rock and thin air. Only his eyes remained the same: black and laughing, clever and kind. He smiled encouragement, and Khalidah burst into tears.

Sulayman took her into his arms and held her while she cried, neither asking nor offering anything in response. After a time, the sound of the river and the shelter of his arms soothed her, and she began to tell him all that Tor Gul Khan had told her. Putting it into her own words did nothing, however, to settle her heart.

"I preferred not knowing," she concluded.

"Are you sure of that?"

"Don't condescend to me!"

"I'm not. It's like Ghassan telling me about my own mother. I was angry with him at the time. I felt it was another burden to carry when I was already overloaded. But now it has settled. It isn't that I don't think of it, or that it doesn't trouble me; only that time has made me see it as necessary. I believe that one day it might lead to some kind of peace."

"I cannot imagine I will ever make peace with this knowledge."

"Very well; but it doesn't change the reasons for your deciding to return to Salah ad-Din. You must hold on to your purpose, Khalidah—if not for your own sake, then for the sake of the people who will follow you."

"What if no one does?" she asked. "What if all of this comes to nothing?"

His face quirked into the expression Khalidah had once thought of as his thief's smile. He indicated the hill behind her. Khalidah didn't know whether to be dismayed or delighted at the stream of people heading toward the rock where she sat, Abi Gul leading the way.

THE volunteers numbered about five hundred: half of the population of Qaf. They ranged from the not-yet-initiated to their grandparents. Tor Gul Khan publicly gave them his blessing on the evening after his conversation with Khalidah. He also gave leave for those not yet of fighting age to join the volunteers, if they had their parents' permission.

When the volunteers had dispersed to make their preparations, one wizened old man made his way toward Khalidah and knelt before her.

"Bibi Khalidah," he said, "my name is Arzou, and I must ask a favor of you."

Trying to remember why the name sounded familiar, she said, "Please, rise—I am no queen. Tell me what it is that you want."

Arzou looked at her for a moment with rheumy eyes and then he said, "Your friend Sulayman has told me that you have met my daughter, Sandara."

It all came rushing back to Khalidah then. "I have had that honor," she said softly.

Arzou nodded sadly. "Sulayman has also told me of her circumstances, and I cannot allow her to live out her life in friendless seclusion. She should be here, and her children should be raised as Jinn. Tor Gul Khan has granted her a dispensation. You will pass by Zabol on your way west, and if I might accompany you so far, perhaps you can persuade Sandara to return with me to Qaf."

"Of course you may come with us," Khalidah said, "but I do not think that you will need any help in persuading Sandara to come back."

Arzou took Khalidah's hands in his and kissed them.

THAT evening, Khalidah's dormitory was as chaotic as it had been on the first night of Psarlay, but this time the turmoil consisted of armor and weapons, saddlebags and bedrolls, rather than finery and face paint. Abi Gul brought Khalidah her things from the cupboard where they had lain since she had arrived in Qaf. Along with her own saddle and blanket and sword, there were two new bows—one for long range and one for close—and a quiver containing three types of arrows. She had leather armor strengthened with fish glue, a metal-and-leather helmet, a suit of plain white clothing cut more closely than what they wore every day, and a set of the silk under-garments she had been so abashed to watch Abi Gul remove on her first day in Qaf. Since then, Khalidah had learned their purpose: the silk was so tough that arrows shot from a long distance would not penetrate it even if they penetrated the skin beneath, and so the arrow could be drawn from the flesh intact by pulling on the fabric around it.

When she had packed, she sat on her bed watching the other girls. The dormitory was half empty, and Khalidah guessed that this was because the missing girls came from families who did not believe in Pamir's prophecy. Though she had heard no one speak out against her, nor against those who were joining her, she felt the absence of the nonbelievers like a dagger in her side.

"You cannot please everyone," came Abi Gul's voice at her shoulder, startling her from her reverie.

"How do you know what I was thinking?"

"Your face is like a clear river—it can't hide the stones at its bed."

"That does not encourage me," Khalidah said.

Abi Gul smiled, stuffing clothing into a saddlebag. "I can't imagine anything that would encourage you at the moment. But it will do you no good to sit here brooding. Take a walk—after all, you might not see Qaf again for a long time."

It was slight, but Khalidah caught the waver in Abi Gul's voice as she spoke the final words.

EVENING had settled over the valley, the last sunlight throwing cypress-colored shadows. By the river the horses grazed as the last of the workers came in from the orchards and the fields. Blue veins of smoke rose from the terraced houses on the hillside. Khalidah walked along the riverbank, looking into water that was opaque now with the falling night. She thought of the first night of Psarlay; there would be no singing and dancing tonight. There was only the hush of anticipation, of speculation and hope and doubt gathering strength with the falling dark.

Khalidah could already feel the hollow chill of the coming night, and she knew that she would never sleep. She also knew then that she could not go back to the dormitory, to the incessant questions and the eager chatter of the girls who had no idea what they were riding into. As the last light faded from the mountains' eastern faces, Sulayman fell into step beside her. They walked for a long time in silence, all the way to the hill above the empty practice field. There the wind was brisker. It blew Khalidah's shawl back against her shoulders and lifted her hair, which was loose for the first time since their journey had begun. It was tradition, Abi Gul had told her, for girls to loosen their plaits the night before setting out on their first mission. There had been some complicated reasoning behind it, most of which Khalidah had forgotten, except that it had to do with virginity; though she wondered now whether she had that wrong, since she couldn't quite see the connection.

"Are you still wondering whether you've done the right thing?" Sulayman asked.

"No—it's too late for that. But I couldn't face them anymore."

"Stay here with me, then."

"What?" she asked. When she turned to look at him, she saw sadness and longing in his face that confused her further. "What is the matter, Sulayman?" And then it hit her. "You don't want to come, do you? You want to stay here. I should have realized—"

But he was smiling, half amused, half sad. "No, Khalidah, don't think that! I have no doubts. It is only that I have missed you."

She shook her head, bemused. "Missed me? But I have been here all the time!"

"Yes—and I have hardly seen you in all these weeks. I know that it's jealousy, and I'm not proud of it, but I have begun to wonder whether you have changed your mind . . . whether the things we promised on our journey have changed for you, now that you have seen this place and the kind of life you could have here."

She felt a rush of remorse, realizing how it must have seemed to him. And what he said was true, to an extent—she had been absorbed and distracted by all that had happened, all that she had learned and become and stood still to become. Yet he had never let his feelings cloud his advice to her. Khalidah reached out to him, and he reached back. And then he was not just clutching her but kissing her, and she couldn't quite believe that it was her own hands reaching for the knot in his sash, as he pulled her down into a hollow in the lee side of the hill. Somewhere in the midst of it, he caught her hands.

"Are you sure, Khalidah? I thought that you feared—"

But she had already counted the days and knew that it was as safe as it could be, and as for the rest she answered, "The only thing I fear now is that I will go to my grave never having known this."

He looked at her for a moment, to be certain that she meant it, that this was not something she would regret.

"I will never regret it," she answered, and then smiled.

Seventeen

Sephoria
Early June

THE Franj castle at Sephoria was hardly worthy of the designation. Numair thought that the small cube of rock looked like nothing so much as the product of some third-rate god's constipation, squeezed out and left to desiccate on the top of an indifferent hill. But if the castle wasn't up to much, the lands around it more than compensated for its shortcomings, and so he had been happy enough to wait there in the weeks between his desertion from the Tiberias detachment and de Ridefort's return. He had lain low, camping in a clutch of trees, hunting at dawn and dusk when he was unlikely to be seen, listening from the shadows of village tea shops and taverns as news rolled in of the massacre at Cresson, Tripoli's capitulation, the Franj call to arms, and, finally, the army that had begun to gather in the town.

When he learned via this same web of gossip that de Ridefort was in residence, he made his way to the castle. Now he sat by a window in what passed for a great hall, sipping a glass of sweet local wine, looking out at the fertile hills of Galilee tumbling toward the horizon. He would have liked nothing better than to relax into the bucolic torpor, but de Ridefort was in no such mood.

"What do you mean, you are not going back?" he stormed when Numair made his announcement, slamming his cup onto the table so that the wine splashed out and over his hand, further stoking his rage.

"Just that," Numair answered with languid arrogance. "I've had enough of army life, and at any rate I've learned nothing in my time in the Sultan's camp that can help you. Besides, your son seems far better placed to provide you with information than I."

Numair had intended for this remark to placate the Master, but instead de Ridefort's anger deepened. "Do not mention that brat to me!"

With the first fluttering of anxiety, Numair asked, "Why? What has he done?"

"He has insulted and betrayed me," de Ridefort answered, "and if you had paid the slightest attention, you would have realized that he deserted us long since for the little Ayyub sodomite. He is of no use to us any longer—if he ever was at all."

De Ridefort's sky-blue glare had settled on Numair with a cast of accusation. Liking this even less than his words, Numair said, "How do you know this?"

"Because he told me."

"He told you?" Numair repeated. "And you let him live?"

De Ridefort paused before answering, convincing Numair that there was more to the story than the Master was allowing. "I was not in a position to do otherwise," he muttered. "But it is worse than that. The Sultan has dismissed me from his service. I hardly need to tell you what that means—for both of us."

"You think that Salah ad-Din holds Bilal in high enough regard to take his advice on such a matter?" he scoffed.

"Do you have a better explanation for the Sultan's sudden change of heart?"

"What does it matter, the reason?"

"It matters a great deal to me," de Ridefort said coldly. "I do not like to be double-crossed."

Numair bristled at the accusation in his tone. "You cannot blame me for this."

"Can't I? You are the one who brought the boy into it."

"So?"

"So, you are the one who is going to take him out again."

"You do not command me," Numair said, slamming his own cup down, his anger finally piqued.

"Oh, but I do," cried de Ridefort, his eyes alight with malice. "You are a Saracen in a Franj castle. One word from me, and your head rolls."

"If Bilal has turned the Sultan against you, do you really think he's left my reputation intact? I won't get anywhere near him."

The Templar stood and leaned over Numair, gripping the arms of his chair, pinning him to it. "Yes, you will. Somehow, you will find a way, for if you don't, your head will decorate my lance." He smiled as Numair glared at him. "And just in case you take it in mind to disappear, remember that there is a good deal of Franj territory between here and your home."

"You are despicable," Numair hissed.

"And that is why we make such good allies," de Ridefort answered coolly. "So, am I to understand that you'll take care of my little problem? You will of course be well paid for your services."

Numair only glowered at him, but they both knew the answer.

Agreeing to it was one thing; carrying it out was another. Depending on how the Sultan had taken the news of his treachery, there might be scouts looking for him even now. Numair knew that he couldn't go near the Muslim camp. His only chance was to draw Bilal out of it.

But Bilal was not the gullible boy he had been on the morning after Khalidah's elopement. For several days, Numair lay in his tent in a wind-ridden wadi to the south of Tal Ashtara, smoking *banj* and ruminating glumly on the impossibility of his mission. And then, with the inexplicable luck that sometimes graces the truly nefarious, the solution fell into his lap.

It was the sixth morning since he'd left Sephoria, and three hours shy of noon it was already sweltering. Numair was seated on the lip of the wadi in the perforated shade of a tamarisk tree, cleaning his weapons and hoping for a breeze, when he noticed a cloud of dust moving along the horizon. It came from the north, and as it drew nearer he recognized the form of a running horse. A few more moments and he could make out its coloring: dark bay. Even as he was telling himself that it couldn't be, he caught a flash of yellow—the rider's flying robe—and the three white spots on the horse's flank.

Grabbing his crossbow and sword, Numair hid himself such as he could behind the attenuated tree. He knew that this chance was likely to be his only one, so he loaded the crossbow carefully and then waited, measuring the distance with the patient acuity that had made him into a formidable hunter. He spared a moment of regret for Anjum—he had bred and broken her himself—and then he fired.

Even before the arrow hit its target, he knew that he had judged the shot perfectly. The horse tumbled, hurling her rider into the sand, and before the stunned Bilal even realized what had happened, Numair was upon him. He drew his sword and shoved it against Bilal's throat, where it turned on the iron links of a mail coif.

"Charmed the prince out of his armor, have you?" Numair snarled, and went to thrust the mail aside.

But Bilal caught the point of the sword in one gauntleted hand, and with strength Numair was clearly not expecting, he forced it back from his throat, until he could roll free. He leapt to his feet, drawing his own sword and hoping that his arm would hold. It had only just healed and was still tender enough that he wrapped it for riding in wet strips of leather, which hardened and stiffened as they dried, protecting it from further damage. He doubted, however, that the bandage would withstand the force of a sword fight, and worse still, Numair had noticed it.

"What was it?" he asked, nodding to the bandage. "A lovers' quarrel?"

"Why are you here, Numair?" Bilal asked coldly, as they circled.

"To kill you, obviously."

"What is obvious? You couldn't have known that I would be here, now."

Numair smiled, shook his head. "I consider that Allah's blessing upon my intention. Now—"

He lunged and Bilal dodged the blow, stumbling. Numair slashed again, and this time their blades clashed in a shower of sparks, which fizzled away into the searing sand. Bilal managed to recover, but Numair had seen the flash of pain on his face as the wrapped arm took the force of the blow.

"If you kneel to me now," Numair said, studying his sweating opponent down the length of his blade, "I promise to make it quick."

"I would suffer the worst of deaths before I would kneel to you!"

"Very well, then . . ."

Numair attacked again. Though Bilal fought with everything in him, he knew that he was beaten. They were an hour's ride from camp—an hour's ride from anywhere—and he would not have been a match for Numair even if his arm had been sound. His fight rapidly deteriorated into a series of desperate parries as Numair forced him back to the edge of the wadi and then, with a vicious swipe, knocked his legs out from under him, so that he knelt after all.

The fall from the hapless Anjum, the heat, and the pain of his arm had all done their work on Bilal. He could not make himself stand. In fact, it was all he could do to keep from toppling into the valley behind him. The blood rushed in his ears with a sound like a flash flood in a wadi; his vision was clouded with the spots and sparks of fleeing consciousness . . . and something else. Something that should not be there, but was: a dark wedge on the horizon that resolved improbably into a band of running horses, all backed by black-robed riders except for one at the front, who rode in a flicker of yellow and a stream of dark hair. For a moment he thought that they were angels come to escort him to paradise, but the subsequent thud of the black-feathered arrow was too visceral to be divine. Likewise the rictus of thwarted vengeance on Numair's face as he stumbled, clawing at the arrow lodged in his back, and pitched over the lip of the wadi.

Bilal clung to the tamarisk's trunk and looked down, forcing his eyes to repeat the truth of the body on the valley floor many times before he believed it. It was only when a hand touched his shoulder that he remembered his liberators. He turned and looked up into Salim's face, still etched with the horror of what had almost happened. But when the prince helped him to stand, he nearly collapsed again, for Salim's entourage had ridden forward and their leader had pulled aside his *kufiyya*.

"*As-salaamu alaikum*, Bilal," said Abd al-Aziz, his narrow, lined face breaking into a smile. "It's a pretty chase you've led us on these last months . . . and it seems we found you just in time."

Eighteen

ABD al-Aziz's men made quick work of Numair's campsite, extracting everything of value and torching the rest. Bilal and Salim stood together, watching the tent burn.

"Are you all right?" Salim asked.

"More or less," Bilal answered, flexing the fingers of his right hand. They were losing feeling as the arm began to swell against the binding.

"Here, let me . . ." said Salim. Drawing his dagger, he cut carefully through the leather strips until they fell away, revealing the livid, swollen skin beneath. He stared at it for a moment and then, looking up at Bilal, he said, "I'm sorry."

"It doesn't hurt much," Bilal answered.

"No—I mean, for the rest."

"The rest of what?" Bilal asked incredulously. "You saved my life."

"Yes, and if I had not been such a self-pitying wretch, I would never have left camp without telling you, and you would not have followed me—"

"And if the last straw had not been loaded, the camel's back would have held," Bilal interrupted dryly. "What's done is done, and we're both alive to tell about it. Besides, we're finally rid of him."

They both looked over at Numair's crumpled body, the ostrich-feather arrow still protruding from his back. For all that they made free with his belongings, none of the Bedu men seemed inclined to touch his body.

"And you?" asked Bilal. "How are you, after—?"

Salim smiled. For the first time since Cresson, it had all the arch brilliance Bilal had first fallen in love with. "Killing him?" he finished. "Surprisingly well, actually. In fact, one might say it was just what I needed to snap me out of the dream I've been in these last weeks."

Bilal wasn't quite certain that he believed this, but he wasn't about to argue with it, either. Salim walked over to the body and prodded it speculatively with his toe. "Do you want his head? You can bring it back to camp as a gift for my father."

Snapped out of the dream, indeed, Bilal thought. He found the matter-of-fact brutality in Salim's eyes at least as disturbing as his earlier torpor. "Leave him for the vultures," he said.

Salim looked at the body with obvious regret, but he resheathed his sword.

DESPITE Abd al-Aziz's protests, Salim led him straight to his father's tent when they returned to camp. While the retainers kicked dust outside with the Sultan's guard, the two leaders eyed each other with cautious respect. After formally thanking the sheikh for his part in Bilal's rescue, Salah ad-Din sent two of his Mamluks to find a campsite for his men, then clapped his hands for tea.

"So then, will you remain here with us, or repair to the south now that you have found your wayward . . . ah . . ."

"I have always considered Bilal a son," Abd al-Aziz said firmly, "whether or not he realized it." Though he was nominally answering the Sultan, Abd al-Aziz looked at Bilal as he spoke the words. The boy nodded mutely, wondering if it would forever be his lot to choke back tears whenever someone offered him a kind word.

Abd al-Aziz gave him a brief smile and then turned back to Salah ad-Din. "As for remaining with you, it would be our honor. I would have come sooner, but certain affairs"—his face darkened momentarily—"have kept me with the tribe. At any rate, I trust that the men I sent to you have proven useful?"

Though it seemed unlikely that he would remember a small band of Bedu cavalry among tens of thousands, Bilal didn't doubt Salah ad-Din's sincerity when he answered, "They have proven serious-minded and stalwart. I thank you for their services."

The two leaders made small talk while they finished their tea, and then the Sultan said, "I imagine that you and Bilal have matters of your own to discuss. Therefore, allow me to detain you no longer."

Abd al-Aziz was astute enough to realize that he had been dismissed. Bowing, he retreated. Salim stayed behind in the pavilion at his father's request; Bilal and the sheikh followed the Mamluk guard who was waiting outside to show them to the campsite. They walked for a time in silence before Bilal found the words with which to break it.

"Do not think that I am not grateful . . . but I cannot help wondering, why did you come for me?"

Abd al-Aziz paused for a moment, then answered, "What I said to the Sultan was true, Bilal—you have always been like a son to me. When I learned that you had left with Numair, I knew that something was not right. I came after you as soon as my brother let up on his raiding long enough to allow it."

"Has it been bad, then?"

Abd al-Aziz sighed. "No worse than usual, though he's been more persistent. It's spite, I suppose. Abd al-Hadi has always been adept at shouldering me with the blame for his problems, and his son's defection was particularly nettlesome to him."

Bilal paused, working up the courage to ask the question that had been prodding him since they met. "How is my mother?"

There was a hitch before the sheikh answered: slight, but not so slight that Bilal didn't notice it.

"What is it?" he demanded. "What has happened to her?"

"I assure you she is well, Bilal," Abd al-Aziz said. "Only

wretched with worry for you. If you do not believe me, you can see for yourself soon enough, for I have sent messengers to tell her that I have found you here. She will no doubt be joining us as soon as she can find a horse to carry her."

Bilal was still convinced that there was something Abd al-Aziz was keeping from him, but for the moment he forced his mind back to the present and asked, "How did you know where to look for me?"

Apparently relieved to have left the topic of Zaynab, Abd al-Aziz chuckled and said, "There aren't many blue-eyed Bedu in Oultrejourdain, and still fewer fighting for Salah ad-Din. You are a bit of a legend in the south by now." Bilal smiled wanly. "We followed the rumors and we met Salim al-Ayyubi this morning, by Allah's grace, as he exercised his horse. The rest, you know."

There followed another long pause that would have been silence, if it had not been so full of the sounds of calling men and clattering weapons, restless horses, and flapping tents. Bilal was keenly aware of all that Abd al-Aziz had refrained from asking him, and grateful for it, but he could not subdue his own curiosity.

Choosing his words carefully, he said, "Please, Sayyid, do not misunderstand me, for you have all of my gratitude, and at any rate I would not choose any life now over the one I have found here . . . but I cannot help wondering, if you really thought of me as a son, why then—"

"Did I not marry my daughter to you?" Abd al-Aziz laughed ruefully and shook his head. "I wanted nothing so much as that."

Bilal stopped, stunned.

"I could see that you loved each other," the sheikh continued, "with the kind of love that may not flash and spark, but that will endure the tests of marriage. I thought that you would temper her and she would inspire you, and that together you would be a pillar of strength to the tribe."

"What happened?"

Abd al-Aziz sighed. "How much does the answer matter to you?"

"I am tired of secrets," Bilal replied. "They bring nothing but grief."

"I will tell you then, though I fear the answer will sow great bitterness in you. So: I did not marry you to my daughter because your mother begged me not to."

A part of Bilal felt that he ought to be surprised by this, but he wasn't. "Because she feared de Ridefort's threat about turning her over to her husband," he said. "She did not want anything to draw attention to us. And a blue-eyed Bedu, as you say, attracts a good deal of attention—particularly if he is clan chief."

Abd al-Aziz looked at him in surprise.

"Yes, I know all about it. It's how Numair enticed me. But how long have you known?"

Once again, the sheikh sighed. "Almost as long as I've known you. Not long before Brekhna left the tribe, she told me your mother's story and made me promise to protect her, and also to keep her secret as if it were my own. I do not regret the first part, but many times I have regretted the latter. If you had known who you were, who your father was, and what your mother feared, so many things might have been different . . ."

Bilal reflected on this as they walked. Things would indeed have been different, but he could not see that they would have been better. At last the Mamluk pointed out the campsite that had been chosen for the Hassan. By the door to the pavilion that had been raised for him, Abd al-Aziz turned to Bilal.

"Thank you for listening to me, Bilal. Now I must rest, and you must have your arm tended. There will be time enough for talk in the days to come. But there is one more thing I would have you know before we part: I have taken a longer view of my daughter's disappearance over these last months. If she should ever return to me, I will hold no grudge over her."

"That is good of you, Sayyid," said Bilal, not quite certain why the sheikh was telling him this.

"Bilal, do you . . . that is to say, if she were to return, and were agreeable to it, would you still wish to marry her?"

Looking into Abd al-Aziz's earnest, solicitous face, Bilal could only wonder how he had ever thought that he was in love with Khalidah, or that marrying her would make him happy. He did not believe that Khalidah would return, and he did not want to hurt the man who had called him a son, but still, after the sheikh's honesty, Bilal could not bring himself to lie.

"Much has changed for me over the last months, Sayyid," he said. "I still hold Khalidah in the highest regard, but you'll understand that I see myself to have a different destiny now."

To his surprise, Abd al-Aziz looked relieved rather than offended. He smiled at Bilal and bowed, saying, "*Ma'as salaama*, Bilal. May Allah bless you in that destiny, whatever it may be."

Bilal watched as Abd al-Aziz turned and went into his tent, ruminating on the fickleness of time and the human heart.

Nineteen

NUMAIR was in hell. He knew it because no mortal realm could encompass such pain. It began as a white-hot point in his upper back, radiating down his spine and into his limbs in skewers of searing agony. But when at last he opened his eyes, he found himself looking not at a fiery world of dancing devils, but at the same empty, sandy wadi he had called home for the last week. He did not know whether to be relieved or disappointed.

It took him the rest of that day to drag himself to the stream. He ascertained in the process that his right leg was broken and his left arm injured, though still workable. The vision in his left eye was hazed red, and he knew that he had at least one concussion to the head. By the time he made it to the water he couldn't raise his hands to drink, so he tipped himself into the stream and lay there, letting the water run into his mouth.

He fell asleep. By some miracle, he did not drown, but he woke shivering violently. The sky was dark. He dragged himself back out of the water and looked for the tent he was certain had been there in the morning, a few paces from the stream. Now there was nothing but a pile of ashes. Digging into them, he found a few glowing embers, to which he fed the remains of the tent poles and some dry grasses until a flame flickered to life.

He lay by the tiny fire until his shudders died to periodic tremors. Then he reached behind him with his uninjured arm, gripped the arrow shaft, and pulled. It seemed to him that he was tearing the soul from his body, but at last it came away. He was so dizzy with pain, it took him several moments to realize what he held in his hand. It was indeed an arrow shaft, with flights of black ostrich feather, but where the point should have been there was only chewed wood. The wedge of iron was still lodged in his flesh.

Numair was no physician, but looking at that arrow shaft he knew without a doubt the course his own death would take. It was almost enough to make him wish that Bilal had let the prince make a souvenir of his head after all. But Allah had spared him, such as it was, and Allah did not spare men without reason. Numair knew with the conviction of the doomed that what time he had left had been left him in order to exact justice on Bilal al-Hassani.

Part Three

One

Qaf–Syria
June

KHALIDAH awakened with the first watery streaks of light in the
east. The mountains were still ghost shapes drawn by the absence
of stars, the birds still slept. There was no sound but the faint whisper of wind through the grasses. She lay on her back watching
the light push subtle fingers into the dark, wrapped in Sulayman's
arms and their discarded robes and the perfect peace of fulfilled
longing.

"Why did I ever want more than this?" she asked.

"You will, soon enough," Sulayman whispered, his lips touching her neck. "No human being ever stops wanting for long."

She could feel his hardness against her leg. "So I see," she said,
grinning, and turned to him, tracing the line of his back with the
tips of her fingers. The light had risen enough that she could see
him shut his eyes, see him shiver as well as feel it. Her own body
leapt to his desire, but he caught her hands as they reached for him
and kissed them.

"There isn't time," he said.

Khalidah sighed. "Since I met you, it seems, we have been riding a horse that is racing time. Will it ever end? Will we ever be
able to lie like this for days and think of no one or nothing else?"

The light caught his smile and seared it into Khalidah's heart.
It was not the old thief's smile, but one of unutterable tenderness;
she knew that whatever happened, he would never smile that way at
anyone else, and it would be with her until the day she died.

"*Inshallah*," he said.

THOUGH the village came out to see them off, there was none of the cheering and weeping that had accompanied the departure of the last mission. The eerie silence that Khalidah had sensed as she walked by the river the previous evening seemed, if anything, to have intensified.

Khalidah rode near the front, behind the guides, with Abi Gul on her left and Sulayman on her right, riding a tall palomino stallion called Sre Zer. Aasifa had come into season during their first week in Qaf, and despite the careful separation of fertile mares from the stallions, she and Sre Zer had been found grazing together one morning outside the pens. Though it was too early to tell whether she was in foal, the stallion's owner had assured Sulayman that Sre Zer's seed never failed to sprout. He insisted that Sulayman leave Aasifa with him and take the stallion in her place.

As they passed the orchards and the houses and finally the practice grounds, Khalidah realized that she had no idea how they would get out of the valley, for she had no memory of being taken in. Abi Gul laughed when she asked her about it.

"Is this the first time you've thought of it?"

"You've kept me too busy to think of anything else," Khalidah answered.

"Poppy juice," Abi Gul said.

"What?"

"Do you not know the effects of poppy juice?"

Khalidah and Sulayman looked at each other and burst out laughing. Abi Gul frowned, unaware of anything humorous in what she had said.

"I'm sorry," said Khalidah, "it's only that none of this would have happened at all if it had not been for the merits of poppy juice. Sulayman used it to drug my tribe the night of my henna ceremony. That was how we managed to escape."

Abi Gul looked at Sulayman with raised eyebrows. "Well, we can claim nothing so dramatic. But when the scouts tell us that someone is approaching Qaf, we make them drink poppy juice before bringing them to the valley. We do not wish the way to be known."

"I do not remember anyone asking me to drink poppy juice on that night," Khalidah said, frowning.

Abi Gul shook her head. "There was no need. They dripped it into your mouths while you slept, and you awakened in Qaf."

They rode on in silence for a long time, winding among the foothills on paths Khalidah would never have found on her own, and for the first time she began to believe that they might actually make it back to Syria as quickly as the Jinn had promised. After several hours the foothills turned into mountains, topped by the snow peaks that had looked so distant from Qaf. They rode along a rocky valley that narrowed continuously, until Khalidah could have reached out and touched both of its sides at once. Great walls of rock reared up, seeming to lean toward each other until at last they did come together, and the little army was riding through the darkness of a cave. There was a dim light coming from somewhere up ahead, and the sound of rushing water. This grew louder and the light stronger as they rode along, until at last Khalidah saw the opening to the rocky passage, curtained by a thundering waterfall.

The horses ahead of her were turning sharply right at the cave mouth. She gave Zahirah her head, letting her follow Tufan. The gray stallion disappeared around the corner and then Zahirah was around as well, picking her way down a narrow, stony incline. At first it was slippery with water and weed, but soon they left the waterfall behind them and reached another valley, this one much wider than the last. It was bordered by dun-colored hills with great rocky mountains behind them, the floor smooth as a racetrack. With a shock, Khalidah recognized it.

"We were here!" she said to Sulayman. "There is a stream up ahead. We camped by it, but that must have been four . . . five days before we reached Qaf?"

"A week," he answered.

"How is that possible?"

He shook his head. "They are the Jinn. This is what they do." He considered this, then added, "Besides, by the time we camped here, we might have been riding in circles for days."

It was possible, Khalidah conceded to herself; but still, it was strange.

They picked up the pace through the valley. Zahirah kept up easily with her larger counterparts; in fact, she seemed eager to best them, for which Khalidah was secretly delighted. They rode through that day until the last light had gone, and then they made camp on a patch of sparse grass by a little green pond.

The Jinn were as efficient in making camp as they were in picking their way through treacherous mountains. Within minutes, it seemed, the horses were stripped, rubbed down, and given their rations of grain. Minutes after that the cookfires were lit and pots of water hung over them to boil. Khalidah shared a fire with Sulayman, Abi Gul, and Hila. They were joined by a few older warriors, cousins of Abi Gul and Hila who regaled them with tales of other missions while they drank their tea and ate their dried mulberries and boiled salted mutton. But nobody had the energy to stay up late, particularly knowing that they would rise again at first light for another day of relentless travel.

Two

A couple of days later they reached Zabol. While the Jinn camped in the foothills outside the city, Khalidah and Sulayman accompanied Arzou to Sandara's house. It seemed to have stood still in time since the morning they had left it: the same leaves rustled above the garden wall, the same smell of verdure came from within. Sulayman rapped on the gate, and once again Daoud opened it. He stood staring suspiciously at the old man.

"You need not be afraid, Daoud," Khalidah said. "This man is our friend, and he would very much like to see your mother. Is she within?"

The boy nodded solemnly and opened the gate to admit them. Sandara sat on the edge of the fountain staring into the falling water, the little girls on either side. She leapt to her feet as she heard their voices, and then she froze. Slowly, Arzou took a step toward her; she took one in return. And then they ran, falling into each other's arms, heedless of all the years in between.

SANDARA wanted them to stay that night, but Sulayman and Khalidah declined, saying that the Jinn must move on early.

"Very well then," said Sandara, looking at her father, "I had hoped to have more time with you alone, but so be it. Father, I entrust my children to you and to my mother. Take them back to Qaf with you and raise them as Jinn—as they should always have been raised."

The twins were too young to catch the ominous undertone of her words, but Daoud heard it and instinctively clung to his mother as she turned to Khalidah. "Bibi Khalidah, I most humbly offer you my services on your mission. If you will allow it, I will join your contingent and go to fight for Mobarak Khan in the west."

"No, Sandara, you cannot!" her father cried. "You have suffered too much already, your children need you, and your mother longs for you so—please, return to Qaf with me."

"My mother longs for the daughter she remembers," Sandara said gently, clasping his hands, "but I am not that girl, and I never will be again. Better to give her three beautiful children to care for than one broken woman. I am sick at heart—sick to my soul—and the only way to end the suffering is to complete what I began so long ago. I will fight my battle and return to Qaf as a Jinni, or else . . . well, the sickness will be ended, one way or another."

The children were distressed now; the girls began to cry. Sandara bent down and took all three of them in her arms. "Do not weep, children; you are going to live in paradise. You will have other children to play with, and two grandparents to care for you, and with Allah's mercy we will be reunited there someday. Now go and pack whatever you wish to bring with you—but not too much for a horse to carry."

After a moment they went, still looking dubiously behind them, as if their mother would disappear. She watched them until they were gone, then she said, "There is little left here that I would keep; but there are some valuables that should go with the children. Can you wait two hours for me?"

Khalidah said that they could, and told her where to find the camp. Then she and Sulayman left Arzou and his daughter to their private farewells.

AFTER that they traveled fast—faster than Khalidah had ever imagined possible. They cut their way across the lands Khalidah and Sulayman had crossed so tortuously, sometimes along the same routes, but more often by different ones, shortcuts and secret paths that even Sulayman had never dreamed were there. The Jinn never consulted maps. The routes were chosen by scouts who had apparently memorized them.

When they came to Jazirah they turned north, so that they bypassed the marshes entirely. They followed the course of the Euphrates for several days before turning west again into the rocky Syrian desert. Now they began to send out scouts, who brought back enticing snips of news. Count Tripoli had abandoned the Sultan and turned back to the Franj after some kind of catastrophic battle; King Guy was mustering his army near the coast; the Sultan was moving his own army south, toward the border with the Franj kingdom. It seemed he might be planning to cross the Jordan. The Jinn could not grasp the significance of this, but to Khalidah it was awe inspiring: Salah ad-Din could hardly choose a more brazen declaration of war.

"The battle you spoke of," said Khalidah to the scout who had brought that piece of news, "the one that made Tripoli turn back to King Guy—do you know any more about it?"

The boy shook his head. "Only that it took place about seven weeks ago, and that a holy order of Franj knights was nearly destroyed in it."

"Which order?" Khalidah asked.

" 'The Order,' that was all the man told me—as if I should know by that what he meant."

Khalidah thought of her nightmare, of the beautiful prince who had cloven the head of the Templar and kissed Bilal by the pomegranate bush. But of course, there was no way to know which had come first.

The army traveled at night now, both for secrecy and to avoid the terrible heat of the desert daytime. The Jinn never complained, but Khalidah could tell that it was hard on them, after their mountain valley. Finally, a week past midsummer, a scout came galloping back to camp one early morning with the news that he had seen the Sultan's army camped by the Jordan.

"And it was vast," he gasped, both from exertion and shock, "more vast than any army you can imagine. Their campfires flickered like lamps on an altar, and I could not see their beginning nor their end."

Many of the Jinn wanted to break the camp they had just made and go to the Sultan then and there; eventually, Khalidah managed to dissuade them.

"It would be suicide," she said. "We would be shot down unapologetically if we were to approach them now, for they are about to make their move, and they will not let anything endanger it. No—we will camp here today, and tonight . . ."

She trailed off, because in fact she had no idea what she would do tonight. Khalidah slept fitfully that day, tossing and turning in the heat. She had forgotten its fierceness, how it sucked the sweat from her skin almost before it was finished forming, leaving it dry and gritted with salt. At last she crawled out of the white tent and walked to the edge of the camp. She stood at the edge of the empty desert, looking for her next step on the scorched and windblown horizon. For a moment it felt as though she had never left—as though the past months had been a dream, and if she were to turn she would see not the white tents of the Jinn but the black ones of her father's tribe, ringed around the oasis.

A slender hand slipped into hers. "What do you see?" asked Abi Gul.

Khalidah squeezed her hand. "Nothing," she answered. "We have come so far, and I still don't know how to bring us to our destination."

Abi Gul considered this for a time, her green-gold eyes slitted against the light and the scouring wind. Then she said, "Perhaps you should listen, instead of look."

"What?"

Abi Gul turned to her, her fairy's face serious for once. "As your mother called you to Qaf, there must be somebody who calls you back. Your father, perhaps? Your nurse?"

"Bilal," Khalidah said softly.

Abi Gul nodded, as if this were obvious; as if it could mean anything to her. "And do you know where to find him?"

Khalidah thought of the Ayyub prince and said, "I think I do."

Abi Gul smiled. "And so, you see, you do know after all."

Three

Tal Ashtara
Late June

AT midsummer, Salah ad-Din knew that his time had come. Battle season was upon them; his army would never be larger or readier to fight, and so he called a review at Tal Tasil. While he and his entourage stood on the hill, the army paraded before them. Salah ad-Din counted twelve thousand professional cavalry plus another thirty-three thousand mixed soldiers, everything from untrained religious volunteers to Bedu cavalry.

"Forty-five thousand souls, gathered to fight for Allah," he said to his emirs in his pavilion afterward. "The opportunity now before us may well never arise again. We must throw ourselves resolutely into the jihad before our troops grow weary of waiting and disperse."

Nobody disagreed, so the Sultan continued, "By our best estimate, we outnumber the enemy three to two—beatable odds for a well-trained, cohesive army, but Cresson culled the best Franj knights, the barons' factions are still barely on speaking terms, and King Guy is as indecisive as ever. They cannot beat us in a field battle, and so that is how we must fight them. It is time to bait the trap, and pray that they take it."

"What trap?" asked Al-Afdhal.

"What bait?" added Al-Zahir.

"Our own arid hills," Salah ad-Din answered, "and their stubborn chivalry."

And however they pressed him, he would say no more than that.

I<small>F</small> Salah ad-Din remained circumspect on the nature of his ultimate plan, he made his primary aim clear enough. He needed to broadcast his intent to fight in a way that the Franj could not possibly ignore, and so, on the twenty-sixth of June, as the Franj bickered at Acre, Salah ad-Din turned his army west. Before the march began he regarded the vast, churning force spreading behind him and, raising his sword, he called, "Victory over God's enemy!" His cry resounded through the ranks as his scribes dutifully scribbled, preserving words that would echo undiminished throughout history.

They spent the first day climbing and camped that night on the Golan Heights. The next day, they put the plain of Hauran at their backs and picked their way along the western edge of the Heights, where the hills become rocky cliffs that drop abruptly down to the Sea of Galilee. Midway through that day they crossed the border into Franj territory, but few marked it. By that point all who had not been told had guessed that the Sultan's aim was not the fickle borderline between their land and the Franj kingdom, but that far more potent barrier, the Jordan River. The moment the Sultan crossed it, the two kingdoms would be at war.

Late in the afternoon the army reached the river Yarmuk. They followed it for an hour in their descent from the Heights before Salah ad-Din turned them north once again, toward the confluence of the Jordan and the Sea of Galilee. That night he pitched his tent at Al-Qahwani, a morose little sore of a village on the lip of the great river, whose mud-brick buildings looked more than ready to rejoin the marshy ground on which they were built. It was damp and fly-infested and equidistant from the recently wronged Tiberias and the great Hospitaller fortress of Belvoir, but perched as it was within spitting distance of the Jordan, it could not have marked the Sultan's intentions more clearly.

Just as Salah ad-Din had intended, the Franj scouts on the other side of the river took one look at the massing Muslim army and turned their horses north toward Acre, pushing them to the limits of their endurance to bring this news to the king. And again as the Sultan had hoped, the insecure Guy immediately moved his knights and nobles to Sephoria, halving the distance between the two armies. At that point, Salah ad-Din allowed himself a cautious sigh of relief. Secure in his position for the moment, he called his own war council together to discuss his next step, which seemed to Salim to be a step backward.

"More raids?" he said to Bilal as they left his father's tent. "I thought that we were finished with all of that."

Bilal shook his head. "It's the same as Amman—the same I suppose as all of our battles with the Franj since they first took Jerusalem. We may outnumber them, but it does us no good if they remain behind their fortress walls. And Sephoria makes a good fortress: plenty of water, open supply routes . . . they would be fools to leave it for a pitched battle."

"Fools indeed," Salim answered dryly, hacking at a withered yucca with his sword. "But I do not think that they are such fools as to come to the call of a few raids."

"There are plenty among them who are hungry for our blood," Bilal said. "They will be happy to come if we call them out, and if enough of them come, the rest will have to follow."

"Perhaps. But there will be no 'we.' I will not let you near a fight until this heals properly!" He touched Bilal's arm, which had been splinted and bandaged again after his run-in with Numair. It had not rebroken, but the physician had warned him that with another heavy blow, it would.

"And do you command me now?" Bilal asked.

"I have commanded you since Busra!" Salim laughed, then dodged Bilal's swat. But his smile died quickly.

They had come to the edge of the water. The light of the campfires shattered and sank into its flow. A few bright points burned like stars somewhere off in the Franj distance. Stabbing his sword into the spongy ground and crouching down beside it, Salim asked, "Why did you tell my father about de Ridefort?"

Bilal sighed. "I had to, Salim. He and Numair could have been planning anything." He paused. "Are you angry?"

"Not that you told him. That you didn't tell me before you did it—yes, a little." He glanced at Bilal, his eyes bright and sharp. "I know that I have not been myself of late, but I am not so weak that I would have shrunk from duty."

Bilal knelt beside him. "That isn't why I didn't tell you."

"Why, then?"

Bilal traced his name in the mud and then, beside it, Salim's. "Because I was afraid."

Salim gave him another keen look. "Don't say that you were afraid for me."

"Well, why not? I love you, Salim. I could not bear a life without you. And since that makes you a target for those who wish to harm me—"

"All right," Salim said wearily. "Well, what did my father have to say?"

"He told me to be careful."

"Of what?"

Bilal shook his head. "For."

"For me?"

"Of course."

"And for yourself."

"He did not say that."

Salim smiled. "It would be like you not to hear it."

"It doesn't signify, anyway," Bilal said, smoothing their names from the mud and drawing an abstract pattern in their place. "A careful soldier is worse than useless."

"We will be like the Thebans, then," Salim said after a moment's thought.

"The what?"

"Thebes was an ancient Greek city-state, and a great military power. They remained autonomous long after their neighbors had fallen to Macedon. The secret of their success was a small band of warriors at the heart of the army: three hundred men, one hundred fifty pairs of lovers. They were talented soldiers, but it was their love that made them great. There is a quote from Plato, I can't remember it exactly . . . it was something along the lines of men bound by familial ties being unwilling to endanger themselves for each other, but those bound by romantic love being invincible. They'll fight fearlessly because they cannot bear to be seen as cowards by their lovers. 'Although a mere handful,' he said, 'they would overcome the world.' The Sacred Band . . . that was what they were called. The Sacred Band of Thebes."

"And what happened to them?" Bilal asked, though he suspected that he did not really want to hear it.

Salim shrugged, but the gesture fell just short of nonchalance. "They were beaten at last by Philip the Second of Macedon and his son Alexander, at the Battle of Chaeronea. It's said that every last one of them fought to the death. I suppose it is no wonder then that Thebes lost its independence that day."

"Hardly an inspiring story," Bilal said with apprehension, because inspiration was exactly what he saw on Salim's face.

"You don't think so?" Salim asked. "That night in Oultrejourdain, when de Ridefort came to challenge you, what made you stand up to him?"

Bilal couldn't speak, not even to ask how Salim knew about that confrontation; but his averted eyes were answer enough.

"Well, if you can fight for me, Bilal al-Hassani, then I can fight for you, too."

Four

ON the first morning in Al-Qahwani, Salim reassembled his cavalry unit. Each day after that they were ready at dawn, awaiting the Sultan's orders. The orders never varied. On the maps he had shown his emirs on the first night by the Jordan, Salah ad-Din had marked out an area the shape of a spearhead, its points at Nazareth, Tiberias, and Mount Tabor.

"Raze it," he had said.

Salim quickly realized that he had been mistaken in calling the raids a step back. These were nothing like their forays in Oultrejourdain, which, though effective, had at times bordered on chaotic. Now the raiding parties struck with quick, brutal precision, torching fields and villages and executing anyone who dared resist them. They took neither prisoners nor plunder. Bilal, listening to their exploits around the campfires at night, was half glad not to be involved.

These lightning raids were what the Muslim army was best at, and Salah ad-Din intended to use them to sow as much confusion as possible before he struck in earnest. But they also had another purpose. The Sultan needed to be absolutely certain that the main body of the Franj army was in Sephoria before he proceeded with his plans, and the raiders were able to confirm this for him.

So, on the evening of the twenty-ninth of June, Salah ad-Din called his emirs together once more and said: "Strike your tents and ready your men. Tomorrow we cross the river."

THEY crossed at the Bridge of Sennabra, and it took them the better part of a day. By the time the last stragglers had put the water behind them, Salah ad-Din had already pitched his tent at Kafr Sabt, one and a half *farsakh*s west of Tiberias and blocking the main road from there to Sephoria. From this position, he would be able to intercept any Franj advance.

Meanwhile, he ordered a detachment to blockade Tiberias ("The bait," he said curtly to anyone who asked why) and sent scouts to Sephoria to gauge the Franj reaction to his day's work. Salim begged to be one of them, and at last, against his better judgment, the Sultan agreed.

"I suppose you will bring Bilal al-Hassani with you," he said warily.

"Well, it's unlikely that we will see any fighting, and he is going mad cooped up in camp."

"It was not his arm that concerned me." The Sultan gave his son a hard look and then sighed. "Salim . . . do not mistake what I am about to say, for I too have grown fond of that boy, and although as Allah's servant I cannot entirely condone the nature of your . . . ah . . ."

Salim could not help smiling; it was the first time he had ever seen his father at a loss for words. Still, he did not like to see him embarrassed when he intended kindness, so he said, "I understand, Father. You need say no more."

Again, Salah ad-Din sighed. "I am afraid that I must, though I would rather not. I know that you love him, Salim, and I would not part you for the world—but the world itself is not so forgiving. You are a king's son and he, though he may not yet realize it, is a Bedu chief's heir. You will both be leaders of men one day, and leaders must sacrifice whatever is required for the welfare of their people. First and foremost, your people will require that you produce successors." He paused, looking closely at his son. "Do you understand me?"

Salim was looking at him, his expression that of an antelope that glances up from its watering hole into the inevitable eye of the hunter. Salah ad-Din knew then that he had told his son nothing that Salim had not already known for a long time, and though he was no champion of the kind of love the boy seemed to favor, he felt for him then as keenly as if he had forbidden him some worthy maiden.

The Sultan tried to smile then, and failed miserably. But to his surprise, the boy reached forward and embraced him. With a pang, he realized that he had not touched Salim with affection since he had been weaned. And before he had quite realized the sweetness of it, Salim had pushed him away again, though he still held his shoulders.

"Thank you, Father," he said.

"For speaking the words you least want to hear?" Salah ad-Din asked with a bitterness he had not intended.

"For your honesty. And for not forbidding me the time I have left with him."

The Sultan passed a hand over his face, suddenly exhausted. "You're welcome, then, and let us speak no more about it until the time comes for . . . but I assume too much in speaking of the future, when we do not yet know whether it will stretch beyond tomorrow. Go now and bring me news of the Franj. And Salim, I don't suppose I need to remind you that de Ridefort will be looking for his son?"

Salim shook his head. "I will watch his back."

"Indeed," said the Sultan dryly. "And make sure that he watches yours."

And so, as the sun dipped beneath the green hills of Galilee, Salim and Bilal rode out with a handful of other scouts toward the Franj camp at Sephoria. The group split up near Tur'an and rode off in a wide semicircle surrounding the south side of the encampment. Bilal and Salim hobbled their horses in a thick copse of trees some distance from the camp and walked the rest of the way. By the time they spotted the first of the tents, night had fallen. They were small, tattered tents, pitched in a rough circle around a fire. A group of soldiers sat in front of them, passing a jar of wine and kicking the dust. They were rough-looking men, as dark as Arabs with long, tangled hair and beards and filthy clothing. Clearly it was not their first wine jar of the evening, for they spoke and laughed with noisy abandon.

"Foot soldiers," Salim said with marked distaste. "They'll know nothing."

They made their way slowly around the perimeter of the camp, retreating when they caught sight of sentries, then creeping cautiously back in their wake. The northern end, where the ground was flat, was the most populated; to the south it tailed away until at last it petered out in a thread of tiny fires on the slopes of the Hill of Nazareth. Bilal was relieved to see no sign of the Templars, though at one point they spotted the black-and-white banners of the Hospitallers, not far from a large pavilion of deep red silk, which Salim told him belonged to the king.

Beyond the central position of the king's tent, there seemed no order to the camp's sprawling constellation. Even at the perimeter they passed everything from the ragged shelters of the untrained infantry to the silk pavilions of wealthy secular knights, heard every language from northern French to the Arabic spoken by Muslim mercenaries.

". . . should go over to the other side while we still can," they heard one of these saying to his fellows. "I heard it from a squire who was with them at Acre—the barons are at each other's throats. Mark me, they won't be happy until they've torn this country apart and fed it to the Sultan for supper."

"The same Sultan you want to defect to?" asked a small, wiry half-breed to his right, taking a swig from a flask and passing it to the bigger man.

"They say the Sultan has a hundred thousand men at Kafr Sabt," said another man morosely.

"There aren't a hundred thousand men in all his lands together!" scoffed the first.

"You're an idiot," said the half-breed. "The Sultan rules a hundred times that many." He shook his head. "The Templar Master is working on the king already—it will be just like Cresson. How many men are we? Twenty thousand perhaps, and only twelve hundred of us knights. The Sultan has at least as many again. God wills it, my arse—that mad Templar and his friend Kerak, they'll call the charge and then stand and applaud while the pigs swallow us whole. Just like Cresson, I tell you."

"Are you sure of those numbers?"

"Sure as I can be. I told you, I spoke to a squire from Acre."

Salim and Bilal crept back into the darkness. If the half-breed was to be believed, they now had an exact count of the Franj army. They walked back to their horses, each lost in his thoughts, and rode back toward camp in silence. Once there, Salim went off to report to his father, and Bilal walked slowly back to their tent. He was so preoccupied that he did not notice that it was brightly lit until his hand was on the flap, and he had lifted it before he thought to wonder why. It took him a good few moments to register the figure sitting on the rug at the center, dark head bent over a book of poetry from which Bilal had been practicing his reading that afternoon.

The figure looked up, and Bilal had a sensation that what he was witnessing ought to make sense to him, and yet somehow did not. For he knew this heart-shaped face intimately, the fine sweep of the eyebrows, the golden eyes beneath; yet time had translated it into something irrevocably foreign. The change went beyond the heavy kohl lining her eyes, the dark patterns on her cheeks and forehead, the warrior's muscle and grace beneath her white robes, and the sword tucked into her sash. But when she stood, offering a hesitant smile, she was once again his childhood friend.

"Khalidah?" he said, stepping inside at last.

"Bilal," she answered, her voice belying the emotion that her face hid. Hesitantly, she reached out her arms to him, and hesitantly he embraced her. But at the contact all the missing months evaporated, all the bitterness and guilt, until they were left at last holding only each other.

※

Five

BILAL wanted to take Khalidah to her father immediately, and interpreted her reluctance as fear. "He will not be angry," he insisted. "He blames himself, Khalidah, not you."

"I deserve his anger," she answered grimly. "But that is not why I do not want to see him now. I have a duty to fulfill before I do anything else: a duty to my mother's people."

"Is that where you've been? With your mother's people?"

She nodded. "With the Jinn."

Bilal blinked at her, and then smiled. "The way you said it, I almost believed you! Now tell me, where have you really been? After the emerald mountains at the end of the world, of course!"

Sighing, Khalidah proceeded to fill him in on all that had happened to her since the night she'd left camp, and the mission of the contingent she had brought with her. As she spoke, Bilal's look of disbelief turned to amazement, then to intentness. Though he stopped her now and then to ask for clarification of one point or another, he took it all in with what she considered remarkable composure.

"So the legends are true," he said softly, when she had finished.

"True, and not true," she answered. "Like most legends, I suppose. But the question is, what will Salah ad-Din make of it? Will he accept us?"

"I don't see why not," Bilal answered. "He has accepted plenty without half so good a reason to be here. Besides, did you not say that he knew your mother?"

"That was a long time ago, and I don't know the circumstances of their parting. Besides, if he is as pious as people say, I am afraid he won't take kindly to the idea of a bunch of infidels worshipping him as a pagan god . . . especially if they call themselves after the tricksters of Islam."

Bilal gave her a smile she did not recognize: a man's smile, its humor cut liberally with irony and regret. "Salah ad-Din deals in realities, not rumors," he said, "and though he is indeed pious—perhaps the most pious man that I have known—he is not parochial. You would be surprised at the things he is willing to accept."

"A Bedu bastard as his son's lover, for example," said a low voice behind them.

Khalidah turned and saw Salim standing in the doorway. She knew him at once, though he had changed since her vision in Alipsha's hut. He was thinner, his black eyes guarded and rather sardonic. She knew that he had intended to shock her with his words, but she didn't flinch at them, nor at the kiss he gave Bilal when he saw that she hadn't—a lover's lingering kiss.

"What is wrong with you?" Bilal demanded, pushing him away in irritation.

"He fears that I will turn you from him," Khalidah answered, before Salim could. Then, to the prince: "But I could not, even if I came with such an intention. Though if you are so blind to the strength of his love for you, perhaps it would be better if I had." Her golden eyes were fierce, almost feral in their thick kohl rims.

Salim scrutinized her for a moment and then smiled. "Forgive me," he said. "You are right. I have always been jealous of you. But you are also wrong, if you do not realize what a wide stake you yourself claim in Bilal's heart. Still, by that very token you deserve my respect and friendship, and so let us begin again." He bowed low to her, hand over his heart, and said, "Welcome, Khalidah al-Hassani; Salim ibn Yusuf al-Ayyubi, at your service." He smiled, his eyes glinting now with humor.

Khalidah smiled back, and bowing as well, she said, "As I am at yours, Your Highness."

"Very well, Your Grace; and from now on, let us dispense with all forms of ridiculous etiquette. Do you smoke?" He produced a pipe of *banj* from a deep pocket of his robe.

Khalidah blanched; then she met Bilal's eye, and they both burst into laughter. Salim looked confused, until Bilal said, "Khalidah and I had a somewhat abrupt introduction to *banj* . . . and it appears her time in the east has done nothing to change her first impression."

Salim shrugged, lit the pipe in the nearest lamp, drew on it, then said, "Wine, then? I hear they drink it like water in Khorasan."

"Tea, please," Khalidah said.

Salim nodded, stuck his head out of the tent flap, sent a servant after refreshments, and then sat down by Bilal.

"Well, Khalidah," he said, "I gather from what I heard before I so rudely interrupted your conversation with Bilal that you are here to make some request of my father. If I can help you in any way, please, allow me the honor."

So Khalidah explained again about the Jinn, about her relationship to them and their beliefs about Salah ad-Din, which had led them to the Sultan's army. As she spoke, Salim's face took on a look of keen thoughtfulness, so like Bilal's when he had first listened to the story that it was eerie. *Do lovers always come to resemble one another?* she wondered, and then wondered on the heels of it whether this might be true of herself and Sulayman.

"It is true," Salim said at last, "that my father will not like to be petitioned as a pagan god. But on the other hand, he is quick to befriend any enemy of the Franj, and if your Jinn are as skilled as you say, then he will be more than glad of their assistance." He paused and gave her another keen-edged look. "I take it that you yourself have not forsaken Allah, despite taking on the guise of an infidel?"

"I will never forsake Allah," Khalidah said firmly, "but this is not a guise. Aside from their religion, I live and fight as one of them."

Salim nodded. "Come here tomorrow morning, then. Can your warriors keep their mouths shut about this messiah myth?"

"Of course they can."

"Very well, then. Bring a few of the best with you, and let me do the talking. I promise you, if it is in my power, your Jinn will belong to this army by midday."

"Thank you, Sayyid," she said, and bowed low to him; this time he did not object to the formality, only looked thoughtfully at her.

"Will you stay with us tonight?" Bilal asked.

Khalidah shook her head. "I must get back to the others. They will be waiting for word."

"Tomorrow, then," he said, taking her hand and squeezing it.

"Tomorrow," she answered, squeezing back. Then she slipped from the tent and into the night.

Six

Kafr Sabt
1 July

THE day dawned as hot and bright as the others of that week. There was no wind, none of the haze of dust it would stir up. The only movement on the vast, searing plain was that of the Jinn's approaching horses, wading through the shallows of a heat-shimmer sea, the dry grass of the plains poking up through the mirage like reeds. The riders themselves, clad in unadorned battle white, all but disappeared into the bleached sky behind them. There were six of them in all: Khalidah and Sulayman; Abi Gul; Sandara; Shahascina's father, Batoor; and his young nephew, Janduli. All of them had been sworn to silence on the matter of Mobarak Khan; none had seemed to need to be told.

Khalidah led them to Bilal and Salim's tent, drawing the stares of the people they passed. They found Bilal outside waiting for them. He told them that Salim was already at his father's pavilion and that they were to follow him there.

"The Sultan is not in good spirits this morning," he said to Khalidah in a low voice, as he helped them hobble their horses.

"Because of the Jinn?"

"Because of the Franj. He is ready to meet them, but they are proving intractable."

"Should we come some other time?" Khalidah asked.

"There is no other time. If it is going to happen, it's going to happen now."

"What can we do, then, to win him over?"

Bilal shrugged. "Just tell him the truth. *Inshallah*, it will be enough." He paused, with a look that Khalidah knew well. It meant that he was deliberating whether to tell her something else.

"Just say it, Bilal," she sighed.

He smiled ruefully. "Very well. Your father knows that you are here."

"Who told him?" she groaned.

"I do not know. I certainly didn't, but news has a way of traveling in this camp."

Grimly, Khalidah resigned herself to a difficult morning. She and the others followed Bilal through the warren of tents until they reached the Sultan's. The front panel was rolled up, with a clutch of Mamluks standing guard at a respectful distance. Inside, Salah ad-Din sat flanked by Salim and his favored scribe, Imad ad-Din. Khalidah walked forward, fixing her eyes on him. He looked back at her, his eyes showing neither emotion nor curiosity. He was smaller than she had expected, but his aura was nonetheless that of a large and powerful man. He wore a mail coat under his yellow silk robe, and a helmet wrapped in a gleaming white turban.

The Mamluks parted to let them pass. Once inside the pavilion, the Jinn bowed to the Sultan and then seated themselves facing him, as he indicated. Bilal sat down by Salim, looking worried; the prince gave her a small, apologetic smile, which told her better than the Sultan's stony countenance what she was up against.

Salah ad-Din looked them all over for a moment, then said, "Welcome, representatives of the Jinn." His voice was cool, polite but expressionless. "I understand that you have a petition for me. Who is your representative?"

"I am, Your Highness," said Khalidah, putting her shawl back from her face.

The Sultan gave a start, though it was nearly imperceptible, and then his eyes narrowed. "And you are?" he asked.

"I am Khalidah, daughter of Abd al-Aziz al-Hassani, and granddaughter of the Khan of Qaf, Tor Gul."

The Sultan frowned. "What business have you here?"

"The same business as you have," Khalidah answered, her voice plangent with the realization that the Sultan had already judged her.

"To fight the infidel with Allah's sword? You are a woman—an outcast, I might add—and your Jinn, from what I have been told, are pagans."

"Yes," Khalidah answered coldly, "and from what *I* have been told, you were once more than happy to accept the assistance of a woman and a Jinni both, Brekhna bint Tor Gul. My mother."

The Sultan looked at her for a long moment, then turned to his scribe, hand outstretched. Khalidah didn't understand until the scribe handed over the sheet upon which he had been writing, and Salah ad-Din crumpled it in his fist, saying, "You are dismissed. Close the flap on your way out." Reluctantly, Imad ad-Din did as he had been told.

When he was gone the Sultan turned back to Khalidah and said, "Yes, I knew your mother. She fought for me, and then she forsook me. The only reason you have this audience is that my son, his friend, and your father, all of whom I respect, have spoken on your behalf." Khalidah was so surprised to hear her father included in this list that she did not heed the menace that had crept into the Sultan's tone. "So tell me now and tell me quickly, why should I listen to the petition of a whore and a tribe of infidels?"

Khalidah was as stunned as if she had been struck, and then the anger flooded in. She saw Bilal and Salim exchange a look of despair, but it was Abi Gul who leapt to her feet, flinging her headscarf aside, and faced the Sultan with eyes blazing. The Mamluks were on her at once, ringing her with spears, but she ignored them.

"How dare you!" she cried. "Do you not realize that this woman is heir to a royal line that stretches back to the beginning of time?"

The Sultan raised his eyebrows and gave her a condescending smile. "And who are your people, to hold such a woman in high regard? Who for that matter are you?"

"My people are a race at least as old and as worthy as yours," she spat back, "and I am no more or less than one of them!"

"As I see it, they must be exceptionally weak in both body and morals to make warriors of little girls."

The next moment the Sultan's guard found themselves ringed by Jinn with daggers in one hand and swords in the other. Khalidah thrust herself into their midst, crying for them to lower their weapons. Miraculously, they listened. She gestured for the Jinn to sit down again, and once they had done so, Salah ad-Din ordered his reluctant bodyguards to lower their spears.

Khalidah had resigned herself to defeat, but when she raised her eyes to the Sultan's, she saw that his look was speculative rather than angry, and a tiny hope flickered into life.

"Tell me, Khalidah al-Hassani," he said, "are all of your Jinn so quick and cunning as these?"

"They are," she said, trying to keep her voice from trembling.

"And why, if they have no quarrel with the Franj, do they wish to fight them?"

"Because they believe that their gods are calling them to it." She paused to steady herself, then said, "Your Highness, though these people do not answer to Allah, and though you have made it clear why you believe my opinion to be of dubious value, you have my word that you would not regret accepting them into your army. The Jinn are loyal and wise, they are the best warriors you will ever see, and they believe that their duty is to fight the Franj—to fight for you. Will you truly turn them away?"

Once again, he studied her. At last he said, "How many do you lead?"

"Five hundred, Your Highness."

"In an hour I leave for Sephoria, to see if I can lure the Franj out of hiding. Send one hundred of your best fighters to me immediately; they shall accompany my division. After that, I will decide. Oh, and I would prefer it if the women among you did not appear as such. I will not have my men distracted by brazen pagan girls." He glared at Abi Gul as he said this. She glared back, but to Khalidah it seemed a small concession if it won them their goal.

"It will be as you wish," she said.

The Sultan gave her a curt nod. "You are dismissed—you too," he said to Bilal and Salim. "Divide these Jinn among the emirs. You," he said, turning abruptly to Sulayman, "stay."

Sulayman met Khalidah's eyes. His were curious, hers worried, but the Sultan had spoken; they had no choice but to do as they had been bidden.

Seven

THE younger Jinn of Khalidah's hundred were giddy with excitement, hardly able to believe their luck at being taken to the Franj camp by the Sultan himself on their first mission. The older ones were subdued, well aware that they had not been chosen so much as tolerated, and that they must conduct themselves perfectly or be sent home in disgrace. They pestered Khalidah with questions about how to speak, how to behave, how to impress, until she thought she would go out of her mind. She had never been so relieved as she was when Salim and Bilal finally came to take them to their emirs.

Sulayman came with them. As they started off, Khalidah asked him, "What did the Sultan want?"

"I still don't quite know," he said. "He remembered me from the time I was taken to his camp and played for him. But he did not talk about that. He asked me questions about my childhood and my days with the troupe."

"What did you tell him?" Khalidah asked.

"The truth," said Sulayman.

"And?"

"And nothing." He gave her a troubled look. "He listened to all of it, and then he sent me away again."

"How very strange. Do you think that he suspects you of something?"

"Perhaps. But he did not detain me, so it doesn't signify."

If Khalidah's journey had taught her anything, it was that almost everything signifies sooner or later; but he still looked worried, and it would not help him for her to say so. She kicked Zahirah to a canter and rode after her people.

THEY were split into ten groups, each put under the command of different emirs. Khalidah purposely separated herself from Sulayman, knowing that they would distract each other if they rode together, but she brought Abi Gul and Sandara with her. The older woman and the younger one bolstered her, each in her own way. They rode in the Sultan's own battalion. Khalidah had insisted, wanting to witness his reaction to the Jinn.

Once they were divided, Salah ad-Din rode down his division, inspecting them. He stopped before Khalidah, giving her a long look. Zahirah danced with days of pent-up energy.

"That's a fine horse," the Sultan said at last.

"Thank you."

"You sit her well." Khalidah waited. After a pause, he continued, "I will not spare you because you are a woman."

"I would not ride with you if you would," she answered.

He narrowed his eyes at her for a moment, then wheeled his horse and cantered back to the head of the column, and they were off. It should have been a short ride to Sephoria, but their progress was slow because of their numbers and their need for secrecy. Abi Gul was quiet, her wide eyes taking in the details of the terrain they passed, and it seemed to Khalidah that she could almost hear her friend's brain whirring as she sorted and stored the information.

Action, however, had made Sandara loquacious. She rattled on to Khalidah about former missions and battles of which her father had told her, her tone almost as giddy as Abi Gul's generally was. Then, at the end of one story, she turned abruptly to Khalidah and said, "You have impressed him."

"Who?" asked Khalidah, who had been only half listening, preoccupied as she was with the other Jinn in her group.

"The Sultan."

Khalidah smiled. "Have you forgotten that he called me a whore?"

"He was testing you. Obviously, you passed."

"If anyone passed," said Khalidah, "it was Abi Gul."

"It was you who put yourself in danger to avert bloodshed. Believe me. He is impressed."

"Then we must live up to it. Until then he is humoring us, no more."

Sandara kept silent, but Khalidah caught the edge of a smile through the fluttering black veil.

By midmorning the castle at Sephoria was visible: a little dirty cube on a stark swell of hill. "It does not look like much," Abi Gul observed, the first words she had spoken since they departed.

"It isn't much," Khalidah answered. "A token only, to show that they hold this place. Many of the Franj castles are like that. The army will be camped on the plain, near the water."

And indeed, it was not long before they could make out the smear of smoke and dust on the sheet-metal sky, marking a place of close-packed habitation. A little later they saw the first of the tents among the low hills. Salah ad-Din stopped them then, to water the horses and decide on the best plan of action. His battalion had converged with the one led by his nephew Taqi ad-Din, in which Sulayman was riding. He sought out Khalidah as the leaders met to discuss their plans.

"How has it been?" he asked Khalidah, but it was Abi Gul who answered.

"Boring," she said. "There hasn't been sign of a single Franji all this way."

Sulayman nodded. "We saw one of their scouting parties in the distance, but they turned and ran back to camp when they spotted us."

"What about Taqi ad-Din?" Khalidah asked. "What is he like?"

Sulayman shrugged, taking a sip from his skin of water. "Just as you'd expect of a favored emir. Assured. Arrogant. His men respect him. It's hard to tell more without seeing him fight."

Khalidah nodded. "The others—how are they?"

"Bored, as Abi Gul says," he answered. "Not quite certain how they are to prove themselves with nothing to fight. But they follow their orders quietly enough."

"That's good," said Khalidah, and she had no time to say more, for the emirs were calling them back into line.

The Sultan and his nephew had decided to continue on toward the Franj camp and try again to lure them forth. Though a wise leader would stay put in Sephoria, King Guy was just volatile enough that he might be goaded forth by the sight of the Sultan so near his lines. So they continued on toward the pall in the sky, slower now than ever, being wary of ambush.

But for all Abi Gul's vigilance, it was the half-blind Sandara who saw it. "Look," she said softly to Khalidah, indicating with a thrust of her chin a slight movement in an olive grove to their right. Khalidah caught a flicker of white, so minuscule and fleeting that it could have been a bird—but she knew instinctively that it was not. She had insisted that the Jinn who rode with the Sultan remain in her sight, and now she was glad of her own caution. It took only a moment to alert them and then they were off, dividing into two groups to gallop down either side of the column and surround Salah ad-Din. He looked at them in anger that turned momentarily to surprise as an arrow whizzed by his right ear, and then to grim determination as he realized what was happening.

As he turned to call his orders, a small band of Franj knights charged from the trees. Judging by the arrows that still flew among the Muslims, they had left a clutch of archers hidden there. The Franj were already engaged with the Sultan's guard, which had clustered around him as soon as they realized what was happening. A quick look told Khalidah that the Franj swordsmen were lay knights, their fighting skills as rusty as their weapons, and that the Sultan's men would subdue them easily. But she was worried about the archers: their aim seemed good. Pulling an arrow from the armor of a man at her side, she examined it. The shaft was smooth, the flights made of neatly cut pheasant feather, the tip of well-forged iron.

Casting it aside, she gathered the Jinn in her sights, caught the eyes of the nearest, and saw that they had come to the same conclusion as she. Immediately they left what they were doing and gathered again into two groups of five, which dispersed to either side of the wood. She caught a glimpse of the Sultan, who glared at her from his ring of Mamluks, no doubt believing that they were deserting, or worse. Then she turned back to the trees and put him from her mind. There was no time to explain, no time to lose.

Once among the trees the Jinn spread out farther, though they always kept within sight of at least one of their fellows. The intermittent arrows she dodged told Khalidah that the Franj archers had seen them enter the grove, but they also gave her a means of locating them. She unslung her short-range bow and fitted an arrow, riding now with her legs only, her reins knotted in front of her. Zahirah had taken to this training like a bird to flight, and she seemed to guess Khalidah's next thought almost before it had formed. They moved slowly, keeping to the thickest trees and undergrowth when they could. At last she located the archer who had shot at her, though by now he had turned back to the battle and the aid of his failing knights. He was only lightly armed, and dressed to blend in with the trees. Khalidah raised her bow, and Zahirah, sensing the motion and its meaning, froze. The arrow hit the man cleanly in the neck. He crumpled without a cry.

Khalidah had begun to ride toward him when she felt an arrow thud into her own armor at her back and then another, with a harder blow and a sting that told her it had pierced through to the flesh. She whirled and saw the archer just as he let another arrow fly. Swerving before the arrow hit, Zahirah sidestepping with sure-footed precision, she nocked another arrow—this time a scissor-headed one—and fired it at the man's drawing arm as he aimed at her again. It sliced straight through his shoddy leather armor, cutting deep into his forearm. He crumpled to his knees, holding the wounded arm to his chest, and Khalidah kicked Zahirah forward, drawing her sword. The archer looked up, but he hardly had time to cry out before his head rolled.

It was only then that she saw the man's long, black beard, the color of his skin, and the shape of the helmet over his glazed eyes. He had been a Muslim—a Turk most likely, given his skill with the bow. A mercenary. Riding back to the one she had felled with the arrow, she confirmed that he too was a Muslim. The thought of Muslims doing Franj work sickened Khalidah more than the violent deaths she had just inflicted.

After that, it was over quickly. Khalidah rejoined Sandara, who reported that the archers she'd killed had also been Muslims, and that their skill had deserted them at close range. They formed a line with the other Jinn and combed the olive grove, but it was as Khalidah already suspected: all of the mercenaries were dead. They rejoined the Sultan's band in time to see the Mamluks cut down the last of the fleeing knights.

Khalidah rode straight up to the Sultan, who indicated to his guard to part ranks for her. "The archers are dead, Your Highness," she told him.

"All of them?" he asked, raising his eyebrows.

"All of them."

He gestured to his guard, half of whom plunged off into the trees. In a few minutes they were back to confirm what Khalidah had said. Salah ad-Din allowed her the hint of a smile.

"Very well, Khalidah al-Hassani," he said, "your Jinn may join my army. But," he added sharply, the smile flattening, "do not ever let me see you break ranks without permission again. If nothing else, my guard might very well have cut you down before you had the chance to prove that you were acting in my defense."

Khalidah nodded, subdued.

"I am aware that your people have done us a great service on this field today, but this is my army, not yours."

Once again, Khalidah nodded. The Sultan held her eyes a moment longer, before the glimmer of a smile returned. "And now we've spent enough time idling here."

"You don't think that the king will send out others against us?" asked Khalidah.

"I know that he will not. He would have done it already, if he meant to. No—it is time to go to Lubiyah."

"Is that not an abandoned village?"

"Very good," said the Sultan. "It is also the best place to put a battalion to block the road between Sephoria and Tiberias."

Khalidah knew that she had ventured into impertinence, but because the Sultan had answered her other questions, she chanced one more. "And why, if your wish is to draw him forth, would you want to do that?"

This time, the Sultan allowed her a full smile. In the shock of its warm luminosity, she nearly forgot her question. But his answer jolted her back to reality like the hard ground after a horse's back: "Because tomorrow, we lay siege to Tiberias."

Eight

THEY returned to Kafr Sabt with the last of the daylight. In all of their days on the road from Qaf, Khalidah had never been so tired. Jinn scouts met them on the road to say that the news had preceded them and the others were already moving into the main camp. She turned with the battalion toward Kafr Sabt, longing for her bed.

However, she'd barely dismounted when Bilal touched her arm and told her that she and Sulayman were wanted in the Sultan's tent.

"What for?" she all but wailed.

Bilal gave her his strange new smile. "To plan for tomorrow," he said. "You are one of his emirs now."

Khalidah was tired enough to wish then that she had never sought the Sultan's favor, but she called to Sulayman and they followed Bilal back through the warren of tents toward the Sultan's pavilion. It glowed like a paper lantern in the falling dark. Inside was crowded with emirs and scribes and servants bringing coffee and food for those who had been out all day.

Khalidah had wound a turban of white linen around her head and stuffed her plaits inside it. As she entered the pavilion, she pulled a tail of the fabric across her face to better disguise her sex, but she need hardly have bothered. The emirs, engaged in their chattering and squabbling, gave her little more than a cursory glance. Apparently the Jinn had been accepted and forgotten as just another band of foreign volunteers.

Khalidah sat with Sulayman far back against the cloth wall,

while Bilal pushed his way through the crowd toward Salim, who was sitting with the Sultan's other sons near his father. Soon afterward, Salah ad-Din called for attention. He looked as exhausted as Khalidah felt, but still his voice was strong and clear as he began to speak, as warm in its assurance as his smile.

"As many of you know," Salah ad-Din said, "I rode out today to the outskirts of the Franj camp at Sephoria, in hopes of luring their army onto the field. In this, aside from a minor skirmish, we failed, and therefore I am left with no choice but to employ the alternative plan I had hoped to avoid. Tomorrow, I am sending a detachment to Tiberias. At the moment the town is lightly guarded, its lord and the main body of its garrison having been deployed to Sephoria, and I have it from good sources that the castle itself is left in the hands of the Lady Eschiva. My intention is to take the town and the castle and thereby goad the Franj army into coming to its rescue."

"Begging Your Highness's pardon," an elderly emir spoke up immediately, "but King Guy would be a fool to give up the security of Sephoria for the sake of one little town."

"And do you doubt that King Guy is just such a fool?" the Sultan answered dryly, followed by a runnel of laughter. "Besides," he continued, "there are those in the Franj camp who will push him toward this decision." He glanced, perhaps involuntarily, at Bilal as he said this.

"And if it works?" said another emir, an Egyptian with a long, pale, lugubrious face. "Our detachment will be trapped between a hostile town and the approaching Christian army."

"That is true," agreed Salah ad-Din, giving the man a cold, calm look, "and it is why I will stay with the heavy cavalry here at Kafr Sabt, until we see how our invitation has been received. Gökböri will lead the Tiberias detachment, and Taqi ad-Din will lead another to the plain beneath the hill known as the Horns of Hattin, to blockade the second route the Franj might take to relieve Tiberias, if they do not choose to engage us here. I have made up my lists already; those of you whose names I call will have your men ready tomorrow at first light to ride to Tiberias."

Khalidah's mind wandered as he began to read out a long list of names and so she almost missed "al-Jinni," squeezed in as it was among the others. It registered only when Sulayman touched her hand. He smiled at her. She felt little but overwhelming weariness.

On the way back to their camp, she kept trying to make herself understand that she would ride into battle tomorrow—not reconnaissance, not a skirmish, but the siege of a town—but she could feel nothing beyond her longing for sleep. Yet even now she wasn't free to give in to it, for as they approached the clutch of Jinn tents, they found it full of light and noise and commotion. Abi Gul appeared at her side and then Bilal, looking as confused as Khalidah felt. Abi Gul was tugging her hand, pulling her away from her dusty little tent and toward another, bigger one, its front flap rolled up and its light spilling out along with the sound of a reed flute and drums.

Abi Gul was chattering to her excitedly, but the words wouldn't penetrate the numb exhaustion. She looked toward Sulayman for help. Sulayman, however, was looking at the large tent, his face sober and strange. Khalidah followed the line of his gaze and saw a small figure come forth, silhouetted against the light, and another, taller one standing hesitant in its wake. It only made sense when Sulayman at last spoke the words that should have been obvious all along:

"It's your father, Khalidah."

Abd al-Aziz approached his daughter. His face looked more deeply lined than she remembered, its bones stood out more starkly, but the wrinkles were lax with relief. It was only as he reached out for her that Khalidah realized he was smiling. He embraced her—clutched her, in fact, as if not quite believing that she was real—speaking her name over and over again. When at last he released her, she saw that the hesitant figure had come up behind them and was hugging Bilal with equal ardor. Zaynab. And then Zaynab was hugging her, praising and scolding at once and weeping through it all.

"But what are you doing here?" Khalidah asked, when she could get a word in. "This camp is no place for you."

"No place for me!" Zaynab cried. "Will you listen to her—as if it were a place for a girl child, either!" She shook her head and said, "No doubt you're right, Khalidah. But I don't have much choice, do I? If it's his place"—she indicated Abd al-Aziz with a jut of her chin—"then it's mine."

Khalidah looked from her father to Zaynab in confusion, and then at Bilal, who seemed equally baffled. But Sulayman, when she glanced at him, had begun to smile; and then she saw that Zaynab and her father had joined hands.

"Children, you must congratulate us," her father said, "and then kiss each other as siblings. Zaynab and I are now man and wife."

ZAYNAB, it seemed, had known for some time what Bilal had only just learned: that her first husband was dead and she was free to remarry. She spoke of protection, Abd al-Aziz of politics, but for all their logical reasons, Khalidah could see that there was a real affection between them.

Still, it was strange. Khalidah could not stop thinking of her father and Zaynab as the opposite poles of her childhood, converging, it seemed, only to battle over points of her upbringing. She had rarely seen them converse without arguing, let alone hold a pleasant conversation. But perhaps, she ruminated as she watched them, she herself had been the impediment to their discovering their true hearts. Without her to divide them—and to remind them of her absent mother—it was not really so odd that Zaynab and Abd al-Aziz would find that they were essentially married already.

All at once, the burden of guilt Khalidah had carried since the night she left her tribe lifted from her. It slipped up and away with the campfire smoke toward the crystalline stars. She felt liquid, giddy, as she did after overexertion; as though her limbs, if she had been inclined at that moment to stand, could not have supported her. But she had no desire just then to stand. Instead, as she listened to Bilal and Abd al-Aziz boast and exaggerate their adventures to one another (Sulayman and Abi Gul had tactfully made their excuses and gone to bed), she slipped her arms around Zaynab's shoulders and embraced her.

"What is this for, child?" Zaynab asked, surprised to find tears slipping down Khalidah's cheeks and into the cloth of her dress.

"Because I'm sorry to have left you like I did," she said.

Zaynab uttered a low chuckle. "I was ready to throttle you at the time, but don't think I don't know why you did it," she said. Then, lower still, "And I'd have done the same, in your place. Tell me, did you find her?"

Khalidah was silent for a moment, still clutching Zaynab, though her tears had stopped. "I suppose I did, in a way; though not to see or speak to her."

"What are they like?" Zaynab asked. "The Jinn?"

"They are like us . . . and nothing like us. Like the legends and unlike them too." She paused, then said, "I am afraid for them, Zaynab. I'm afraid for myself."

"Of course you are," she soothed. "All of us are. But you're living your truth, Khalidah. That is what matters. Oh, don't start again! Why are you crying?"

"Because I'm so glad," Khalidah answered, "to finally be able to call you Mother."

Nine

❧❧❧

Kafr Sabt–Tiberias
2 July

It seemed to Khalidah that she had hardly shut her eyes before the trumpets and drums were waking her again and the muezzin wailing. She rinsed her sleep-fuzzed eyes with water, then her arms and feet. Finally she ran her wet hands across her head. The actions were stilted with disuse, and she wondered whether she would even remember the prayers. But as she knelt among the camp's handful of Muslim women, bowing to the still-black southern sky, she found the words tumbling from her lips as a once-familiar tune would come back to her fingers on the oud if she did not think about it too hard.

By the time she returned to camp the Jinn had risen and pulled together a breakfast of sorts. Khalidah's stomach turned at the thought of food, but she drank the glass of tea Abi Gul handed to her, grateful for its heat in her cold hands and knotted stomach. By the time the red sun prized the sky from the horizon, they were on the road to Tiberias.

The weather was clear, the wind slack, and before long the day had grown hotter even than the previous one. Khalidah felt the sweat running down her back inside her layers of clothing and armor and wished for nothing so much as to tear all of it off. Yet she knew that the Jinn leather was still preferable to the nobles' mail and metal. The doctor had grudgingly declared Bilal's arm fit enough for battle, and she had caught sight of him as they rode out, fine and shining in armor and brocade fit for a prince. She wondered how he was faring now.

Despite the heat, they made good time. By midmorning Lake Tiberias had shimmered into view, and with it the bleached stone walls of Tripoli's castle, bright banners slack in the windless heat. To Khalidah it looked impressive, but to those who had lived for weeks as the castle's guard, and the others who had ridden beneath its walls on the fateful reconnaissance two months earlier, it seemed an eerie, desolate place. With the garrison and their women gone to Sephoria, its numbers had dwindled, and the Countess Eschiva had brought most of the remaining citizens inside the fortifications as soon as Salah ad-Din had crossed the river. The town, therefore, was silent.

The detachment encircled the walls, the siege engines and towers rumbled into place, and still there was no sign of life. Khalidah had begun to wonder whether Tiberias would surrender without a fight when a volley of arrows, pitifully thin, whizzed out from the walls. The Muslim army surged into action: emirs began calling orders, and the sky darkened briefly as the archers sent a cloud of arrows in response. There were cries from beyond the walls to tell them that the arrows had found their marks, and then the catapults were firing, the air filling with the shriek and dust of shattering masonry.

Far back in the fidgeting ranks of the light cavalry, Khalidah wondered how long it would continue. The Muslim detachment was easily strong enough to obliterate the vulnerable castle by midday, but they were being careful. "Spare the town as best you can," the Sultan had said, for he had no interest in the little Galilean port other than as a means of drawing out the Franj army, and no wish to harm the family of his old friend Tripoli. So the Muslims flung their stones until the few men of Eschiva's guard retreated to the keep, and then they fired the town. No knights rode forth to challenge them. There was no point, and both sides knew it.

Khalidah's Jinn, like most of the detachment, never drew their weapons that day. They watched the catapults take halfhearted shots at the castle's towers as the town burned. Khalidah herself saw the messenger pigeons released from the roof. They fluttered for a moment above the flaccid banners, finding their bearings before turning south and west toward Sephoria with their inevitable message. There was nothing for Salah ad-Din's men to do then but return to camp and wait to see how it would be answered.

Ten

Sephoria

City lost. Confined to citadel. Quite well. E.

TRIPOLI sighed and rubbed his forehead. It felt as if someone were trying to drill through his skull. The headache had begun when they heard of the Muslims' march toward Tiberias, and it had not shifted since. Still, he could not help smiling grimly to himself as he handed the note back to Guy. That Eschiva would approach a siege with the same pragmatic nonchalance as she would a pile of dirty linens was worth more to him than her beauty and money combined. Tripoli could not imagine a woman less in need of saving than his wife; nevertheless, he knew that this was exactly what the barons would propose.

"I suppose we must go to her aid . . ." the king began doubtfully.

"Unquestionably," agreed Kerak, delighted as ever at the possibility of spilling Arab blood, particularly after so many days of inactivity.

"We might even leave today," de Ridefort mused. "There is light enough left for a few hours' travel—"

"Why bother," asked Tripoli dryly, "when we could simply hand the Sultan our kingdom on a silver platter?"

"Do you intend then to leave your wife to the mercy of the Saracens?" asked de Ridefort, with studied horror.

As he considered the possible answers to this, Tripoli revised his opinion of his headache: it was not, after all, the work of something external trying to penetrate his skull, but the pent-up words of reason trying to escape. He had held them back all day, know-ing that they would fall on deaf ears, or worse, fuel Kerak's and de Ridefort's latent accusations of treachery. Now at last he spoke them, not because he expected to be heeded or even heard, but because the pain left him no choice.

"I tell you just what my wife would if she were here: to march on Tiberias is folly at best, but to do it tonight is suicide." He held up his hand to stay de Ridefort's protest and was bolstered to see, from the corner of his eye, that the brothers d'Ibelin were nodding and most of the other barons were at least listening. "Can you not see that this is a trap? Here we are well watered, our supply line is secure, our position is strong. Between here and Tiberias there is nothing but barren desert, with only two springs to break it—that is, if this heat has not caused them to run dry. If we leave tonight, I tell you, by morning we will be at Salah ad-Din's mercy."

"At his mercy!" roared Kerak. "He will be begging ours!"

King Guy looked nervously at Tripoli, but the count kept his composure, his anger showing only in the sudden heat in his black eyes. "We are outnumbered," Tripoli said, "and very nearly out-maneuvered. We are unlikely to beat Salah ad-Din's army in a field battle, still less so if we are hungry and thirsty and surrounded on a desert plain. But if we can maintain our patience for a few days more, we can fell the Sultan by his own sword."

Kerak opened his mouth to retort, but Balian d'Ibelin said sharply, "Stay! I would hear what the count would say; then you will have your turn."

Tripoli plunged on, "The strength of the Sultan's army is also its greatest weakness. He is in enemy territory now. Soon he will run out of supplies. When he does, he will be forced to attack us here or to retreat. Sephoria is a secure fortress. If he attacks it, we have a good chance at beating him. And if he retreats, well, the battle is won with no bloodshed."

"Spoken like the traitor you are," de Ridefort said, his voice supple, sibilant with hatred.

"I would beware how I bandied that word, Messire," Tripoli

returned, with only the barest hint of sarcasm. "The same has been said of you not long since. What better way to revive the suspicion than to urge this army on to another fool's mission?"

"You accuse me?" bellowed de Ridefort, the vein standing out on his forehead, his fury buffeting Tripoli's calm like the sea raging around an ancient stone. "You, who would leave your own wife and children to the mercy of the heathens? You are not only a traitor, Count, but a coward!"

Rather than rise to the taunt, Tripoli merely shook his head, his face stoic, almost beatific in its acceptance. "Tiberias belongs to me," he said softly, "and it is my wife who is besieged. Not one of you here can imagine how I love that woman, or our home. But I would allow the citadel to be taken and my wife to be captured if I could be sure that Salah ad-Din's offensive would stop there; for in God's name, I have seen many a Muslim army in the past, but none as numerous or as powerful as the one Salah ad-Din commands today. I tell you, if we march from here it will be to our deaths, and the destruction of God's kingdom."

De Ridefort was shaking his head, Kerak sneering, but the king, for once, seemed to have seen beyond bravado to reason.

"I believe that Tripoli may be right," he said, looking to the nobles for affirmation, "and at any rate, things always look clearer in the morning." He laughed feebly, hoping perhaps for encouragement that was not forthcoming. "Let us put off any decision until then. You are dismissed."

Not quite certain they believed it, the nobles drifted away, though de Ridefort remained behind, his angry eyes boring into his hapless king.

Eleven

TRIPOLI knew when he left the king's tent that nothing had really been settled, and therefore that it was a mistake to do so. He had long suspected that de Ridefort was playing both sides, and since Cresson he had been certain of it. But he had no way of proving it, not even any clear idea of how the treachery manifested, and more than anything he was exhausted, worn down by the constant debate and indecision and the brutal pain in his head. So he left Guy to the mercy of de Ridefort and Kerak—a decision he would spend the rest of his days regretting.

It seemed he had barely closed his eyes when his stepson, Hugh, was shaking him awake again. He read the whole story on the boy's face, but allowed Hugh to tell it anyway on their walk back to the red pavilion.

"They say that de Ridefort has been hounding him since we left," Hugh said, "and Kerak with him."

"As they were before," Tripoli answered. "What, then, has changed his mind?"

The question was rhetorical; Tripoli knew that little but persistence was required to change Guy's mind. So he was surprised to hear the boy answer, "King Henry's money."

"What?" he demanded.

"The king held firm until de Ridefort reminded him that they had spent the money that Henry of England had given into the keeping of the Templars, in penance for murdering Thomas Becket, without consulting Henry. They spent it on mercenaries, to fight the Saracens," the boy added helpfully, though Tripoli knew this already. "He said that since we'd spent it in God's name, then we'd best act on our promise or consider ourselves damned."

"Idiot," Tripoli grumbled. He said no more, but strode out with renewed vigor, leaving his stepson to wonder whether the count referred to Guy or de Ridefort. In fact, Tripoli had been referring to himself: his own stupidity in not having foreseen this tactic. Likewise, the anger with which he entered the tent was self-directed, though none of the others could have known this. Even de Ridefort recoiled from the palpable force of Tripoli's wrath.

"What is this about?" Tripoli demanded. "How can you change your orders in the middle of the night?"

"It has taken exactly this long to undo your handiwork," retorted de Ridefort, "and to remind the king of his duty."

Guy smiled wanly at Tripoli, who pointedly ignored him. "And so you would break camp now? Could it not wait until daylight?"

"You yourself reminded us about the heat we will encounter tomorrow," said de Ridefort. "Is this not, then, the best time to march?"

Tripoli glared at the Templar Master. "It is madness," he said, "unless perhaps you have an appointment to keep."

De Ridefort smiled. "Only with God, Count . . . for we Templars are appointed by God to protect this kingdom, and we would sell our mantles rather than let a Christian city fall to the Saracens."

Tripoli was shaking his head. "You will live to rue this night."

"We've heard your song, Tripoli," Kerak snapped. "You try to frighten us with talk of the strength of the Muslim forces simply because you like them and prefer their friendship. Otherwise you would not proffer such words. If you tell me that they are numerous, I answer: the fire is not daunted by the quantity of the wood to burn!"

There were nods, murmurs of agreement from the sleepy barons jostling for space in the red tent. Tripoli might have ignored them all and argued further if he had thought that Guy might still be swayed by reason. But one look at the king's face told Tripoli that he had been captured by Kerak's crude images of glory. He glowed with his imagined victory in a battle that Tripoli knew was lost already.

"Very well," he said, too weary now for bitterness, "as I am one of you, I will do as you wish. I will fight at your side, but you will see what will happen." And he went to rouse his men, leaving a vacant silence in his wake.

Twelve

Sephoria–Tiberias
3 July

IF King Guy had decided to ignore Tripoli's advice, he had at least remembered some of his warnings. Despite Salah ad-Din's shrewd positioning of his forces, there were still several routes open between Sephoria and Tiberias, and Guy realized that his choices were limited to those with water. Therefore, they must go by either Tur'an with its small spring, or Lubiyah and Hattin, which possessed a larger one as well as access to the lake. In the end, Guy chose to march south toward Kafr Kana, then northeast, where they would rejoin the main road to Tiberias near Tur'an.

Tripoli, wedded now to this doomed mission, insisted on leading the advance guard. The king rode at the center, flanked by the bishops of Lydda and Acre, who carried the golden reliquary containing the shard of the True Cross, which had been brought from Jerusalem for the purpose. Though the Templars rode in the rear guard, its command was given to Balian d'Ibelin rather than Gerard de Ridefort. That de Ridefort didn't argue this was suspicious at best, but Tripoli didn't have the energy to wonder anymore what his old rival was up to. Nor, in the end, did it particularly matter.

Guy's midnight glow of inspiration quickly dampened as the tired soldiers formed ranks. They knew by the stars' crisp clarity the nature of the hell that awaited them when the sun rose. Their grim mood turned black when the horses refused to drink before setting out. The water was tasted and pronounced sweet, but nothing would induce the animals to take it. The men whispered to each other that it was an omen. Then, just as they were about to move out, there was a commotion toward the front of the ranks. Tripoli, who had positioned himself near the center of the vanguard, pushed through the knights and surrounding infantry to see what was causing it. What he found sent a chill down his spine, a cold portent of disaster so far out of keeping with its cause that he knew it must be heeded.

An unveiled Saracen woman in a tattered dress was struggling against the restraining arms of two infantrymen. Her eyes were wild, and as soon as she spotted Tripoli she began screaming at him: "By Allah and His Prophet Muhammad, I curse you! By all the prophets before Him and all the angels in heaven, I curse you! Lead your men forth this day and you are damned, every last one of you, to the fire of hell—"

"Enough," he said to her quietly in Arabic.

She spat in his face.

"You'll burn for that, you heathen whore!" snarled one of her captors, at which she turned to him, smiled, and then sank her teeth into his arm.

"You'll burn!" the man screamed. Some of his fellows had already broken ranks to stoke one of the dying campfires.

"There is no time for this!" Tripoli cried, furious. "Leave her, she is of no account!"

"The devil is in her," one of the men replied. "Witches must burn!"

"Stop this, I tell you—"

But they had already lashed the woman's hands and feet and were dragging her toward the fire. Tripoli could only watch with appalled resignation as they lifted the woman like a sack of barley and hurled her into the flames. Her clothes and hair caught at once and burned away, but she did not scream or cry out. In fact, her skin seemed impervious to the fire. The flames ran off of her like rain as she struggled into a sitting position. When she met Tripoli's eye again she was smiling.

"You see, you have no power over us," she cried. "We are like the deep-rooted tree that grows back after each cutting. You who survive this day will find that you have lost everything. Your blood will water this land and we will drink it, we will—"

At that moment one of the infantrymen, his face twisted by rage and fear, lifted his battle-axe and split her head in two. The woman's body toppled into the flames, but one eye still stared up at Tripoli as he turned his horse and barked at the foot soldiers to rejoin ranks or face his sword. Yet all his fury could not erase that mocking, taunting eye from his mind. He did not know it, but it would hound him, waking and sleeping, until the day he died.

Thirteen

THE Muslim scouts rode into Kafr Sabt just after dawn with the news that the Franj army was moving. At first Salah ad-Din could hardly believe that his plan had worked so well, and he found himself wondering whether there could be a trap somewhere within the Franj's apparent gullibility. But when his son Al-Afdhal voiced this same suspicion, it polarized the Sultan's opinion.

"*Alhamdulillah!*" he said to the gathered emirs. "We must thank God for this gift, for that is what it is. Break your camps this morning and take your men to the plain between the Horns of Hattin and the lake. Make certain that there is no gap by which the Franj might reach the water. We will fight them there tomorrow."

"Why not just march out and fight them today?" asked Al-Afdhal, querulously.

His father gave him a cold look and said, "Why not, Salim?"

Startled, Salim surfaced from his reverie. "Because they aren't thirsty yet?"

"Indeed," his father answered dryly, still looking at his eldest, who was crimson now with shame and fury. "The Franj, by their decision to relieve Tiberias, have declared a war of attrition upon themselves—for who among you remembers a week of such brutal heat, or can name a road so poorly watered as the one the Franj have chosen?" He waved his hand, as if these matters were trifles rather than the lynchpin of his plan. "Still, we cannot leave our victory entirely to nature, or even to the Franj king's stupidity. We must do everything we can to intensify the infidels' misery on their march, everything to make sure that by the time they see my army between themselves and the lake, they will beg to be taken prisoner. I want the horse-archers mounted within the hour. They are to harass the Franj ranks from both sides and slow the march as much as possible."

Khalidah, squeezed in among the emirs, felt a shiver run down her spine. Beneath the folds of their robes, Sulayman took her hand and held it tightly. In its taut muscles, she could feel her own fear and excitement. The Sultan looked out at them all for a moment, his golden-brown eyes stern, without the hint of a smile, but benevolent all the same.

"In the name of Allah, Most Gracious, Most Merciful," he said, "go now and tell your men that the time has come. Tomorrow, we will win back Jerusalem."

Fourteen

THE Jinn rode out with the Turkish horse-archers, half of them in each of the two main battalions. Even before Khalidah saw the Franj army, she had begun in a corner of her heart to pity them. The country over which they had chosen to march was rocky and harsh, not quite desert but a far cry from the green hills that made up so much of Galilee. It was less than three *farsakh*s from Sephoria to Tiberias—less than a day's march for a fit army—but without water or fodder for the horses it would be a march across hell.

At last, with the sun a finger's width above the horizon and buzzing in the sky like an angry hornet, Khalidah had her first sight of the enemy. Her detachment crested a wooded hill between the villages of Lubiyah and Shajarah and found themselves looking down through the trees onto the Franj vanguard. Even so early in the morning, the heat was having its effect. The Franj division, which should have appeared as a tight formation of knights boxed by infantry, was instead stretched like a frayed and threadbare runner along the plain between the hills to the north and south.

Across the valley to the east Khalidah could see the stacked cubes of the village of Tur'an on its wooded hillside. She knew that they must be heading there, for it possessed the only spring in the area. Khalidah's band of Jinn had been put under the command of a Turkish emir who was obsessed with the arrow and therefore enamored of their skills. Dividing his detachment quickly into smaller groups, each with an equal number of Jinn, he said:

"The time has come to commit ourselves to our Sultan and to Allah. Strike quickly, strike hard. Aim for the horses—without their mounts, they are easy prey. But remember, Count Tripoli leads the vanguard, and the Sultan has commanded that we spare him at any cost. *Allahu akbar!*"

He kicked his horse and hurtled off down the hill toward the hapless knights on their scorching plain. *"Allahu akbar,"* Khalidah whispered, and unslung her bow.

Fifteen

RAYMOND of Tripoli looked up at the group of shrieking raiders galloping toward him. He could muster no more than a weary sigh in response. He was stewing within his armor, his head pounded as if to burst his helmet, and he could barely see for the glare and the rivulets of sweat running into his eyes. He watched with dreamlike disconnection as the arrows whizzed past, barely noticing as two of them lodged in his armor. On all four sides the infantry were crumbling against the onslaught, barely managing in their exhaustion to raise their shields before they were shot down. The count rested one gauntleted hand on his sword but made no move to draw it; there was no point. By their skill alone he could tell that these archers were Turks, and as such they had no interest in close combat. They would fire off their arsenal and then turn tail and run, disappearing back into the trees from which they had come. And indeed, almost before he had finished thinking it, it had happened. The whiz and thud of the arrows fell silent, leaving only the sound of his fallen men crying out in confusion and pain.

Now Tripoli roused himself to action. He pushed through the ranks to survey the damage. It was considerable. The infantry had been sluggish in their response, numbed by weariness and thirst and perhaps already by the realization that their mission was doomed, and they had paid for it. All around him men lay wounded and dying, the lucky ones pierced cleanly through their throats or hearts, many more gut-shot or broken-limbed and screaming in agony.

And then he saw something else, something that should have had no place in the aftermath of an archers' skirmish: a severed arm. The man to whom it had belonged was already dead, but Tripoli dismounted anyway and examined the wound. It was a clean cut, and if he had not known that it was impossible, he would have said that it had been made by a sword. A quick assessment of the dead showed that it was not the only one. He scoured the ground until at last he discovered the culprit—an arrow with a forked head, not unlike his wife's sewing shears.

Before his men could see it and panic, he cried, "Back in line! Onward!" But the command was halfhearted, and halfheartedly obeyed.

From the woods to which her division had retreated, Khalidah watched as the Franj leaders tried to pull the scattered troops back together with the last frayed threads of order remaining to them. As the battered division stumbled forward, her pity was genuine.

Sixteen

THE rest of the Christian army was faring little better. Even before the Muslim onslaught they had been far too spread out for safety, their formations sabotaged by the heat and their own thirst and exhaustion. Now, as they neared Kafr Sabt and the Muslim front, more and more raiders were sent to harass them. Their horses succumbed to heat or arrows, and the knights were forced to walk in their armor. Some collapsed beside their horses; others simply cast the armor aside, preferring to expose themselves to Muslim artillery rather than slowly cook to death.

By ten o'clock in the morning, the king's center division had reached Tur'an. Those of his men who had not dropped away had, for the past several hours, marched with the sole purpose of reaching this town, with its promise of water and respite from the terrible heat. The left flank broke ranks as soon as they spotted the springs, paying no heed to the commanders who called them back.

"What are they doing?" cried Guy from the center of his formation, where he rode behind the reliquary of the True Cross, surrounded by packhorses carrying water skins. "They cannot stop here!"

"They have seen water, Your Highness," one of his knights answered. "They have marched a long way without drink."

But Guy had grown increasingly panicked over the course of the morning, as the Muslim onslaught became fiercer and his own army stumbled and straggled. Now that panic obliterated what little reason he possessed.

"They cannot stop here!" he repeated, his voice rising. "We are too close to the Saracens. We must press onward!"

"Sire—" the knight began patiently, but Guy interrupted.

"I order you onward! Send someone to bring the left flank back into line, and do not allow the others to break ranks!"

"Your Highness," the knight answered, and spurred his horse forward to do the king's bidding.

To be so near the antidote to their suffering and yet be denied it did more to degrade the Franj army's morale than any number of Muslim arrows could have done. By the time they crossed Salah ad-Din's front, they were barely moving. Even for the few who were lucky enough to have access to water skins the heat was maddening, intensified by the blowing dust and the steady pounding of drums from the Muslim lines, which seemed to rise up from the parched ground like a heartbeat from hell. At noon, Tripoli and the vanguard reached the village of Miskinah. As they paused there, a messenger reached them with the news that the rear guard had been forced to halt. Leaving the division temporarily under the command of his stepson Hugh, Tripoli turned and retraced his steps until at last he reached the center division. He picked out Guy's standard at the center and forced his way toward it until he rode beside the king.

Without ceremony he said, "We cannot possibly continue on this road, for if we do, we will meet the main body of the Muslim army, and my men can barely stand, let alone fight. We must find them water and a place to rest, or we are finished."

Guy's eyes were dull and far away. There was neither emotion nor curiosity in his voice when he asked, "Well, what, then?"

"Not far from here a track leaves the main road to the left. If we follow it we will come to Hattin village. It is only a few leagues, and there are springs there. More than that, it is close to the lake. We could reach it the next day, and with the water on our side we just might salvage this disaster."

Kerak, riding at the king's other side, had been listening to Tripoli's proposal with a darkening countenance. Now, at this insult, he burst forth: "The only disaster would be for Your Highness to listen to this—"

But to both Kerak's and Tripoli's surprise, Guy interrupted, "Silence! It was *your* advice that landed us here." He glowered at Kerak with uncharacteristic vitriol. "I ought to have listened to Tripoli when he told us to remain at Sephoria. As I did not, I can at least heed him now. Give the command: we ride now for Hattin."

Though it was unclear to whom this order was directed, Tripoli wasted no time in which Guy might once again vacillate. "Your Grace," he said, and with a curt nod he turned his horse and rode as fast as it would take him back to the vanguard with their new orders.

Seventeen

"**HAVE** they gone mad?" Al-Afdhal asked his father.

They sat on their horses atop a hill above the camp, watching as the Franj army in the valley dissolved into chaos. Salah ad-Din watched for several moments without comment, eyes slitted against the brightness. The emirs around him stood equally silent, awaiting his judgment (and perhaps the chastisement of his arrogant son).

At last the Sultan spoke. "They have realized that they cannot reach Tiberias," he said, "and now they are trying to change direction. They are making for Hattin."

"How do you know?" Al-Afdhal persisted.

The emirs expected a sharp retort, but the Sultan maintained his odd serenity when he answered, "Because they are dying now of thirst, and Hattin has the only springs within their reach." He turned abruptly to face his emirs. "Taqi ad-Din!"

The Sultan's nephew had engaged the Christian vanguard already that day, skirmishing with the stragglers among Tripoli's men. He had ridden back into camp only half an hour earlier to report to the Sultan and take new orders. He was dusty and sweat-stained, his yellow robe rent and blood-spattered over his mail, but the look in his eyes was as fresh and eager as it had been at dawn.

"Your Highness," he answered, urging his horse forward.

"Your division is still blocking the main road to Tiberias, by Lubiyah?"

"It is."

"Take them now and block the road to Hattin instead."

"It will not work," Al-Afdhal muttered. "The Franj are much closer to Hattin than we are."

"The Franj are closer," his father said shortly, "but we are faster."

"Your Highness," Taqi ad-Din repeated. Bowing to the Sultan, he turned his horse and rode toward Lubiyah, flanked by his guard.

"Will you leave the main road to Tiberias unguarded, then?" Salim asked his father quietly.

Salah ad-Din shook his head. "I must move the center division to cover it. We will make camp tonight at Lubiyah." He spurred his horse, and as they rode down the hill the Sultan recounted their position, though it seemed to his listeners that he spoke more to himself than to any of them. "Taqi ad-Din and the right wing at Hattin; Gökböri and the left wing in the hills near Shajarah. If all goes well, Gökböri will attack the Franj rear guard and Guy will be forced to order a halt."

"But if the Franj make camp at Hattin," Salim persisted, "will it not be the same as Sephoria? Worse, since they have learned their lesson: we will never draw them forth."

"We will not need to."

"How can you be sure?"

The Sultan gave his son a smile of beatific wisdom. "Because by then, we will have them surrounded."

Eighteen

THE Franj rear guard had been under constant attack by Gökböri's division for eight hours when the order came. The halt boded no relief for the men, for without water or shade it only prolonged their misery. While the troops hung and wavered on the shimmering road, swatting at the intermittent Muslim arrows as if they were flies, Balian d'Ibelin and Joscelin d'Edessa called a hasty meeting with Gerard de Ridefort.

"We cannot go on like this, my lords," de Ridefort said, before either of his commanding officers could take control. "We must strike back, or be cut down little by little."

D'Ibelin had never liked de Ridefort, and since Cresson he had not trusted him either. Now the Templar Master's face was eager, florid, little reflecting the gravity of the situation. If he had not known better d'Ibelin might have attributed this to religious fervor, but as it was he smelled treachery.

"Your haste has condemned us to this march, de Ridefort," he said. "Let us not now allow it to finish us."

Immediately, de Ridefort was fuming. "If I had allowed the king to listen to that traitor Tripoli, the Lady of Tiberias would be a Muslim whore by now!"

"And who is to say that she is not?" d'Ibelin asked. "We have certainly not succeeded in delivering her."

"Which is why we must act now, and act decisively!"

"With what, Messire?" d'Ibelin cried, his fractured patience finally shattering. "Look around you! The foot soldiers are finished.

Let the Saracens say the word and they will convert for a cup of water. As for the knights, they are little better off, and I will not order mine to charge an enemy so superior to them in their present condition. I might as well order a foundering ship to steer for the rocks!"

"Well, d'Ibelin," de Ridefort answered coldly, "not all of these knights are yours to command. Mine answer to God, and God demands that His soldiers do more than make themselves willing pincushions for heathen arrows."

"Do you call yourself God, now?" d'Ibelin hissed.

"Enough," d'Edessa broke in at last. "We have enemies enough among the Saracens without making more of each other. I agree, d'Ibelin, that a charge is unlikely to win us much ground. On the other hand, it will certainly be more effective than sitting here and succumbing to the heat. If de Ridefort wishes for his Templars to engage the Saracens, we may as well let them. If nothing else, it will give us a few moments' relief from their arrows."

D'Ibelin's head swam with heat and exhaustion. D'Edessa's words had deflated him as a needle would a pig's-bladder balloon. He could not even muster words to answer, just waved his hand in acknowledgment of his defeat, and watched de Ridefort gallop away with a deepening sense of doom.

Nineteen

To General Gökböri it was Cresson all over again, the only difference being that this time he was prepared. Even so, he could hardly believe his eyes when he saw the little wedge of white-robed knights galloping toward his lines, lances couched and ready to shatter on the infantry's shields—which, a moment later, they did. He caught the flash of drawn swords, and then the scene succumbed to its own raised dust.

It was over before it began. The Templars had spent themselves in the initial charge. By the time they joined ranks they were swaying in their saddles, hardly able to draw their swords, let alone use them. It was like picking fruit, thought Sulayman, who was fighting in the front lines: a comparison that he could not subsequently banish from his mind, though as the dust turned to crimson mud and his horse's hooves sucked and squelched in a mire of tattered flesh and spilled entrails, he wished he could. There was no second charge. The Templars who survived the first retreated as quickly as their tired horses could carry them, leaving their fallen brethren to the vultures and the captured or wounded to the mercy of the Muslim swords.

Meanwhile, to the east, the king's division had at last caught up with the vanguard near the village of Miskinah. They were still nearly two *farsakh*s from Tiberias when the news of the Templars' charge reached them. When he heard it, Tripoli cursed himself bitterly for accepting the command of the vanguard and thereby separating himself from de Ridefort. He ought to have stayed by him, where he might have had a chance of curbing his impulsiveness.

"Lord God, the war is over," he said bitterly. "We are betrayed to death and the land is lost."

"Betrayed?" asked Guy, his voice thin now and showing cracks.

Tripoli had forgotten the king in his self-recrimination. Now he looked over at him. Seeing the whiteness of Guy's face, the tremor of his hand on the reins, he knew that he must act quickly and decisively if they were to retrieve anything of this disaster.

"Betrayed," he answered coldly, "by those whose hot blood burns away reason. If you would salvage anything of your kingdom, Your Grace, then you will order a halt immediately."

"Another halt? But that cannot possibly help us. Perhaps we ought to turn back to Sephoria . . ."

Tripoli gave a derisive snort. "It's a bit late now, Your Highness, to think of Sephoria. Even if the Sultan's men would allow the retreat, our own would never make it so far. Order them to set up camp for the night by Miskinah. We will wait there for the rear guard to catch up, and we will try for Hattin spring in the morning."

"This is travesty!" cried Kerak, who had ridden up to listen when he saw Tripoli speaking with the king. Heat and sun had already ruddied his face; now fury deepened it nearly to the color of his hair. "We must attack the Saracen pigs' main position now while we are near it—it is our only chance of victory!"

"Victory?" said Tripoli. "Is it possible that you are still so deluded as to imagine we might escape from this with our lives, let alone as conquerors?"

"You speak blasphemy, Tripoli, to suggest that God would see us vanquished by heathens!"

Tripoli looked not at Kerak but at the king. Guy's hands were shaking harder now, and his face, if possible, had gone whiter. He looked as if he would gladly hand over his crown to the first taker, if only to escape the crushing responsibility for this mess. But Tripoli had no pity left for him.

With a voice like the strike of a blacksmith's hammer, he said, "You have succumbed time and again to bloodthirsty fools, Messire. You might as well fall on your own sword as listen to this one now."

Kerak reached for his sword, but at the rasp of metal, Guy spoke: "Stand down, Kerak."

It was so unexpected that for a moment, Kerak's vitriol dissolved. But only for a moment. "Your Highness, would you have this lover of heathens dictate—"

"Silence," said Guy, and if he did not sound entirely certain of himself, his hand had at least stopped shaking. "Your advice has proven worthless. Let us see if Count Tripoli's serves us better. We will halt now and make camp as he has suggested, and let us all pray that tomorrow the Lord sees fit to deliver us."

Twenty

BY nightfall, the Franj army was surrounded by the Muslim one. They were camped within speaking distance of each other, had either side been inclined. But the Franj were thirsty to the point of madness or despair, depending on each man's particular inclination, and the Muslims taunted them with raging drums, with prayers and songs broadcast by the surrounding hills, and most of all with the knowledge that they were replete with water. For as soon as his troops were installed in their new position, Salah ad-Din had organized a camel caravan to bring water from the lake, which was emptied into temporary reservoirs.

As the Muslims drank to their hearts' content, their laborers collected brushwood and dry thistles, lining them up in piles along the windward side of the Franj camp and setting them alight. They laid more brushwood along the road the Franj were expected to take the following day, to be lit at dawn. As the smoke and heat from the fires began to do its work, the Sultan had water pots placed at the edges of camp where the Franj could see them. He ordered them filled and then emptied in view of the miserable Christian soldiers. Many of the Franj infantry gave in then, throwing away their weapons and pledging their souls to Allah for the privilege of a mouthful of muddy water salvaged from the dust.

"What will be done with them?" Bilal asked Salim as they sat watching the wretched converts being led away.

Salim shrugged. "They'll be put to work with the camp laborers."

"Even the knights?"

"Have you seen a knight surrender yet?"

"No," Bilal answered, "but I imagine they will. They have little choice now."

"They won't surrender without some attempt at a fight."

"Surely even the Franj are not so arrogant as to imagine that they have any chance at victory now?"

"I cannot claim to know what they hope for, but I do know that they won't lay their faith aside so easily." He shook his head. "They believe that God wills this war, so even now they must believe that God will provide them with a victory."

"Those infantrymen don't seem to believe it."

Salim waved a dismissive hand at the trickle of converts. "Those men are poor and ignorant, and most of them are probably half-breeds anyway."

As soon as the words were out of his mouth Salim realized what he had said and turned stricken eyes on Bilal. Bilal only smiled. "Don't say it, Salim."

"Truly, Bilal—"

"Don't. It doesn't matter. Very little matters now."

Salim's eyebrows drew together. "What does *that* mean?"

"It means that by tomorrow all of this will be over one way or another and, *Inshallah*, you and I on our way to someplace better."

Thinking of his father's words, Salim gave Bilal a troubled smile. "You have discovered that land, then, that we spoke of long ago?"

"We will find it," he answered.

"Do you truly believe that?" Salim asked, without a trace of a smile now; in fact, with something very like desperation. A darkness seemed to have gathered around him, and Bilal shivered, wrapping his arms around Salim.

"When I am with you, I can believe anything," he said bravely.

Salim seemed about to say something else, but in the end he only nodded, then rested his chin on Bilal's shoulder as they watched darkness fall. At the foot of the Horns of Hattin Khalidah sat similarly between Abi Gul and Sandara, watching their camp-fire burn and thinking of Sulayman far off down the valley with Gökböri's division, just as Sulayman thought of her. And on the muddy shores of the Jordan a strange, filthy figure with a splinted leg and a devil's eyes pulled himself from the water, turning west toward the sound of beating drums—and revenge.

Twenty-one

Near Hattin
4 July, Morning

NEAR dawn King Guy, who had sat through that night in his red tent with his head in his hands, called his commanders to him. He looked around at them as if searching for somewhere to lay blame, his eyes coming to rest at last on de Ridefort.

"You," he said, and if his voice hadn't trembled it might have held accusation. "You have brought us here; now it is up to you to get us out."

"Out, Sire?" de Ridefort repeated incredulously. "We came here to fight the Saracens, and it is God's will that we are now so placed that there is no way out but by doing so."

"God's will?" the king repeated, shaking his head. He looked around for Tripoli, and found him back in the shadows by the doorway. "Count? What do you say?"

Tripoli raised his head and looked at the king. After a moment he smiled, and it was like the grimace on the face of a dead man. "What is there to say? If we stay here we will die of thirst by nightfall. To reach Hattin spring we must march straight through enemy lines. It is up to you to choose our doom."

"Very well," Guy trembled. "Yes, I fear that you are right. We must fight our way out. Mobilize the troops!"

And so it was that Count Tripoli was given the first division and rode once again at the front of the army. Balian d'Ibelin and Joscelin d'Edessa kept command of the rear guard, and the king rode at the center with the other nobles, his bishops, and the relic of the True Cross. As dawn streaked the sky with light the color of blood, they turned toward Hattin village and their last hope.

"SIRE, they are moving!"

Salah ad-Din, who had lain all night in his armor, came immediately to the Mamluk's call. From his position at the top of the camp he had a clear view down into the valley, where the Franj army had indeed re-formed and resumed its shuffling march northeast. After a time his sons joined him, but it was several moments before any of them ventured to break the silence.

"Are we not going to stop them?" Al-Afdhal asked at last.

Salah ad-Din looked at his eldest. The boy's face was taut with anticipation and real anxiety. It stifled the caustic reply that was forming on his tongue. "We will wait," he said. "I need to know whether they intend to try for Hattin village or to launch an attack on us before I decide our next move."

"Then we must sit idle?" Al-Afdhal asked incredulously.

Taking pity on him, Salah ad-Din answered, "Send word to the laborers to light the fires along the road. Tell them to light them in sequence, as the army moves, so that they do not burn out too soon to do their work."

Inclining his head to his father, Al-Afdhal ran off. When he was gone, the Sultan surveyed his remaining sons with a distracted look. At last his eyes settled on Bilal, who stood behind Salim like a pale shadow.

"Al-Hassani," he said.

"Sire?" Bilal answered, stepping forward.

"Do you know the whereabouts of the minstrel Sulayman, who rides with the Jinn?"

Bilal raised his eyebrows in surprise, then quickly recovered himself, saying, "I believe that he went with Gökböri."

Salah ad-Din gave him a curt nod. "Gökböri is camped at Miskinah. Go and find the minstrel, and bring him to me." Catching Bilal's glance at Salim, he added, "No, you must do this alone. I need Salim here."

"Of course, Your Highness," Bilal answered, and cursing Sulayman all over again, he went to saddle his horse.

The horse was a fine black mare, which Salim had given him to replace Anjum. She was fast and sure-footed, and even in the dim dawn light it did not take him long to reach Miskinah. But a search of the camp there turned up not a single Jinni. Bilal rode on past the town to the north, where yesterday's brush fires still smoldered. Beyond them was a smaller camp, and on its fringes, a cluster of white tents. Bilal found Sulayman untying the guy ropes of one of them.

"The Sultan wants you," he said.

Sulayman looked up at him as the tent collapsed. He was dressed in his armor already, his sword slung through his sash. "Why would he want me?" he asked.

"The Sultan is not in the habit of confiding in his servants," Bilal answered irritably.

"I am coming," Sulayman sighed. He called something to a small, slight Jinni in a language that Bilal didn't recognize. The boy—or girl, Bilal couldn't tell—ran off to do whatever Sulayman had ordered. Then he went and spoke for a moment with an older man, who nodded and put his hand on Sulayman's shoulder for a moment before Sulayman turned away.

The little Jinni returned, leading his horse. Shoving his helmet onto his head, Sulayman said, "Let's go."

By the time they returned to Salah ad-Din's camp, it was full daylight. Bilal approached the Sultan's pavilion, with Sulayman a step behind. Turning to his sons, Salah ad-Din said, "Go and ready for battle. I must speak for a moment with this man, and then I will join you."

When they were alone, Salah ad-Din gestured for Sulayman to sit down by him in the shade of the pavilion. Sulayman was grateful for this: the sun was already strong, and he was sweating inside his armor. He knew that the heat of the coming day would be brutal, but for the moment he tried to focus on the present.

"Thank you for coming," said Salah ad-Din.

"You are welcome, Your Highness."

"You are wondering why you are here."

"Of course . . ."

The Sultan paused for a few long moments. "How much do you remember of Cairo, Sulayman?" he asked at last.

Sulayman looked up at him, surprised. "I remember it as a heaving, filthy, vibrant, and beautiful place."

The Sultan smiled fondly, and Sulayman suddenly recalled that the young Salah ad-Din had begun his political career in Egypt. "I could not have put it better," he said. "Few people know this, but I loved it there." He paused, shook his head. "Did you ever see the Jewish quarter?"

Sulayman felt suddenly cold. He could not make himself speak, so he shook his head, his eyes fixed on Salah ad-Din. The Sultan met them squarely.

"It was my favorite part of the city," he continued. "The caliph was by that time an old man rotting on his feet, infecting everything with a terrible lethargy. But the Jewish quarter was different. Alive. I used to walk through it in the mornings, when the bookshops and apothecaries were opening and the streets smelled of baking bread . . . well, you do not care about that. You want to know how I met your mother."

Sulayman sat very still, afraid that if he moved or even breathed the Sultan might change his mind and retreat into silence.

"She was far from home. Her family was Persian, from Shiraz, but her sister had married an Egyptian physician the previous year, and had just borne him twins. Haya had been sent to Cairo to help her . . . and no doubt to find a husband of her own."

"And instead," Sulayman heard himself saying bitterly, "she found you."

Salah ad-Din looked at him calmly. "We found each other, Sulayman. I have never had any woman against her will. Haya was young, but she was not a child. She chose me, as I chose her."

"And then you abandoned her, pregnant, to fend for herself."

The Sultan raised his eyebrows, smiled humorlessly. "Is that what you have been told? I'm sorry to disillusion you, Sulayman, but the truth is that she abandoned me. I could not marry her—our religions forbade that—but I had made it clear that I would take care of her. She could have lived with me as part of the harem, and I told her as much; but then she disappeared.

"For a long time I didn't know why. By the time I traced her back to Cairo she was dead, but I did learn that she had had a child. A son called Sulayman. And that is the nearest I can come to an explanation: that her faith made it impossible for her to live as a concubine, or to raise her child as anything other than Jewish. I assumed she had gone back to her family."

Sulayman nodded. "She was on her way back to them when I was born, in a Ma'dan village in Jazirah. She left there not long after. I suppose she went to her family, and they would not have her, and that is why she returned to Cairo; but I do not know."

Salah ad-Din sighed. "I looked for you, but you too had disappeared. I had long since given up any hope of finding you when you stumbled into my camp in the mountains that night, the very image of your mother."

"Why didn't you tell me this then?" Sulayman asked.

Salah ad-Din shook his head. "It took time for me to believe it. But also, I suppose, because you were a grown man with your own life. I did not think you needed to know."

"Then why are you telling me now?"

"Because Allah keeps setting our paths to cross, and I cannot keep ignoring it. Because we might die here today, and it does not seem right that I should take this knowledge with me to my grave. And because if I cannot recognize you as a legitimate son, I can at least honor the blood we share. I would like you to fight with me today."

Sulayman looked at his father for a long moment. He felt as if he were dreaming, but the blowing smoke and dust, the sweat running down his back and neck, the crying of buzzards overhead, were too mundane for that.

"I thank you for telling me this, Sire," he said, "and you honor me by your request, but I have promised to fight with the Jinn in this battle, and I do not break promises. Perhaps, though, when this is finished"—here at last his voice trembled—"we may speak to each other again?"

The Sultan studied him for a moment, and then smiled his rueful smile. "*Inshallah*, we shall have that chance. Here, take this." He handed him a silken robe of Ayyub yellow. "Good luck, Sulayman."

Sulayman accepted the garment. "Good luck to you too, Sire," he said, and bowing low, he retreated.

Twenty-two

AFTER he had dismissed Sulayman, the Sultan's first action was to send orders to his generals by carrier pigeon instructing them to anchor their divisions on nearby hills. Taqi ad-Din and his right wing would position themselves between the foot of the Horns of Hattin and Nimrin village, to cut off the route to the springs at Hattin village. Gökböri would station his own division between Lubiyah and Tur'an, making it impossible for the Franj to retreat west to the springs at Tur'an. The Sultan's center division would complete the triangle around the Franj, spreading out between the foot of the Horns and Lubiyah, thereby blocking the main road to Tiberias.

"Do not underestimate the motivating power of despair," Salah ad-Din added at the end of his orders to both generals. "The Franj will try to break out toward water—quite likely the lake—and they must be stopped at any cost. Hold firm. Leave Tripoli and de Ridefort alive if it is in your power. *Allahu akbar!*"

When the pigeons had disappeared into the searing sky, Salah ad-Din took the helmet proffered by the Mamluk on his left and mounted the horse held by the one on his right. He looked out over the glittering expanse of his army, its banners fluttering proudly in the hot wind, then down at the Franj army, crawling along the valley in its ragged square formations like some great, ailing insect. The disparity did not deceive him. He knew exactly what kind of day lay before him. He knew that he must not be defeated.

"*Allahu akbar*," he repeated softly, and then spurred his horse forward.

SALAH ad-Din's center and Gökböri's left flank were the first to attack. The Franj rear guard had a momentarily perfect view of the endless ranks charging down upon them before the raised dust and the smoke of the bonfires obscured it. The Muslim army slammed into them with the force of a sandstorm. Only the Templar line held, doggedly standing their ground as the Muslim cavalry hacked their way through the infantry and Turkish arrows felled their horses. For a moment in the midst of the chaos, de Ridefort wondered if he had made a terrible mistake. But he balked at the brink of that chasm.

"Countercharge!" he cried against the shriek and whine of metal, the thuds of arrows, and the screams of fallen men and horses. "Regroup and countercharge!"

The smoke and the dust and the forest of flailing weapons were too thick to accurately assess the Muslim position or even the extent of either side's losses, but de Ridefort had been fighting in this land long enough to have developed an instinct for it. He sensed a lessening in the onslaught and once again shouted his orders into it. This time they were heeded. The knights who still had mounts formed a line behind what remained of the infantry.

"God wills it!" cried de Ridefort, spurring his horse. Though few repeated his cry, the surrounding thunder of hooves told him that they were with him. They slammed into Gökböri's lines, crushing foot soldiers and toppling the lighter Muslim cavalry. The dust and smoke swayed this way and that, like a curtain in a crazed breeze. For every Muslim soldier that de Ridefort cut down, three more seemed to spring into being. They came like a river behind a burst dam, rank upon rank of them, a blackness on the hills; and then suddenly they were gone. A tattered remnant of some Muslim battalion was all that stood between de Ridefort and freedom.

"Messire, we are through!" cried one of his knights. "Call another charge, and their line is broken!"

Broken, thought de Ridefort. His head was ringing with the din of battle, with the heat and thirst and exhaustion that had at last caught up even with him. He could not make his mind work. The internal compass that infallibly pointed to whatever path would lead to his greatest benefit had failed.

"Messire!" cried the knight, a voice bleeding despair.

But it was already too late. The gap had closed again, filled in by apparitions in white with marks on their faces and bows in their hands. *Retreat.* The word crawled across de Ridefort's sluggish mind. By the time it penetrated, his horse had been shot from under him. At last he came back to himself. To his right he saw the knight who had tried to rouse him to call the charge, fighting one of the white riders. Perfunctorily, he shoved the boy from his saddle and onto the Saracen's sword and then, hurling himself onto the horse, de Ridefort turned and raced back into the valley.

Twenty-three

FROM the slopes of the Horns of Hattin, Khalidah looked down into the valley, where the two armies darkened the bright sands. There were the wooded hills, there the vastness of water; there even the standards waving in the morning breeze, though the colors had lost their visionary clarity to the reality of smoke and dust. Still, she could see the Templars' bloodied white and the Hospitallers' black, the colorful banners of both sides' warrior houses, the brilliant yellow of the Ayyubids and Mamluks, the green and white of the Fatimids, black again for the Seljuqs. There was a charge and a countercharge, and Khalidah knew that had she been nearer the ground would have trembled. But she did not cry "Now!" She did not cry anything. She sat on Zahirah's back, still as a statue, with Sandara on one side and Abi Gul on the other, watching the storm of flesh and steel, awaiting orders.

"So much for prophecy," she said, not realizing that she'd spoken aloud until Abi Gul answered, "What do you mean?"

Khalidah only shook her head. She knew that somewhere down in the dusty valley everyone she had ever loved—everyone but the few Jinn who waited with her now—had cast their lives to the mercy of Allah. She knew that in a moment she would do the same. She was wondering why she had ever thought that she could be anything more than fodder to her land's battling gods.

"Nearly time," Sandara said calmly. "The vanguard is lining up to charge."

Khalidah looked down to see the closest Franj square spreading out, the horsemen lining up behind the infantry. Her heart came into her throat.

"Don't be afraid, Khalidah," Sandara said gently. "The Jinn have taught you well."

With numb fingers, Khalidah fumbled for her bow. And then the Franj vanguard was charging, heading straight for Hattin village, straight for Khalidah and her Jinn. Once she was moving she forgot her fear, firing her arrows with speed and precision equal to Sandara's, if not to Abi Gul's. The Muslim force was larger, but as Salah ad-Din had pointed out to his generals, the Franj had the motivation of despair. Once the two divisions had joined ranks, the Franj fought with formidable strength.

Khalidah had long since changed her bow for her sword. Blows rained down on her seemingly from all sides, but her armor held. She rained blows in return, but in the raging of tight-packed men and horses, the smoke and dust and the deafening clash of metal, she had little concept of their effectiveness. She did not even know which side was prevailing, though at some point she felt the tidelike push against her slacken and then reverse, so that slowly, slowly, she was pushing forward. Then the man whom she was fighting turned and galloped away, and she looked up to see that all down the line the Franj were retreating. She didn't know whether to be elated or disappointed.

Their emir was calling them to re-form ranks, and Khalidah turned Zahirah back up the hill with the others. The diverging armies left a detritus of bodies in their wake, as the retreating tide leaves weed on the strand. There were white-robed figures among them, but both Sandara and Abi Gul had survived the charge. There was blood seeping through Sandara's right sleeve, however, and Abi Gul looked pale and drawn beneath her helmet.

"All right?" Khalidah asked them as they resumed their position on the hill.

Abi Gul nodded mutely, but Sandara shook her head. "This is not going to work."

"What isn't?" Khalidah asked.

"If the Franj charge again, they will break through. You must speak to the general."

"Taqi ad-Din?" Khalidah asked incredulously. "And tell him what?"

"Have you forgotten already, Khalidah?" Sandara snapped. "Yield where the opponent is strong; attack where he is weak. We will gain far more right now by yielding."

"You mean that we should let them through?"

Sandara nodded.

"But—"

"But nothing! The Franj charge, we open our ranks, they ride through the gap and we close them again. They will find themselves on their way down a steep, narrow cleft in the rock of this hill. They would be unable to charge back up it again even if they had the will. And with water in their sights, they'll have will for nothing else."

It made sense, but the idea of her approaching Taqi ad-Din was preposterous. "What reason does he have to listen to me?"

"He has as much reason as he has to listen to any of us."

"It was your idea," Khalidah said.

"It is a Jinn idea. It belongs to us all, but you are our leader. Now go, Khalidah, or you will lose your chance. They are lining up again already."

Khalidah glanced down at the Franj and saw that this was true. Taking a deep breath, she turned toward the waving Ayyubid banner that marked the general's position and kicked Zahirah into a gallop. In seconds, it seemed, she was there.

"I must speak with the general," she said to the Mamluk guard.

He looked at her as he might a scorpion he intended to crush.

"Please," she said. "I have a message from the Sultan."

She didn't like to lie, but she knew that she had no choice. The Mamluk looked at her for a moment, and then barked something over his shoulder. A moment later Taqi ad-Din rode up. He was streaked with sweat and blood, his eyes irritable on either side of his helmet's filigreed nasal.

"What is it, Jinni?" he demanded.

Show no weakness, Khalidah thought, then said, "I can tell you how to defeat Tripoli's division, Sayyid."

"Indeed?" said the man, his look and tone now mocking. "And perhaps you can magic this entire Franj army back to their pox-ridden country . . . or better yet, to hell!"

"That I cannot do," Khalidah answered, forcing herself to remain calm, "and there is no magic involved." She repeated Sandara's idea.

"You suggest allowing the entire Franj vanguard to go free?" Despite the incredulous words, his tone held a flicker of interest.

"Free?" She shook her head. "Perhaps for a few hours. But without the vanguard the king will be an easy target, and when the king surrenders there will be no freedom for any Franji in this country."

For a moment, Taqi ad-Din wavered; and then his face hardened. "Back to your battalion, Jinni, and leave the strategizing to the generals!"

With a sinking heart, Khalidah rode back to her position and took up her place between Sandara and Abi Gul. Neither of them needed to ask her how the interview had gone. Once again they readied their bows, and once again the Franj charged. Khalidah was caught in the thicket of swords and spears, hacking and stabbing with her mother's sword before she could be hacked and stabbed herself. But something was different this time. The onslaught was not as fierce, and instead of the tidal reach and retreat, the force of the action seemed to be spiraling away to her left.

When she killed the man she had engaged she found herself momentarily clear, and looked in the direction that the Franj seemed to be heading. A gap had opened in the Muslim ranks where an entire section of the line had swung aside, and the Franj were pouring through it, disappearing like water into parched sand. A moment later the last Franj horsemen had been swallowed, and the Muslim ranks had closed again. And when Khalidah turned again to face the infantry, she found nothing but their retreating backs.

Twenty-four

THOUGH Tripoli and his knights were now expunged from the battle, his initial charge had weakened the Muslim triangle where Taqi ad-Din's division met Salah ad-Din's. Tripoli's abandoned infantry could see Lake Tiberias to the right of the Horns, and they began to move east toward the thinned patch in the Muslim ranks, hoping to break through. It was a delusional hope, and for the Franj it had devastating effects. Seeing their brethren deserting, the infantry of the remaining center and rear guard began to follow them. Before long there were no infantry left to defend the knights. The Muslims concentrated their arrows on the Franj horses then, until most of the Franj knights were fighting on foot.

"We must form some kind of barrier against their cavalry," said Guy to anyone who might be listening. Nobody answered him. All of his men were either fighting or sunk too deep in their despair to soothe the qualms of their king.

"The tents," Guy said to himself after a moment, and then cried, "the tents! We must pitch the tents between ourselves and the enemy, for surely that will slow them."

Ignoring the withering looks of his commanders, Guy proclaimed the order. His men turned grudgingly from the battle to obey it, but they only managed to pitch the king's tent and two others at the foot of the Horns before the rain of arrows grew too fierce for them to continue. Guy huddled inside his pavilion, trying not to hear the screams of the failing cavalry, trying not to breathe the smoke that rolled over him thicker than ever, trying to make his mind work. He wanted nothing more than for someone else to take responsibility. He cursed the nobles who had pushed him toward the throne to thwart Tripoli, cursed Sibylla who had put the crown on his head. It never occurred to him to curse himself.

After a time a squire came in, a skinny boy dripping sweat and blood onto the fine carpet. "Sire, I am to tell you that all of the infantry is now on the northern Horn. We have sent your orders for them to come down, but they refuse. The bishops have threatened damnation if they will not defend the Cross, but still they will not listen."

"Oh?" said Guy faintly. "And what do they give as their reason?"

The squire made a helpless gesture. "They say that they are dying of thirst."

Guy smiled bitterly. "And will death spare them on the northern Horn? No, never mind. I will come."

When the king emerged, he found the remaining cavalry fighting solely to keep the encroaching Muslim forces away from his tent. The rest fought on foot, though more for their lives, it appeared, than any cohesive goal. Looking east, Guy could see the Horns of Hattin: the larger southern one flat-topped and pristine, the nearer northern one crawling black with his own infantry. He was reminded of a rose he had once seen in his mother's garden, so infested with blackfly that its color was no longer discernible.

He turned to the squire. "What is your name, boy?"

"Ernoul," the young man replied.

"Ernoul," the king repeated. "I know that name."

"Perhaps, Sire. We have met before. I am squire to Balian d'Ibelin."

Guy raised his eyebrows. A knight, for some reason missing his helmet, stumbled past them with an arrow protruding from his forehead, and died. "Then why are you here, and not with him?"

"There was no one else to bring you the news, Sire."

Guy nodded, as if all of this information were perfunctory. "And what would you do, Ernoul?"

"Do, Sire?"

"Yes. If you were in my shoes, what would you do right now?"

Ernoul looked around at the chaos, the dwindling Franj forces and the surrounding host of the Saracen army, bristling with weaponry and bitter intent. "Well, Sire," he sighed, "it seems there is little that can be done, except perhaps to follow the infantry onto the Horns and hope that then they will remember their duty."

"Very well," Guy said. "Let it be known."

"Sire?"

"Go and tell the rear guard that we are moving onto the Horns."

Twenty-five

KHALIDAH was glad of the sudden respite in the fighting, though she could not immediately see what had caused it. It was Abi Gul who first realized the truth.

"Look!" she cried, shaking her plaits back over her shoulders. "They have pitched the king's tent on the Horns!"

Khalidah watched for a moment as the red fabric billowed on the hilltop and then stretched taut. "They are taking the army after the infantry," she said. "But we will surround them and, *In-shallah*, that will be the end."

For a few minutes they watched as what was left of the Franj army took up position on the flat-topped southern Horn. Then their commanding emir rode up with the order they were all expecting:

"Surround the Horns! Move out!"

They turned their horses to follow the rest of their division toward the hill. The Franj center seemed to be heavily burdened, and the Muslims wasted no time in capitalizing on this, engaging them wherever they could, which slowed progress. The Jinn detachment was toward the back of the division and therefore free of the fighting for the time being. As they rode, Sandara, who had been silently studying the Franj for some time, suddenly asked:

"What is the significance of the cross?"

Khalidah looked in the direction of Sandara's gaze. A short distance away a golden cross bobbed on a long pole at the center of a cluster of Franj, surrounded by waving banners. Though it had been there throughout the battle, Khalidah had not really registered it until that moment.

"That is the reliquary containing the fragment of the True Cross—the cross on which Iesu was killed. Or so the Franj believe."

Sandara nodded. Though she wore her black veil even with her helmet, Khalidah could tell by the tilt of her head and the very stillness of her hidden gaze that she was plotting something. "And so, that golden cross is precious to them?"

"More precious than anything," Khalidah said slowly, for she saw now where Sandara was heading, and she did not like it. "To them it is a piece of God. They always carry it into battle. I suppose it motivates them."

"So, if they were to lose it," Sandara concluded, "then they would lose their will to fight?"

"Sandara," Khalidah said, "you cannot."

"Why not?" the older woman asked.

"Because you are unlikely to succeed, and very likely to be killed. Think of your children."

"I am thinking of them, Bibi Khalidah," she said. She pulled her veil away and jettisoned it to the churning hooves. For a moment the dust-laden air gave the illusion that her face was whole, her smile a perfect curve of certainty. "I am going to the front now. I need to be near the Franj the next time we charge. Good luck, daughters. Sing of me to my children."

And before Khalidah or Abi Gul could say anything, Sandara had plunged off into the roil of men and horses in the direction of the Franj cross.

WITHIN the hour the Franj were surrounded on the hill. The north and east slopes were too steep for horses, but the Muslim right and center divisions fought their way up from the south and the west. Early in the afternoon the Muslim foot soldiers, who had been marching toward the northern Horn, finally arrived and engaged their Franj counterparts. There was little contest. The Franj who did not immediately surrender were easy targets for Muslim swords, or else they were thrown down the steep hill to their deaths.

Salah ad-Din was cautiously pleased. His sons were fighting well. Salim had apparently recovered from his ennui and was cutting down Franj like a demon, and even Al-Afdhal was managing to hold his own. Sulayman had proven a strong, steady swordsman, and his men—men and women, the Sultan corrected himself, for he must not forget that the heathen Jinn were both—followed his lead with obvious respect. There were definite possibilities for the boy, the Sultan thought. This was not the time to consider them, however, and of course he had not yet survived the battle.

Evaluating his situation once again, Salah ad-Din saw two things clearly. The day would not be won until the king was taken, and the king could not be taken without an action more decisive than their current slow trundle up the slopes of the horned hill. There were two possible routes for a charge. The southern one, guarded by his own division, was the steeper. It might tire the horses unduly before they engaged, which could give the Franj just enough of an advantage to repel the charge. Though longer, the western slope had a gentler incline. The west was also Taqi ad-Din's position, and this decided the matter for the Sultan. If he could not make the final charge himself, he could think of no one better to entrust it to than his nephew. If the fact that Khalidah al-Hassani rode in that division was also present in his mind, he did not acknowledge it even to himself.

Upon receiving his orders, Taqi ad-Din wasted no time. The Jinn rode at the back of the division, but still Khalidah's heart was in her throat as they lined up and the call sounded. Then the horses were moving forward, gaining momentum as they climbed the slope toward the flat saddle between the horns where the Franj knights had gathered. There were not many of them, but there were enough to form a solid line, and far too many of them wore the Templar white. She didn't have much time for anxiety, though.

Within moments they had joined ranks and then they were fighting, even the Jinn. Khalidah soon found that the Templars' reputation was justified. It was all she could do to fend off their swords. But gradually she became aware of the tide she had felt that morning during Tripoli's doomed charges, and it was moving slowly but inexorably against the Franj.

During a lull in the fighting she looked up. Ahead of her the Franj banners fluttered red and gold and purple, and behind them the king's tent trembled in the wind of the heights like a coward's heart. In between them was a bright spark, which resolved as she watched into the golden reliquary of the True Cross. For a second it hovered above the banners. Then it swayed drunkenly to the side, swung wildly for a moment, and sank beneath the churning waves of the battle.

"Did you see—" Abi Gul began.

"I saw," Khalidah interrupted. And more important, the Franj had seen. Many of them had thrown down their weapons to run back to the place where the cross had fallen. But they would not find it—Khalidah knew that with as much conviction as she knew that she would never see Sandara again.

Twenty-six

LATER on, thinking back on the battle, Khalidah would realize that they had won it the moment that cross fell. At the time things weren't so clear. After its loss and the initial confusion, the Franj knights still in possession of horses regrouped between the Horns and made two countercharges that fell on the join between the Muslim right and center divisions. They knew that their only chance now to salvage the day was to take Salah ad-Din himself, and in fact, one of their charges came so close to the Sultan that the men around him disbanded their offensive in order to surround and protect him. But Salah ad-Din sent them angrily back to their work, crying, "Away with the Devil's lie!"

Not long afterward the Muslim cavalry charged again up the western slope. This time they succeeded in driving the enemy off the saddle between the Horns. Watching from the valley with his father, Al-Afdhal cried out, "We have conquered them!"

Salah ad-Din turned to him and growled, "Be quiet! We shall not have beaten them until the red tent falls, and as you can see, it is still standing."

Up on the hill, the assessment was much the same. "Onto the southern Horn!" the emirs were crying. "Take the tent—take the king!"

The Muslims battered their way onto the flat-topped hill where the final few mounted Franj knights attacked them with the wild abandon of the doomed. The hot wind blasted the hilltop, the sun beat down, and Khalidah felt as though she'd slipped into a nightmare. The hill was so crowded that movement was nearly impossible, and she could think of little beyond the brutal heat and her own exhaustion. She kept catching glimpses of familiar faces as one does in dreams, ghostlike and gone in an instant, but disturbing and somehow indelible despite it. There was Bilal, leather arm bandages in tatters, fighting on foot with blood running down his face. By him was Salim, his yellow robes torn away and his long hair slick with sweat or blood. There was Abi Gul, still clinging to Tufan and hacking doggedly away at a black-robed Hospitaller twice her size. She saw Jinn fighting and Jinn dead beneath Zahirah's hooves, neither penetrating far into her consciousness. She even saw Sulayman once, but this, she was sure, had been a hallucination, for over his white Jinn trousers he seemed to be wearing a tunic of Ayyubid yellow.

For a time she succumbed to the eddies of the battle, allowing them to shunt her one way and another. And then something else swam into her field of vision; something red. It took her another moment to realize that it was the king's tent, and she was almost upon it. The next moment someone was attacking her, but she had regained her clarity of purpose. Looking down, she saw that her attacker was an unhorsed knight. She hacked down on his sword arm when he raised it and wheeled Zahirah as he dropped away howling. She knocked away the subsequent arms raised to stop her and then it was there before her, mundane and solid: a thick hemp rope tied hastily to a wooden peg hammered into the dry earth. A shadow fell on her. She looked up. It was Sulayman, and this time there was no mistaking the yellow tunic. For a moment this distracted her. Then he smiled.

"Well, are you going to do it or should I?"

She blinked at him, then raised her mother's sword. The yellow jewel caught the light for a moment, flashing like a Jinni's eye as she brought it down, severing the rope. For a moment as the king's tent drifted to the ground there was perfect silence. And then, the deafening roar of victory.

Twenty-seven

Near Hattin
4 July, Evening

I F King Guy ended that day as Salah ad-Din's prisoner, he was in good company. Along with countless of his knights and barons, the Muslims had taken Gerard de Ridefort and Kerak. Despite the victory, the Sultan left the field in rather more circumspect a mood than his soldiers. He repaired to his tent amid their rejoicing and ordered that the high-ranking Christian prisoners be brought to him. He also requested the presence of his scribes, his sons, Bilal al-Hassani, and the minstrel Sulayman.

When Salah ad-Din and his attendants were settled, the erstwhile Frankish nobles were brought before him, each with his own Mamluk guard. King Guy, de Ridefort, and Kerak were among the first to be presented. Salah ad-Din looked them over and then, his eyes settling on the king, he said, "Come, Your Grace, and sit by me."

The Sultan's words were translated for the king, who spoke no Arabic. He looked as though he did not quite believe them, or anything that he was seeing. In fact he looked, Sulayman thought, much as Aasifa had looked on the night he stole her from the Hassan camp. Trembling with fear or exhaustion or perhaps with both, Guy obeyed the Sultan and knelt beside him on the fine carpet.

"And you," Salah ad-Din said to Kerak. "Sit beside him."

Kerak gave the Sultan a long stare after the interpreter had spoken and then, so slowly that the movement itself was an affront, he sat down beside the king. Salah ad-Din subjected him to a long scrutiny, during which Kerak met his gaze with one of unflinching venom.

"How many times," the Sultan said at last, his voice calm but steely, "have you sworn an oath and then violated it? How many times have you signed agreements that you have never respected?"

Kerak answered, and the interpreter spoke hesitantly: "Kings have always acted thus. I did nothing more."

Salah ad-Din said nothing to this, but turned to the Franj king beside him. Guy's water skins had long since run out, and if he was not quite as beleaguered as his soldiers he was at last coming close. He swayed drunkenly, his head hanging like a beaten mule's.

"You are thirsty, Your Grace?" Salah ad-Din said gently. "And afraid, I see. You have nothing to fear from me." With a glance at Kerak as short and sharp as a poisoned dart, Salah ad-Din gave a quiet order to one of the servants. The man slipped away and returned a moment later with a cup of shaved ice. The Sultan took it from him and handed it to the king, but Guy would not accept it.

"Ah," said Salah ad-Din, "you fear treachery . . . and so might any man in your place, though I have told you already you need not fear me."

He took a sip from the cup himself, then handed it back to Guy. This time the Franj king received it with good grace. He drank his fill and then he handed the cup to Kerak, who finished it off. To the Franj, Salah ad-Din appeared to take all of this in with calm circumspection. Those who knew him better, however, recognized the sudden coldness in his eye.

When Kerak had set down the empty cup, the Sultan turned to Guy. "You did not ask my permission before giving him water. I am therefore not obliged to grant him mercy." For it was Arab tradition that a prisoner who had been offered refreshment must then be spared—a nuance of the culture of which Guy had been ignorant.

As the interpreter was attempting to explain this to him, Salah ad-Din lifted his right hand and Salim placed the hilt of his own sword into it. With a smile that had nothing of its usual warmth and welcome the Sultan stood, raised the sword, and brought it down between Kerak's neck and shoulder blade. Several of the Franj knights cried out. Guy shut his eyes and moaned, shaking now like a man with quartan fever. Kerak fell forward, his eyes bulging and his hands fluttering around the wound in his neck. The Sultan's sword had severed an artery, and dark blood poured forth, soaking the carpet. But the job was not finished, and so Salah ad-Din raised the sword again. With an almighty strength he brought it down on his old enemy, and this time Kerak's head rolled free, fetching up at the feet of the Franj king.

Salah ad-Din handed the bloody sword back to Salim and turned once again to the miserable Guy. "This man was killed only because of his maleficence and his perfidy. But you have nothing to fear. Kings are not generally in the habit of killing kings." Salah ad-Din bent then and dipped his fingers into the blood that had drenched the carpet. He sprinkled it on his head as tradition demanded, in recognition of the fact that he had taken vengeance on the dead man.

"Take his head to Damascus," he ordered the Mamluks when he had finished, "and drag it through the streets, so that all might see that vengeance has been taken upon this vile man. Take the prisoners to the city as well and confine them as befits their station. I will tolerate no mistreatment of any of them."

And then, leaving his interpreter to attempt to explain, he strode from the tent to supervise the return of the troops.

Twenty-eight

KHALIDAH and Abi Gul intended to find Sandara's body and give her a Jinn burial, but even before dusk made the job impossible they had given up. The magnitude of the slaughter was beyond anything that Khalidah had ever imagined. Whereas the valley and the horned hill had earlier been a forest of swords and spears without apparent beginning or end, now it was a carpet of mutilated bodies. A horse could not move without stepping on squelching human remains, and there was little to distinguish one bloody, muddy tunic from the next. Besides, the camp laborers had already begun digging graves for the Muslim dead, and it was entirely possible that Sandara would be under the earth before they ever got near her.

"It does not seem right," Khalidah said to Abi Gul as they turned at last from the terrible field and headed back toward the Sultan's camp. "The Jinn would not wish to be buried beneath the earth."

"No doubt there are many here who will not be laid to rest according to their customs," Abi Gul answered. "It is one of the many casualties of war. At any rate, Khalidah, do you imagine that we usually carry our dead back from our missions?" She shook her head and smiled sadly. "It is part of being Jinn—the knowledge that our bodies may well come to rest far from home. But wherever our bodies lie, our souls are free. Once the two are separate, nothing can keep us from rejoining our gods in Hewad."

It made sense, and there was a generosity to the philosophy

that Khalidah envied. Nevertheless, she did not like the thought of being buried by anyone who would not understand and implement her own faith's traditions. Sighing, she turned to her friend. Abi Gul looked more exhausted than Khalidah had ever seen her. Her eyes were wide in shadowed hollows, there were countless gashes in her armor and skin, and she was favoring her left arm; but still she rode upright and proud.

"How are you?" Khalidah asked.

Abi Gul smiled. "Alive, praise the gods! You?"

Khalidah's own smile was grim. Her right shoulder had been wrenched sometime in the final charge, and now she could not lift her sword arm. There were lacerations on her arms and legs, and she'd had cause to put her silk underwear to the test when a Franj arrow had lodged in her upper left arm. And yet the pains didn't seem to belong to her; her own body didn't seem hers. Yes, she was alive, but as detached from herself as if her soul had flown.

Khalidah had seen plenty of brutality over the last half year, and she'd known that any clash between the Sultan's army and the Franj's would be cataclysmic. Yet somehow, the result was still unspeakably shocking. It was difficult to witness such rampant destruction and not wonder why she had been spared to ride over the bodies of the countless thousands who had died. And when she considered the trinkets for which all of these men had given their lives—a gold-leaf cross that might or might not contain a holy relic, a red pavilion, even the city that was not in the end the holiest or even the second holiest in Islam—she had to wonder whether it had been worth it.

She told herself that she needed to sleep, that morning would clear her head. But when she and Abi Gul finally located the Jinn camp, they found that the Sultan had given out apricot spirits in honor of the victory. Those who were not drunk already were well on their way. Khalidah used her portion to clean Zahirah's wounds, and then, when the horse had been fed and watered, she retreated to her tent. She was stripping off her armor when the flap opened and Sulayman's flushed face peered in.

"You cannot mean to go to bed!" he cried.

"That is just what I mean to do," Khalidah said shortly. She wasn't sure whether her irritation was a result of her exhaustion, her grim search through the bodies of the fallen, or the fact that Sulayman still wore the yellow tunic, tattered and bloodied as it was. But it was on the last that she seized. "Have you tired already of the Jinn?" she demanded. "Is it more glamorous to be the Sultan's man—ah!" Rancor turned to a yelp of pain as she tried to pull her tunic over her head and her wounded shoulder screamed protest.

"Let me help you." He tried to ease the tunic over her arm and shoulder, but in the end he had to cut it off. "Let me find a physician," he said, gently touching the swollen joint. "This doesn't look good."

"No," she answered. "There are others who need them more tonight." She lay down in her silk underclothes, pulling the blanket up to her chin. Though the tent was close with the residual heat of the day, she was shivering. Sulayman came and sat beside her.

"I have not tired of the Jinn," he said in a tone Khalidah could not quite read. "It is only that I learned something today that changes everything."

"What?" Khalidah asked, not really wanting to hear the answer.

Sulayman paused, then said, "Salah ad-Din informed me this morning that he is my father."

Khalidah had thought that she was beyond shock, but these words were like the thud of an arrow into armor. Slowly she sat up, looking warily at Sulayman. He looked back with equal bewilderment.

"How could he possibly be your father?" she demanded.

"He and my mother were in Cairo at the same time in their youth, it seems—"

"No, no," said Khalidah crossly, "that is not what I meant to ask. How is it that he could know this?"

"How did you know that a sword in a junk shop in a desert town was your mother's?" he asked, exasperated. "Blood calls to blood, Khalidah."

She was silent for several long moments. "Very well; but I do not see that it changes very much. He cannot recognize you, so you cannot inherit, and even if you could, there would be all those other princes to challenge you."

"It is true that he cannot recognize me publicly," he said. "But he loved my mother, and because of that he wants to do something for me."

"Like what?" Khalidah asked, her gut heavy with foreboding.

"He has offered me land—not much, just a little town near Edessa and the surrounding farmland—but it is enough to give me a name and the rank of emir in his army."

Abruptly, Khalidah began to cry. "So that's it? All that time pining for Qaf and you'll give it up for an indifferent town and title and a chance to kill yourself in Salah ad-Din's name?"

"Have we not all come here today for that chance?"

"I have not," Khalidah said bitterly. "Nor have the Jinn." She turned her back to him and lay down again.

"Khalidah," he said, the hurt and confusion in his voice so strong that she almost gave in and pitied him. But then he continued, "This way, I can give you the life you deserve."

She laughed. "If I had wanted that life, Sulayman, I would have married my cousin, not followed you to Qaf."

"Khalidah, please try to understand . . ."

"If this is your decision, then I will never understand! The Jinn too have offered you a name and a country, one far worthier than the Sultan's. But if you are so fickle that his favor can blind you to it, then you are not the man I thought you were."

No matter how he coaxed and pleaded, Khalidah would say nothing more to him. At last he lay down beside her, listening to her sob all through that long night of their victory.

Twenty-nine

THE next day Salah ad-Din began his reconquest in earnest. The first thing he did was issue a declaration that the Countess Eschiva and those of her people who were still holed up in the citadel at Tiberias were permitted to leave the castle and to go unmolested wherever they wished. Count Tripoli had not joined his wife at Tiberias after his disastrous charge the previous day, but had gone on north to the city of Tyre. Tiberias passed to Salah ad-Din peacefully, Eschiva personally handing him the keys.

This bloodless conquest would set the scene for others in the days to come, but before the Sultan could continue his redistribution of the Franj kingdom, he had a pressing problem to solve. Among the many prisoners taken the previous day were more than two hundred Templars and Hospitallers. Muslim chivalry forbade killing prisoners of war, but Salah ad-Din knew very well that these knights were the Franj's only means of challenging his newly won authority. As such, he could not allow them to go free. And so he issued another, darker decree. Saying, "I shall purify the land of these two impure races," he ordered them all beheaded.

He had wondered whether some of his more devout followers might raise objections, but before the morning was out his little white pavilion was swamped with men begging to be allowed to play the role of executioner. The Sultan found himself dispensing the task as a privilege to those he wished particularly to thank or impress, and therefore one of the first invitations was issued to Sulayman.

"You are not thinking of accepting?" Khalidah said when he told her.

"Why shouldn't I?"

"Because it is barbaric! It flies in the face of Muhammad's teachings!"

They bristled at each other for a long moment, but Sulayman was the first to drop his eyes. "I hope that the Sultan is impressed by your zeal," she said, and though she had intended sarcasm, her tone was flat.

"Khalidah, please try to understand . . ."

"How?" she cried. "How can I possibly understand?" She shook her head. "A woman does not change her mind frivolously! There is no allowance for it. I made my choice the night I left my father's camp with you, and I knew that I could never revoke it."

"But he has forgiven you, Khalidah," he pleaded, "and at any rate, what would it matter to anyone once you are my wife?"

She laughed mirthlessly. "Do you really think that I could be a nobleman's wife, having been a Jinni?" She shook her head. "Consider my parents, Sulayman, and tell me that you think it could work."

The silence between them cauterized. Sulayman picked up his sword and turned toward the Sultan's tent.

"**What** has happened?" Abi Gul asked Khalidah later as they cleaned their armor and weapons by one of the reservoirs at the edge of camp.

Khalidah considered denying that anything was wrong, but Abi Gul was too good a friend. "Sulayman has left me," she said.

"What?" Abi Gul cried. "Do not tell me that he has found another woman—I won't believe it!"

Khalidah smiled grimly. "Not a woman," she said. "A man. The Sultan—his father." She filled Abi Gul in on what Sulayman had told her, and when she was finished Abi Gul sat thinking for a long time.

"It does not make sense," she said at last. "Sulayman is not fickle. Are you certain you aren't mistaken about his intentions?"

Khalidah shook her head. "He has been perfectly clear. To give him his due, I do not think it is fickleness. Until you have dreamed of a lost mother or a father, it is difficult to understand the power its realization can have over you."

"And yet you are the woman he loves," Abi Gul said gently. "You are his future, not this aging Sultan."

"I am afraid," Khalidah answered, her voice wavering dangerously toward tears, "that he does not see it that way."

"And you could not stay here, for him?"

Khalidah smiled sadly. "Could you?"

"Ah, Khalidah," Abi Gul said, and she might have said more if something had not caught her attention then. "Look—what a strange man! Do you think that he is a stray Franji?"

Khalidah looked up distractedly, but a moment later her frayed attention focused on the man Abi Gul pointed out. He rode a skinny, mangy cart horse, swaying in the saddle as though he were drunk, and he seemed to be accompanied by a swarm of flying insects, though with the distance it was hard to be certain.

"No, he is not a Franji," Khalidah said, dropping her armor as she stood up.

"How do you know?" asked Abi Gul.

"Because he is my cousin, to whom I was once betrothed."

"But what is he doing here?"

Khalidah did not answer, for she had seen something else: two figures walking toward camp from the direction of the execution field, leaning together with the complicity of lovers. Without waiting to see whether Abi Gul followed, she took up her sword and ran.

"Khalidah," Bilal said when he caught sight of her, "what is—"

"Numair!" she cried. "Behind you!"

Bilal turned, blanching as he saw the fly-ridden wraith with the swollen, grinning face, the tattered clothing stained with old blood and filth, the sword held high. He raised his own sword as

Salim laughed: "That is impossible! I killed him. You must be—"
But Salim would never finish that sentence or any other. He sank
to his knees as Bilal screamed, a look of startled wonder on his face
as Numair's sword sank into Salim's back.

For a moment the world seemed to stop. Then it resumed into
chaos. Khalidah could not make sense of what had happened until
Bilal's sword fell from his flapping, useless arm. He was senseless of the bones piercing his skin, reaching for Salim as Numair
wrenched the sword from the prince's back and he fell lifeless into
the dust. Bilal fell with him, beating at him and wailing for him to
wake, heedless that Numair had raised his sword again. But Khalidah had reached them at last. She knocked Numair's sword from
his hand and his legs from under him, waiting only to make certain
that he knew her before she plunged her mother's sword into his
throat.

Thirty

BILAL did not cry. He could not. He would have believed that he had turned to stone in that moment when Salim fell if it had not been for the deep, rending ache within him. Unable to think of anything to do but keep moving, he made Khalidah tie a sling for his broken arm and between them they carried Salim's body back to the tent. He had to be dragged from the dead prince to let the physicians see to his arm, and he submitted then only because Khalidah promised to keep vigil in his place.

Even so, the arm was barely bound before he was working again. He allowed no one to help him as he drew the water for the ritual bath, washed Salim three times, then dried him and wrapped him in the white linen shroud. He didn't speak except to drive away everyone who came to comfort him, from his mother to the Sultan himself. Khalidah's was the only presence he would tolerate, but as a woman she was forbidden to enter the place where a man was being prepared for burial. So she sat just outside the tent as he worked, making his apologies for him, listening for any sign that he needed her. But still, he didn't cry.

When Salim's brothers came to carry him to the grave site, though—a blood-bound honor he could not deny them—Khalidah entered the tent to find Bilal curled into a ball, sobbing tearlessly on the bloodstained bed that was now his alone. She lay down beside him and put her hand on his head, expecting him to pull away. Instead he moved toward her, clutching the skirts of her black dress as an infant clutches for comfort at whatever is nearest to

hand. When a servant came to tell them that the funeral prayers
were about to begin, he was crying still.

THE grave had been dug on the hill above the camp. It was one of
many, and it seemed to Khalidah as they threaded their way among
them that the earth had opened a thousand mouths to weep for
all the vast hordes of dead. Nevertheless, she felt that it was not
enough to account for the suffering of those left behind. Looking
from Bilal's ravaged face to the still-smoking valley, she wondered
if there were enough tears in all the ages of man to account for
what had been sacrificed to the Sultan's victory.

The imam was already facing Mecca, the lines of mourners
forming behind him. Khalidah saw Sulayman standing near the
Sultan, the late sun burnishing his yellow tunic. He looked back
as she and Bilal approached. She met his eyes for a moment, then
took her place between Bilal and her father. Though women were
forbidden to accompany a body to the grave, nobody questioned
her right to be there.

The imam raised his hands to his ears, and in a low voice he
began, *"Allahu akbar."* Khalidah repeated the words and then, with
the other mourners, she folded her right hand over her left. As the
imam continued the prayers Khalidah's mind drifted with the sun-
stained smoke, so that she only half heard the words: "O Allah!
Forgive our living and our dead, those who are present and those
who are absent, our young and our old, our males and our females.
O Allah! To he among us to whom You grant life, help him to
live in Islam, and to he whom You cause to die, help him to die in
faith . . ."

Khalidah wondered how many imams were reciting these same
words that evening in the surrounding hills. She wondered what the
Christians were doing with their dead. When the prayers ended,
Salim's brothers lowered his body into the grave. Though the Sul-
tan had beckoned to Bilal to join them, he remained in his place by
Khalidah's side, still clutching the fabric of her dress in his good

hand. Salah ad-Din looked puzzled, but Khalidah understood: this was a finality that Bilal could not bear. And so the Sultan himself stood in the grave and laid his son down on his right side, his head propped on a stone and his face turned toward Mecca.

"In the name of Allah and with Allah," Khalidah whispered with the others as the earth claimed the body, "and according to the sunnah of the messenger of Allah upon whom be the blessings and peace of Allah . . ."

Al-Afdhal heaved a shovelful of earth into the grave. It fell with dull irrevocability. Bilal turned and ran.

KHALIDAH sat with him through the three days of his official mourning. His wound was swollen and hot, he raved with fever, and the physicians stopped pronouncing and began whispering beneath furtive glances. He refused all medicine, leaving Khalidah to deal with the inevitable visitors. Their questions and condolences seemed to fall on him like dust into a dry well. When the mourning period was over and he was left alone once again, Bilal at last accepted a dose of opium, and with it he broke his silence.

"He had no child," he said in the voice of an old man.

Khalidah started, dropping the cloth with which she'd been sponging him to try to bring the fever down. "What?" she asked, so shocked to hear him speak at last that she had not heeded the words.

"The Prophet," he continued, his words thick and ponderous with illness and the drug, "peace and blessings be upon him, says that at death, everything in the earthly life is left behind except for charity given during the dead one's lifetime, knowledge that will benefit others, and a child who prays for him." He paused, his good hand rambling aimlessly over the blanket. "Salim was not given to charity, and I do not think that he much influenced the world's knowledge, nor had a child."

Khalidah thought for a long time before she answered. "He

had little time to give materially, nor to come up with worthy phi-losophies, nor yet to procreate . . . and yet he loved, Bilal. From the little I knew of him, I could see how deeply he loved. And is love not a greater gift than money or knowledge? Is it not a kind of progeny? For though he is gone, the love you shared with him will remain as long as you are alive to feel it."

"Perhaps you are right, Khalidah," Bilal said wearily.

"But it is poor consolation?"

"It is no consolation at all."

Khalidah sighed, looking at the stone boy who had been her dearest friend. "I would do anything to ease your pain, Bilal."

He gave her a terrible smile. "Then poison my next draught."

"You know that I cannot!"

"Then give me a world where he would not have died," he said bitterly.

Again there was a long silence. At the end of it she said, "Do you know, Bilal . . . I think I can."

SULAYMAN was waiting for her in her tent when at last she returned to it. He wore his yellow tunic, and Khalidah's deathly weariness flared immediately to anger. "Why are you here, Sulayman?" she asked.

"What if I told you that I am not the only one?" he asked. "Half of the Jinn want to stay here and help the Sultan with the rest of his conquest."

"Conquest?" she repeated dully, wiping the smudged kohl from her eyes with a wet cloth. "I thought that they came here to find Mobarak Khan."

"They did," he answered, growing angry at last, "and they have, and that is why they want to stay. His mission is not finished, so neither is theirs."

"And the others? What do they think?" she demanded.

"Like you," he said with a trace of accusation, "they believe that their duty to the Sultan finished at Hattin."

"My duty was never to the Sultan, Sulayman," Khalidah said softly, "but to Allah, and to the Jinn, and perhaps to myself." He opened his mouth to retort, but she pressed her fingers to his lips. Silenced, his eyes filled with despair. "It is no use. You will not sway me, nor I you. We have traveled a long way together, but our road parts here."

"That is all you can say?" he demanded when she withdrew her hand.

"Nothing more can be said. Please, Sulayman, leave me now."

"Does love mean so little to you that you would cast it aside for duty?" he demanded.

"I could ask the same of you."

"Khalidah—"

"Leave me, Sulayman, if that is what you mean to do!" she cried, her eyes filling at last. "I cannot bear any more!"

He looked at her for a long moment, but in the end, of course, she was right: there could be nothing else to say.

Epilogue

SALAH ad-Din's army moved on with his reconquest, leaving only a handful of black Hassan tents and white Jinn ones in the ruins of the camp. Bilal's fever finally burned itself out, if it didn't burn out his grief. When his arm had healed enough for him to travel, he packed his things with the Jinn's, mounted the horse Salim had given him, and prepared to leave his past behind.

Abd al-Aziz and Zaynab were there to see them off. Zaynab muttered blessings through her tears, but the sheikh seemed to be taking their departure with remarkable equanimity.

"I am sorry, Father," Khalidah said to him as they faced each other for the final time.

"For what?" he asked.

She smiled. "For not being a boy; for not having pure Bedu blood; for proving everyone right about my mother . . ."

"Ah, my daughter! I would not change anything about you."

"Truly?" she asked.

He shook his head. "You are everything a father could hope for in his child."

"Headstrong, impulsive, and intractable?" she smiled.

"Resolute, courageous, and loyal. And I believe that despite everything, you are still devout." Khalidah bowed her head. After a moment he said, "You are so like her, it breaks my heart."

"Better, then, that I am going," she said with a shaking voice, but she smiled and kissed both of his cheeks. "Good luck, Father. By Allah's grace, we will meet again. And if not I wish you joy in your new marriage, and many children who are nothing like my mother!"

She kissed Zaynab once more and then turned Zahirah toward the rising sun.

NEWS of the Sultan's campaigns followed them until they were deep into Persia. They heard how he took the Franj towns and castles in quick succession until at last he reclaimed Jerusalem. They heard that Gerard de Ridefort had alone been kept alive of the captured holy knights, to be used as a barter piece in the surrender of the more stubborn Templar castles. They even heard that the Pope in Rome, after learning of the Franj's terrible defeat at Hattin, had died of grief, and how his successor immediately called for a new holy war. After that the chain of whispers fell silent.

Though neither Khalidah nor Bilal spoke of their grief, they found comfort in one another's presence. They rode side by side during the day, and at night they slept with their backs together as they had in their earliest childhood, their breathing assuming a common rhythm. One mild, moonlit night in the foothills of Khorasan, Bilal finally broke his heart's silence.

"I would not mind as much," he said, "if he had died in battle. The way it was, it seems such a terrible waste."

"I thought the same of Sulayman at first," Khalidah answered.

"And now?"

"Now, I am not so certain that we didn't both lose our loves to Hattin." She laughed ruefully, then sighed. "We all thought we won the war that day, but really, it was only the beginning. And sometimes I wonder if there can ever be an end—for when two gods claim the same piece of earth, how can either win?"

"It is all very well to talk of gods," Bilal said after a moment, "but I miss him, Khalidah, as if I'd been torn in two. Sometimes I don't think that I can survive it."

"Sometimes I don't think so either."

But when Bilal reached out through the darkness to squeeze her hand, Khalidah knew that both of them would.

By the time they reached Qaf, Bilal's arm had healed, but it had healed crooked, with a deep, cratered scar where the bones had broken the skin when he tried to fend off Numair's blow. The doctors said that it would never be strong enough again for battle. He didn't mind. He asked to be given a flock to tend in the high pastures, and for a long time that was where he stayed.

Likewise Khalidah took up residence in the temple with the celibates, hoping to forget her grief. But she soon grew bored, the peace she had hoped to find there continually eluding her. So she went back to training with the cavalry, and the first time a request came for help, she asked to be included in the mission. Tor Gul Khan hesitated only a moment before he agreed, and so Khalidah began her life as a Jinn warrior; but still she was no closer to finding peace.

One evening, nearly a year after she first came to Qaf, she was walking among the horses when she came upon Aasifa lying prostrate and breathing hard. Khalidah knew at once that she was in labor, and a moment later that she was in trouble. A single tiny hoof extended beneath her blood-matted tail, flexed upward toward it: a hind leg, a breech birth, as dangerous in horses as it was in humans. Kneeling by the mare's side, Khalidah lifted away layers of thick membrane and tail, and found as she had feared that the foal's other leg was still inside the mother.

Rolling up her sleeve, she pushed her hand inside the horse's birth canal past the protruding leg until she felt the other, bent and wedged at the top. She waited until the current contraction relaxed, and then slowly she straightened the leg and guided it down beside the first. Khalidah waited to see whether the next contraction would push the foal farther out, but it didn't move. Sighing, she unwrapped her sash and used it to grip the slick little legs. With the mare's next contraction she pulled downward toward her hooves in hopes of rotating the foal's pelvis to a better position. After three contractions with well-timed pulls the foal began to come, first the long matchstick legs, then the rump, and finally, in a rush of fluid, the head and forelegs. Khalidah pulled the remnants of the sac from the foal's face and body. He was a colt, a palomino beauty like his father, with four white socks, a white star on his forehead, and a snip on his nose. He wasn't moving.

Wearily, Khalidah picked up her ruined sash and began vigorously rubbing the colt's nose and sides, pressing to expel the fluid from his lungs. "Breathe!" she yelled at him. "Please, breathe!" She hardly believed it when at last he obeyed, drawing a shuddering gasp and coughing up a lungful of fluid. He lay there, as exhausted as his mother, but breathing with increasing regularity. Khalidah looked at the umbilicus still joining him to the mare, but without a knife and cords to tie it off this was beyond her.

Looking up then she saw a small, middle-aged man standing watching her. His name was Emal, and he was the owner of Sre Zer, the foal's father, which for all she knew Sulayman was still riding in Salah ad-Din's battles. Emal pulled his dagger from his belt and handed it to Khalidah. Tearing strips from her sash, she bound the cord and cut it.

"That was well done," he said, kneeling to inspect the mare and foal.

Khalidah shrugged. "My father bred horses. Any child of our tribe could have done the same."

"Still, you have saved two fine horses. I would have been sorry to lose them." He looked at the little colt, which was already struggling to raise itself, and then back at Khalidah. "What will you name him?"

"Is it not left to a horse's master to name him?" Khalidah asked.

"You brought him into the world; he is yours."

"But you have lost his father."

"And gained a broodmare," he said gently, "whereas I think that life has not treated you so fairly."

Khalidah looked around at the hills and houses and trees, but saw nothing to suggest a name worthy of what would no doubt be a beautiful stallion. Then, high above their heads, she caught sight of two birds drifting on the valley's warm updrafts. Eagles.

"Shahin," she said, turning back to the little man and his horses.

He nodded. "A fine name," he said. "Leave him to me now, but come back in a few hours and see him standing."

Khalidah nodded, still overwhelmed. "If you change your mind—"

"A Jinni does not go back on his word," he said sharply.

She looked at him for a moment, then touched her forehead and her heart, and bowed deeply, a Jinn gesture of the highest respect. "Thank you, Sayyid. You have honored me."

He shook his head, smiling. "Do you not yet realize, Bibi Khalidah, that it is you who have honored us?"

SHAHIN grew into as fine a stallion as Khalidah had imagined, and he took to his training quickly and easily. With time his coat darkened to mahogany, though his mane and tail remained silvery white. The crossing of the Jinn and Hassan horse lines had proved so successful that Aasifa and Zahirah and Bilal's black mare were soon in great demand as broodmares, and Khalidah took to riding Shahin on her missions.

She was not the best of the Jinn warriors, but she fought doggedly and dealt fairly with the enemy, and in the end even the skeptics accepted her as one of them. When she wasn't fighting she spent time with her grandfather, who instructed her in the history and customs of the Jinn. Little by little she felt her Jinn self eclipsing the Bedu, until even their religion ceased to seem strange.

She did not think that she could ever be entirely a Jinni, but at the same time she knew that she was no longer entirely a Muslim. When she voiced her concerns about this to her grandfather, he only shrugged.

"All things change, Khalidah. Even beliefs."

"But how can I be Khanum to the Jinn if I am still partly Muslim?"

"As I told you long ago, our survival has always relied on the Khan's taking an even view of our clashing beliefs. I do not see that this is much different, as long as you respect and uphold our religion, and I know that you will do that."

Khalidah couldn't argue with this, and when at the end of her first six years in Qaf Tor Gul Khan contracted the pneumonia that would kill him, she no longer balked at the thought of taking his place.

"I have two regrets," he said to her during one of their last conversations.

"If there are only two, then you may count yourself luckier than most," she answered, smoothing the wispy hair back from his forehead.

He sighed. "They are plenty, for they are the two things dearest to me."

"It is sad about you and Brekhna," she said gently, "but as my father's people would say, it was written. You cannot regret what is inevitable."

"Perhaps not," he said, "and yet I regret not having the chance to tell her that I am sorry."

"I think that she knows, Grandfather," she answered. "But if ever I should meet her, I will tell her for you."

He squeezed her hand. "You are a good granddaughter, Khalidah. Too good."

"Don't tell me that you regret me?" she asked, smiling a little.

"I will never regret having known you," he answered, "but I regret very much what I have taken from you by calling you here."

"What?" she asked. "A life of drudgery in a nomad camp? A

husband I did not choose, and children he would turn against me?"

"I know that you left Sulayman to come back here," he said softly.

Khalidah had to swallow hard to loosen the knot that still formed in her throat when she thought of him. "That, too, was written," she said at last. "And at any rate, there was nothing much left to leave."

"And still, you are very young to be so resigned to solitude."

"Don't worry about me," she said. "I am contented."

"Precisely, Khalidah. Contented is never quite enough."

THEY buried Tor Gul Khan two weeks before Psarlay, and Khalidah wondered how she would be able to get through that most important of Jinn ceremonies on her own. A few days before the festival, as she was sitting in her rooms in the hermitage reading, there was a soft knock on the door. It was Bilal. He was hardly recognizable as the heartbroken boy who had ridden beside her out of Salah ad-Din's camp. He had taken to herding, and he was good at it. His sheep always threw live lambs, and he had a talent for seeking out the best grass so that his ewes gave the richest milk in the valley.

Early on he had befriended Abi Gul's brother Arsalan, and at first Khalidah had thought that they might become more than friends. But Bilal had only laughed when she suggested it, saying, "Arsalan is a good man, but as hairy as a sheep! Besides, he likes girls. He is my friend; no more, no less." And she had never brought up the topic again.

"Well, Bilal," Khalidah said as he stood before her now, "what brings you down from the mountain?"

He knelt on the carpet across from her. He wore the traditional clothing of the Jinn, plus a long dagger in his sash and a heavy woolen waistcoat against the predators and the cold of the mountains. The waistcoat, Khalidah noticed, was covered with intricate embroidery, brilliant blue poppies on a deep red ground. The poppies were the color of Bilal's eyes, brighter than ever in his sun-darkened face.

"That is a lovely piece of embroidery," she commented, "and I think I could put a name to the artist, for no woman of this valley plies a needle like Abi Gul."

To her surprise, Bilal blushed deeply. "Yes, Abi Gul made it. And it is because of her that I have come here today."

"Oh?" Khalidah asked, with the sudden feeling that the ground beneath her was sliding away.

Bilal nodded once toward the floor and then looked up at her. He was smiling. Beaming, she might have said, if she could have thought clearly. "Khalidah, I am here to ask you to marry us—Abi Gul and me. I would like to announce our betrothal at Psarlay."

Khalidah hesitated, and Bilal's face fell. The next moment she recovered herself, forcing a smile. "Of course you may marry; you are both adults and free to choose. Forgive me if I seem startled, it is only that I thought . . . I assumed that your inclinations . . ." She stopped, uncertain how to continue without offending him.

But Bilal only smiled again. "I do not claim to be much of an expert on love, Khalidah," he said, "but it seems to me that it is about the soul within rather than the body containing it. Salim and Abi Gul could not be more different on the surface, and yet their spirits are alike as any two people I have known."

Khalidah looked at her hands, trying to swallow her jealousy. She knew that it was ridiculous. She had never been in love with Bilal, and would not have wished to marry him even if their parents' marriage had not made it impossible. Besides, Bilal had suffered at least as much as she, and he deserved to be happy now. Yet his joy threw a spotlight onto her own loneliness and the shallow grave of her sorrow. It was very hard to look past them to her duty.

"Let me be the first to congratulate you, then," she said at last, leaning forward to embrace him. "Nothing could make me happier than joining my two dearest friends in marriage."

He held her tightly for a moment, then stood. "Thank you, Khalidah."

"You're welcome, Bilal," she answered. "Send Abi Gul to me, so that I may congratulate her, too." And she managed to hold her smile until he had shut the door.

KHALIDAH shook when she had to address her people on the first night of Psarlay, but as soon as she began speaking, the words rushed back to her and her confidence with them. After that it was almost as if she had always done it. She saw the festival through, a few days later she married Abi Gul and Bilal, and life returned to normal.

And then at the end of May the news reached Qaf that Salah ad-Din had died the previous March, not on the battlefield but in his bed in Damascus, of a short illness. The Jinn took the news silently—those who had believed in him as Mobarak Khan for grief, the rest for relief and, perhaps, for vindication. Nobody spoke of the warriors who had stayed behind to fight for him. Nobody dared to wonder whether any of them would return.

The first of them arrived at the beginning of June. There were not many, but they continued to come in a steady trickle throughout that summer. They'd been battered by the hard fighting they had seen, first to take back the Franj territories, and then to secure them against the new waves of invaders sent from Europe to recapture Jerusalem. All of them spoke well of the Sultan, but they had little good to say about his sons. It was because of them, and the chaos into which the once-mighty sultanate had dissolved as they fought each other for sovereignty, that the Jinn had at last turned for home.

Khalidah steeled herself after the first few arrivals. None of them had news of Sulayman. She had no reason to hope that he was even alive, yet each time she caught sight of a ragged pilgrim riding up the valley she hoped all the same, and every disappointment was more painful than the last. When it became unbearable she did what she had done since childhood: she rode, galloping Shahin up the valley and into the hills, the wind and the motion dulling her mind and heart for a little while.

She was riding like this one August evening as the shadows deepened when she saw a solitary figure stumbling up the valley on foot. He leaned heavily on a walking stick, and she thought at first that he was a supplicant looking for military aid, though she could not see how he could have come to the valley on his own. She turned Shahin toward the figure. As she approached he stopped, and then she froze too.

Slowly she slid down from the saddle and stood clutching Shahin's mane. She could not speak; she could only stare at him, wondering if grief had at last driven her mad. For it was Sulayman standing before her: older, thinner, scarred by his countless battles, and with something very near despair in his eyes. But he was alive.

After a moment, he offered a tremulous smile. "Is it you, Khalidah?" he asked, his voice equally unsteady.

"It is me," she said.

He looked at her for a long moment, taking in the plain white robes and fine, gold-striped headscarf of her rank, the thick kohl around her eyes, and the blue-black *harquus* on her face.

"You are Khanum now," he said, half wonderingly.

She nodded.

"Then it is you whom I must ask for sanctuary."

Again, she nodded. Slowly, painfully, he knelt before her. "Khalidah Khanum, I am sorry, sorrier than words can ever express, for abandoning you and the Jinn. I have no right to ask this, but if you could find it in your heart to let me stay here, if only for a little while . . ."

He trailed off, looking at her. In his face she saw all the hell of the years he had lived since they parted, and the greater torment of his regret.

"Stand, Sulayman," she said sternly.

He stood, trembling. She looked at him for a long moment. And then she took him in her arms.

"Welcome back," she said.

ACKNOWLEDGMENTS

Many people have helped in many ways to bring this book to light, but I'd particularly like to mention Elaine Thomson and Jeanie Goddard for their enthusiasm and their meticulous reading of the manuscript at various stages of completion; Professor Peter Jackson of Keele University for patiently answering all of my obscure Crusade questions; Fiona Walling of Cumbria Arabians for sharing her horses (and their Bedouin tack); Dr. Maktoba Omar, Latifa Mohamed, and Asim Shehzad for help with Arabic language and Muslim culture; Lubna Asim for checking the Pashto; Abdullah Chhadeh for the recordings of his *qanun* playing (amazing!); Colin for his ability to untangle the most horrific plot problems and for generally picking up the slack. Any mistakes or diversions from historical fact are mine and not theirs. Last but far from least, I want to thank Gilly, Emma, and the crew at Snowbooks for their support and hard work, as well as Emily Rapoport and her colleagues at Berkley Books in New York for giving this book a new life across the pond.

SELECTED BIBLIOGRAPHY

Though there isn't space to name all of the resources I used in researching this novel, listed below are a few books that provide interesting further reading about some of the subjects involved in *Sand Daughter*. For those interested in the Battle of Hattin, there are numerous firsthand accounts from both Muslim and Christian perspectives. The Jinn—their military tactics, culture, and religion—are based on traditional Pashtun, Kalash, Mongolian, and Tibetan culture and mythology, all of which make fascinating reading material.

Afghanistan: A Companion Guide, by Bijan Omrani and Matthew Leeming
An Arab-Syrian Gentleman in the Period of the Crusades, by Usamah Ibn-Munqidh
Arabia of the Bedouins, by Marcel Kurpershoek
Before Homosexuality in the Arab-Islamic World, by Khaled el-Rouayheb
The Book of Saladin, by Tariq Ali
The Crusades through Arab Eyes, by Amin Maalouf
Desert Tracings: Six Classic Arabian Odes, translated by Michael A. Sells
A Short Walk in the Hindu Kush, by Eric Newby
A Traveller on Horseback, by Christina Dodwell
A Vanished World, by Wilfred Thesiger
Veiled Sentiments, by Lila Abu-Lughod

ABOUT THE AUTHOR

Sarah Bryant is originally from Boston, Massachusetts, and now lives in the Scottish Borders with her husband, daughter, son, horse, dog, and cats. In her free time she knits obsessively, plays and teaches the celtic harp, and runs a small press specializing in handmade mixed-media books.